SHE HAD NO INTENTION OF BOWING TO ETHAN BODINE'S ORDERS.

Wilhemina walked up to Ethan Bodine, unmindful that she was still in a state of undress, and stared him right in the eye. "I will not be dictated to, Ranger Bodine, not by you or any man. I have no intention of giving up my pursuit of your brother. I will not be bullied, nor do I need you for a protector. I am perfectly capable of taking care of myself, thank you."

Ethan listened to every word Wilhemina spewed forth. But he was having a heck of a time concentrating, for his eyes had a mind of their own and were roaming over every delectable inch of her body.

The sunlight streaming through the window bathed Wilhemina's body in a warm glow. Desire filled every inch of him, overpowering his common sense and good judgment. Shocking not only Wilhemina but himself, Ethan grabbed her, pulled her to his chest, and proceeded to kiss her senseless.

Please turn the page for praise for Millie Criswell's other outstanding romances. . . .

RESOUNDING ACCLAIM FOR "ONE OF THE BEST IN THE WESTERN ROMANCE GENRE"* MILLIE CRISWELL

"Nobody does a better Western romance with style and panache than Millie Criswell. As the Bard would have said: 'All's well with a Criswell.'"
—Harriet Klausner, *Affaire de Coeur*

"Millie spins an absolutely delightful yarn."
—Janelle Taylor, author of *Destiny Mine*

. . . AND HER WONDERFUL PREVIOUS NOVEL *DESPERATE*

"Tightly plotted. . . . Readers will be hooked the moment Rafe addresses Emmaline as 'little lady,' and images of John Wayne at his most gallant come to mind."
—*Publishers Weekly*

"Five stars! This warm-hearted, gritty Western simply steals its way into your heart. . . . Millie Criswell's sweet sense of humor, combined with poignancy and an unforgettable cast of characters, touches you and brings you a smile and a sigh."
—*Romantic Times*

"Four stars! This Western runs the full gamut of emotions, with ample doses of humor and heroism."
—*Affaire de Coeur*

* *Literary Times*

"A handsome ex-ranger on the run, a socialite with five orphan children—Ms. Criswell delivers another fast-paced, rollicking Wild West adventure. Enjoy!"
—**Kat Martin, author of** *Innocence Undone*

"A riveting, tender tale that leads readers on an absorbing Wild West adventure. Full of spellbinding action and vibrant passion. A wonderful romantic treasure."
—*Rendezvous*

"Packed with emotion and tender humor, a wonderful page-turner you should not miss."
—**Patricia Potter, author of** *The Marshall* **and** *The Heiress*

"Five bells! Fantastic!"
—*Bell, Book & Candle*

"A touching, emotional, fast-paced story that will leave readers thirsty for more. The story will stick with you long after you've read the last page. Fans will not want to miss the continuing adventures of the Bodine brothers."
—*Writers & Readers Romance Group*
(Web site magazine)

"This book is going right into my 'keeper' pile. I never wanted this book to end. Criswell has created characters throughout this book that are memorable and leave you wanting more."
—**Gayle Fine,** *Under the Covers*
(Web site magazine)

BOOKS BY MILLIE CRISWELL

FLOWERS OF THE WEST TRILOGY

Wild Heather
Sweet Laurel
Prim Rose

THE LAWMEN TRILOGY

Desperate
Dangerous

Coming August 1998

Defiant

Published by
WARNER BOOKS

MILLIE CRISWELL

DANGEROUS

WARNER BOOKS

A Time Warner Company

WARNER BOOKS EDITION

Cover design by Diane Luger
Cover illustration by Ron Broda
Hand lettering by Carl Dellacroce

Warner Books, Inc.
1271 Avenue of the Americas
New York, NY 10020

Visit our Web site at
http://warnerbooks.com

W A Time Warner Company

Printed in the United States of America

First Printing: February, 1998

10 9 8 7 6 5 4 3 2 1

To my hardworking Warner sales rep,
Paul Leahy, who does an
outstanding job of selling my books.
Thanks for the extra
effort you always put forth!

ACKNOWLEDGMENTS

The author wishes to acknowledge Susan Broadwater Chen for her valuable assistance in the writing of this book. Her expertise and willingness to provide information on a variety of subjects is greatly appreciated.

Prologue

Justiceburg, Texas, Autumn 1879

Slamming THE DOOR TO THE SHERIFF'S OFFICE BEHIND him so hard the windows shook, Texas Ranger Ethan Bodine stepped onto the wooden sidewalk, puffing his cigar with agitation. Staring out at the driving rain, he tried to control his fury with Elmo Scruggs.

The man was a fool to think Ethan's brother, Rafe Bodine, had shot Bobby Slaughter in cold blood. Ethan had let him know in no uncertain terms what he'd thought of both his misguided opinion and that damned Wanted poster Elmo had printed.

Both Ethan and Rafe had ridden with the Texas Rangers for years, but Rafe had resigned a few months back—against Ethan's wishes—to marry their neighbor Ellie Masters, a lovely young woman they'd known most of their lives. Rafe's wife and unborn child had been brutally murdered by Hank Slaughter's gang, the ruthless criminals who held Rafe responsible for putting Hank in prison five years before for robbing the bank in Misery, Texas. Now Rafe was on the outlaw trail himself, seeking revenge against the four men.

Ethan couldn't blame Rafe for wanting to avenge his wife's murder. He might have been tempted to do the same if he'd been married—a situation not likely to happen in his lifetime. But he also couldn't allow Rafe to take the law into his own hands. The day Rafe decided to go after Hank Slaughter was the day he became an outlaw in the eyes of the law. And it was the same day Ethan had been forced to ride down his brother like a common criminal—the saddest day of his career as a Texas Ranger.

He hadn't taken a full step toward the street when two elderly white-haired ladies accosted him. One was as thin as a rail, with skin so parchmentlike that he could see tiny veins beneath the surface of her cheeks; the other was plump as a peacock and almost as colorful.

"Mister," they called out in unison, waving frantically to gain his attention.

Drawing to a halt, Ethan touched his hat brim in greeting to the two women, flicked the ash off the end of his cigar, and deposited it in the pocket of his sheepskin jacket.

"Afternoon, ladies. What brings you out on such a dreary day?" The rain was pouring down with no end in sight, but Ethan knew he had to leave anyway before Rafe got too far ahead or some crazy bounty hunter caught up with him.

"Something terrible has happened, sir, and we need your immediate assistance," explained the plump one with the god-awful hat. Flowers, bows, and feathers in every imaginable color decorated the crown. Ethan tried to keep a safe distance.

"Isn't that right, Birdy?" the peacock asked.

The other lady twittered, fluttering her thin arms in the air as if she couldn't quite decide what she should do, then nodding, reminding Ethan of a hummingbird. It wasn't difficult for him to understand why she'd earned such a nickname. Birds of a feather and all that.

The last thing Ethan needed right now was to play knight in shining armor to a couple of elderly damsels in distress.

"I ain't the law in these parts, ladies. 'Fraid you'll have to speak to Elmo Scruggs if you've got a problem." He started to leave, but the next question stopped him in midstride, and he turned back.

"Aren't you the Texas Ranger who's following that murderer?"

"Eunice! Don't be so blunt." Birdy smiled apologetically. "Eunice isn't known for her tact, so you'll have to forgive her."

Ethan didn't intend to remain in town long enough to forgive anyone, but he sure as hell didn't like these ladies calling his brother a murderer. "Whether or not a man's found to be a murderer is decided by a jury, ma'am. But yes, to answer your question, I'm going after him."

"We're the Granville sisters. I'm Eunice, and this is Bernadette. But we call her Birdy, Mister . . ."

"Bodine, ma'am."

"Mr. Bodine, we need your help," Eunice Granville stated. "Our niece has gone and done something rash, and we fear for her life."

"Her life," Birdy parroted, nodding in agreement.

"I'm sorry to hear that, ladies, but you'll have to inform the sheriff. I don't—"

"Wilhemina has gone off to hunt down the man you're looking for, Mr. Bodine. She has become a bounty hunter." Both women stared at each other, wringing their gloved hands nervously.

"What?" Incredulity punctuated his words. "You're joking, right?" A woman bounty hunter? He'd never heard of such a thing.

"It's true," Birdy assured him. "We've been experiencing some financial difficulty of late, and, well . . ."

"And our niece decided to take matters into her own hands," Eunice finished, clutching his arm with surprising strength for such an elderly woman. "Wilhemina's always been a bit impulsive, but she's never done anything quite as drastic as this. You've got to help us, Mr. Bodine. Wilhemina could be in grave danger."

"Of all the harebrained, stupid things I've heard of in my lifetime, this takes the cake." Women didn't have a lick of sense about them as far as he was concerned, and this Wilhemina Granville sounded more empty-headed than most. "How experienced is your niece at tracking?"

Eunice swallowed. "Not very. You see, Wilhemina is a horticulturist by profession. And—"

"A what?"

"She studies plants, things like that," Birdy said. "And she's very good at what she does."

"Wilhemina has always been a tad headstrong. She gets that from me, I'm afraid," Eunice confessed. "And from our brother, her father, God rest his soul. And when that horrible man at the bank, Mr. Bowers, threatened to foreclose on our home . . ."

Birdy dabbed at her eyes with a frilly lace handkerchief. "Well, I'm sure you can understand why she felt compelled to go after this criminal. The price on his head is awfully appealing." Pointing at the Wanted poster of Rafe now hanging in front of the sheriff's office, which offered a reward of five hundred dollars, dead or alive, she dabbed at her eyes once again, as if the sight of him were just too much to bear.

"What if he tries to kill our Wilhemina?" Eunice clutched Ethan's arm tighter. "She's so young, so full of life. I just couldn't bear it if anything happened to her."

Ethan's voice chilled to arctic proportions, and he extricated himself from her hold. "My brother isn't a murderer."

He heaved a frustrated sigh, for he wanted to put Justiceburg behind him and be on his way to find Rafe. He'd been on his brother's trail for over a week. But he'd been stuck in the two-bit town for days. He'd come here to talk to the prostitute who'd sworn that Rafe had shot down Bobby Slaughter in cold blood. Ethan needed to interrogate Judy DeBerry, Bobby Slaughter's former lover, before he could depart, but the woman hadn't been the least bit cooperative in making herself available to him, and her stubbornness had cost him precious time.

Now it seemed these little old ladies would cause more of a delay.

Both women gaped at Ethan, then turned to stare at the likeness on the poster, noticing for the first time the name printed there. "Why, we didn't notice that he has the same name as you do, Mr. Bodine," Birdy pointed out. "How silly of us."

Ethan sighed at the understatement. "Yes, ma'am. Rafe is my younger brother."

The woman's blue eyes brightened, even as they reflected and calculated the possibilities. "Why, that's wonderful, Mr. Bodine! Now you and Wilhemina will have a common goal."

His forehead wrinkled at the woman's convoluted logic. "I'm not following your drift, ma'am."

"You obviously want to find your brother and bring him back safely"—Eunice took up where Birdy left off—"before someone else does. So it only stands to reason that since our niece is going after your brother to collect the price on his head, it's in your best interest to find her first."

"Wilhemina's not a crack shot," Birdy interjected, piping up for her sister, "but she's proficient enough with a gun to hit what she aims at. And she'll be aiming at your brother, Mr. Bodine. We're sure you'll want to stop her from hitting her mark."

The two women smiled in complete satisfaction, nodding at one another as if they had just solved their immense problem.

Ethan frowned, wondering if the two women were touched in the head. Because there was no way in hell that he was going after some errant horticulturist when his brother's life was in jeopardy. And he doubted very much that this Wilhemina Granville could sneak up on Rafe and shoot him anyway. He was a Texas Ranger, after all— ex–Texas Ranger, Ethan amended. It wasn't likely that Rafe would allow some fool woman to get the drop on him.

"Sorry to disappoint you, ladies, but I'm going after my brother and no one else. It's my sworn duty to bring him back to Misery to stand trial, and that's just what I intend to do." Judge Barkley had already issued a writ of habeas corpus giving Ethan the right to bring him back to Misery, though the murder took place in Justiceburg. And he wasn't about to get sidetracked by some mindless female.

"It's doubtful your niece will get very far. She'll probably come home this evening. Women don't like being out in inclement weather. It tends to muss their hair."

Eunice's double chins quivered in indignation. "I think you may have misunderstood us, Mr. Bodine. Just because Wilhemina isn't an experienced tracker doesn't mean that she isn't the most stubborn young woman on the face of this earth. Once she sets her mind to doing something, she does it. And she's an excellent horsewoman. Why, she's won several blue ribbons for her equestrian abilities at the county fair."

"Is that a fact? Well, she'll just have to ride back here on her own, then, because I don't have the time to find her.

Now, if you ladies will excuse me?" He stepped into the street to where his horse was hitched to the post.

"But, Mr. Bodine," Birdy implored with a shake of her head, "what about our niece? Wilhemina is all we have left in this world. If she were to perish . . ."

Tears rolled down both women's cheeks, and Ethan wished to God he had Wilhemina the horticulturist in his clutches so he could strangle the inconsiderate woman.

What kind of person would ride off and leave two old ladies to fend for themselves?

He mounted the large black stallion. "If I come across your niece in my travels, I'll be sure to let her know that you're worried about her."

"And you'll send her straight home?" Birdy looped her arm through Eunice's, and both women smiled bravely.

"You can be sure of it, ladies."

Tipping his hat, Ethan rode away, wondering how many more strange encounters he would have before finding his brother and thinking that Rafe had a lot more to atone for than the alleged murder of Bobby Slaughter.

Chapter One

On the Trail, Texas, Autumn 1879

CAMPED NEAR THE NORTH FORK OF THE DOUBLE MOUNtain River, Wilhemina Granville shivered uncontrollably in her bedroll, despite the fact that her campfire still blazed brightly under the trickle of falling rain. She wondered again at the wisdom of her decision to hunt down the outlaw Rafe Bodine, though she knew she had little choice.

The man was wanted for murder. Though she was proficient in the use of a firearm, she was out of her element in dealing with a vicious outlaw. Calling oneself a bounty hunter was a lot more impressive than actually being one. And circumstances being what they were, she needed the five-hundred-dollar reward to pay her aunts' debt. She needed to bring the outlaw back to Justiceburg or her aunts would lose their home.

She tossed another stick onto the fire; it hissed, caught, and burst into flame. In the distance a coyote howled, seemingly as unhappy with his surroundings as

Wilhemina was at the moment. She cursed aloud the banker Rufus Bowers, whom she held responsible for her present set of circumstances.

If it hadn't been for the lecherous coot, she'd still be safe and warm back in Justiceburg, savoring one of her aunt's delicious sweet-potato pies before she retired to her own comfy feather bed, instead of shivering her behind off out here in the middle of nowhere.

Three days ago she had gone to the bank officer at the Justiceburg Savings and Loan, asking him to extend the repayment period on her aunts' mortgage.

Money was tight. Her father's death a year ago had revealed the sad state of his financial affairs. She had come home to Texas disillusioned in any case by the lack of career opportunities in Boston. After attending college north of Boston, she had secured a position as a horticulturist at the renowned Boston Horticultural Society. But she'd soon discovered that women weren't welcomed into a man's domain.

Employment prospects weren't any better in Justiceburg. There wasn't a need for a horticulturist in the small provincial town. Her inability to find a job had only added to her family's monetary woes.

Wilhemina felt it was her responsibility to render her aunts' only domicile safe and secure. Eunice and Bernadette Granville had raised Wilhemina after her mother died in childbirth and had provided comfort after her father succumbed to a lingering illness last year. They'd been kind and caring, supporting her decision to pursue a career in horticulture though it was thought of as an unconventional choice for a woman. She wasn't about to repay those two dear souls by abandoning them to the likes of Rufus Bowers.

Wilhemina had tried her best to deal civilly with the bank officer, but the man had been anything but businesslike. Mr. Bowers's suggestions had been lewd and revolting. Even now, as she recalled his improper advances, the memory of his flaccid face and puffy lips nauseated her.

"What type of collateral do you offer to secure the mortgage, Miss Granville? The mortgage money is due and payable on the first of every month, and your aunts are now several months behind in their payments. We are not a charitable institution, as you well know."

Wilhemina stiffened, doing her best not to lash out at the man's arrogance, for she knew it would not accomplish her goal. "I'm not asking for charity, Mr. Bowers. I'm merely asking for an extension on the loan. Surely you wouldn't consider putting a couple of elderly women out on the street. My aunts' home is all they have in this world." And they were all she had left.

He stood and came around to the front of the impressive mahogany desk, then perched on the edge of it, his knee precariously close to Wilhemina's. He was sweating profusely, and she could detect the distinctive scent of sensen on his person. She would never again be able to eat a piece of licorice without thinking of him.

"You're an attractive woman, Miss Granville, and I am not a heartless man. I'm sure we can find some mutually satisfying solution to this problem." His leering gaze made her skin crawl, as did the way he rubbed his chubby thighs.

Knowing a proposition when she heard one, Wilhemina rose. She fought to keep her voice impassive, which was extremely difficult considering how angry she felt. "The only solution to this problem, Mr. Bowers, is an extension on my aunts' loan. Anything else you may be suggesting is out of the question."

He *tsk*ed several times, shaking his head. "That's a pity, my dear." Reaching out, he attempted to caress her cheek, but she stiffened and pulled back. "A little cooperation from you and I could tear up the Granville mortgage altogether. Your aunts would never have to worry about losing their home. And you, my dear, look old enough to know the ways of the world."

At twenty-eight Wilhemina was definitely old enough to know which way the wind blew. And this was an ill wind blowing at best. She had already made a foolish mistake back in Boston with a colleague, a man whom she'd trusted and admired. That mistake had cost her her virginity, not to mention her faith in men. And she had no intention of allowing some corpulent banker she had no tender feelings for whatsoever to place her in a similar circumstance.

Moving toward the desk, she smiled deceptively as her hand crept closer to the flower-filled vase. "I'm indeed old enough to know the ways of the world, Mr. Bowers. I'm also old enough to know a lecher when I see one, and I'm not stupid enough to be taken in by the likes of you."

Anger stiffened his spine. "Really? Well, since you're so smart, Miss Granville, I hope you'll be able to come up with the money to save your aunts' home. Perhaps you should consider going after that outlaw who has a price on his head. I hear bounty hunting is a very lucrative profession." His malicious laughter filled the room, and her hand stilled.

"I'd rather become a bounty hunter than allow a man like you near me."

"In that case, that is exactly what you must do." With a feral smile, he reached into a stack of papers and extracted one, handing it to her. "In order to pay off your aunts' debt, you must bring this outlaw back to Justiceburg to stand trial."

Staring at the Wanted poster of Rafe Bodine, she gasped in outrage, but he ignored her and continued. "If you are unable to do so, I will evict your aunts and toss them out on the street. And it will give me great pleasure to do so."

"But you can't do that!"

With a shrug, he held up the mortgage to her aunts' home, taunting her with it. "I assure you, Miss Granville, that I can. And it's perfectly legal. When your aunts signed the loan papers they agreed to abide by the terms and conditions that I set forth, should they ever become delinquent or default on their loan.

"I've hereby decided that one of the conditions to satisfy their delinquency and repayment of the loan is that you bring back this ruthless criminal. If you can. Otherwise . . ."

Picking up the vase, she noted that it was a cheap Meissen reproduction. Not allowing herself time to reconsider, she poured the contents—water and yellow sunflowers—over the banker's balding head. "I accept your terms, Mr. Bowers," she stated before marching out the door and slamming it behind her.

Wilhemina's only regret now, as she stared into the dancing flames of the campfire, was that she hadn't turned around to see the outrage on his face. No doubt he had turned three shades of red. She could still hear his gasps of outrage, and the memory filled her with satisfaction.

She rarely lost her temper and was inordinately proud of the fact that she held tight rein on her emotions, but this was one time she was glad she'd let herself go. Though it was a pity about the flowers. They had been too lovely to waste on a scoundrel like Mr. Bowers.

Ah well, she told herself, she would make it up to the lovely *Helianthus annus* next time she crossed its path.

The little town of Santa Rosa, New Mexico Territory, was too much like Nogales, Mexico, to make Ethan feel any too comfortable. Lorna Mae Murray, the woman who'd deceived him, the woman he'd fancied himself in love with, had been from Nogales. And anything or anywhere that reminded him of Lorna Mae was something to avoid.

Licking the salt from the web of his hand, he tipped back the glass of tequila and downed it in one gulp, squinting his eyes as the pungent liquor went down hard; then he sucked the lime and tossed it into the empty glass.

He'd ridden hard since leaving Justiceburg a week ago. He and his horse needed a good night's rest, and Ethan knew he could find it in Juan Campos's cantina. He'd known Juan for many years and could count on the man for a hot meal and warm bed—provided, of course, he had the money to pay. Juan never did anyone a favor for free.

"You would like another tequila, *Señor* Bodine?" Juan's weathered face held a hopeful expression, and Ethan could almost hear the pesos being calculated inside the man's head.

"Might as well give me the whole damn bottle, amigo. I'm feeling kinda melancholy, and shooters always lift my spirits."

"*Sí, señor,*" Juan agreed with a nod, his grin knowing. "And they will also lift you off the floor after you drink too many and pass out, no? But you no worry. Juan will cart you to the back room like the last time."

Ethan had a vague memory of the "last time." If he recalled correctly, his head had pounded for three days straight and had swelled so big, it wouldn't have fit into a horse corral.

"*Grácias, amigo.*" He grasped the neck of the bottle and sauntered off to the table at the rear of the adobe building, where he could keep an eye on things and still have his back to the wall. A man couldn't be too careful these days.

Rumor had it that Texas outlaw Clay Allison, a deranged son of a bitch who liked beheading his victims, had started up a cattle ranch in Colfax County. If the gunfighter was in the territory, Ethan would watch his back, for Clay had a score to settle, like so many others Ethan had hunted during his career.

Shootists, as some gunmen referred to themselves, didn't have any rules when it came to killing. And shooting a man in the back was a hell of a lot easier than looking him in the eye and pulling the trigger.

A man couldn't be too careful. That creed had kept Ethan alive longer than most in his profession.

Near the entrance to the cantina, Juan's brother, Carlos, sat on a stool and strummed his guitar. The Spanish love song he played brought back memories best forgotten.

To think he'd allowed a woman like Lorna Mae, with her sweet smiles and seductive laughter, to dupe him. She'd passed herself off as virtuous, but Ethan discovered soon enough that Lorna Mae was no virgin. Far from it. The lying hussy had tried dragging him to the altar by claiming he'd stolen her innocence to hide the fact she was carrying another man's child.

"Sweet Jesus!" He belted back another shot of liquor and shook his head, wondering how a man who prided himself on having excellent judgment and common sense had been taken in by such a conniving female.

Was it any wonder these past two months that he felt not the slightest bit of desire where women were concerned? Lorna Mae had taken his pride, his manhood, and smashed it beneath her dainty slipper, and now he had no use for women, in any way, shape, or form. If he never laid eyes on another member of the female sex, it wouldn't bother him in the least. He was through with women once and for all. Lorna Mae had buried his manly urges under a mountain of lies and deceit.

Sucking on his cigar, Ethan blew smoke rings at the ceiling. After summoning Juan to the table, he ordered a plate of frijoles to accompany his bottle of tequila, then settled back in his chair to enjoy the rest of the evening and get drunk. There was nothing like a dose of snake poison to take a man's mind off his troubles, and tequila had a deadlier bite than most.

The Texas Ranger had just eaten the last of his tortilla when the cantina door swung open and four men entered. Armed and covered with sweat and trail dust, they looked as though they'd been riding hard and fast. Hinges creaked, spurs jingled against the wooden floorboards, and the few patrons in the small restaurant became immediately wary of their presence.

Through glazed eyes Ethan stared at the tall forms, then blinked several times, hoping he was having some kind of alcohol-induced hallucination. He was surely having a nightmare of gigantic proportions.

The sinking feeling that formed quickly in the pit of his stomach had nothing to do with the refried beans he'd just eaten, but rather with the realization that Lorna Mae's brothers, who'd vowed to avenge their sister's so-called honor, had found him.

The oldest, Jacob, was the first to realize their good fortune. "Bodine, you rotten, no good, egg-sucking dog! We've been looking all over for you." He turned to his brothers and grinned, indicating with a nod of his head where Bodine was seated. "Looks like our search is over, boys.

"We'd heard from a whore over in Justiceburg that you was headed this way, but we never figured on catching up to you so soon. Guess we owe her one."

As a reflex, Ethan's hand went to the Colt .45 Peacemaker at his hip. It was the weapon of choice for the Texas Rangers, who had a saying: "God didn't make men equal, Colonel Colt did."

Ethan wasn't afraid of much, but common sense dictated that only a fool would relish these odds; he didn't withdraw the gun from his holster.

"Howdy, Jacob." He nodded in greeting at the other three brothers—Joseph, Jedediah, and Jeremiah. Obviously their mama had thought there was something spiritual about her sons when she'd named them. Ethan thought Lucifer or Beelzebub would have been more fitting for the no-good sons of bitches.

He tried to keep his tone casual. "Heard you were looking for me. What's on your mind?"

The stockily built Joseph stepped forward and sneered. "As if you didn't know, Bodine. You dirtied our little sister, and we aim to get our revenge agin you. You shouldn'ta done what you did to Lorna Mae. Now she's in a family way and we aim to make you pay."

"She was that way before I ever laid with her, boys," Ethan explained, shaking his head, mostly to clear the cobwebs from it. "Lorna Mae lied to you, and she lied to me, too." Jedediah, the youngest at nineteen, looking like he had a great deal to prove to his older brothers, stepped toward Ethan with murderous intent flashing in his dark eyes.

"You calling my sister a lying whore, Bodine? Ain't no way I'm gonna let no Texas Ranger who screwed my sister get away with calling her a lying whore."

By this time Carlos had ceased strumming his guitar and was making his way to the door, while Juan moved tables out of the way, hoping to avoid breakage.

Ethan pushed back his chair and stood, his hand resting on the ivory butt of his gun. "Lorna Mae was no innocent when I bedded her, is all I'm saying. And seeing as how I'm the one who'd know, you'll just have to take my word on it."

A stiff wind could have toppled Jeremiah's rangy frame, and he spat a wad of tobacco on the floor before saying, "That's just plain bullshit, Bodine. Lorna Mae told us how you promised to marry her and all. She cried her eyes out the whole time she was tellin' the tale. Our sister's a brokenhearted, fallen woman, that's what she is, and we aim to see that you pay for what you done."

All hell broke loose just then as the brothers rushed Ethan and knocked him to the floor. Somebody's fist landed in Ethan's left eye, blinding him momentarily. He lashed out and caught Jedediah's chin with a right uppercut.

"He knocked my tooth out," the disgruntled man yelled as blood poured from his mouth. A yellowed tooth bounced unceremoniously against the floorboard and out of sight.

Ethan knew that his only chance was to get to his feet and to his horse. He was outnumbered, and it didn't take a genius to figure out that he was going to get the crap beat out of him if he stuck around much longer.

He managed to get to his feet, but someone—Joseph, he thought—broke a chair over his back, knocking him to his knees. He grunted in pain but managed to tackle Jeremiah on his way down.

"Señors! Por favor!" Juan shouted, raising joined hands imploringly to the ceiling. "Take your fight outside. I am a poor man and cannot afford to have you break more of my furniture."

A few moments later Juan got his wish as Ethan was hauled to his feet by two of the brothers and thrown bodily through the front door and into the street. He landed with a thud in the dirt.

Fights in Santa Rosa were as commonplace as fleas on a mangy mutt. Despite the angry shouts and curses from the Murray brothers, and Ethan's loud protests of innocence between bouts of spitting dirt out of his bloodied mouth, no one in the town paid any attention to the ruckus going on.

No one, that was, except the apparition coming toward him.

Through swollen eyes, Ethan could barely discern the form of a horse and rider. The figure was shrouded in darkness. No street lights illuminated the area, and though the moon shone half-full, it was still difficult to see who it was.

As the heel of Joseph's boot came down hard on his side, Ethan prayed that his rescue was at hand.

Chapter Two

OUTRAGED BY THE SIGHT BEFORE HER, WILHEMINA nudged her heels into the side of her mount and urged the mare into a gallop. In front of the cantina, a large man was being brutally beaten by four equally large men, and it was clear that he was not only outnumbered, but bearing the brunt of the altercation. Her sense of fair play and justice could not abide the uneven odds.

"Stop! Stop this at once!" she shouted, reining her mare near the fighting men. But she might as well have been talking to the wind, for no one paid her the least bit of attention.

She dismounted hastily and pulled her umbrella from the rifle scabbard. Rushing forward into the melee, she brandished it enthusiastically, as if it were the shiniest silver saber. "Stop beating that man!" she screamed again, hitting one of the attackers on the back of his legs.

Jacob paused, fist in midair, and turned to stare at the stranger who'd struck him. Then he grinned. "Lookee here,

Bodine. Looks like you got yourself a champion. And a purty one at that."

The other brothers turned, then Jeremiah laughed aloud that Bodine's champion was a woman. "Whoooeee! Look at that fancy lace umbrella. I'm quaking in my boots."

The cowboy's laughter halted abruptly when Wilhemina jabbed the point of her weapon straight into his midsection; he grunted in pain. "You should be ashamed of yourself! You should all be ashamed. This isn't a fair fight."

"Yeah? Well, it weren't fair when Bodine dishonored our sister, neither," Joseph pointed out, making Wilhemina blush to the tips of her sturdy boots.

She glanced at the man sprawled on the ground. There was nothing in his swollen, discolored face that spoke of handsomeness or cadlike behavior, although the mustache he wore made him look a tad sinister. But there was nothing that indicated the man giving the beating was telling the truth, either.

When the tip of the man's boot plowed into the injured man's stomach, Wilhemina decided that she'd had enough and swung her umbrella wildly at Joseph, catching him in the eye and making him curse loudly.

"You'll pay for that, you hellcat. You hear me?" Joseph stepped forward, flashing her a threatening look, and Wilhemina reached inside her reticule to withdraw the derringer hidden there. Aiming it near the man's feet, she fired.

Wilhemina had never actually fired a gun at an animate object before and was breathing hard. At her father's insistence, she'd learned to shoot to protect herself, but her targets had been empty bottles and tin cans, never a human being.

Joseph jumped higher than a cockroach on a hot skillet. "Hey, lady! Watch it. You almost hit my foot."

"I would have hit your foot, mister, if I'd been aiming at it. Let me assure you that I'm a very good shot."

The men stopped what they were doing and eyed her warily—except the youngest, Jedediah, who took umbrage at being bested by a woman and shook his fist at her, screaming, "You shouldn't get involved in something you know nothing about, lady. We owe Bodine a beating. Now run home and attend to your knitting." A cocky grin split his face.

"I'm already involved. And I don't knit. So why don't you boys call it a night. This man has been injured enough, and I'd hardly call this an equitable fight."

"Yeah. But what he did to Lorna Mae wasn't eq . . . eq . . . fair, neither. She's in the family way now, and this no-good varmint is to blame."

Shocked by the unexpected revelation, Wilhemina's eyes widened, but she held firmly on to her gun and her convictions. "I'll count to three. If you're not gone from here, I'm going to start shooting, and I'm going to start with the baby-faced boy over there." She aimed at Jedediah, who started toward her but was held back by his brother.

Joseph snatched his hat from the ground and swatted it against his pant leg; a billow of dust rose in the air. "We'll leave, lady, but this ain't over. Not by a long shot. Only now we'll have the two of you to get even with instead of just Bodine."

Watching them stalk off down the street, Wilhemina breathed in deeply and thanked the Almighty that they were gone. Replacing the small gun in her reticule, she approached the man on the ground.

Ethan coaxed one cautious eye open and stared up at his rescuer. He would have opened two, but the other was swollen shut tighter than a corset on a two-hundred-pound whore, and it smarted like the dickens.

The woman, for all her ferocity, wasn't much bigger than a minute. But she was definitely so well rounded in all the right places that even a blind man would have noticed. And he wasn't quite blind, just slightly impaired. Ethan had always prided himself on having a discerning eye when it came to women.

Not that he cared a whit about that sort of thing at the moment, he reminded himself.

Dressed in a white shirtwaist—still spotless despite the altercation—and navy skirt, with her chestnut brown hair peeking from beneath the crown of a felt hat, she appeared to be a no-nonsense kind of woman. She'd certainly been zealous in her defense of him—something he hadn't expected from a member of the opposite sex.

Most females of his acquaintance were helpless creatures, more concerned about their appearance than with helping a fellow human being. None of them would have lifted a manicured finger to aid in his defense. Apparently this woman was different.

In many ways she reminded Ethan of his mother: headstrong, unafraid, taking on more than she could possibly handle, doing for others without a thought for herself. Patsy Bodine had been a true helpmate to his father before her death. In fact, in a rare display of emotion on the first anniversary of his mother's death, Ethan's father had actually credited his wife with the success of the Bodine ranch, saying that all he had accomplished had been because of her love, support, and physical labor. For Ben Bodine, a man of few words and even fewer compliments, to have made such a statement was nothing short of extraordinary.

Wilhemina blushed under the scrutiny. "Perhaps you'll allow me to assist you to your feet. The way you're staring at me, I feel like I've just grown two heads."

"I can barely see your one head, ma'am, as swollen as my eye is. And if I'm staring, it's only because I'm not used to having a woman help me."

She wrapped her arm gently around his middle and assisted him to his feet. "I can't abide an unfair fight."

Wincing in pain, Ethan finally managed to stand. His brow was sweating so profusely, his ears ringing so loudly in his head, he thought surely he'd embarrass himself by passing out cold, puking, or both.

"I think some of my ribs might be broken."

"If you'll allow me to assist you, I know a place where we can get help. I'll be able to tend your wounds there."

Though it picked at his pride to be rescued by a woman, and twice in the same day, Ethan decided to take her up on her offer. His pride was bruised all to hell, but his body was in much worse condition.

"I don't think I can ride."

"And I wouldn't allow it even if you could," she stated matter-of-factly. "Just hang on to me. I'll lead the horses and guide you to the convent. The sisters of the Sacred Heart aren't that far away."

Ethan attempted to widen his one good eye at the mention of the convent, then thought better of it after pain shot through it like a hot arrow.

He and God had been on pretty shaky footing these last few years, and Ellie Bodine's murder hadn't helped matters much. Ethan wasn't at all comfortable about holing up with a bunch of pious nuns. Not even for a night.

Wilhemina was all too conscious of the warm body pressed against her side. The man was leaning heavily against her, and she could smell sweat and stale cigars, the leather of his sheepskin jacket mingling with the spicy scent of his cologne. For some reason she couldn't quite understand, the manly odors were not only reeking the night air, they were wreaking havoc on her composure.

"It's not much farther." Out of the corner of her eye she saw him nod, and the pained look on his face indicated that it had cost him to make even that tiny movement.

His face was as discolored and puffy as his eye, but she thought there lurked the possibility of handsomeness beneath all the bruises, now that she'd had a closer look. The one good eye he'd flashed at her was the most startling shade of blue. She hadn't quite been able to put her finger on the exact flower it reminded her of, but she would. If there was one thing she possessed, it was an excellent memory.

Wilhemina had put her memory to good use while in Boston, impressing many of her colleagues during the formulation of the herbarium at the Boston Horticultural Society's Botanical Garden, where various specimens of flowers and plants had been collected for study and comparison. It was during the collection and drying of plants for the herbarium that she'd come into close contact with Thomas Fullerton, her mentor and former lover.

Studying the man next to her, she could see he was nothing like the urbane, fussy Thomas, who would never have engaged in anything so common as a brawl or dirtied a pair of neatly pressed trousers to the degree this man had.

The color of the stranger's pants was nearly obliterated by dirt. His dark hair was mussed beneath the Stetson he wore, giving him a rumpled appearance. But if it weren't for the roguish mustache, he would look almost approachable. His boots and jacket were scuffed and well-worn, and she knew both, as well as the man himself, had seen rough use over the years.

Not at all comfortable with her thoughts, she was grateful when the convent came into view. The white, baked-clay structure shone like a welcoming beacon in the moonlight, and she knew that she and the injured stranger would be welcomed there.

Wilhemina had visited the Sisters of the Sacred Heart on many occasions since her return from Boston, advising them on their fruit orchards and vegetable gardens. Though it was a two-day trip on horseback, she relished the time spent there and had grown friendly with many of the nuns, especially Sister Theresa, a pretty novitiate who had yet to take her final vows of poverty, chastity, and obedience.

Wilhemina had decided long ago that she was not cut out to be a nun. Obedience had never been part of her vocabulary.

Ethan opened his one good eye to find a group of nuns hovering over him, whispering and shaking their heads. His shirt was off, and a white bandage had been wrapped securely around his midsection, which made his injured ribs feel slightly better. He was covered to his neck with a wool blanket, mostly for their modesty, not his, he suspected.

"You passed out," his pretty rescuer said, bathing his brow with a damp cloth. Her soothing drawl stamped her a Texan. "I think it was for the best. You wouldn't have been able to stand the pain otherwise."

"What happened to the herd of buffalo that trampled me?" His attempt at humor was met with confused looks by the nuns, who slipped out of the room silently, leaving Ethan and the woman alone.

The corners of her mouth tipped up slightly, indicating that *she*, at least, had a sense of humor. "I'm sure you'll be stiff and sore for a few days. You took quite a vicious beating, so that's to be expected. It'll take a while for the swelling to go down on your face, and your eye will no doubt be black and blue by tomorrow. And, as I'm sure you already realize, several of your ribs are cracked."

The woman's warm brown eyes were filled with kindness, and the intentness of her gaze sent shivers of awareness darting through him. She was truly lovely. Not beautiful and flashy, perhaps, like Lorna Mae. But lovely and serene, like the calm waters of a sun-dappled pond.

Her lavender scent drifted down to tease Ethan's senses. When she bent over, her long brown braid brushed across his chest, and he feared that the swelling on his face wasn't the only swelling he was going to have to contend with.

Damn the contrariness of my maleness! Hasn't it learned a dad-blamed thing?

He grabbed her wrist before she decided to bathe more than his forehead and awaken "the beast," which was how he and Rafe had jokingly referred to their male members when they were kids. She had a disturbing effect on him that wasn't purely sexual, and that scared him far more than the prospect of meeting up with the Murray brothers again. "I think you've washed enough dirt off my hide for now."

She set aside the washcloth and basin of water, saying, "I'll leave you to rest. I'm sure that will be the best restorative for the time being." She turned to leave.

"Wait!" he said almost as an afterthought. "I forgot to ask your name. My manners usually aren't this bad, but under the circumstances . . ."

Her smile was unexpected, kind, and blinding as the rays of the sun, which would be up in just a few short hours. Ethan felt as if he'd just been gut shot. But that reaction was nothing compared to the one he experienced when she calmly announced, "It's Wilhemina . . . Wilhemina Granville."

He recognized the name instantly, grimacing at the realization that this was the woman bounty hunter—the one the old ladies had told him about—the one they'd cried over. The one who was hunting his brother—dead or alive.

"You're Wilhemina Granville!" She didn't look like any bounty hunter he'd ever seen. But she could shoot. He'd witnessed that firsthand. And she didn't have the sense to be afraid. He'd witnessed that, too.

"Why, yes. Have we met? You act as if we know each other."

"You could say that, Miss Granville. I had the pleasure of meeting your elderly aunts a few days back. They're worried to death over your welfare."

"My aunts? You know my aunts?" She shook her head, confused by the censure in his voice. "I'm afraid I don't—"

"It wasn't very considerate of you to ride off and leave them alone and afraid. I thought that birdlike woman was going to expire right on the sidewalk in front of me."

Wilhemina smiled inwardly at the reference to Birdy. Everyone thought Bernadette would topple over in a heavy wind. "My aunt may appear frail because of her slight build, but let me assure you that she's as tough as nails. Both my aunts are, in fact. But I do appreciate your letting me know about their concern." What she didn't appreciate was his rude manner. For someone whose life she'd just saved, he was extremely ungrateful. She had half a mind to tell him so.

"Hand me my vest, will you, Miss Granville? I need a smoke."

"I don't think you—"

Ethan's fierce look, which he'd used quite effectively to make more than one criminal comply, made short work of Wilhemina's protestation.

She reached for the pile of clothes on the chair, and it was then she noticed the shiny silver Texas Ranger badge attached to his vest.

To protect her modesty, Wilhemina hadn't been allowed in the room when the sisters had removed the stranger's shirt and vest, or she would have understood immediately his new-found hostility. Lawmen didn't like bounty hunters. And her aunts had no doubt informed him about her present occupation and the subject of her search.

"Bodine's the name, Miss Granville. Ethan Bodine. Does the name sound familiar to you?"

She swallowed, handing him the garment. "I've heard the name before."

"I venture you have, as it's the same last name as on that Wanted poster back in Justiceburg." He pulled a cigar out of his vest pocket.

Wilhemina felt heat creep up her neck, but she wasn't about to let the lawman intimidate her. She had every right to hunt down a criminal, even if that criminal shared the last name of the man before her. And she had responsibilities to her aunts—the same aunts this man was so incensed over her leaving behind.

"I know the name, Mr. Bodine. I assume my aunts told you of my decision to turn bounty hunter and collect the five-hundred-dollar reward."

He scoffed. "They did. It's the most ridiculous, dad-blamed, foolish thing I've ever heard, and I told them as much. You've got no experience hunting animals, Miss Granville, let alone the two-legged variety. You're bound to get yourself hurt if you don't put aside this crazy notion of yours and ride back to Justiceburg. Your aunts need you. And there's not much your horticulturist learning will gain you on the trail. Unless you got a hankering to be pushing up daisies."

She felt her face flush redder than a claret cup cactus flower. "I'm well aware of my limitations, Ranger Bodine. And I appreciate your concern, but I'm quite capable of taking care of myself, whether in a botanical laboratory or on the trail." She'd battled male prejudice before. The Ranger's chauvinistic attitude toward women was nothing new. It was the main reason her relationship with Thomas had soured: she had refused to allow her career to take a backseat to his.

"I've never known a woman who wasn't a stubborn, mule-headed—" He shook his head and drew a breath, then lit his cigar to calm himself. The Granville woman was going to be a problem, he could already tell that.

"Look, Miss Granville, I appreciate your help tonight with the Murray brothers and all, and I owe you for that. But I can't allow you to interfere in a criminal investiga-tion. I *won't* allow it, Miss Granville. Do I make myself clear?"

Finding it easier to stare at the smoke rings curling toward the ceiling than at him, she nodded. "Perfectly, Ranger Bodine. Now I think you should rest. We can discuss this further tomorrow, when we've both had time to sleep on it. I always think clearer in the morning."

Maybe she could be reasoned with, Ethan thought, pleased he'd been able to talk sense into her. "You can be sure we'll take this up in the morning, Miss Granville. I'm not a man who allows himself to be sidetracked. Even by a pretty woman."

His compliment was unexpected, and she felt an unwelcome surge of pleasure. She doubted Ethan Bodine was a man given to making compliments. But he was definitely all man. Even injured and lying flat on his back, he exuded virility. And though she'd done her best to ignore his rugged good looks, doing so was as difficult and formidable as his disposition.

"I understand totally," she said finally. "I shall see you in the morning."

But when morning came, Wilhemina Granville was nowhere to be found, and Ethan was stark raving mad and cursing loud enough to wake the dead.

Sister Theresa stood in the doorway, looking distraught and embarrassed, covering her ears against the man's profanities. "You must not take the Lord's name in vain, Mr. Bodine. Mother Superior will be very upset and ask you to leave if she hears you."

He looked at the nun as if she'd lost her mind. "Do you think I care about that? Where's Miss Granville? How long ago did she leave?" He should have known better than to trust the woman—any woman.

The novitiate twisted the material of her dark habit nervously. "Willy left last night. She sensed that you would not be happy with her this morning and made the decision to ride out ahead of you. I fear she was right about your being upset. Willy's not in trouble, is she?"

Willy. Cute, he thought disgustedly.

The tears in the young woman's dark eyes gave him pause. He'd been bellowing like a two-day-old calf and had probably frightened her out of her wits. "She's not in trouble with the law, if that's what you're asking, ma'am. Now, if you'll do me the kindness of fetching the rest of my clothes, I'll be out of your way."

She looked horrified by his request. "I must report this to Mother Superior right away, Mr. Bodine. You are injured badly. It would not be good for you to leave so soon. Your ribs are not yet healed, and you could hurt yourself more seriously if you attempt to mount your horse."

"Well, I guess I'll have Wilhemina Granville to thank for that if I do, Sister. The woman out-and-out lied to me." But then, there was nothing new about that when it came to dealing with women.

Sister Theresa's face filled with regret. "Yes. Willy said as much last night and confessed her transgression. She's usually very honest and forthright, and not given to such behavior.

"Please don't be too hard on her when you catch up to her, Mr. Bodine. Willy has been very good to us here at the convent. If it wasn't for her assistance, we wouldn't have apples in our orchard, or half the amount of vegetables in our garden to sustain us. She knows everything there is to know about plants."

And nothing about being a bounty hunter.

And there was still the matter of the Murray brothers, who'd vowed their revenge, not only on him, but on Wilhemina as well. He couldn't live with that on his conscience, not after she'd risked her neck to save him.

"I'm sure Miss Granville's attributes are legion, Sister Theresa," he said. "But the woman doesn't have the sense God gave her. Now, if you'll leave me be, I'll dress and go find her, before she gets herself into more trouble." If that was at all possible.

Unfortunately, it was.

Chapter Three

STRUGGLING AGAINST THE BONDS THAT HELD HER hands and feet tied securely to the chair, Wilhemina stared up at the water-stained ceiling of the dingy hotel room and inwardly cursed her stupidity at riding into a trap.

She'd allowed her frustration at Ethan Bodine to overrule her good judgment. And because of that lapse she was now at the mercy of the Murray brothers, who had vowed their revenge.

Her unceremonious entry into Los Alamos, New Mexico, had been on the rear end of a horse. And not just any horse, but one belonging to none other than Joseph Murray. The same Joseph Murray who now sported a black eye patch because of her overzealous umbrella assault.

To add insult to injury, the leering men had bound her roughly to this chair, taking great delight in passing the last ten minutes describing to her the hideous acts they would perform upon her body.

The only reason she'd been spared till now was that Jacob, the eldest, had gone to the telegraph office to send a wire. No doubt to his vengeful sister, Lorna Mae. But when he returned . . .

Wilhemina shivered at the thought of what would happen when he returned. She had tried to reason with the brothers, to apologize, but they would not listen. But knowing the alternative, she had to try one more time.

"Please, Mr. Murray"—she directed her comments to Jeremiah, who seemed a bit more civilized than the others—"I never meant you any harm. I was merely coming to the aid of an injured man."

Spittle ran down Jeremiah's chin as he moved closer to the chair. He smelled of whiskey and stale cigars and didn't appear to be entirely sober, driving Wilhemina back to despair. "You ain't so high and mighty now, without that peashooter and that fancy stick of yours, lady.

"Jed done told you to mind your own business. You shoulda listened to him."

"Yeah," interjected the youngest Murray. "And you shouldn't have threatened me with a gun. Now I'm gonna have to give tit for tat." He laughed at his own joke, staring at her breasts and licking his lips, then elbowed his brother in the arm. "Get it, Jeremiah: tit for tat?"

"Yeah. I get it."

"Wish we didn't have to wait for Jacob," Jed complained. "It don't seem fair to me."

Panic filled her as the threat became imminent, and she struggled harder; the chair creaked and moaned in protest to her frantic movements. "Please! Please, let me go. I promise never to bother any of you again."

Why, oh why had she interfered? Why hadn't she minded her own business, as they had suggested? Her aunts were forever cautioning her that her impetuous ways would one day be her ruination. But how in good conscience could she have stood by and watched an injured man being brutally beaten, possibly to death?

She couldn't have. Not and live with herself. If she had it to do over again, even knowing the horrible circumstances she would face, she would assist Ethan Bodine without hesitation.

Seated in a chair by the window, Joseph fingered his eye patch and snorted. "We ain't gonna kill you, if that's what you're worried about. We're just gonna have us a little fun. Sort of payback for what Bodine did to Lorna Mae."

Tears clouded her vision. "But I don't even know Mr. Bodine, or what he did to your sister. You shouldn't revenge yourself on me because of him. It wouldn't be fair." But life wasn't fair, or her father wouldn't have died. She would have been able to remain in Boston, a well-respected horticulturist, honored for her knowledge and her worth, not chastised and ridiculed for being the wrong sex.

If life were fair, Thomas would have loved her, accepted who she was, and treated her as equal in all respects.

But life wasn't fair, which was why she was in the predicament she was in.

"A man don't think much about fairness when he's got a hankerin' for a little female companionship, little lady," Jedediah said. "But don't worry. We're going to show you a real good time. I give you my word on it."

Ethan fought against the stabbing pain in his chest as he rode into Los Alamos. He'd ridden hard and fast, following Wilhemina Granville's tracks to about ten miles outside of town. There her tracks had joined up with four other mounts at that point, and he suspected that the woman was in a great deal of danger.

The Murrays had revenge on their mind. And men being men, he had a good idea how they would plan to get even. Wilhemina Granville was an attractive woman.

He entered the dilapidated building that passed for a saloon and ordered a whiskey to dull the pain in his ribs. It was approaching noon, and he was the only patron in the seedy establishment, so the barkeep seemed pleased to have his business and his company.

"New in town, stranger?" The man's red eyebrows lifted as he recognized the silver badge on Ethan's chest. "Or should I say 'Ranger'?"

"It's Bodine. And I'm looking for some information about a friend of mine." He tipped back the whiskey, welcoming the burning liquid into his belly, hoping it would ease the searing pain. He remembered Sister Theresa's admonitions about not riding and knew he had only himself to blame. And Wilhemina Granville.

"Bodine. I heard that name before. Ain't you that Texas Ranger who's tracking his brother? The one they say killed Bobby Slaughter in cold blood over Justiceburg way?" He swatted at a pesky fly that buzzed near his head, but he missed.

Ethan held out his glass for a refill. "One and the same. But it ain't my brother I'm looking for at the moment. It's a woman."

The barkeep smiled knowingly, indicating the curtained partition at the back of the room. "Well, hell, why didn't you say so? If it's a whore you're needing—"

"I ain't lookin' for a whore. I'm looking for a woman—a decent woman—who may have been in the company of four cowboys. They probably rode in early this morning."

"I seen her—the woman you're talking about." He indicated the grimy window with a nod of his head. "They got her in a hotel room across the street. The youngest one came in a while ago to buy a bottle of whiskey, bragging about how they was going to have them a poke for free. I didn't pay him no mind. Thought he was bragging."

Rage filled Ethan, though he tried to appear nonchalant. There was nothing worse in his opinion than a man who would take a woman by force. It was the ultimate act of cowardice.

"That's probably just as well."

"What's this woman to you? You sweet on her or something?"

Ethan shook his head. "She's nothing to me but someone who helped me once when I needed it. Now I'm returning the favor." He checked his gun to make sure it was fully loaded, and the barkeep's eyes widened.

"You aim to do some killing Bodine? I heard you Texas Rangers were a ruthless bunch. *Los Tejanos Diablos*, the Mexicans call you—the Texas Devils."

Ethan was aware of the nickname, and he supposed the Mexican bandits who'd suffered at the Rangers' hands had good cause to fear them. But they'd deserved everything they'd gotten. A Ranger didn't dispense justice without good reason.

"I won't be doing any killing unless my hand's forced. Who's the local authority in town? I want to inform him of the situation." And it would help to even up the odds if the Murrays decided to get trigger-happy.

"That'll be Marshal Bob Heggan. He's over at the café getting hisself a bite to eat. Marshal likes to have hisself a big meal in the middle of the day. Says if he eats too much too late in the day, it gives him gas."

Ethan thanked the bartender and headed toward the café, wondering how pleased the marshal would be to know that his stomach problems were the topic of conversation at the saloon.

It was tough keeping a secret in a small town. Ethan and his brothers had learned that lesson well while growing up. Every time the Bodine boys would get into a scrape, let "the beast" loose at the whorehouse when they should have been working, or have a drink of whiskey with the undertaker, Sammy Willits, who was usually more embalmed than his customers, their pa would know of it before they got home. And crossing Ben Bodine was not a smart thing to do.

Ethan had inherited not only his pa's wisdom, but his orneriness as well. He guessed the Murrays would find that out soon enough.

Wilhemina's eyes widened in fear as Jacob Murray entered the room, having just returned and given his brothers permission to proceed.

She wanted to scream, to cry out in protest, but they'd stuffed a dirty rag in her moth, rendering her powerless to resist even that much.

"Time for some fun, little lady," Joseph said, and his younger brother laughed.

Suddenly the door burst open, startling the two men. With gun drawn, Ethan Bodine stepped across the threshold, and Wilhemina released the breath she didn't know she'd been holding.

Ranger Bodine looked mad enough to bend nails with his teeth, and she couldn't remember a more welcome sight.

"Freeze!" Ethan gave a quick glance at the men standing statuelike in place. Joseph and Jedediah were near the bed in various stages of undress. Jacob was seated near the window, looking concerned but not overly surprised that they'd been found out. Jeremiah was in the midst of relieving himself in the corner.

"You're all under arrest for the kidnapping and violation of Wilhemina Granville."

"But we ain't done nothing to her," Joseph protested, pulling up his pants. "You didn't give us time to poke her."

"Yeah. We ain't done a thing." Jed reached for the ceiling, looking as cowardly as a green bronc in a thunderstorm.

"You think that gets you off the hook?" Ethan's eyes narrowed. "I should shoot you all now and get it over with." He cocked his gun to make good on his threat, and the click of the revolver sounded ominous and loud in the ensuing silence.

As if on cue, the marshal entered, took one look at the disheveled woman tied to the chair, and shook his head in regret.

Pointing his rifle at the Murray brothers, the lawman said in a voice as cold as steel, "You boys are under arrest. I don't hold with this kind of uncivilized behavior in my town. Tie 'em up, Captain Bodine, and I'll escort them to jail. They're gonna have a long wait for the circuit judge to come to town. Old Judge Willoughby just died, and they ain't appointed a new one yet. Yep, it's going to be a right good while till these boys have their cases heard."

When the door closed behind the marshal and the Murrays, Ethan moved to the chair. Untying the bonds at Wilhemina's feet, he tried not to notice the trimness of her ankles, bruised slightly by the rope.

She made a muffled sound, and Ethan realized the gag was still in place. He moved to untie it. And that's when his gaze zeroed in on her lush breasts. With her hands tied behind the chair, her chest was thrust forward. His hands faltered momentarily, as if they had minds of their own and would rather attend to her perfectly formed mounds than to removing the gag in her moth.

"Goddamn it!" He cursed his lack of control. For a man who had sworn off women, he was doing a piss-poor job of ignoring this one.

Wilhemina bolted upright as soon as her bonds were released and draped her arms around Ethan's neck. "Oh, thank you, Ranger Bodine! I'm so grateful you came when you did."

"Are you all right?"

She blushed as his meaning became clear. "They told the truth when they said there hadn't been time to—" She blushed even deeper.

The firm little body pressing against his chest was playing havoc with Ethan's composure. Instinct had him wrapping his arms about her small waist and pulling her into him. He inhaled deeply of her lavender scent and felt the wetness of her tears on his neck. Only his extreme self-control, and the knowledge of what she'd just gone through, prevented his hands from creeping up to explore those tempting breasts and capture her mouth beneath his.

Extricating himself abruptly from her stranglehold, he pushed her gently down on the bed. "Get hold of yourself, woman!" His tone was brusque and filled with the tension of unfulfilled desire.

"Oh, dear! I'm so sorry, Ranger Bodine. I forgot all about your injured ribs. I was just so grateful. I don't know how I can ever repay you. I—"

"Forget it." He scowled. "We're even as far as I'm concerned." He turned his back on her and stalked to the window, trying to get his mind on something other than how good Wilhemina Granville looked. Even the pain in his ribs couldn't obliterate the anguish that settled much lower.

"As soon as you're ready, Miss Granville, I want you to get on your horse and get yourself back to Justiceburg. You've got no business being on the trail by yourself. Your recent encounter with the Murrays should prove how totally incapable you are of defending yourself against ruthless individuals.

"Leave the finding of Rafe to me. It's my job to bring him back to stand trial."

Cheeks flushed hot in indignation, Wilhemina stared at him, unable to believe the man's high-handedness in ordering her home as if she were a mere child, incapable of taking care of herself.

She may have been momentarily upset, even stunned, by what had happened, but she was in full control of her faculties now and had no intention of bowing to Ethan Bodine's orders. No matter how fierce and determined he looked.

Deciding that the arrogant Ranger needed to be taken down a peg or two, Wilhemina walked up to Ethan Bodine and stared him right in the eye. "I will not be dictated to, Mr. Bodine, not by you or any man. I have no intention of giving up my pursuit of your brother. I will not be bullied under any circumstances, nor do I need you for a protector. And despite what just happened, I am perfectly capable of taking care of myself. Which I've been doing for years, quite successfully, thank you."

Ethan listened to every word Wilhemina spewed forth. But he was having a heck of a time concentrating on what she was saying, for his eyes had a mind of their own and they were roaming over every delectable inch of her body.

The sunlight streaming through the window bathed her body in a warm glow. Her shapely form stood out in stark silhouette. Desire filled every inch of him, overpowering his common sense and good judgment. Shocking not only Wilhemina, but himself, Ethan pulled her to his chest and proceeded to kiss her senseless.

The kiss was wet, warm, and masterful, and Wilhemina felt its power clear down to the tips of her toes. Ethan tasted of tobacco and whiskey, and she found the combination heady. His soft mustache felt good against her face, and when his thrusting tongue sought entry into her mouth, she parted her lips slightly, allowing her dormant passions to be brought to life.

Wilhemina was powerless to stop the hunger within from spreading. From her hard, throbbing nipples to the moistness between her thighs, her body craved, lusted, on a purely physical level. And all her years of learning, all the studies she'd conducted of the sex life of plants, all her sorry experience of lovemaking with Thomas Fullerton, couldn't explain why.

Her soft moan of surrender brought Ethan back to his senses, and he set Wilhemina away from him. Her mouth was swollen and red from his kisses, her eyes glazed with passion and confusion, and he knew in that instant that he could take her, make love to her if he wanted to, and she wouldn't resist.

The stinging slap to his cheek shocked him to his senses.

"How dare you take such liberties! You are as vile as the Murrays. Only you hide behind a badge, Ranger Bodine."

The insult to his profession enraged Ethan. A Ranger was honorable above all else, and this self-proclaimed female bounty hunter wasn't going to tell him any differently.

"You're the one who wrapped yourself around me like a morning glory vine, Miss Granville."

She gasped, her cheeks turning as red as his where she'd slapped him. "I did no such thing! How dare you say I did." But despite her protests, she knew there was a kernel of truth in his statement. Her outrage had completely overshadowed her modesty and common sense. It struck Wilhemina suddenly that for a woman who rarely lost her temper, she'd been in a foul mood and a state of turmoil since meeting the Texas Ranger.

Inhaling deeply, she said, "I may have put temptation before you, Ranger Bodine, but I assure you it was not intentional. And I would have thought that a man such as yourself would have greater control over your base instincts."

No one was more disgusted with his behavior than Ethan, not even Wilhemina Granville. He'd lost control, allowed himself to be taken in again. And by a woman.

He patted his burning cheek, decided that this snip of a woman packed quite a wallop, and wondered what the hell he was going to do with the horticulturist.

The apology he knew she expected stuck in his throat like dried beef jerky. "Guess we were just caught up in the moment."

Her eyes flashed fire, but she said nothing more on the subject.

"You won't catch Rafe, you know," Ethan told her. "He's an ex–Texas Ranger, and almost as good as me at tracking and all. He'll evade your attempts to bring him in."

She picked her hat up off the floor. "You'll not dissuade me, Ranger Bodine. I'm determined to go after your brother and bring him in for the reward money."

His sigh was full of frustration. "You'll get yourself killed if you do. If a snake or a mountain lion doesn't get you, the elements surely will."

She shrugged. "It's a risk I'm willing to take." One that was necessary to protect her aunts, thanks to Rufus Bowers's unreasonable and ridiculous demands.

Ethan cursed, plowing agitated fingers through his hair. It wasn't a risk *he* was willing to take. And he couldn't stand the thought of having the woman's death on his conscience, especially after she'd saved his hide. There was only one solution to the problem. And though it galled him to say it, he did.

"I think it would be best if you threw in with me, Miss Granville. There's safety in numbers." He could keep an eye on her and at the same time prevent her from shooting Rafe should she find him. Which would be nothing short of a miracle in his opinion. But miracles had been known to happen.

She shook her head, her chin jutting out stubbornly. "I don't have any intention of throwing in with you, Ranger. You're a bully. And I like doing things my own way."

"Now listen here—" He bit back his words, knowing from the mutinous glint in her dark eyes that she wouldn't respond to threats. He tried reason instead.

"You have to admit, Miss Granville, that I'm much better at tracking and outdoor survival than you. Would you know what to do if a blue norther suddenly came upon you, or a mountain lion attacked? And what if you were taken ill, or became snakebit? Would you know what to do then? Because I can assure you, Miss Granville, I do."

Wilhemina chewed upon the indisputable facts that Ethan presented. And rather than choke on his wisdom, she accepted it for what it was: common sense and the truth.

She was out of her element, and he knew it. They both knew it. And to deny it was just plain foolish. Besides, she'd already had a taste of what being a defenseless woman was like. Being logical in the extreme, Wilhemina knew that there was only one thing to do.

"All right, Captain Bodine. I will agree to accompany you. But I want it understood from the onset that I will be treated like an equal partner and not one of the men under your command. Do you agree?"

Wilhemina Granville should have been turned over somebody's knee years ago and spanked soundly on her curvaceous little rump, Ethan thought. But since that obviously hadn't been done, and since he wasn't a man to administer corporal punishment to a woman, he was stuck.

He held out his hand to seal their uneasy alliance. "Agreed."

Fortunately she couldn't see that the fingers of his other hand were crossed behind his back.

Chapter Four

LEAVING LOS ALAMOS AND THE UNPLEASANT MEMO-ries behind them, Wilhemina and Ethan made camp the first night beneath a stand of cottonwoods near a small, fast-running stream.

Ethan had just started to make a campfire when the pain in his broken ribs he'd been fighting all day overcame him. He clutched his side and slumped to the ground with a moan.

"Mr. Bodine!" Wilhemina dropped the tin coffeepot and rushed to his side, alarmed by the chalkiness of his complexion and erratic breathing.

"My . . . my saddlebag. There's whiskey. Get it."

She rummaged through his gear until she found the amber bottle of liquor, then handed it to him.

It was her fault that he was in such a state. If he hadn't been forced to come after her, if they'd stayed put at the convent and his ribs had had adequate time to heal, he wouldn't be suffering so now.

"I'm so sorry, Mr. Bodine. This is all my fault."

He tried to nod in agreement, but the effort cost him dearly and he cursed aloud, clutching his injured side. "Jesus! I'd like to shoot Joseph Murray straight between his beady eyes." Holding the bottle, he took a healthy swig. The whiskey made his eyes water. "There's nothing worse than cracked ribs, except being gut shot." His ribs would heal eventually, if he could stay off his horse for a few days.

And therein lay the problem. If Wilhemina suspected he was incapacitated, she might ride off and leave him again. Unless he could convince her not to.

"There's a storm brewing. It's likely we'll be camped here a day or two," he lied.

Wilhemina glanced up at the cloudless sky, her brow wrinkled in confusion. "I think you must be mistaken, Ranger. I see no indication of rain."

"I believe I know a bit more about reading nature's signs than you do, Miss Granville. I say we're in for a storm. We'll stay put until I say otherwise."

"Are you sure? I just don't—"

Used to command, Ethan hated having his authority questioned by anyone, even if he was lying. His voice hardened. "Of course I'm sure. I've been riding trail a lot longer than you. And if you think I'm not anxious to be on my way, you're dead wrong, Miss Granville. There's more at stake here than a measly five-hundred-dollar reward. I have my brother's life to think about."

Her cheeks heated at his words, but, noting the anguish in his eyes, the paleness of his complexion, she re-

frained from retorting. The Ranger was obviously still in a
great deal of pain, and she had no intention of adding to it.

"I'm sure a slight delay won't hamper our efforts to
find your brother, Captain."

She obviously didn't know Rafe if she thought that,
Ethan decided, but he was grateful that she'd chosen not to
argue the point.

His brother was savvy and trailwise. He'd use their
every delay to his best advantage. Rafe's trail would be
much more difficult to find the longer they stayed, but it
couldn't be helped. A broken rib could puncture his lung
and do some permanent damage. Then he'd be good to no
one, least of all Rafe.

"I'm glad you've decided to be sensible, Miss
Granville."

"I pride myself on being sensible, Ranger Bodine.
Though I'm sure you must think otherwise, due to my recent actions."

He thought she was headstrong, foolish, impulsive,
and very brave, but he refrained from uttering any of his
opinions. If they were going to be riding together, then
they needed to get along. "You might as well call me
Ethan. Looks like we'll be spending some time together."

She brightened at that. "And you must call me Willy.
That's what my friends call me."

She looked a little too feminine to be called by such a
tomboyish name, but if that's what she wanted, Ethan
would comply. He could be accommodating when the situation warranted. But he intended that *Willy* should know
exactly who she was dealing with and who was in charge.

"I'll finish getting this fire going before it gets dark. No telling what animals might be lurking about. You can take over the cooking chores. Anyone riding with me has to pull their own weight."

"I can make a decent pot of coffee, and there're beans and bacon in my saddlebag. I'll get supper started. I assure you, Ethan, that I am quite capable of pulling my own weight, as you say."

"Good. See that you do. There's nothing worse than a shirker, in my opinion."

She bit her lip and took a deep breath, unwilling to be bated. Either Ethan's ribs were ailing him or he just naturally had a nasty disposition. She was inclined to believe the latter.

"Where do you think your brother is headed, Ethan?" Wilhemina tossed a few strips of bacon into the frying pan, separating the pieces with a fork. It sizzled and browned, and the aroma made Ethan's stomach grumble.

He found it pleasurable to watch her work. She was efficient and seemed to know her way around a campfire, something few women could claim. Lorna Mae Murray knew her way around a bedroom and could heat things up in there pretty darn good, but he doubted the woman had enough sense to rub two sticks together to make a campfire.

"That's hard to say," he replied. And he wouldn't tell her anything specific even if he knew. Once Wilhemina found out where Rafe was headed, she might take matters into her own hands and take off again. He wasn't about to let that happen. Women, he'd found, were notorious for saying one thing and doing another.

"Tracks indicated Rafe's heading north. And I don't think he's alone. I've seen signs of more than one horse." Which surprised Ethan. A man on the run usually rode alone and fast. But Rafe, whose horse's shoe had a missing nail and made a distinctive marking, wasn't riding by himself.

"Does he have a gang?"

Knowing that the woman didn't know anything about Rafe's character, Ethan tried not to let it rankle him. "My brother's not a criminal. He's out to avenge the murder of his wife by a gang of ruthless outlaws."

Gasping, she nearly dropped the pan of bacon into the fire. "How dreadful! Why did those men kill your brother's wife?"

"Rafe and I put the leader, a man by the name of Hank Slaughter, in prison five years ago for bank robbery. Hank's a sadistic son of a— He's mean as a snake," he amended, remembering that she was a lady. "A man like Hank Slaughter and the men who ride with him don't care if their victims are young or old, male or female. They kill for the pure joy of it. Guess they decided to take their revenge out on poor Ellie, Rafe's wife."

"I'm terribly sorry for your brother."

"Don't be. He broke the law when he shot Bobby Slaughter. Though I suspect it was done in self-defense. Rafe's not one to murder a man in cold blood."

The bacon and beans were done, and Wilhemina put them on a tin plate and brought Ethan his share. Anguish rode the Ranger's face hard when he spoke of his brother, and love shone deeply in his eyes for the man he'd been forced to hunt down.

"I'm sorry you have to go after your own flesh and blood, Ethan. That can't be an easy thing to do."

"It's my job. I can't allow Rafe to take the law into his own hands. That wouldn't be right."

"And you want to protect him from himself, don't you?"

He seemed uncomfortable with the question, as if she'd probed too far beneath his exterior and found some truth. "I guess you could say that."

They finished their meal in companionable silence, each lost in thoughts neither cared to express. The sun had gone down, the ebony sky still clear and glittering brilliantly with an endless array of stars. Ethan hoped Wilhemina was too absorbed in her thoughts to notice that there wasn't a raincloud in sight.

He set aside his plate. "Guess we'd better think about turning in." Being careful not to strain himself, he reached for a log and tossed it onto the fire, hoping it would last through the night. Tomorrow would come early, but he refrained from adding that. As poorly as he felt, he wasn't certain he'd be able to ride tomorrow.

Wilhemina nodded. "You need to rest. And after my recent ordeal I could use some peace and quiet, too."

"I'm sorry about what happened. The Murrays shouldn't have taken out their anger on you. It's me they hate."

Though she knew that the Murrays' hatred stemmed from their sister's fall from grace, Wilhemina didn't feel like probing the topic at the moment. The one she had to deal with, the problem uppermost on her mind, was going to be equally uncomfortable.

"Before you bed down for the night"—her color rose—"I think it would be wise if I checked your bandage. It may have loosened, which would explain why you've been having so much pain and discomfort."

She moved closer, before he had a chance to protest, and squatted beside him. "You'll have to remove your shirt."

Ethan arched a brow. "Well now, except for those nuns, I haven't taken my shirt off for a pretty woman in a right good while." His fingers moved to the bone buttons, and he wanted to laugh at the mortification on her face. He'd always been something of a tease—Rafe and his youngest brother Travis, had been the butt of his humor many times—and it was proving fun to needle the head-strong, proper horticulturist.

Wilhemina was embarrassed and wished the ground would open up and swallow her whole. But she wasn't about to let the Ranger know it. She'd seen the twinkle in his eyes and suspected he was having fun at her expense. Men, she'd found, always enjoyed getting the upper hand.

As she slipped off his vest and shirt, her fingers brushed his warm skin and darts of awareness shot through her. The kiss they'd shared had been on her mind most of the day. She'd replayed it, relived it, in every glorious detail, then cursed herself a thousand times for being a fool.

Men like Ethan had a woman in every town, and he was hardly the type of man who would view her as an equal, despite his words to that effect. She'd already experienced the full force of a man's egomaniacal need to control—to be first and best. Now she needed to remind herself of that experience and learn from it. Repeating past mistakes was a sign of stupidity, and Wilhemina prided herself on not being a stupid woman.

Ethan's tan skin glowed like burnished copper in the firelight. She swallowed several times as she unwrapped the long length of bandage, trying to keep her mind on other things besides the soft furring of his chest, the rock hard muscles of his abdomen. Intentions were a whole lot easier to set than to keep.

Ethan was having similar thoughts. Wilhemina's innocent ministrations were driving him wild. Another minute and he would toss her on the ground and—

"Does your bandage itch, Ranger? Because if it does, I can prepare a salve to place under it. I spotted some laurel plants nearby. I'll collect them and—"

"Never mind. Just rewrap the damn thing and be done with it." Ethan's tone had turned downright testy, owing to the fact that he had a bulge in his pants the size of Texas. The touch of Willy's hand burned into him like a hot branding iron, and her warm breath on his chest made his toes curl heavenward. He was already experiencing shortness of breath thanks to his injury. A few more minutes of her tender care and he just might pass out cold.

"There." She cinched the bandage tighter, then tied it off. "How does that feel?"

Surprisingly, it felt much better, and he said so. At least he thought he had. Then he realized that he'd been holding his breath and thinking the response.

"Better," he said, loud enough to wake the dead.

Willy rocked back on her heels. "You needn't shout, Ethan. I'm close enough to hear you."

"Sorry." He had the grace to look chagrined.

"Is there anything else I can do for you before we turn in?"

A thousand responses came to Ethan's mind, none of which were decent, and he cursed himself and this woman who had slipped so easily beneath his newly erected guard.

"Hell, no!" he replied, wrapping a blanket around himself for protection and lying on the ground.

The dampness of the earth would chill his ardor. The hardness of his makeshift bed would serve to remind him that a Ranger couldn't be sidetracked by the scent and touch of a woman. He just wished someone or something would relay those messages to "the beast."

Time hadn't improved Ethan's disposition a day and a half later, and neither had Wilhemina's penchant for taking control.

"I cannot allow you to chop firewood, Ethan. You could reinjure yourself and delay our departure another day. Now give me the ax and I will take care of chopping the wood."

He stared at the bossy woman, whose arms were folded across her chest in a no-nonsense manner, and wondered where she'd gotten such an exalted opinion of herself. Just because she had beaten him badly at poker last night was no reason for her to think that she could now emasculate him by ordering him about. No one ordered a Texas Ranger about and lived to talk about it.

"I'm on the mend. And we're leaving at sunup, so I don't see the difference. Besides, chopping firewood is men's work, not women's. Why don't you go gather weeds or something." She'd been wandering around in the woods since they'd arrived at camp.

"They are not weeds, for your information, but interesting forms of plant life. I will use the wild mushrooms and mustard to add flavor and nutrition to our stew this evening. The others I will catalog for future reference.

"And don't try to change the subject." She held her hand out for the ax. "Quit being so stubborn and . . . and masculine. You need to give your ribs time to heal properly."

His eyes narrowed. "Maybe you should try being more womanly, *Willy*, and a little less masculine yourself. Didn't your mama ever tell you that it's men who wear the pants in the family?"

"My mother died giving birth to me, and I have been raised to believe that a woman is equal to a man in all things. I believe I proved more skillful than you last evening when I beat you at poker." She dared him to deny it.

"You were lucky, that's all. It was the draw of the cards and had nothing to do with skill. And how do you know that I didn't let you win?"

She smiled sweetly. "Because your large ego would never have allowed that, Ranger Bodine. I've had dealings with men's egos before."

He resented this woman's astuteness. It was as if she could read his mind at every turn, and it gave him a downright unsettling feeling. "I said I'd chop the damn wood." He picked up the ax, swung it over his head, and quickly doubled over in pain, dropping the offending implement to the ground. "Jesus!"

"You are a stubborn, foolish man, Ethan Bodine. I am quite capable of cutting firewood. I'm sure you'll discover while on our journey that I am capable of a great many things."

Yeah, like driving a man insane! Ethan kept that thought to himself as he straightened and took a deep breath. "Suit yourself. But if you chop your damn foot off, don't come crying to me," he retorted, and stalked toward his horse. At least his horse knew better than to mouth off at him. He doubted he would ever get the last word with Wilhemina Granville.

Grasping the wooden ax handle as though she'd been born to it, Wilhemina felt the thrill of victory rush up her arm. She had actually won the disagreement with the hardheaded Ranger. Though she knew it was only the first of many to come. Ethan wasn't a man to give in easily, and he had a very low opinion where women were concerned. He was a Neanderthal—a caveman totally out of step with the times.

Women were gaining respect in the fields of law, medicine, dentistry. They'd been given the vote in

Wyoming, and other states were likely to follow suit one day. It was time for men like Ethan, who viewed women as helpless, mindless creatures, to take another look and form some different opinions. Wilhemina was going to be instrumental in teaching the arrogant lawman a new way of looking at things.

She glanced across camp to where his horse was tethered to a piñon tree and found it amusing that he was talking to the creature. The big black stallion seemed to be taking in every word of Ethan's animated conversation, bobbing his head now and then. Wilhemina couldn't contain her smile.

She was sure he was giving the steed an earful about her, and women in general. Well, it was high time Ethan learned that a woman could be his equal.

Wilhemina always enjoyed a challenge. Maybe it was the scientist in her, but she thought it would be fascinating to peel back the outer layers of Ethan's brusque exterior to explore the man beneath.

She was sure that behind his gruff outer shell lurked a kind and gentle man. She'd seen glimpses of it from time to time, like when the Murrays had assaulted her. And even the fact that he talked to his horse affectionately proved his heart was softer than he let on.

Despite the fact that Ethan Bodine was somewhat uncivilized, extremely arrogant, and a far cry from someone she would consider an ideal mate, Wilhemina found him to be extraordinarily handsome, now that the swelling on his face had gone down. It was hard to ignore the way the sunlight glinted off his ebony hair, the way his mustache twitched when he found something she said amusing, the way his eyes captivated and held her gaze. And there was something about all that raw masculinity that set her pulses pounding whenever she got near him.

Dangerous. He was dangerous. And she found that very appealing after her safe, staid life. He was a rare find, like a wildflower that had yet to be discovered, named, and categorized.

He was uncharted territory, and Wilhemina found herself wondering what it would be like to explore an unknown entity, to study every detail, to satisfy her natural curiosity and budding desire.

Meanwhile Ethan curried Buster's coat to a high sheen. "Damn infernal woman!" he cursed beneath his breath. He'd known Wilhemina Granville would be nothing but trouble, and she sure as hell was proving him right. For her to imagine that a woman could be equal to a man . . . He shook his head. "Damn fool woman."

He glanced to where she was swinging the ax with far more proficiency than he ever imagined possible. In fairness to her he had to admit, even grudgingly, that Willy did possess some unusual traits for a woman. He'd never met any females, save for whores, who could play a decent hand of poker, and she'd beaten him soundly. She could sit a horse well—the old ladies had been right about that—and she handled a gun pretty darn respectably.

He admired the way she had stood up to him after her abduction, though he would never admit that to her—the woman was too full of herself as it was—and she did have a fair amount of knowledge about plants, and not just flowers.

She could tell the difference between poisonous mushrooms and good ones. He'd always been afraid to pick the damn things for fear of killing himself.

"Willy does have a few good points to consider, Buster," he admitted, and the horse nudged his shoulder, as if agreeing with him. "But I'd say the bad ones still outnumber the good."

Ethan enjoyed his own company when riding the trail and the silence that went along with it. But he soon discovered that quiet and his companion didn't go hand in hand.

"Did you know, Ethan, that by the end of the eighteenth century there were sixteen hundred botanical gardens in Europe? Of course, gardens have been around forever. There were the Hanging Gardens of Babylon and, of course, the Garden of Eden.

"And did you know that St. Louis had the very first botanical garden in the United States? I just find those facts so interesting, don't you?"

Ethan was far more interested in the fact that Willy's eyes sparkled and her face radiated joy whenever she talked about plants, and he couldn't help wondering if she'd be as responsive to other earthy topics that had nothing whatsoever to do with horticulture.

"Is that so?"

She nodded, warming to her topic. "Man has always been dependent on plants for food and shelter. And for the very air we breathe. Plants give off a gas known as oxygen."

"You don't say?" He'd studied something about that in school—the times he'd actually attended—but he couldn't recall exactly. Studies and Ethan didn't go together too well. He'd learned to read, write, and do sums, but he'd found life outside the schoolroom far preferable to life within.

His youngest brother, Travis, was the scholarly one in the family. With Rafe's and Ethan's help, and against their father's wishes, the boy had left the ranch to attend one of those fancy universities back east and study law. He was now a full-fledged practicing attorney in Misery, and Ethan couldn't be more proud.

His youngest brother wasn't cut out for rangering, not like he and Rafe. Travis had taken a shine to the law, but in his own way and on his own terms.

"I hope I'm not boring you. I do tend to go on when I'm talking about horticultural topics."

"I like flowers well enough. We've got the prettiest Texas bluebonnets back home. My ma was real partial to them."

"I'm quite familiar with *Lupinus texenis*. The plants grow about two feet tall. They are dark blue, two-lipped, with five petals. The upper petal has a white—"

"I like them because they're pretty when they bloom along the hillsides and valleys in the spring. Don't really need to know their inner workings, ma'am."

Willy's cheeks flushed scarlet at the mild rebuke, but she was determined not to let Ethan's rudeness bother her.

After all, he was not as scholarly as she, and not everyone appreciated and found as fascinating the botanical makeup of plants. "Are bluebonnets your favorite flower, then?" she asked, suddenly realizing that bluebonnets had been the flower she'd been thinking of earlier—the ones that reminded her of Ethan's blue eyes.

He shook his head. "Nope. I'm a sucker for morning glory vines. I don't think there's anything that suggests home and family more than a pretty pink vine climbing up the side of a house."

"You're the one who wrapped yourself around me like a morning glory vine, Miss Granville." Ethan's words came flooding back in Willy's mind, along with memories best forgotten. "And . . . and does your home have a vine growing up the side?"

"Don't have a home of my own. I go where the work takes me. But if I did, it'd have a morning glory growing up next to it."

"Doesn't that get kind of lonely? I mean, not having a home? Everyone needs somewhere to put down roots. A tree or plant would die if it couldn't sink taproots into the ground for nourishment. I think a person's the same way. We get our strength and sustenance from home and family."

"I'm partial to the life I've chosen for myself. I've got my horse, the camaraderie of men when we're out on a mission. And there's always my pa's ranch, if I feel the need for company, which I don't very often. Too many roots can get tangled up and strangle a man."

"Well, you're certainly entitled to your opinion, but I don't agree with it at all."

That was no surprise to him; he smiled inwardly. "There are few things in life men and women are likely to agree on. We're too different to find common ground. And most times women don't look at things in a rational way, like men do. They're ruled by emotion, not common sense."

"First of all, Ethan, I doubt that you've ever looked for a commonality where women are concerned. And second, I resent your generalization regarding women. I have a great deal of common sense."

"Like riding into a fracas that was no concern of yours, when you could have gotten yourself killed? That don't make no sense to me."

"You would have done the same for me, if the shoe had been on the other foot."

He considered her comment for a moment. "Maybe. But then, I'm a man and it would be my nature to protect a helpless, outnumbered female."

"And what is so different about me? Do you think I could have stood by and watched those men beat you to death? And all because I'm supposed to be a helpless female?" She snorted indignantly. "I've never heard such poppycock and drivel in my life. There is little difference between men and women."

Ethan knew it was pointless to argue with the woman. Any woman, for that matter. Once they made up their mind, there was no reasoning with them. But it just wasn't in his nature not to have the last word on a subject.

"Sometime when you're in the mood, Willy, we'll strip down naked and stand in front of a mirror together. That way you'll be able to see the difference between the two sexes." His smile was naughty, and it caused a flush that stained her cheeks bright red. "I'll be more than happy to point them out to you."

Recovering quickly, she replied, "Really, Ranger Bodine? Isn't that kind of you. I am a scientist, after all, so perhaps at some future time we'll have to conduct a little experiment. Hands-on research, Ethan, is the horticulturist's byword." She smiled sweetly, adding, "You'd best close your mouth. You're likely to catch flies if you don't."

Ethan snapped his mouth shut and stared bullets at the woman's retreating back as she rode away. Not only had she gotten in the last word, but she'd managed to give him an erection as hard as his saddle horn. And as big as his mouth!

Chapter Five

ETHAN AND WILHEMINA ENTERED THE TOWN OF Never Die later that day. Having passed by a sign on the outskirts that proclaimed the former silver mining town's credo—"The sun never sets, the fun never stops, the residents never die—" Ethan decided that this would be the perfect place to take his mind off the horticulturist and the temptation she presented and maybe discover something about the whereabouts of his brother.

Not that he had much choice. Willy's horse had thrown a shoe, and they weren't going anywhere until it could be shod. They had agreed to spend one night in the town while it was taken care of at the livery.

Rafe's substantial lead and the unforeseen delays they'd been experiencing gave Ethan cause to worry. If Rafe were to catch up with the Slaughters before Ethan could find him, he was likely to kill them. Then there'd be no saving his hide. No jury in Texas—or anywhere else, for that matter—was likely to be sympathetic to his brother's cause if he took the law into his own hands again and dispatched another Slaughter to hell. The law was still the law, even to a Texan. Rafe was going to swing by the neck until dead, and Ethan had to find him before that could happen.

As they rode down the main street, passing by the many shops and buildings, there seemed to be an underlying restlessness in the air. It was quiet, too quiet for a town the size of Never Die, and neither Wilhemina nor Ethan could discount it.

"Even though there are people milling about, this place seems like a ghost town." Wilhemina observed two neatly dressed matrons hurrying across the street in front of her, looking nervously over their shoulders as if they were in danger of being accosted.

An air of prosperity hovered about the small farm and ranching community. The false-fronted buildings had been recently painted. The millinery shop had an attractive display of hats in the window and a lavender-checked gown that made Wilhemina's heart palpitate with longing.

Ordinarily she wouldn't get all agog over the latest fashion creations, but riding the trail in nondescript clothing had given her a yen for something pretty.

Although she'd never admit it, not even to herself, Wilhemina now had someone to look pretty for.

A few of the locals sat in front of the barbershop, reading the evening edition of the *Never Die Gazette*. But the usual jocularity and social atmosphere you'd expect from the regulars of the tonsorial parlor was missing, and Wilhemina thought that as odd as everything else she'd observed about the town. Something wasn't quite right, but she couldn't put her finger on it.

Ethan shrugged, dismounting in front of the livery. "After Santa Rosa and Los Alamos I'd think you would appreciate a little peace and quiet. There's just no pleasing some women."

"If you want to please me, Ethan Bodine, you can find us a restaurant and something to eat. I'm starving."

Her stomach grumbled, and he grinned. "A woman with a big appetite is a woman after my own heart, Willy." His rakish wink made her blush all the way down to her toes. "But first we need to take care of your horse. Hopefully the blacksmith will be able to reshod your mount so we can be on our way by morning."

She nodded. "I'm as anxious as you to find your brother."

"I doubt that," he said before disappearing into the stable.

A short time later they registered at the hotel, procuring separate rooms, then proceeded to the Iron Kettle Cafe, where the hotel manager had assured them they could get a steak as big as a lead bull in a buffalo herd.

Ethan had just sunk his teeth into a rare, juicy sirloin, just a shade smaller than the hotelier's description, when a stout older man approached their table. Wearing a garish brown-checked suit, he was perspiring profusely and dabbing his balding pate continuously with a linen handkerchief, though the ceiling fan circled in full motion.

"Excuse me, but I noticed you're wearing the badge of a Texas Ranger," the man said, staring at Ethan's chest with unconcealed interest.

"So?" Ethan wasn't in the mood for polite conversation and kept eating. He was hungrier than a bear after hibernation, and he didn't like having his meal interrupted, unless it was a dire emergency. And by the looks of the dandy, the only emergency likely to happen was the overweight man falling over in a dead heap from a heart seizure.

Noting the man's nervousness, Wilhemina kicked Ethan under the table. "Mr. Bodine is a Texas Ranger. Are you in need of assistance, sir?"

Smiling kindly at the young woman, the stranger failed to note the hostile look Ethan directed at both of them. "I'm Mayor Herbert T. Bradley, ma'am." He reached up to tip his hat but realized he wasn't wearing one, and his face reddened again.

"I'm terribly sorry to interrupt your meal, but there is a serious situation going on in Never Die, and I could use some help from the law."

Chomping off a piece of bread, Ethan talked around it. "Where's the local authority? This isn't my jurisdiction."

The man swallowed nervously. "May I sit down, Captain Bodine?"

Ethan was about to reply in the negative when Wilhemina patted the chair next to her. "Of course you can, Mayor Bradley. We'd be delighted to have you join us. Wouldn't we, Ethan?"

If there was one thing Ethan hated, it was someone putting words in his mouth. The thing he hated more than that was when those words were uttered by a woman—an interfering woman.

"There's no local authority, I'm afraid," the mayor began. "Sheriff Wilbert left a few weeks back. Just packed up in the middle of the night and took off for parts unknown." He shook his head at the unconscionable, totally unacceptable behavior of the lawman. "There's been so much upheaval and strife in the town that no one wants the job."

Ethan straightened and gave the man his full attention. Ranchers meant rustlers, range wars, and vigilantes. And the cost of life in those situations was high. "What's the problem?"

The mayor removed his spectacles and cleaned them with the edge of the red-checked tablecloth. The dark circles under his eyes revealed a man who'd spent more than a few sleepless nights fretting about the town's problems.

"It's the women of the town, Ranger Bodine. They have gone on strike."

"Strike?" Ethan's eyes widened, and he felt almost giddy with relief at the news that there was no range war. "Your women are on strike and you want the law to intervene?" He chuckled and shook his head in disbelief. "Since when can't the men of this town handle their own women?"

"Spoken like a true Neanderthal," Wilhemina muttered, staring in disgust at her dinner companion, who was grinning like the Cheshire cat.

"It may appear amusing to you, Captain, but I assure you it's not. I haven't had my clothing washed for over six weeks." He sniffed the air and gave an apologetic look that said he hoped he hadn't offended them. "I've been forced, as have most of the other men in town, to take my meals in restaurants because our wives refuse to cook. I can't begin to tell you how expensive it's become. The only one benefiting is Clyde Hammermill, who owns this place. He's a widower," he added, though no one had posed the question.

"And it's not just our wives who have refused to perform their duties, but our daughters as well. Sisters have turned against brothers, grandmothers against grandsons. It's truly horrible. And we need your help to rectify the situation, Ranger Bodine."

Noting Wilhemina's sympathetic expression, Ethan knew she was totally taken in by the man's plight. Heaving a sigh of disgust, he resumed eating. "Don't see as how I'd be much help, Mayor. This here's a problem for the clergy, or one of those social welfare people. I'm used to settling disputes of a different kind. And I'm in pursuit of someone. I don't have the time to get involved in petty squabbles."

And he knew that he didn't have the power to intervene. Rangers could only support civil authority in cases of bloodshed, arrest criminals indicted by the courts, and reestablish civil government in the frontier districts. But as far as he knew, he didn't have the authority to interfere in disputes between husbands and wives. Nor did he want it.

"It would be terrible to have to use your brain instead of your brawn to settle a dispute, wouldn't it, Ranger Bodine?" Wilhemina asked, unwilling to believe that Ethan would so casually turn his back on these people, who obviously needed his help.

She ignored his look of outrage and turned to the mayor. "What have the men done to incur such wrath, Mayor Bradley? Surely the women have not gone on strike for a frivolous reason."

Ethan snorted disdainfully. "With women it's always frivolous."

"They want to be treated as equals, ma'am. They want to attend the town meetings and have a vote on the issues that are discussed."

"What's wrong with that?" Wilhemina asked. "If they're citizens of this town, then why shouldn't they have a say in how they are governed and what decisions are made? It seems only fair and certainly reasonable."

Herbert Bradley sighed. "I'm only the mayor. The town council has decided unanimously not to allow the women a vote. I'm only one person. And though I may be slightly sympathetic to their cause—I say slightly because I consider myself to be a fair man—I can't overrule a majority vote.

"And in my heart I don't believe Violet Bradley has the common sense to decide important issues. She's a bit flighty, my wife is."

Wilhemina's eyes darkened. She'd heard these kinds of comments before, but then they had been directed at her.

"Don't be ridiculous, Miss Granville. There's no place in horticulture for a woman."

"Though your research paper is well written, Miss Granville, I'm not sure the Botanical Society will publish it. They're a very old and established organization. Very male oriented, if you get my meaning?"

"You'd be surprised, Mayor," she finally said, unable to disguise her disgust. "Your wife obviously had the common sense to stop doing your laundry. You should at least give her credit for that."

Ethan shot the outspoken woman a quelling look. "That's enough, Willy! I think you should stay out of this matter."

"I'm sure you do. Men always side with one another. Especially when their creature comforts are disturbed. Not to mention the other *comforts* that are no doubt lacking."

The mayor turned as red as the beets on Wilhemina's plate. "Really, miss! You know nothing of what you're talking about."

"And you think that's going to stop her from stating her opinion?" Ethan's laughter was derisive. "Not likely. You obviously haven't met a horticulturist turned bounty hunter before, Mayor. It's a very interesting combination. Miss Granville's bluestocking views will no doubt butt up against your own."

Wounded by the comment, Wilhemina stood, her appetite suddenly gone. "Just because you don't like my views is no reason to be insulting. I assure you that I'm not a bluestocking, merely an independent woman with a mind of my own." She pushed back her chair. "And I'm not at all interested in your opinion of me, Ranger Bodine." She stomped out of the restaurant, slamming the door behind her.

Fortunately for Ethan, only Herbert Bradley and a few of the other patrons were there to bear witness to her display of temper. "Women are a pain in the butt, Mayor." Ethan shook his head as he stared down at his half-eaten steak and knew now he would never finish it.

Willy would have to be appeased. There was just no getting around that. The woman was as volatile as a stick of dynamite, and he couldn't afford to let her go off and explode on her own. There was no telling what kind of damage she might do.

"Guess I'd have to agree with you there, Ranger Bodine. I never thought my sweet-tempered Violet would turn into a shrew."

"They're born that way. It's just hidden until they find some poor man to fool into thinking they're sweet as molasses. Once they get their hooks into you, then watch out. That molasses turns quickly to vinegar."

"Sounds like you speak from experience."

Ethan's lips flattened into a thin line. "Yeah, I do. And coming here has reminded me of just how manipulative and cunning women can be.

"Take my advice, Mayor Bradley: Do your own laundry."

The insistent pounding on the hotel room door had Wilhemina reaching for the white fluffy towel she'd left at the foot of the bed. The door burst open before she could grab it, and she sank quickly into the tub of hot water and gasped in outrage at the sight of Ethan standing just inside the doorway.

"How dare you come in here without knocking!" She brushed strands of damp, matted hair away from her face.

"I did knock. Rather loudly, as a matter of fact. You must have been preoccupied." He shut the door behind him and allowed the aroma of lavender to wash over him. The caustic lecture he intended to deliver momentarily evaporated like steam rising from the bathtub.

"Well, get out!" She crossed her arms over her chest. "As you can see, I don't wish to be disturbed. I'm taking a bath."

Staring into the water to observe the outline of a plumb breast, he arched his right eyebrow. Despite her nickname, Willy was anything but masculine. "I can see that."

If looks could kill, Ethan would have been planted six feet under by now. Dragging the towel into the water to cover herself, Wilhemina said, "You are certainly no gentleman, Ethan Bodine!"

He grinned, unfazed by her observation. "You'll get no argument from me on that point. But then, ladies don't usually voice their opinions as openly as you do, either, Willy. Mayor Bradley was left speechless by your shocking insinuation that the men of this town were being . . . How shall I say it? Deprived of their physical pleasures. *Tsk, tsk.* Such a naughty comment for a lady to make. And in public, too."

The heat rising from the water had little to do with the scarlet hue of Wilhemina's cheeks. "If you've said what you came to say, then get out. I'd like to finish my bath in private."

He pulled up a chair and straddled it, crossing his arms over the back and leaning on them as if he had all the time in the world and nowhere else to go. "I'm just getting started, so I'm afraid your bathwater and your temper will have to cool off some."

The impropriety of being naked in a tub of water with a man seated only a few feet away was not lost on Wilhemina, and her mouth went momentarily dry. This was not a situation a respectable woman should find herself in. Although, she amended silently, respectable women didn't usually turn themselves into bounty hunters.

"Please state your views and get out. The water is turning cold." Was the man deaf or just horribly obtuse?

"I'd be happy to assist you out of the tub if your skin's starting to shrivel."

Her nipples were beginning to pucker, but she thought that had more to do with the lecherous gleam in Ethan's eyes than the temperature of the water. She clutched the towel to her chest, hoping he would get the point and leave. "That won't be necessary," she said, her voice pitched so high that it sounded strange to her own ears. "I'm perfectly fine."

Remembering why he'd come, Ethan dropped his teasing demeanor. "I don't want you interfering in this town's problems, Willy. I know you're just itching to share your bluestocking views with the women of Never Die, but you'll only make things worse if you do. I want you to stay the hell out of things here. Do I make myself clear?"

Wilhemina bit the inside of her cheek, swallowed all the vile things she wanted to say to the arrogant, egotistical lawman, and smiled innocently. "Why, Captain! I'm surprised you know what a bluestocking is. Thank you for admitting that I have some intellectual prowess."

"You're too damn smart for your own good, woman. And if you don't mind your tongue, I won't be responsible for my actions."

Her heart began to pound hard at the mental image of Ethan pushing back his chair and hauling her wet and naked body out of the tub, then kissing her lips and unruly tongue into submission. She stared speechless, expecting him to pounce on her at any moment, until she noticed that he was now standing by the door.

"You mind what I say now, Wilhemina. We can't get involved in these folks' problems. We've got a mission, in case you've forgotten. Time is of the essence, and we can't afford to waste any of it on foolishness."

His callous words snapped her out of her fantasy and back to reality. "It was my understanding that a Ranger is sworn to help those in need, to administer justice when necessary, and to put others' welfare before his own. Am I mistaken in that, Ethan?"

Giving her a look that could have heated her bathwater to boiling, Ethan cursed under his breath and slammed out of the room.

Wilhemina didn't know whether to feel disappointed or disgusted. She opted for both.

* * *

The following morning Wilhemina did what any self-respecting horticulturist would do: she paid a visit to the Ladies' Garden Club's monthly meeting, which she had seen advertised in the local paper the night before.

Ethan's admonitions about not involving herself in the local dispute had crossed her mind a time or two while she dressed in the one decent outfit she'd brought with her, but in the end she decided to ignore them.

The Ranger was not going to boss her around. She was an independent woman with a mind of her own, capable of making her own decisions, and she didn't need some imperious lawman dictating what she could and could not do or say. This was a free country, even if Ethan Bodine thought he was in charge of it.

She also intended to ask a few questions of her own about the whereabouts of Rafe Bodine. Though Ethan had insisted she leave the investigating to him, Willy knew that women were often far more astute and attuned to the goings-on in their town than the men. She would start her interrogation with the ladies of the Garden Club.

The autumn air was crisp as Wilhemina hurried up the front steps of St. Paul's Methodist Church hall, where the meeting would be held. She opened the door and stepped across the threshold just as the meeting was called to order.

The large room was lit by several kerosene lanterns, and she could detect the odor of burning candle wax. Someone had gone to the trouble of placing containers of gold chrysanthemums about; their distinctive fragrance was overpowering.

The room full of women turned in unison to stare over their shoulders at her, eyes wide with curiosity. Wilhemina, grateful she had donned a clean white shirtwaist and serviceable navy serge skirt for the occasion, smiled tentatively.

"May I help you, miss?" The white-haired matron at the podium posed the question, a kind smile on her face.

Shoulders back, and bolstered by the friendliness she heard in the older woman's voice, Wilhemina strode confidently toward the head of the hall. She was used to addressing groups of people—mostly male horticulturists—and felt confident in her ability to relate to an audience.

"My name is Wilhemina Granville, recently of Boston, and late of Justiceburg, Texas. I arrived in town yesterday and learned of the difficulties facing you. Though I realize that I'm a stranger, and none of what's happened here is any of my business, I'd like to help if I can."

Violet Bradley set down her gavel and came forward to shake the young woman's hand. "Herbert mentioned he'd met a headstrong, outspoken woman yesterday." She smiled impishly. "I suppose he was speaking about you, Miss Granville. I'm pleased to say that you made quite an *un*favorable impression on my husband."

Having little doubt that the mayor found her abrasive and outspoken, Wilhemina nodded in acceptance. "I'm a horticulturist by profession, Mrs. Bradley. So when I saw the notice for your meeting of the Garden Club, I viewed it as an omen of sorts. I felt I should come and offer my assistance. I'm an ardent and firm believer in the equality of women."

Several of the women whispered among themselves, and a few clapped, albeit somewhat nervously.

"We really ain't here to garden and such," a plump, red-haired woman who introduced herself as Ophelia Toomey stated in a voice that reminded Wilhemina of fractured glass. "We've got more serious problems to consider."

Wilhemina turned to face the assemblage and noted the grave expressions on many of the faces. Young and old alike had come to the meeting to air their grievances and seek a solution. The mayor hadn't exaggerated when he'd mentioned grandmothers and sisters, as there were just as many elderly matrons as young girls in attendance.

"Although I'm a horticulturist by profession, I've studied the teachings of Elizabeth Cady Stanton and Susan B. Anthony and became somewhat involved in their women's movement while living in Boston. I don't profess to have all the answers, but I do know that when women band together in a unified cause, such as you have done, they usually get results." Her comment produced a chorus of cheers and loud clapping.

"Well, Miss Granville," Violet said, "we're happy to have you with us. Will you be staying long in Never Die?"

"I'm afraid not. I rode in with Mr. Bodine of the Texas Rangers. I know this is going to sound rather unorthodox to most of you, but I'm traveling as a bounty hunter in pursuit of his brother."

An attractive blonde with cornflower blue eyes stood up in the back row and waited a moment to be recognized. "Did he jilt you, ma'am? 'Cause if he did, you have every right to go after him and drag him back to the altar and see that he does right by you. Tommy Lowell did the same thing to me, but my pa hunted him down and dragged him back to Never Die. We're married now." She smiled sweetly until the woman seated next to her, obviously the young woman's mother, elbowed her in the side and declared:

"Hush, Louella! Your mouth is running again."

Wilhemina shook her head. "No. I'm not even acquainted with the outlaw Rafe Bodine, and I only just met his brother Ethan less than a week ago, quite by accident. I'm after the reward money that's being offered for the return of Mr. Bodine." At the women's shocked gasps, Wilhemina went on to explain about the circumstances in which her aunts found themselves. Then she asked if anyone present had knowledge or information about the whereabouts of Rafe Bodine. Unfortunately no one could remember seeing the outlaw.

"My, my, but you're a brave woman," Ophelia stated, clucking her tongue like a brood hen. "We could all learn something from your tenacity, young woman. I'm not saying I approve of your riding off after some outlaw, but you should be lauded for putting your aunts' welfare above all else."

Clarice Dabney wiped the tears from her eyes with a pristine handkerchief. "Old people are so carelessly discarded by the young these days. My grandson Lloyd will rue the day he sided with his pa and grandpa against me. You should be commended for your efforts, Miss Granville."

Another round of applause went up, and for the first time since starting this foolhardy trek, Wilhemina felt her efforts might be justified.

While Wilhemina was being touted by the ladies of Never Die for her courage and compassion, Ethan, seated in the vacated sheriff's office, was being raked over the coals by the members of the town council for his reluctance in wanting to assist them with their plight.

"It's plain to see you ain't never been married, Bodine," commented the barber, Will Sharpe, toying with the scissors he'd forgotten to remove from his apron pocket in his haste to attend the meeting. "My wife's made my life a living hell. Sally won't cook, she won't clean, she won't—" He rolled his eyes, and everyone understood his meaning and nodded in empathy. "You just got to help us." Will wasn't a man who liked going without, and he'd been going without nigh on to two weeks now.

A headache was starting to form at the base of Ethan's skull, and he rubbed it to ease the tension. The barber's comments were one of many he'd heard this morning. And finding Wilhemina gone from her hotel room had only added to the pounding in his temples.

According to the hotel manager, the headstrong woman had left word that she would attend the monthly meeting of the Ladies' Garden Club, and Ethan had no doubt that the topic discussed would be not flowers but anarchy.

And who was better qualified to lead a revolt than Wilhemina Granville?

"As I explained to the mayor yesterday, I'm in the middle of a murder investigation. I don't have time to referee some domestic squabble. I'm sure in a reasonable amount of time the women—"

Simon Toomey, the undertaker, burst through the doorway, his face bright red with anger, halting the lawman's explanation. "That woman you brought here is counseling my wife and the other women of this town on how to stand up to us, Ranger Bodine. We were having enough troubles before you came, but now they've all banded together like an angry mob."

"We're in a fix now," Will stated angrily.

Simon continued, "I was listening outside the window of the church, and I heard Miss Granville say that the women must present a united front and not back down in any way, shape, or form to their husbands, lovers, brother, fathers, or whomever. She said they was to put on the '*no* pillowcase,' whatever the hell that means."

"You know what it means." Morris Jones's lips thinned in disgust beneath his bushy mustache. "It means we don't get no lovin', that's what it means. And if Martha ain't gonna see fit to grace my bed anymore, I may as well pack up and leave this town. I ain't gonna live like a damn monk!"

"You can't leave here, Morris. You own the mercantile. What the hell would everyone do if you was to leave?"

Stu Packer rubbed sweaty, callused hands on his overalls. "I need supplies to run my farm. I can't buy everything I need out of the Montgomery Ward catalog."

A tall, barrel-chested man stood at the rear of the room. Ethan recognized him as Farley Strange, the black-smith, and a sinking feeling formed in the pit of his stom-ach. "Don't think I can shoe that horse you brung in, Ranger. I'm a mite busy. It may take several days, even a week, before I can get to it."

It was blackmail, plain and simple, and Ethan's face reddened in anger.

"Ranger Bodine," Herbert Bradley stated, clasping Ethan's shoulder to calm him down, "I think you can now see the seriousness of this situation. If we don't get our problems solved and soon, Never Die is going to dry up and blow away like a ghost town."

Easing himself off the corner of the desk, Ethan stood to face the agitated men, vowing silently to get even with the sharp-tongued horticulturist. If Wilhemina had only stayed the hell out of things, they could have been on their way to find Rafe. But no. She had to interfere, butt in, go directly against his orders. Now they couldn't even get the damned horse shod.

Damn the woman!

"Ordinarily I wouldn't take sides in a matter like this. But since my companion has decided to stick her two cents into the fracas and upset the delicate balance of things around here, then I guess I'd better side with the men of this town to even up the score." The men nodded their ap-proval, and he went on to say, "In my opinion, women have no head for business, or things of a political nature. They're ruled by emotion instead of logic."

"That's just what I told Ophelia," the undertaker said. "Of course, she told me to shut up. Said I was a damn fool."

Ethan frowned. "Women are never lacking in opinions. What we need to find is a way to placate your womenfolk so that they'll think they are contributing to the matters at hand. Maybe then we can put an end to these hostilities."

Herbert scratched his balding head, a look of confusion on his face that was mirrored by the others in the room. "But how we going to do that, Captain? We've been trying for weeks to come up with a solution. Why, we even invited the ladies to sit in on one of the council meetings, as long as they promised not to chatter during the proceedings. Of course, they still weren't allowed to vote."

All heads nodded in unison, as if that were a given.

"I'm going to need some time to see if I can come up with a solution. Maybe I can convince Wilhemina Granville and the ladies of this town that they're making a big mistake." Talking sense to Willy was like facing an armed bandit with an empty gun. What he needed was some ammunition. But what?

"I'll walk over to the church and pay a surprise visit to the Garden Club. Maybe I can convince the ladies that they're totally out of line in wanting to be on equal footing with the men of this town."

"I guess it's worth a shot, Captain Bodine, but stay clear of Ophelia," the undertaker warned. "She packs a

mean punch when she's riled, which is most of the time."
Simon had decided long ago that dead people were far easier to deal with than his wife.

Ethan smiled confidently, wondering how a group of
grown men had become so fearful of a bunch of silly
women.

Chapter Six

"Fear is what we need to instill into the men of this town. Fear of retribution, if they do not take us seriously in our fight for an equal voice." Wilhemina's voice grew louder as she stood at the podium, addressing the women of Never Die, trying to infuse them with the spirit to succeed in their quest for equality.

The ladies were hanging on to her every word, urging her to continue. "The women of Wyoming already have the power to vote in national elections. Why then should it be any different for the women here? You're not asking for more than what is already a God-given right: to be on equal footing with a man, whether it be in the boardroom or the boudoir."

A loud gasp went up, then Clarice Dabney rose and propped herself against her cane, stating in a voice full of censure, "Miss Granville, we are all ladies here, and I don't believe that discussing matters of the bedroom should enter into our desire for an equal voice."

"And why not, Clarice?" Ophelia asked, her double

chins swaying in time to her wagging head. "We've been put in our place too long as it is. Told what to think, how to react, when and how we should find pleasure. I, for one, think Miss Granville is absolutely right. We need to start taking control."

Wilhemina knew she was treading on dangerous ground. She wasn't a free thinker or an advocate of free love, and she certainly didn't want to give that impression. Nor was she qualified to counsel anyone on marital problems, especially those dealing with the bedroom. Her own brief love affair had been nothing short of disastrous.

"What does or does not happen in the bedrooms of this community is a highly personal matter, and I'm not advocating that anyone reveal something so delicate as what goes on between a husband and wife. That is a sacred matter. What I'm saying is that a woman has the right to demand as much pleasure and satisfaction from a man as he demands from her. Women are not merely receptacles for a man's pleasure any more than they were put on this earth to breed solely to increase the surface population.

"A woman has a right to expect . . . no, to *demand* that her needs are met in every area of her life."

A loud clapping ensued from the rear of the hall, stealing everyone's attention. Wilhemina observed Ethan standing in front of the door with an amused grin on his face, and she felt her own flame scarlet.

"Hear hear, Miss Granville! I wholeheartedly agree."

"This is a private meeting, Captain Bodine," Wilhemina informed him haughtily. "You were not invited, nor are you welcome here."

He strode forward despite her protests and was tempted to point out that she hadn't been invited, either. "I came here to talk to the ladies of this town. I think we need to try to reach some type of solution to the problems that presently exist."

Wilhemina didn't look convinced. "You mean a capitulation, don't you, Captain?"

Ethan's forehead wrinkled in confusion. "I'm not sure—"

"Your solution to the problem would be for the women of this town to give in and give up their quest for equality. Isn't that right?"

"My mama always taught me you can catch a lot more flies with honey than vinegar. Maybe your approach to the matter is wrong, is all I'm saying."

"Oh, so you're saying it is the women who must smile and fawn over their men instead of the other way around, in order to convince them to grant rights that by nature should be theirs to begin with?" She rolled her eyes in disbelief.

The Ranger's voice hardened. "I cannot allow this stalemate to continue, Wilhemina. And you should have stayed out of it like you were told."

"You are not in charge of me or anyone else, Ranger Bodine."

The women cheered enthusiastically, and Ethan's eyes narrowed dangerously. "You are making my job a lot more difficult than it needs to be."

"And you, Ethan, are as obtuse as every other man in Never Die, if you do not concede that these women should have a say in what goes on in their own town. I think you need to convince their husbands of that fact."

"Miss Granville is absolutely correct, Mr. Bodine," Violet Bradley stated. "We are in no hurry to end this stalemate, as you call it. In fact, we are prepared to escalate matters if our foolish husbands don't come around to our way of thinking."

"Son of a—" Ethan wiped his hand over his face and swallowed his curse, remembering where he was and whom he was with.

"We're not asking for all that much, Ranger," Ophelia chimed in. "Just a vote on the matters that govern our lives and those of our children. Why shouldn't we be allowed to decide what months the children go to school? How many hours a day they should attend? Who knows these things better than a mother?"

"And why shouldn't we be able to suggest that a garbage collection policy be implemented in the town?" Clarice added, tapping her cane insistently to make her point. "Something needs to be done with the refuse in this town, and the members of the town council have turned a deaf ear to our pleas, saying it's too costly to consider. *Hmph.* It's going to be a whole lot costlier when we all come down sick."

"And who says we shouldn't have a vote to see who's elected mayor?" chimed in Violet, "I never would have voted for Herbert, and he knows that, which is why he's being so obstinate about this whole situation. I've always thought Clyde Hammermill was far better suited to the position."

"That's just because Clyde's always been sweet on you, Violet," Clarice reminded her with a knowing smile, bringing a bright blush to the woman's already rosy cheeks.

What the ladies said made sense, as much sense as what their husbands had said earlier. Ethan sighed at the impasse. At least he'd made up his mind about one thing: Violet Bradley was far from flighty. She was intelligent and sensible. The mayor had been wrong about that.

Willy studied Ethan's face intently for some sign of acquiescence. "Well, Mr. Bodine, what do you think we should do now? It's clear that these women have some legitimate complaints. Wouldn't you say?"

He was thoughtful for a moment, then replied, "I'm going to have to rethink my position on this matter."

Seeing that he was weakening just a bit, Wilhemina decided that now was the perfect time to woo him to her way of thinking. The only way to convince the men of the town that the women's grievances were just was to convince Ethan first.

"Why don't I accompany you back to the hotel, Ranger? Perhaps once you've heard more of our position, you'll be able to make a sound judgment."

Ethan knew that if he was ever going to get back on the trail again, he would have to find a solution to the situation at hand. Especially now that Wilhemina had stirred up the ladies to a militant degree.

"Yes, Ranger," Violet urged. "We have no problem with Miss Granville presenting our case to you. She's one of us now."

His thin smile held no trace of amusement. "Wilhemina does have a way of placing herself smack dab in the middle of things, doesn't she?" He didn't wait for an answer, but held open the door for Wilhemina to proceed him out.

The interfering woman was going to rue the day that—

Damn, but her smile was dazzling!

And why was she looking so pleased with herself? Did she really think she could convince him to change his mind? And what did she plan to do to accomplish that fact?

Women were known for using their wiles. Did she plan to try hers out on him? If so, the evening ahead could prove mighty interesting.

After pulling the hairbrush through her long sable tresses until it shone in the lantern light, Wilhemina grasped the thick mound of hair with one hand and a few pins with the other, intending to twist it into a bun at the nape of her neck, which was how she usually wore it. Gazing at her reflection, she suddenly let the thick mantle drop down past her shoulders to her waist and looked at herself critically. The style definitely made her look younger, softer, and she remembered how Thomas had always loved it when she wore her hair down. How feminine he'd said it made her look.

The knock at the door took the decision out of her hands, and she gave one last look in the mirror before hurrying to answer it. Ethan was taking her to dinner this evening to discuss the women's difficulties, and she didn't want to keep him waiting. Especially now that she had a solution to present.

Opening the door, she found him standing hat in hand, like an anxious suitor—a handsome suitor. The musky scent of his cologne sent her pulse racing and created havoc in her midsection, where a hornets' nest had settled. Pasting on an uneasy smile, she wondered who was wooing whom this evening.

"You look very nice, Ethan." She ushered him in, noting how his damp hair shone like obsidian in the lamplight, how his shoulders seemed wider than usual.

"I took a bath. Cleaned up some."

"Yes, well . . . I'll just grab my coat and we can be off."

The intense way he studied her made her mouth go dry, until he said, "You've still got on your same clothes. I changed mine."

She had hoped he wouldn't notice and felt her cheeks blush hot in embarrassment. "This is the only decent outfit I have with me. The others are for riding and not appropriate for dining out."

"You smell nice anyway."

Anyway. Meaning that she smelled nice but didn't look nice. Was that what he was trying to imply? "Thank you. I added a little lavender scent to my bathwater. I find that it refreshes me."

Ethan found that it was refreshing him to the point where his manhood was stirring something fierce. He bit down on his lower lip to control himself. He had Wilhemina off-kilter for the moment, and that's just where he wanted her. And he wasn't about to let her know how her scent, and that glorious hair that a man could lose himself in, was playing havoc with his emotions.

He held the door open for her. "Did you lose your hairpins? You don't usually wear it loose like that."

She gritted her teeth as she walked past him. "I couldn't find a single one," she said, and he smiled inwardly at the obvious lie.

The night air was biting as they stepped onto the sidewalk, and Wilhemina shivered despite the wool coat she wore.

"Cold?" Ethan welcomed the frigid air, hoping it would cool his ardor and restore his control.

"A little. But I've always enjoyed the brisk evenings of autumn and look forward to winter. Summer is not my favorite season, though it does have some of the loveliest flowers, and the trees are in full foliage."

"What made you want to become a horticulturist? That's a mighty peculiar profession for a woman." He thought it peculiar enough for a man.

"I was raised on a small ranch. My father was a great lover of plants, and we would explore the land from morning till night, searching out wildflowers, finding various herbs, planting different types of grasses to see which offered our cattle the best nutrition.

"Father was a scholarly man who loved to read. He strived to learn everything he could from books, and what he learned he taught to me. It was his idea that I go to Boston to further my studies, and with his help I did. I guess I just inherited his enthusiasm for nature and botanical things." Unfortunately she hadn't inherited all of his wisdom or patience. That was dramatically evident by her harebrained scheme to become a bounty hunter. Not that she had much choice, she reminded herself.

When Ethan remained silent, she added, "Horticulture isn't really such a peculiar profession for a woman. After all, women and flowers have gone together for centuries."

"I guess when you put it that way . . ."

"What about you? Why did you decide to become a Texas Ranger?"

He shrugged. "I wasn't cut out for ranching. My pa wanted me and Rafe to work the ranch. It was his dream that we would inherit the property one day and pass it on to our young'ns. Pa was always talking about leaving something for future generations of Bodines. But that was his dream, not mine.

"I wanted adventure. And I wanted to get away from home. So when the opportunity presented itself, I talked Rafe into joining the Rangers with me."

"I bet your father was furious." She could well imagine Ethan Bodine as a brash young man eager to make his mark in the world and chafing at the bit to do it.

Ethan smiled at the understatement. "He still is. We never got on all that well. It got worse after my mother died. Ben Bodine doesn't like to be crossed, and he blames me for taking Rafe away from the ranch."

"And does he blame you now for what's happened? For Rafe being in the situation that he's in?"

"He's never said, but I can sense the hostility and anger in his words. Rafe always had the most promise for ranching. In fact, he and Ellie had just started a small cattle ranch before she was murdered." His mood turned pensive as he thought of his brother and dead sister-in-law and the recent turn of events. He wondered if he would ever see his brother alive again.

Wilhemina found Ethan's background fascinating and wanted to ask him more about it, but they had reached the restaurant and the subject changed quickly to the situation in Never Die.

"Looks like the ladies of this town have taken you into their confidence," Ethan said not fifteen minutes later as he savored the pot roast that the restaurant owner had just set before him. It was peppery, just the way he liked it. He liked many things hot, including women with feisty tongues. Of course, he preferred those tongues to be occupied with something other than harping and lecturing, as Wilhemina was wont to do.

"I'm quite pleased with the way the meeting went today. What did you think about what the women had to say? I'm sure you must agree that they have some legitimate complaints."

He sopped a piece of bread in gravy and bit into it before answering. "Some. I guess I can understand why they'd want to have a say in things that relate to their young'ns and such. And the garbage situation the old lady talked about was something I hadn't thought of before."

"I'm glad you can be fair-minded when the situation warrants."

"I'm always fair, or try to be."

Wilhemina smiled to herself, unsure of whether to believe that about him or not. She strongly suspected that Ethan liked having his own way, and if fairness came into play . . . well, she wasn't sure which would win out if push came to shove.

"Since you profess to being so fair-minded, I think I might have a solution to our problem, or at least the beginnings of one."

He arched an eyebrow and leaned back in his chair, noting the animation on her lovely face, how her eyes sparkled with enthusiasm. "I'm listening, but don't expect me to agree with everything you say. The men had their good points, too. And you weren't privy to hearing those."

"I was thinking that if the women elected one member of their group to attend the monthly council meetings and have a vote that would represent them all, it might satisfy their need for representation. It would give them a chance to present their views, and at the same time allow the men to decide whether or not those views are sound.

"I believe that if given the opportunity to hear the women's views on various topics, the men of this town are going to side with them. Sound logic and good ideas will be listened to no matter the gender presenting them."

Ethan mulled over her idea. "It's got merit, I'll give you that, Willy. I wasn't sure you'd be willing to compromise."

"Whether or not you believe me, Ethan, I am just as eager as you to be on my way to find your brother. My aunts are in danger of losing the only home they have ever known. If I don't return with the money soon to pay off their debt, that horrible Mr. Bowers from the savings and loan is going to kick them out on the street. And he's made my bringing Rafe back to Justiceburg a stipulation for forgiveness of my aunts' loan." She explained further her encounter with the banker and his lurid advances.

Ethan's brow arched in disbelief, even as his face darkened in anger. "I'll present your suggestion to the council tonight. We're meeting at the sheriff's office at nine o'clock to discuss the situation."

"Shall I come with you?"

He shook his head emphatically. "No! You've had about all the say you're going to have in this matter, Wilhemina. Now leave the rest to me."

She sighed in defeat. "There's just one more thing."

"And what's that? You thinking about running for mayor? Herb Bradley won't like that." She grinned impishly, and the strangest fluttering began in his chest. Heartburn, he decided.

"I think once these matters are resolved to everyone's satisfaction, the town should hold a dance. That'll give everyone a chance to make up without losing face. There's a lot of hostility and hurt feelings around here that need to be diffused. And quickly."

"That could take time. Time we don't have."

"I've already thought of that. A harvest dance had been planned some time ago by the ladies' auxiliary of the church for Saturday night, which is only two days away, but it was canceled because of all the problems. I'm sure it could be resurrected quickly. All we need is a fiddler and some refreshments to get it going again."

"You speak as if we're going to attend this shindig."

"I think we need to be there to make sure that all goes as planned, don't you? Besides, it's been ages since I've danced. How about you?"

"I don't dance."

"How come? Don't you know how?"

"Of course I do. My ma made sure all of us boys knew how. I just don't like it, that's all."

She smiled knowingly. "Too sissy for you, Ranger?"

His lips thinned at her unerring perception. "Something like that."

They finished their supper in silence, then made their way back to the hotel. When they reached Wilhemina's room they paused in the hallway.

"Thank you for dinner, Ethan. I enjoyed myself very much. Good night. I'll see you tomorrow."

"You mean you're not going to invite me in?" He looked genuinely surprised at the dismissal.

"I thought we had finished our conversation."

"But you wore your hair down. And you put that smelly stuff in your bathwater. I just figured—"

"You just figured that I was going to lure you to my way of thinking by using feminine wiles, didn't you?" It was all she could do to keep a straight face, for the thought had crossed her mind. Fortunately common sense had prevailed. She was no femme fatale, and she knew it.

"I much prefer using logic to make my point, Mr. Bodine. Perhaps the women you're used to dealing with are dishonest or more adept at womanly wiles than I am. I find that the straightforward approach to a situation is always the best."

He wondered how she would find his straightforward approach if he pushed her up against the door and kissed her senseless. He was tempted to try it and see.

"My mistake."

"You will let me know the outcome of the meeting, and the decision that's made about the dance? I'll need to inform the ladies as soon as possible."

He leaned forward, his hand resting against the door alongside her head, a hopeful look on his face. "Shall I come back later and give you a full report? We can discuss *things* in depth."

She swallowed nervously, gazing at lips only inches from her own. "Morning will be soon enough to let me know."

"Are you sure? I'm only right next door, and it'll be no trouble to—"

"Perfectly sure." She reached behind her to open the door, then ducked inside before she had a chance to change her mind. The sound of Ethan's laughter floated through the door, and she cursed herself for allowing him to toy with her emotions again.

Men!

"Learn from experience, Wilhemina," she scolded,

flinging herself back on the bed and covering her eyes with her forearm.

But that was easier said than done when faced with a virile man like Ethan Bodine—a man she was finding very difficult to resist.

Chapter Seven

WILHEMINA FLITTED ABOUT THE CHURCH HALL AS IF she'd been a member of St. Paul's for years, rearranging dishes of food on the table, adjusting the flowers in the arrangements just so, checking and rechecking to make sure everything would be perfect for the dance.

She glanced at the gold watch-brooch pinned to her bodice—an heirloom once belonging to her mother—and noted the time: seven forty-five. In just a few minutes, if everything went as planned, the men would pour in and the conflict separating the ladies and gentlemen of Never Die would begin to heal.

Ethan had slipped a note beneath her door after his meeting with the town council, explaining that the men had agreed to accept her terms and would allow the women to have a voting member on the council. It was an auspicious beginning, she thought.

Violet Bradley approached, looking lovely in a purple and rose calico gown. "I feel as giddy as a schoolgirl, Wilhemina." Her face radiated unconcealed joy. "I know that must sound silly to a young woman like you, but I haven't been this nervous since the night Herbert proposed."

Smiling, Wilhemina patted her hand. "You look lovely, Mrs. Bradley, and I'm sure the mayor will be swept off his feet when he sees you."

"Your idea for the women to come to the dance an hour earlier than the men was truly brilliant. I think it gives us a definite advantage, don't you?"

"I thought we needed time to settle our nerves, and to make sure everything was in place for the festivities."

"Is that handsome Ranger Bodine coming tonight? You make an awfully attractive couple, my dear."

Blushing to the tips of her newly purchased shoes, which were a size too small and cramped her toes, Wilhemina didn't know how to respond.

Ethan was indeed a handsome man. But they were too different in nature and ideals to be compatible as a couple should be. Ethan liked being footloose and free, while she coveted roots and family. He was brash, arrogant, and used to having his own way. She preferred using logic and calm reasoning to settle a problem and was a great believer in compromise.

They were definitely unsuited.

Weren't they?

She was saved from answering by the arrival of the musical entertainment.

The ladies had managed to secure the services of rancher Slim Wattley and his two brothers for the evening's entertainment. Slim, Wilhemina had been assured by Ophelia, played a mean fiddle, while Tiny and

Shorty, accompanying him on the banjo and guitar, were equally skilled.

Nodding in greeting at the trio, she made her excuses to Violet, then took her place near the refreshment table, feeling on edge.

Mrs. Bradley's nerves had nothing on hers, Wilhemina decided. Not only was she anxious for the evening to be a success, she'd spent money she could ill afford to purchase the lavender-checked dress she'd seen displayed in the millinery shop window, and which she now wore. It had a scooped neck and puffy sleeves trimmed with white eyelet lace. She still wasn't quite sure what had prompted her to make such an extravagant purchase.

Just then Ethan walked in, looking devilishly handsome. Black wool pants hugged his muscular thighs, his blue chambray shirt was nearly the same color as his eyes, and the black leather vest enhanced the width of a very impressive chest. She forcibly shut her gaping mouth, knowing without a doubt what had prodded the acquisition of her dress.

Ethan stirred her in ways no one ever had before, including her former suitor. It was as if he'd cast some magical spell over her. She couldn't think rational thoughts when she was with him, only feel. Logic and common sense seemed to vanish into thin air, like wishes gone unfulfilled.

The man was Dangerous, with a capital *D*. And if she wasn't careful, she was going to lose her heart and be hurt again, as she'd been with Thomas, the man who had professed to love her.

Wilhemina and Thomas Fullerton had talked of marriage and had made wonderful plans for their future, but her refusal to give up her career for his had quickly soured their relationship. In a few short months minor disagreements and petty squabbles turned into full-fledged, bitter arguments, and soon there was nothing left to be said but good-bye.

It had been a painful lesson for a young, naive woman who'd fancied herself madly in love with an urbane gentleman of good breeding. Painful but productive, for she'd decided never again would she allow herself to be blinded to the frailties of human nature. Her own included.

The menfolk started to file in, interrupting Wilhemina's disquieting thoughts, and she busied herself by pouring lemonade punch into glasses. She tried to ignore Ethan's virile presence, but it took him only a moment to find her.

"Well, well." He eyed Wilhemina appreciatively, paying particular attention to the large expanse of creamy skin her neckline revealed. "You look good enough to eat, woman."

Blushing under his scrutiny, she swallowed, wiping sweaty palms on the skirt of her dress. "Thank you. You look very nice yourself."

"But your hair . . ." His frown had her reaching up self-consciously to pat her chignon. "How come you didn't wear it down? I like it long and hanging to your waist."

"But you said—" She caught herself just in time and shrugged, as if his opinion were of little importance. "It looked too girlish the other way. I prefer it this way."

"A man likes to have a woman's hair wrapped around him."

The image he put forth was too provocative, too tempting, for Wilhemina to consider. She pushed it aside, forcing a nonchalant pose. "Really? Well, it does tend to tangle quite easily when it's left to its own devices, I'm afraid."

"Pity," was all he said before moving away to talk to the mayor, leaving Wilhemina more confused than ever.

Time floated by quickly as couples dressed in their Sunday-go-to-meeting finery whizzed by Wilhemina, circling the dance floor. She observed the barber with his wife, looking as contented as a cat with a full bowl of cream. She supposed that Sally Sharpe had already appeased her husband in ways that counted.

Ophelia and Simon appeared to have put their differences aside as well—for how long nobody knew. Their life together was just one ongoing argument. But it seemed they had called a truce, for they were laughing at something Violet Bradley said.

Things in Never Die seemed to be improving. Wilhemina smiled in satisfaction, glad that she'd played a small part in bringing that about.

"You're lookin' mighty pleased with yourself, Willy. Are you taking credit for all the happy faces I see here tonight?"

Lost in reverie, Wilhemina started at the sound of Ethan's voice, nearly spilling her glass of lemonade punch all over her brand-new dress. She clutched her chest, took a deep breath, and turned to him.

"I wish you wouldn't sneak up on me like that, Ranger. For a man who's as light on his feet as you are, I'm surprised you don't dance."

He removed the cup from her hand and set it on the table. "I've decided I will, if you'll be my partner."

Her eyes widened at the unexpected offer; a warm, fuzzy feeling spread through her all the way down to her toes. "You want to dance with me?"

"I just asked you, didn't I?"

She smiled brightly. "Yes. I guess you did."

Floating on air as they circled the dance floor, Wilhemina noted the envious looks she received from several of the women, including pretty Louella Lowell, who paid far more attention to Ethan than she did to her young husband. But she couldn't really blame her. Ethan possessed manly good looks and was a wonderful dancer. Being held in his arms was every bit as thrilling as she'd imagined, and Wilhemina found herself sighing at notions too impractical to consider.

Ethan mistook her wistfulness for something else. "Are you tired? All these preparations must have tuckered you out. You and the other ladies did a fine job, by the way."

His compliment pleased her. "No. I'm not tired at all. I'm having a delightful time. You're a very good dancer, you know."

"Dancing's only one of the many things I'm good at, darlin'."

"If you're referring to riding and shooting, I already know that."

His voice grew husky. "I wasn't."

"Oh!" she exclaimed, making a misstep and stomping down hard on his foot. She blushed furiously. "Guess I should have paid more attention to my dancing instructor back in Boston." Mr. Tutley would have been horrified to see his most promising student prancing about like a cow.

"Tell me about your life in Boston. Did you like living among so many people? I'm not much for crowded spaces."

"It's quite different from Justiceburg, but I enjoyed the many museums and cultural things the city had to offer. There's so much of our country's history there. I never grew bored. And, of course, I enjoyed my work."

"You must be pretty smart about flowers, trees, and such, for them folks to want you to come work for them."

"Oh, they didn't want me," she said ruefully, "despite the fact that I had a degree in horticulture. And they did everything in their power to convince me to give up on my career choice. I wasn't very popular with my colleagues."

"They were jealous, huh?"

"No, Ethan. They were just men who didn't feel it was a woman's place to become involved in a field that had always been exclusively a man's domain."

"Why, that's just plain stupid, seeing as how you were qualified and all. You were, weren't you?"

"Yes. I'm extremely qualified. I have a college degree, and I did better in school than many of my colleagues. But I was guilty of the one sin they couldn't forgive: I was born a woman."

Ethan looked chagrined. He'd always thought of women in the same way—inferior to men, not as smart or as qualified. And all because they were women. But Wilhemina disproved that notion somewhat. There wasn't an inferior bone in her body. In fact, her body was put together in a rather extraordinary—

"Ethan"—Wilhemina tugged his shirtsleeve to gain his attention—"the music has stopped." She turned to discover that they were the only ones on the dance floor and the object of everyone's amusement.

The Ranger nearly tripped over his feet in an effort to leave the dance floor. "Now you know why I don't like to dance."

"I think you're very adept. Thank you for asking me."

There were a number of other things he wanted to ask her, far more provocative things, but he had to wait until the dance ended. And that couldn't come soon enough as far as he was concerned. He'd had enough of pleasantries and small talk. Now it was time for action.

The Bradleys approached, looking the very image of happiness and contentment. "Herbert would like to dance with you, Wilhemina." Violet gave her an encouraging wink that said her husband was trying to make amends. "And while you're gone I'll keep this handsome Texas Ranger company."

"Of course. I'd be delighted." Wilhemina held out her hand to the mayor and wondered nervously what Violet was up to. The woman seemed bent on matchmaking, and that worried her greatly.

"Are you enjoying the dance, Ranger?" Violet asked, moving to stand next to him.

"It's just fine, ma'am."

"I noticed you and Miss Granville took a turn around the dance floor."

Ethan nodded. "Yes, ma'am. I thought it would be the polite thing to do."

"I doubt that dancing with someone as lovely and kind as Miss Granville is too great a hardship. Wouldn't you agree, Ranger?" She pinned Ethan with a knowing look, daring him to deny it.

Ethan had enjoyed himself more than he'd care to admit. He hated dances. But Wilhemina's company, her witty conversation, had actually made this one fun. He had no intention of confessing that to Mrs. Bradley, who seemed intent on butting into things that were none of her concern.

"It's a pretty good shindig. And Wilhemina makes a fine partner."

"I think you make a most attractive couple. If you don't mind my saying so, a man could do a lot worse than to wed someone like Miss Granville."

Ethan felt the noose Mrs. Bradley had tied being lowered around his neck, and he swallowed. "I guess that's true, if a man was in a marrying mood, which I'm not. I have no intention of ever marrying." Might as well set the woman straight once and for all.

"And why not? It's a perfectly fine institution. Oh, I'm not saying there aren't problems now and again. You've just witnessed a whopper of one. But the good definitely outweighs the bad. And living life alone can't be that great a prospect to look forward to."

She placed her hand on his forearm. "I'm not usually one to interfere, Ranger Bodine, and please excuse the advice of an old lady, but I've seen the two of you together, and I can't help but think that you make a perfectly lovely couple." She clasped her hands together. "Oh, the children you would have!"

Ethan's face paled considerably, and he felt for the flask in his pocket, grateful when the music finally ended. *Marriage? Children? Was the woman out of her mind?*

The mayor returned Wilhemina to Ethan's side, and then he and Mrs. Bradley moved on, but not before Violet gave Ethan a knowing wink and encouraging smile. His response was no more than a grimace.

"Looks like you've made a conquest in Mrs. Bradley. Careful you don't make the mayor jealous."

Ethan snorted at Wilhemina's attempt to tease. "The woman is far too opinionated and should mind her own business. Interfering busybody."

"Oh? Did you and Mrs. Bradley have a disagreement?"

"I'd rather not discuss it. Are you ready to leave this shindig? I'll walk you home if you are."

Whatever Violet had said to Ethan had not sat well at all. Wilhemina would have given a lot to have been a fly on the wall during their conversation, and she prayed silently that she had not been included among the topics.

"I suppose I am. My feet are killing me."

"That must be the reason you stepped on mine so many times tonight." He grinned at her indignant expression.

"It's these stupid shoes. They're too small, and my toes feel as though they're going to fall off. I can hardly wait to take them off."

"Why don't you make your excuses and say your good-byes and we'll be off."

Ethan seemed awfully anxious to quit the place, so Wilhemina nodded. "All right. I won't be long."

A short time later, Ethan pulled open the front door for Willy to precede him into the empty hotel lobby. "Why not take off your shoes, if they're hurting your feet so bad? No one's around to see you."

Wilhemina cast a furtive look around, saw not a soul, and didn't wait for a second invitation. After slipping off the offending slippers, she wiggled her toes in absolute contentment. "*Ah.* That feels so much better." She had gritted her teeth the entire walk home, and all because she had foolishly paid more attention to vanity than comfort when purchasing the slippers.

"I thought it might."

Glancing at the stairs, she groaned aloud. "That staircase might as well be Pike's Peak, as tired as I feel right now." Before she could take a step, Ethan scooped her up in his arms and strode toward the stairs.

"Allow me to save you the walk."

"Ethan! Put me down at once. I never meant for you to carry me up the stairs. I was merely making conversation."

"*Sssh.* You don't want to wake everyone, do you?"

He cradled her to his chest, holding her close, and Wilhemina thought she smelled alcohol on his breath.

"You're light as a feather."

"I doubt that, after two servings of Violet's applesauce cake."

He hefted her weight, as if reconsidering. "Well, maybe a pound of feathers."

"Have you been drinking, Ethan? You're acting awfully strange, not at all like yourself." His playfulness, though not unwelcome, was definitely unexpected.

He shrugged, as if it were of no consequence. "I had a few nips of whiskey from my flask while you were saying good-bye to everyone." He'd needed the fortification after his disturbing conversation with Violet Bradley.

"Good heavens! Have you a flask? I hope no one saw you. I'm not at all approving of spirits. They make folks act dull-witted and foolish." She abhorred spirits. The few times she'd imbibed, she'd been rendered every bit as mindless as those she'd just described.

When Ethan reached her door he didn't set her down as she expected. "Good thing I don't need your approval then, isn't it?"

"You can put me down now, Ethan," she insisted more firmly. "I can manage from here."

He ignored the request. "I think that such a good deed as mine deserves a little reward, don't you?"

Her right eyebrow arched. "A reward? I have no money. I spent it all on this dress and these horrible shoes." She waved them at him.

"And it was worth every cent, darlin', let me assure you. But I don't need your money. You've got something a lot more valuable that I want."

At his ardent look, her heart went into double time. "I . . . I do?"

"I'm going to kiss you now, Willy. So don't go screaming your head off or nothin'."

She was appalled that the thought to refuse his advance hadn't even entered her mind. The one kiss they'd shared had been burned into her memory, and she brought it forward whenever she needed something wonderful to contemplate.

"I'm not going to scream," she whispered right before his mouth descended to hers.

His lips were soft, his mustache a tickling feather, as he captured her mouth in a mind-melting kiss. Soon his lips were trailing down her neck as he placed tormenting kisses on her throat, nuzzling the sensitive skin of her chest, then moving up to capture her mouth once again.

Wrapping her arms about his neck, she leaned into him and their kiss deepened. It was a wondrous kiss, full of passion and tenderness, and Willy wished it would never end. When it finally did they were both breathing hard, and Wilhemina's bones felt as if they'd completely dissolved; she doubted her legs would support her.

"I want you, Willy. Hand me your key."

Heeding her heart and not her mind, she reached into her reticule and handed him the key, saying not a word as he unlocked and opened the door.

The large brass bed loomed before her when they entered, and she swallowed nervously as he set her down gently upon it and covered her body with his.

"I've been thinking about making love to you all night," he whispered, removing the pins from her hair. "Remember what I said about wrapping myself in your glorious hair? I wasn't just making idle talk."

"You planned all along to seduce me?" She didn't know whether to be flattered or incensed.

"Since the moment I cocked my one good eye open and found you bent over me."

His hands covered her breasts before she had a chance to tell him that this was all a mistake, that ladies didn't invite gentlemen into their rooms, even if those ladies weren't in jeopardy of losing their virtue.

But his tongue thrusting into her mouth, his fingers plucking her nipples into taut peaks, made coherent speech impossible, so Wilhemina gave in to the glorious sensations Ethan evoked and allowed herself to enjoy the moment.

Rolling to his side and taking Willy with him, Ethan unhooked her gown and pushed the garment down past her hips. She wore no corset, only a chemise and drawers, and the sight of her creamy flesh, the outline of her dark nipples, shot sparks of desire through him.

"God, woman, you make me hard as a brick. Feel." He placed her hand upon his crotch, covering it with his own, and untied the ribbons of her chemise with his teeth, freeing her breasts to his mouth.

The long, hard length of Ethan's member beneath her palm sent warning signals to Willy's brain. They had to stop before it was too late—though by the feel of Ethan, it already was. But the tongue tormenting her nipples, the fingers slipping past the waistline of her drawers, kept her from saying the words that would end it all.

The passion burning within her was like nothing she'd ever experienced. She was hot, wanting, filled with an uncontrollable desire that would soon render her senseless. As his fingers inched down to explore the center of her being, Wilhemina realized that things had gone too far too fast and she let loose a strangled cry, pushing him from her.

"Stop, Ethan! We can't do this. It's not right."

"I'll be gentle, darlin'," he coaxed. "It's always scary for a woman the first time, but I'll make it good for you."

Of that, she was positive. "I've no doubt that you're a considerate lover, but I can't go through with this. I'm not ready."

"You sure as hell seemed ready a moment ago."

"I should never have let things go so far. And neither should you. We're business partners, Ethan. Making love will only complicate things." And things were already quite complicated.

Ethan thought she was a virgin, and she hadn't disputed his assumption. What would his reaction be when he discovered that she wasn't?

It was one thing for a man to be experienced and worldly, to sow his oats, but for a woman to have done so was considered scandalous and shocking.

And she knew that Ethan's opinion of her mattered. It mattered a great deal.

There was also the matter of Lorna Mae Murray, supposedly pregnant with Ethan's child. Wilhemina had no intention of ending up the same way as that poor unfortunate woman.

A pregnant, unmarried woman was a pariah in the community and brought shame upon her family. Wilhemina had worked too hard and long to accomplish what she had to throw it all away on a moment of passion.

She had decided to never again make love to a man outside of marriage. She had made that mistake once before with Thomas. Only then, she had thought marriage imminent. They had been very discreet. No one had known of their brief alliance but her and Thomas, and he was too much of a gentleman to ever speak of it to anyone. And he wasn't about to admit that he had failed at something as inconsequential as a relationship.

Her illusions shattered, Wilhemina's good reputation was about the only thing she had managed to salvage out of the whole sordid mess.

Despite all that, Ethan had proven by his behavior with Miss Murray that he was not the kind of man to take responsibility for his actions.

Men wanted pleasure and none of the pain.

"I'm willing to risk it," he said, confirming her opinion.

"Well, I'm not." Moving off the bed, she clutched her dress to cover her nakedness.

"You want me, Willy. You know you do; there's no sense in denying it."

She didn't, but neither did she confirm it. "You'd better go, Ethan. I'll see you in the morning."

His eyes glittered with desire and frustration. And there was a hint of anger at the rejection. Ethan was not a man used to taking no for an answer.

"I'll go, Willy. But know this: We will be together in that bed or another before this trip comes to an end. You have my word on it."

"And if I refuse, will you take me by force?"

His laughter was sardonic as he stepped toward her and held her face in his hands. "You'll come to me willingly, darlin'. Your body betrays you." He kissed her. "Good night, Willy. Sleep tight, if you can."

She stared at the door a long time after he'd slammed it behind him. Feeling bereft and utterly wretched in her righteousness, she knew that there'd be no sleep for either of them this night.

Giving credence to Wilhemina's prediction, Ethan sat in a chair by the window, smoking a cigar, staring out at the darkened street below, and wondering why he'd allowed his life to become so damn complicated.

For a man who'd recently sworn off women, who had vowed to lead a celibate life, he was feeling pretty hypocritical about what had occurred between him and Willy.

Had his memory of Lorna Mae and her deceitful ways faded so quickly? Had he forgotten how women liked to tease and torment? How they enjoyed twisting a man into knots, making him sweat and feel miserable?

He thought Willy might be different. She seemed honest in her dealings with him, not coy or devious, like other women he'd known. And he'd known quite a few.

But she was just like the others, leading a man on, pretending she cared, and then pulling the rug out from under him when the time came to demonstrate the depth of her feelings.

Well, Wilhemina Granville was going to find out that he wasn't the kind of man to toy with, the kind of man to take for granted. Let her test out her womanly wiles, her virginal protestations, on someone else.

He was a man who expected payment for promises made. And though she'd never uttered the words, her actions had spoken volumes about what she was willing to give. He hadn't been joking earlier when he'd told her they'd see this affair through. He intended to have Willy in his bed, to take what she offered, to get his fill of her; then she'd be free to find another more malleable partner.

Willy would soon find out that if she played with fire, she was going to get burned.

Chapter Eight

*S*AYING GOOD-BYE TO ALL HER NEW FRIENDS HAD BEEN difficult. Violet had been beside herself with tears at their parting and had made Wilhemina promise that she would eventually return to Never Die and pay a visit when her business was concluded. Even Ophelia had shed tears upon her departure.

But none of that was as difficult as riding next to a brooding, sullen Ethan Bodine, who'd spoken not a word to her since they'd left town early this morning and who had totally ignored her few attempts at civil conversation.

He was punishing her for her rejection of him last night. But it was a small price to pay to retain her dignity and to keep her heart from getting broken. Which it would eventually. That was an inevitability she'd already accepted.

What other man but Ethan would admit to having planned a seduction from the moment of their first meeting? His startling confession had touched her. Instead of being outraged, incensed, as she should have been, she'd been warmed by the knowledge that he found her attractive, that he wanted her. It was a balm to her battered ego, and it made her feel womanly again.

Though she hated to admit it, to even acknowledge the possibility, she had fallen in love with the audacious Texas Ranger. Felled like a giant Sequoia laid low by a logger's saw, Wilhemina knew there was nothing to be done about it. Not that she would want it any differently.

Maybe she was naive in thinking that something good could come of loving a man like Ethan Bodine, but Wilhemina knew she had to try. Her heart had dictated that she must, her future happiness depended on it.

"I think we should talk about what happened last night, Ethan."

He flashed her a disdainful look. "You mean what *didn't* happen, don't you?"

"I'd still like us to be friends."

"A man and woman can't be friends. It's not possible."

She turned her collar up against the cold wind that blew determinedly. The oak leaves had turned a deep brownish red, signaling that winter was not far off. "Why not? I had several male acquaintances back in Boston who were friends—two, not counting Thomas." One was nearly eighty, but Ethan didn't need to know that. "I think you are mistaken."

"Did these men want to make love to you, Willy?" She turned varying shades of crimson, but he ignored her mortification and continued. "Because I do. And I'm telling you that we can't be friends. Men can be friends with each other. Women can be friends. But men and women who are close can only be lovers. That's just the way of it. I didn't make the rules."

She was astonished by his reasoning. "But surely you know women who are merely friends."

"Some. But they were lovers first. I can't recall a one who wasn't."

The idea that others had come before her hurt. "Well, I'm determined that we can be friends while keeping our relationship strictly platonic."

He shook his head. "Nope. First chance I get I'm going to strip you naked and finish what we started last night. I'm giving you fair warning. If you want to go back home and save yourself, then go ahead. But be warned: If you stay, we're going to end up in bed. And we won't be sleeping."

The way he talked about their lovemaking, so matter-of-factly, as if it were already a foregone conclusion, had Wilhemina squirming restlessly in her saddle. Goodness! The man was a walking, talking stamen, ready to pollinate the unsuspecting ovule. He knew how to keep her off balance, that was for certain.

She'd been riding wave after wave of emotion since meeting Ethan, and she could only hope that she wouldn't drown in the end.

"I believe you're just trying to scare me off again, and you know that's not going to work. I'm bound and determined to collect the reward on your brother's head."

"Darlin', the only reward you're likely to collect is the long, hard one I'm going to give you." His smile was purely sexual, and Wilhemina's heart thundered like a herd of stampeding buffalo.

"And, Willy, you're going to enjoy it a whole lot more than that five hundred dollars you're after. I promise you that."

He rode off ahead of her, which was just as well in Willy's opinion, because she didn't want him to see how overheated she had become. She poured water from her canteen onto her neckerchief and mopped her face and forehead with it in an attempt to cool off. Even the cold wind blowing couldn't compete with Ethan's heated rhetoric.

She adjusted herself in the saddle, but the feel of that hard leather between her thighs only made things worse.

"Damn you, Ethan!" she cursed, nudging her horse into a trot. "I wouldn't have you for a friend if you were the last man on earth."

But that left only the alternative.

Misery, Texas, Autumn 1879

The door slammed shut, and Travis looked up to see an aging Ben Bodine entering his law office. Judging by the consternation on his father's face, and the fact that he now had more lines across his forehead than the map of Texas, the latest news from Ethan hadn't been good.

"You've had word?" he asked, knowing that his older brother had made it a practice to telegraph their pa from time to time to keep him apprised of his efforts to find Rafe.

Ben dropped into the chair fronting his son's desk, his massive shoulders sagging dispiritedly. "None good, I'm afraid, boy. Ethan's had no luck in tracking Rafe down. It's like the boy's fallen off the face of the earth. I confess, Travis, I'm worried to death. Even Lavinia's given up on cheering me. My temper's been sour of late."

Ben's temper and disposition hadn't been that good during normal times—Ethan used to say that Pa was usually mad enough to eat the devil with his horns on—so Travis had little doubt that poor Lavinia was having difficulty coping. His stepmother's heart was generous and kind, but there were limits as to what even saints could endure.

"I can still go after him. You know I'll do whatever's necessary to help Rafe and Ethan." He'd offered as much many times before, but each time his father had insisted that Ethan was the more competent of the two when it came to tracking and had talked him out of it.

Travis knew his limitations, knew he couldn't compare with his older brothers when it came to hunting and horsemanship, but it was damn difficult having it thrown in his face every time he offered.

"Your job defending Rafe will be hard enough, son, if and when your brother brings Rafe back to Misery to stand trial. My boy's going to need all your legal expertise then."

Travis had never tried a murder case before, and he still had doubts as to his ability to do so. Settling land disputes between ranchers and farmers and handling last wills and testaments was a whole lot different from conducting yourself in front of a judge and jury and having a man's life in your hands. Especially when that man was your own brother—a man whom you loved and respected, a man you had always looked up to and emulated.

"Perhaps you should think about hiring a lawyer from back east. Get someone with more experience than I have in criminal matters. I want Rafe to have the best representation possible."

Leaning forward, Ben braced his hands on the desktop and looked his son right in the eye. "You'll do fine, boy. I know you won't let any of us down. I'm just praying that Ethan can find Rafe before he has a chance to kill someone else. I doubt anyone will be able to help him then."

Travis had drawn the same conclusion, and it was almost a relief to hear someone else say it. Rafe's killing of Bobby Slaughter could be explained away by the duress of his wife's death, or as self-defense, as Ethan suspected it was. But if Rafe were to purposely execute another member of the Slaughter gang, the best lawyer in the world wouldn't be able to keep him from hanging.

"Ethan will find Rafe, Pa. He's good at what he does. I know you haven't always agreed with his methods, or his career choice, but he's a damn good lawman. I've got every confidence in his abilities to find my brother."

"You mama always said that me and Ethan were too much alike, and that's why we were always butting heads."

Travis chuckled. "I suspect that's true enough, though I'm sure Ethan would deny it with his dying breath."

That made Ben smile. "True. Your brother has always fancied himself to be more Ranger than Bodine. But blood always tells. It will in Ethan's case, too."

"He loves you, Pa. Ethan just doesn't show his feelings like other men."

"One day he will, when he meets the right woman. I used to hold everything in, same as him, but your ma taught me that saying the words didn't make a man any less a man, and Lavinia's devotion has humbled me. I'm no longer as hard as I used to be."

Travis's brows shot up in disbelief. If Ben Bodine had gentled, he sure as hell hadn't noticed. And Ethan meeting the right woman and confessing his undying love was about as likely a possibility as mortals flying to the moon. It just wasn't going to happen.

Ethan and Wilhemina entered the town of Red Dog late in the afternoon but stayed only long enough for Ethan to visit the saloon to gather information.

While Ethan was preoccupied with his investigation, Willy slipped upstairs to the brothel and did a little sleuthing of her own. There she found a strange German woman by the name of Frau Muehler, who claimed to have traveled with Rafe and a woman by the name of Emmaline St. Joseph.

Miss Muehler had been hired, she'd said, by Miss St. Joseph's deceased brother to act as nursemaid to five eastern orphans. On the trek west, the brother had succumbed to heart failure, leaving her, the children, and Emmaline St. Joseph stranded in the wilderness.

Miss St. Joseph, Frau Muehler insisted rather harshly, not bothering to hide her dislike of her employer, had been totally incompetent at caring for the children and didn't know anything about surviving in the wilderness. Mr. Bodine had come along and saved them all from certain death.

The German woman went on to say that Mr. Bodine might have decided to accompany Miss St. Joseph all the way to Sacramento, California, to assist with the opening of the St. Joseph Home for Foundlings and Orphans.

Ethan was astonished at the details Willy had discovered all on her own. Over the fire at their campsite that night, he grudgingly complimented her on obtaining such a good lead. Of course, he also took her to task for going off on her own and "risking her skinny neck," as he so kindly put it.

"I can hardly believe that woman was telling the truth. Why in hell would a man running from the law saddle himself with a woman and five children? It just doesn't make any sense." Ethan was thinking aloud, tossing sticks into the campfire, and watching them go up in smoke.

"And if Frau Muehler was the children's nursemaid," Wilhemina responded, "then why is she now working in a brothel as a laundress and cook? That doesn't make much sense, either.

"And she claims your brother didn't seem very fond of children. If that's true, then why, as you say, is he accompanying them?"

Ethan merely shook his head at the perplexing questions—questions he had no answer for.

As far as he knew, Rafe liked kids well enough and had always talked about having a son one day, but that still didn't explain his association with the St. Joseph woman.

"The German woman also claimed Rafe was anxious to be rid of them, that he was bossy and demanding," Willy said, grinning. "Now that I can believe. Bossiness must be a Bodine trait. Hard to believe you have brothers as ornery and opinionated as yourself."

"You should meet my father. Now there's a man who has the corner on orneriness."

"Your mother obviously doesn't think so."

"My mother's been dead these last eight years. Pa remarried about five years ago. A fine woman by the name of Lavinia. She's been good for him." Though Ethan was at a loss as to understand how she could put up with his father's autocratic, demanding ways. In his opinion, the woman was an angel, and too good for the likes of Ben Bodine. Though Ethan knew she was madly in love with his father.

"And your other brother? Is he married?"

Ethan snorted. "Nope. He came close once. Travis was courting a strong-willed woman by the name of Hannah Barkley, but they broke off their relationship." Just as well, Ethan thought. Hannah would have been more than a handful for Travis.

"That's too bad. Do you know what happened?"

He shook his head. "No. In those days I was gone a great deal of the time, so I really didn't get in on all the details. Rafe claims Travis got mad about something or other, which was probably a good thing."

"What does Travis say?"

"Nothing. Travis is unusually closemouthed for a lawyer."

She leaned back on her hands and measured her words carefully. "Sometimes what a person doesn't say is as telling as what he does."

"Meaning?"

"That perhaps it's too painful for him to talk about. That maybe he's still in love with this woman and regrets what's happened."

"I don't know why women always have to sentimentalize everything and read things into situations that just aren't there."

"Because we're astute and know things about the human condition. Men are just too obtuse to figure things out sometimes. If they were less concerned with the physical side of a relationship, with their own selfish wants and needs, they might notice more of what is going on."

Ethan studied her closely in the firelight, watching the flames flicker across her wounded expression, and wondered who the man was who had hurt her. He didn't like the thought of Wilhemina and another man and decided he might have to kill the fool for hurting her, if he ever made his acquaintance.

Surprised by his own thoughts, he said gruffly, "We'd better turn in. We'll be in Jansen tomorrow, and it's likely Rafe passed through there since he's traveling with a woman and children. I need to question the local authority, find out if they've heard anything." On second thought, maybe he should let her question the authorities. Willy seemed to have far better luck finding things out than he did. It was a damn galling thing to admit.

"I hope this Jansen has a hotel, because I'm already tired of sleeping on the ground."

"That's because you don't know how to bed down properly." He disappeared for a few minutes, and when he returned he was holding an armful of grass, which he placed beneath her bedroll. "That'll keep you from getting chilled. Always keep something between you and the cold ground." He held out his hand to help her to her feet. "I'd be happy to volunteer."

"I was thinking more of a bed."

"There ain't nothing like bedding down beneath the stars, drinking in the cold, invigorating night air. No stuffy hotel room can offer you that."

"Maybe not. But at least they have blankets and bathtubs."

His blue eyes twinkled. "Ah . . . yes . . . bathtubs. I seem to remember . . ."

She sucked in a breath of that very cold air and found nothing invigorating about it. "Good night, Ethan."

"Night, darlin' Willy. And don't worry, we'll find us a hotel room tomorrow. I'm about ready to pick up where we left off."

"The only thing you'll be picking up, Ethan Bodine, is your prostrate body off the floor when I shoot you in your very large"—she looked meaningfully at his crotch, and his brow shot up—"ego."

Chapter Nine

Upon entering the southern Colorado town of
Jansen, Ethan headed directly for the only hotel. The establishment looked very much like an old whore—one
who'd been ridden hard, unloved, and sorely used.

A brief examination of the Occidental's guest register
confirmed that a family by the name of St. Joseph had
stayed there several weeks before. The hotel manager remembered the family because of the children. From his description, Ethan was sure his brother had been there. The
hotel manager also unwittingly provided Ethan with the
perfect means of getting Willy into his bedroom, if not his
bed.

"Man here says the hotel's full up. He's got one room
left." Ethan looked over his shoulder at Wilhemina's horrified expression and cocked an eyebrow. "Well, are you
willing to share?"

Willy's suspicious gaze flew to the proprietor, whose
look was innocent enough. She yanked Ethan's shirtsleeve,
pulling him out of earshot. "If I didn't know better, Bo-

dine, I'd say you prearranged this whole thing. Well, I might have to share your room, but I don't have to share your bed. I'll sleep on the floor."

Cocksure and mighty pleased with the fortuitous circumstances, Ethan wasn't the least bit fazed by Willy's anger. "Suit yourself, darlin' Willy. I always enjoyed the floor myself, so that shouldn't prove to be a problem a'tall." He grinned at the fury flashing in her eyes, wondering if she'd be as volatile in bed.

While Willy unpacked and settled in their room, Ethan headed down the main street and straight for the sheriff's office, hoping to discover a substantial lead that would take him to his brother.

"Long time no see, Ethan," Sheriff Dixon said when he entered. "What brings you to Jansen this time of year? I thought you'd settled down in Misery. Heard you were through rangering."

"You're confusing me with my brother, Sheriff. I've no intention of quitting the Rangers or settling down." Ethan had never cared much for Rory Dixon. The man was an overweight braggart who usually smelled like he hadn't bathed in a month of Sundays. Today was no exception. The man smelled as strong as sheepherder's socks.

"I've got good reason to believe my brother's been here recently. Heard in Red Dog that Rafe's traveling with a woman named St. Joseph and five children. A family by that name was registered at the hotel sometime back. I'm wondering if you know anything about it."

A young deputy seated behind the desk answered him by pulling open the right-hand drawer and searching

through a pile of papers until he found what he was looking for: a Wanted poster of Rafe. "If this is your brother,
Captain Bodine, then I'm pretty sure I've seen him."

Hope filled Ethan, for this was the first real clue he'd
had since starting out. "When?"

"Three, maybe four weeks ago. He was standing in
front of the mercantile with an attractive redheaded
woman. Had five young'ns with 'em. Two were pretty little girls, about the same age as my daughters, so I took particular notice of them. There were two older boys and a
baby, if I recall correctly."

The deputy didn't look old enough to be married, let
alone have a family. Ethan decided it was not only a
shame, it was a damn waste of a lawman.

A man shouldn't have women and children on his
mind when he was tending to the law. There were enough
widows and orphans in the world as it was. A man needed
to keep a clear head when he was in pursuit of despera-
does, instead of worrying about families and sweethearts.

And female bounty hunters who stirred their blood.

"Did you interrogate him?"

The deputy nodded. "I surely did. But he was
bearded, and didn't look exactly like the picture on the
poster. And him being with that woman and children . . .
Well, I confess, it really threw me for a loop. And he
seemed to have a reasonable explanation for being in town,
so I let him go."

"Even though you were suspicious and thought you
recognized him?" Ethan suspected the young man had received his inadequate training from lazy Sheriff Dixon.

Embarrassment flooded the deputy's face. "Yes, sir."

"Either one of you heard anything about the Slaughter gang? It's possible they came through here not long ago."

"Haven't seen hide nor hair of them, Bodine," Rory stated, looking a mite put out that the Ranger would question their abilities. "We might have missed your brother, but the Slaughters are a different story."

The sheriff went on to explain, "There was some trouble down in New Mexico a while back. Eagle's Nest, to be exact. A whore was found murdered. She'd been butchered up pretty bad. The Slaughter gang is suspected in the killing. I'm told the bastard who knifed her even cut off her hair." His face registered disgust and disbelief. "Guess he fancied himself a trophy or some such."

Ethan's visage darkened like the thunderclouds rolling off the mountains. The same hideous thing had happened to his sister-in-law. Ellie's long blond braid had been missing when Rafe found her.

What kind of sick son of a bitch would do something like that to a woman? To anyone, for that matter?

"Sounds like the Slaughters all right. I suspect they're long gone from here by now." And there was no doubt that Rafe was hot on their trail.

But where had they gone? That was the question uppermost on Ethan's mind. Where?

"Rafe was here, but those damn fools failed to arrest him." Disgusted with the recent turn of events, Ethan tossed his jacket on the bed and hunted his pocket for a cigar. He'd half hoped to find Willy in her bath again—a definite diversion to take his mind off his troubles. But she was fully clothed and seated in a chair by the window, reading the newspaper.

"I'm so sorry, Ethan. I know how much this troubles you. Is there anything I can do?" She moved toward him and placed a hand on his arm to offer comfort, and he was damn tempted to take it.

"I doubt you're thinking of the same kind of comfort I am, Willy darlin'." He heaved a sigh and dropped to the bed dejectedly, holding his head in his hands and looking as though he'd just lost his last friend.

Ethan's despondent mood worried Wilhemina. He was usually so self-confident and hopeful about finding Rafe. "Why don't we go downstairs and get something to eat? Things always look better on a full stomach."

"You go on. I'm not very hungry, and I'd rather just lie here and brood awhile."

"Can I bring you up something to eat when I'm done?"

He forced a smile he didn't feel. "Just your sweet kisses, darlin'."

Wilhemina was very tempted to stay and give him just what he wanted, but she was hungry and decided that dining would be the wisest course for the moment. It would give her time to think, to decide if she really wanted to go through with making love to Ethan.

She'd been thinking about little else all day. Her mind had strayed from the newspaper a hundred times, the words blurring in front of her as Ethan's image appeared from the pages to haunt her. She wanted him more than she'd ever wanted anything. Probably even more than he wanted her.

Desire was a dangerous thing. It crept up on you when you least expected it. Then it stayed to torment, to tease, to crumble all the inhibitions and logic it had taken a lifetime to build.

Though there were hundreds—no, thousands—of reasons not to make love with Ethan, there was no denying what was in her heart. She hungered for him deep in her soul, the way a starving man hungers for food to sustain him. Her need was as great as the air she breathed to keep her alive. If she denied her body and her heart, then surely she would die.

Ethan paced across the pine-planked floors like a caged animal. Restless, unsure of what to do.

He'd never had any trouble making decisions. Hell, his whole life as a Ranger had been one decision after another. Men placed their lives in his hands and always trusted him to figure out the best plan, the wisest thing to do.

But now he was at a loss.

He wanted Willy. Wanted her until his belly ached with a need that consumed him, until he couldn't concentrate on anything but her and how it would be to hold her in his arms, kiss her, and make love to her.

He needed a woman. But it wasn't a whore he wanted. He wanted Willy.

Searching his saddlebag, he found the bottle of whiskey he'd recently purchased and was about to pull the cork when the door opened and there she stood. She looked nervous, unsure of herself, as she bit her lower lip and closed the door quietly behind her.

"I thought you were getting something to eat?"

Wilhemina stepped forward, and there was a look of resolve on her face. And trepidation. "I changed my mind."

He sucked in his breath, not daring to hope. "About the dinner?"

She shook her head, and his heart thumped loudly in his chest, ringing all the way up to his ears.

"You're sure?" he asked. "You didn't seem so certain before."

Wilhemina still wasn't certain. But the horrible debate she'd been having with herself over Ethan had provided no answers to her dilemma. And at twenty-eight she didn't have a whole lot to lose. Certainly not her virginity.

She considered herself to be a modern woman with a mind of her own. And she'd made up her mind that she was going to have Ethan Bodine one way or the other, despite her earlier beliefs to the contrary.

She knew it was foolish, and that it went against everything sane, sensible, and morally right. There was also the possibility that she could get pregnant. But this was one time she would listen to her heart, not her head.

It might not be permanent, it might not be forever, but she'd take what he was offering and enjoy it while it lasted. Few things were forever, anyway. And those who waited might wait in vain and never experience life or love.

He had removed his shirt, and his tanned, muscular chest appeared like burnished copper in the lantern light. The hair on his chest was as soft as his mustache, and her fingers itched to touch him all over.

"Come here."

The softly spoken words were like a velvet rope tugging gently on her heart, but she remained rooted. "I want to change first, freshen up. I'll only be a minute." She slipped behind the wooden screen and stripped, sponging herself with water from the pitcher and washing herself as best she could. From her saddlebag she removed a small bottle of lavender perfume and dabbed some between her breasts, behind her ears, between her thighs, blushing all the while.

"What's taking so long?" he called out, and she heard the impatience in his voice.

Nerves made her hands shake, and she quickly pulled on her lawn nightgown. "I'll only be another minute. I have to brush my hair."

"Bring the brush here. I'll do it."

She clutched it in her hand, weighing the idea, then slid from her hiding place. Her unbound hair hung past her waist to her hips.

"You've got the prettiest hair I've ever seen," he said, holding out his hand to her.

She sat beside him on the bed and handed him the brush. "It's a mess of tangles. Are you sure you want to do it?"

He lifted the heavy mass off her neck and kissed the nape, making gooseflesh rise on her arms. "Very sure,

Willy darlin'. I'm going to know every inch of your sweet body before we're through, including every strand of hair." He pulled the brush through her hair with long, smooth strokes, and after a few moments Willy felt the tension in her neck and shoulders start to dissolve.

"*Hmmm.* That feels wonderful." She nearly purred, sounding very much like her aunts' cat, Minnie, when she had her belly rubbed.

"Don't be making sounds like that, Willy, or this brushing business is going to be over in a flash." With one hand he continued to brush, but the other moved around to cup her ample breast and toy with her nipple.

Willy's tension returned, centered quite a bit lower than her shoulders.

"You've got nice breasts, Willy. And your nipples are made for—"

She grabbed his hand, for those very nipples he rhapsodized over were turning hard as pebbles. "I don't think we need to discuss all of my womanly attributes, Ethan. You're embarrassing me."

He put down the brush and turned her to face him, noting the faint blush to her cheeks. "Why should you be embarrassed? You have a lovely body—a body just made for loving." He kissed her then, a long, drugging kiss that made her toes curl heavenward.

Easing her down on the quilt, he covered her body with his own. "I want to look at you, Willy. All of you."

She hesitated a moment, then nodded, and he pulled her nightgown up over her head, removing the last defense she had between them. "Turn off the light," she whispered.

Weighing her breasts in his hands, he shook his head, then thumbed the nipples into hard peaks. "No, darlin'. I'm not quite finished yet." He demonstrated by bringing first one breast, then the other, into his mouth and suckling until Willy thought she would fly straight to the ceiling.

"Ethan!" Her heart began beating so fast, her breathing grew so rapid, she thought surely she would faint. Thunder boomed outside the window, but Willy thought it was the pounding of her heart.

He grinned. "Lay back against the pillow. I want to look at you."

Mortified that he planned to examine every inch of her, she shut her eyes tight and felt the heated blush that consumed her entire body. She couldn't see what he was doing, but she heard his murmurs of appreciation when he parted her thighs and separated the dewy folds of her womanhood. She tensed and tried to bring her knees together.

"Just relax, darlin'. We're going to take our time so we can both enjoy the experience."

He pulled her legs apart and suddenly his tongue replaced his fingers and he was tasting her with his mouth. She wanted to cry out, to tell him what he was doing was wrong, but it felt so wonderful, so exquisite, she couldn't bring herself to do more than groan aloud in ecstasy.

She felt the mattress move, heard his boots hit the floor one by one, then his pants, and she knew that he was now as completely naked as she.

Unable to resist, she opened her eyes and drank in the glorious splendor of his body, of his rigid manhood jutting forth proudly from the dark, springy curls. Tentatively she reached out to touch him and heard his sharp intake of breath, and she was glad she affected him as strongly as he did her.

That knowledge was heady and bolstered her confidence.

"I've never felt this way before," she confessed. And it was true. The few times she had made love with Thomas had been rushed and unfulfilling. It had been nothing as erotic and sensual as this. Certainly not as romantic. Or wicked.

The rain pelting against the glass, the bolts of lightning streaking outside the window, electrified the room and Willy's passionate mood.

When her fingers closed around him, he groaned as if in pain and grabbed her hand, bringing it to his mouth for a kiss. "You'll unman me if you keep that up, and this'll be over before we get started."

In an awe-filled voice she declared, "You're beautiful."

He chuckled. "I don't rightly recall ever being called beautiful before, darlin'."

Her eyes widened in appreciation. "You are. You're like a statue I saw once in Boston. All hard and chiseled and perfect." But definitely not cold. Quite the contrary, Ethan was hot, so very hot. And velvety to the touch.

He smothered her praise with his mouth, covering her body fully with his, placing his erect member atop the juncture of her thighs. "Open for me, darlin'," he coaxed. "Open and let me inside you."

He thrust his tongue into her mouth and replicated the motion as he plunged deep inside her. He paused, as if expecting something to hold him back, then continued on as her frantic pleas and his own desire obliterated everything but the moment.

Wrapping her legs about his waist, he drove in to the hilt, harder and faster, sliding in and out until Wilhemina nearly lost consciousness. The tension mounted, her breathing accelerated, sweat poured off his brow into her chest, until with one final burst, one deeply delectable plunge, he took them to the top and they climaxed together.

"Jesus!" Ethan murmured when he finally got his breath back and his heart quit pounding.

Wilhemina stared speechless, for never in her life had she experienced anything so breathtakingly beautiful. Her heart felt full to bursting with love for this man who had taken her to places she hadn't thought possible, who had made her feel every inch a woman.

Smiling in complete and utter contentment, she sighed deeply and reached out to caress his cheek, to touch the mouth that had given so much pleasure. "That was wonderful, Ethan."

But Ethan pulled back, disappointment and anger etched clearly on his face. "You weren't a virgin! You said you were a virgin."

Dread filled Willy as her worst fears were confirmed; she tried to explain. "I . . . I never said that, Ethan. You just assumed I was."

He rolled off the bed and reached for his pants, wondering why in hell he cared. He'd just had the best sex of his life, and now he was quibbling about a piece of flesh. But still, it mattered. Someone had come before him. And Willy had allowed him to believe he'd been her first.

Dammit to hell! He had wanted to be her first.

"You acted all virginal back in Never Die when we almost made love."

"Because I wasn't sure I wanted to be with you back then. Now I'm sure."

His look of contempt wounded her to the core. "You lied. All women lie to get what they want. Just like Lorna Mae." He laughed derisively and shook his head. "I never learn."

"Don't compare me to other women, Ethan. I never lied to you, and I never pretended to be something I'm not."

"Did you know Lorna Mae said she loved me, insisted that we get married, then turned around and tried to pass off another man's child as my own? I must be the biggest damn fool in the world."

Wrapping a sheet around herself, Willy moved off the bed to stand next to him. "I'm sorry you were hurt, Ethan. But don't you dare suggest that I'm anything like that conniving woman. I'm not. And you're the biggest fool in the world if you think so."

He snorted. "All women are the same, darlin'. You were just a bit more clever in your deceit. Must be that college education you're so damn proud of."

She wanted to scream, to smack that supercilious smirk off his face, to hit him alongside the head with a lamp and knock some sense into his thick skull. But she did none of that. Instead she said, "I refuse to stand here and listen to another word of your stupid tirade. You've made me eternally sorry that I chose to compromise myself with you. It was a huge mistake, and one that I'll likely regret for the rest of my life."

Her words hit their mark, and Ethan rocked back on his heels as if slapped.

"I'm going to bed now, Ethan, and you may sleep on the floor, since you find it so agreeable and my presence so abhorrent." She marched to the bed, fetched her nightgown, and put it on, then burrowed beneath the covers without uttering another word.

It took Ethan only a moment to regain his equilibrium. "I've got just as much right to sleep in that bed as you do, Wilhemina. And don't think you can keep me out of it." He turned off the lamp and waited for her response, which was to turn away from him and face the wall, then he stomped over to the bed.

Sliding in next to her, he yanked the covers. Smelling the lavender scent of her body, the muskiness of the sheets where they had so recently made love, feeling the heat of her warmth, he cursed himself for being such a goddamn stupid fool.

And spent the rest of the night staring at the ceiling.

Chapter Ten

WILHEMINA AROSE BEFORE THE ROOSTER'S CROW, which was a good thing, considering she'd been sprawled across Ethan's chest when she awoke, her hand tangled in his hair, his hand resting between her thighs.

Oooh! she thought, struggling to yank on her boots as quietly as possible. If she never saw Ethan Bodine again, it would be too soon. She had every intention of escaping his company before the irritating lawman woke up and had a chance to mention their humiliating encounter and his lowly opinion of her.

She'd been devastated by his cruel and callous treatment and had vowed to put many miles between them before this day was through. To think he had thought her capable of such deceit, had compared her to his paramour.

Wilhemina had come to the conclusion that men were far more trouble than they were worth. She had no doubt that Rafe Bodine was making poor Miss St. Joseph equally as miserable as Ethan had made her, so she'd decided to single-handedly save the woman and herself from the clutches of the Bodine brothers. Hannah Barkley didn't realize just how lucky she'd been to escape marriage to Travis Bodine.

"What the hell do you think you're doing?" Ethan bolted upright, noting that Wilhemina was dressed and ready for traveling. "We haven't had our breakfast yet."

Ignoring his bellow, she continued buttoning her jacket. "I'm leaving, Ethan. Without you. I've decided that our partnership should be dissolved here and now. I'll be going after your brother by myself."

"Like hell you will!" He reached down for his pants, but they were nowhere to be found. Then he noticed her sly smile of satisfaction. "What have you done, woman?"

"I'm afraid your clothes took flight this morning, Ranger Bodine. They appear to be on the sidewalk in front of the hotel."

Before he could jump from the bed or utter the vile curses threatening to burst from his tongue, Wilhemina stalked out of the room, slammed the door firmly behind her, and disappeared.

"Son of a bitch!" He'd been bested by a woman. Again.

He rushed to the door and threw it open. The woman staring back at him, wide-eyed and gasping at his nakedness, was not Willy. He slammed the door in her face, right before she fainted.

Wilhemina had no doubt that Ethan would come after her, which was why she'd been riding as fast as she could to put distance between them. The previous night's rain had made the ground a muddy mess, and the horse was having difficulty maintaining his footing. Twice he had stumbled, almost unseating her and tossing her to the ground, but she held on, determined not to be thrown by her mount, or life in general.

She didn't know exactly where she was headed, but the positioning of the afternoon sun told her she was still going in a northerly direction.

If Rafe had decided to accompany Miss St. Joseph and the children to California, he would need to find a city large enough to accommodate train travel to the west. Figuring that Denver was the closest metropolis to her current location, she decided to head there.

Ethan thought she needed him to find Rafe, but he was wrong. She was perfectly capable of making her own way in the world and of mending her own broken heart. She'd done so before; she would do it again. Only this time it was likely to take a bit longer.

She knew now that she loved Ethan. His harsh accusations and totally unfounded opinions of her character had wounded her deeply, cutting to her core and injuring not only her pride, but her heart as well. It was going to take a long time to get over the heartless Texas Ranger. A very long time.

So long, in fact, that the institution of spinsterhood was looking more and more agreeable to her. Though failure had never before been part of Wilhemina's vocabulary, she had failed miserably with Thomas, and now Ethan, and had come to the sad but logical conclusion that she wasn't cut out to be with a man for any length of time. She had the worst luck when it came to choosing a mate, and it was just fortunate that she had discovered that fact before saddling herself with someone for life.

And, of course, she and Ethan had never been truly compatible. He'd been the wrong man from the beginning. They had nothing in common on which to build a successful relationship. On the other hand, she and Thomas had had a great deal in common and that hadn't worked out, either.

She sighed, thinking that maybe she'd be better off with the Sisters of the Sacred Heart. At least there she would have only women to deal with.

The horse was lathered and blowing hard, and Wilhemina's stomach was grumbling louder than an angry bear. She was hungry, tired, and dirty. So when she spotted the lovely wooded glen with the small stream running through it, she decided to make camp for the night.

There had been no sign of Ethan, and she supposed that maybe he'd been slowed down by the rain or his lack of clothing. She smiled at the latter, trying to imagine him buck naked and searching outside in the rain for his pants and shirt.

It was a comforting thought.

Ethan was fully dressed, madder than a wet hen, and on Wilhemina's tail. He'd been riding hellbent-for-leather for hours, trying to catch up to the headstrong horticulturist. And with every hour that passed his temper worsened.

His clothes were soaking wet, thanks to her spiteful prank. And she'd done a pretty good job of hiding her tracks, slowing him down considerably. Once the rain stopped he had managed to pick up her trail and had just spotted the smoke from her campfire.

The little fool should have known better than to make a bonfire any rustler or outlaw might have noticed. He swallowed hard at the thought of the Slaughters catching up to her, especially after learning what they'd done to that whore back in Eagle's Nest.

Wilhemina didn't realize the danger she had placed herself in by riding off in a snit. He knew he was partially to blame for her impulsive action because of the way he'd spoken to her after they'd made love. He had only to close his eyes to see the wounded look on her face, and he felt like he'd taken a boot to a puppy.

But dammit! She'd deserved every word of his anger. Willy had lied to him. Played him for a fool. Made him think she was special. And when he caught up to her he was going to strip her bottom bare, take her over his knee, and . . .

And what? Spank her? Not likely, Ethan thought. When he got his hands on that curvaceous mound of smooth, silky flesh he was going to do a lot more than spank her.

He recalled the sweetness of their lovemaking, her deep sigh of pleasure when he entered her warm and willing body, her radiant smile of bliss when she'd told him how wonderful it had been between them.

And it had been wonderful, exciting, and the most fulfilling sexual experience of his life.

"Dammit!" he cursed, feeling himself harden at the memory of making love to Willy. And the thought of doing so again.

When he reached the glen where she had set up camp, he dismounted, tied Buster to a tree, and went in on foot. He picked his way forward carefully until he spotted Wilhemina standing in the river.

His mouth fell open.

Naked as the day she was born, the foolish woman was bathing in a stream whose water was rushing much too fast to be safe, giving no thought whatsoever to her welfare or the fact that anyone could happen upon her.

She was singing. Running the bar of soap over her breasts, between her thighs . . .

"Jesus!" he choked as he made to move forward.

Just then the loud cry of a hawk startled Wilhemina as it came swooping down from the branches of an oak tree. She flailed her arms, lost her footing on the slippery river bottom, and went careening into the rushing water.

At Wilhemina's frantic screams, Ethan ran toward the stream. Spying her valiant attempt to keep her head above water, he cried out, "Hold on, Willy! I'm coming to get you."

"Ethan! Ethan!" she screamed. "I can't swim."

"Holy shit!" He yanked off his boots and gunbelt as fast as he could and waded into the water. The stream was swollen to twice its normal size because of the recent rain and was moving rapidly, carrying Wilhemina downstream.

"Hang on, Willy," he shouted to be heard above the rushing, turbulent water, fear clutching his heart at the prospect that she could very well drown before he could reach her.

With swift, sure strokes he swam in her direction, noting that she was having a difficult time keeping her head above water. "Grab on to a rock, Willy," he shouted.

Wilhemina was terrified as the cold water lapped up to cover her face once again. She was tired, too tired to grab a rock as Ethan had suggested, though she made a pitiful attempt. Too tired to care that her lungs were near bursting from holding her breath and that her arms and legs felt like rubber as she tried to withstand the fast-moving current.

She tried to raise her arm once again to signal where she was, but the water kept beating her back down. "Ethan!" she screamed.

Wilhemina's cries for help were garbled. Then there were no more sounds and no more movements that he could detect.

Panic twisted Ethan's gut into knots, and he raced through the water like a man possessed, grateful he'd always been a strong swimmer. He caught up to her a few moments later, pulling her listless body against him and making his way to a shallow portion of the stream.

When he finally reached the riverbank he gave no thought to his burning lungs and leaden arms and legs. After depositing Wilhemina on the ground, he rolled her onto her stomach and, placing the flat of his hands on her back, pushed down hard, trying to force the liquid out of her lungs.

Ethan had never been a praying man—he'd always believed that, as a man, he himself and not some spiritual entity was in charge of his own destiny and that religion was for those too weak to accomplish things on their own. But he prayed now, prayed hard, willing Wilhemina to live, begging God to spare her life.

Over and over he pushed hard and prayed, until finally she began to sputter, cough, and spit up water. "Thank you, God!" he declared, rejoicing in the life sounds she made and the relief rushing through him.

"Ethan . . ."

His name came out as a whisper, but the sound of it had his heart beating fast. "*Sssh*, darlin'. Save your strength." She attempted to pat his cheek, but her arm fell back to her side and she closed her eyes in exhaustion.

As if he were toting a fragile and rare piece of porcelain, Ethan lifted Wilhemina and carried her back to camp, placing her near the fire. After retrieving a blanket from his saddlebag, he dried off her damp skin, paying special attention to her long mop of hair, which was dripping wet and tangled. Remembering how last night he had brushed the glorious locks into submission, he swallowed with some difficulty.

Now that Wilhemina had survived near drowning, Ethan had no intention of losing her to pneumonia, and he would do everything in his power to see that she recovered fully from her ordeal.

Her lips were blue, and he kissed them tenderly before carefully wrapping her in the warm blanket. It was much too large, but her own clothes were still down by the river's edge, splayed over bushes to dry. Apparently Willy had decided not only to bathe, but to do her laundry as well.

Wrapped in a blanket and sleeping the sleep of the dead, Wilhemina appeared to be breathing almost normally, so Ethan left to fetch his boots and gun and to retrieve his horse. Once Buster was unsaddled and fed, he set about fixing supper.

Willy would need nourishment when she awakened, and he was so hungry he could eat a horse. Buster whinnied just then, as if he could read Ethan's mind, and the Ranger smiled. "Don't worry, ol' fella. Your time's not up yet."

The sun peeked out just before it dipped low into the horizon, and Ethan knew that night would be upon them soon, and with it colder temperatures. After adding more wood to the fire, he prepared a supper of canned peaches, stale biscuits, and beef jerky for himself and some cornmeal mush for Willy. Not exactly a culinary delight. Though he'd tried several times to rouse her, she hadn't awakened yet, so he ate his meager meal and kept hers warm by the fire.

Seated on a log, he studied her while she slept, watched the fluttering of her lashes, how her breath fanned her cheeks, and his heart clenched at the thought that he'd almost lost her today. He didn't know why that should matter so much, didn't want to question the reasons he cared, but he did.

And he'd cursed himself a thousand times for not learning his lesson where women were concerned. There was a saying among the Rangers that a man should never trust women, fleas, or tenderfoots. It was sound advice, if impractical.

Wilhemina seemed a combination of all three. She was certainly all woman—he'd found that out firsthand, much to his delight—and a bigger tenderfoot he'd yet to meet. She'd also gotten under his skin and irritated the hell out of him, just like fleas were apt to do.

But damn if he didn't trust her more than most women of his acquaintance. It was true she'd deceived him about her state of virginity, but maybe it had been hard for her to explain things to him. For all her other dealings with him had been straightforward and aboveboard.

He'd accused her without knowing all the details. And that hadn't been fair. Ethan always prided himself on being fair. After all, Willy hadn't been privy to his dealings with Lorna Mae, and she had borne the brunt of the Murray brothers' anger unjustly.

Staring at her angelic face in repose, he decided that when she recovered, the first thing he'd do was ask her how she'd lost her virginity. He figured he had a right to know.

Wilhemina awoke slowly, and the first thing she realized was that she was quite warm and feeling very comfortable. The second thing that came to her attention was that she was naked and sleeping in a bedroll with a man who felt naked, too!

It all came flooding back to her in the space of a heartbeat: her fall into the river, Ethan's arrival and dramatic rescue of her. But she hadn't counted on being compromised while she slept.

Ethan was sound asleep, his hands wrapped securely around her waist and cupping her breasts, as if he had every right to touch her so intimately. If things had been different, if *he* had been different, she would have welcomed his attentions and protective posture; but they weren't. Nothing had changed since she'd walked out on him yesterday morning, and nothing would.

"Let go of me, Ethan!" She squirmed against the restraint of his arms.

Awakening with a start, he noted her anger and his hold grew firmer. "Now, darlin', don't go getting all mad again. It's not good for you to get yourself so worked up. How are you feeling? I was worried about you."

She shot him an accusatory look. "Is that why you thought it necessary to stuff me into your bedroll and cocoon us together? I doubt it was my health you were thinking of, Ethan Bodine."

Reluctantly he released his hold. "Is this any way to act after I saved your life? You're pretty ungrateful for a woman who almost drowned. And you would have, had I not been there to rescue your pretty hide."

Her cheeks flushed. "I'm grateful that you saved me from drowning, Ethan, truly I am. But you've taken much upon yourself to think we should sleep together."

"You were freezing last night, and I only did what I thought best."

"*Hmph!* I'm sure of that." She sat up, and he followed, looking a bit sheepish.

"I think we need to talk about the other night."

"What's there to talk about? You made your feelings perfectly clear."

"I . . . I decided that maybe I'd jumped to conclusions. Maybe I should have given you a chance to explain."

Her eyes widened in surprise and then filled with confusion. "Explain what? I have no explanation for your outlandish behavior."

He shook his head, realizing that he hadn't made himself clear. "I meant about you not being a virgin, Willy. Maybe there's a reasonable explanation for it and you just haven't told me."

Her mouth fell open and her face reddened; then she rolled out of the blanket and stood, unmindful of the provocative picture she presented.

But Ethan was very mindful of the fact that his shirt barely covered her thighs.

"You have the nerve, the audacity, to ask me how I lost my virginity!" She shook her head, unable to believe the man's gall. "You are either insane, stupid, or more obtuse than I had originally suspected."

Obtuse. Audacity. What the hell was she talking about? The woman used more ten-dollar words than a preacher at Sunday sermon. "I'm giving you a chance to explain yourself, woman. I'm giving you the benefit of the doubt. I figured since we're going to be sleeping together, I have the right—"

"The right! Sleeping together!" She gasped aloud, almost choking on her words, her eyes narrowing as she brushed the hair out of her face and worked herself into a frenzy. "I don't need to explain myself to you. And you don't have any rights at all where I'm concerned. I made love with you because *I* wanted to." She thumped her chest. "Me, Ethan. Do you hear me? It was my idea, not yours. And the fact that I wasn't a virgin is none of your business. You weren't one, either, if one can believe the Murray brothers, and I didn't take you to task for it and accuse you of vile things."

Her logic astounded him. He stared at her as if she'd lost her mind, then said, "I'm a man," as if that explained everything.

She shrugged. "So? Is that supposed to make me feel better that you went to bed with Lorna Mae Murray and numerous other women, I'm sure, before you made love to me?"

"Men are supposed to be experienced, Willy. It's the way of things."

"And women are supposed to remain ignorant? Is that what you're saying?"

"Women are supposed to remain pure and untouched until their wedding night."

"Oh, really! So you were married to all those women you bedded? I find that hard to believe, Ethan."

He threw off the blanket and stood to face her, not caring that he was stark naked and that his member was sticking straight out like a barber pole. "You're twisting my words." He took a step toward her, and she put up her hand.

"I'm going to twist more than your words, Bodine"— she stared meaningfully at his maleness—"if you don't stop right where you are. I have no intention of resuming a relationship with you. It's obvious that I need to remain in your company for my own protection, but I do not have to sleep with you. I'm sure you'll find others who'll be more than willing to accommodate your needs."

Her words deflated his ego and his sexual ardor quite effectively. "You can try to ignore what's between us, Willy, but sooner or later you'll come begging for more. And you're right, I won't have any difficulty finding someone to warm my bedroll in the meantime. I know plenty of women in Denver."

The thought of him making love to another woman twisted her heart and made her absolutely miserable, but Wilhemina wasn't about to reveal the depth of her emotions. Ethan was a heartless, hardheaded, arrogant man, and she wouldn't give him the satisfaction of knowing how much he'd hurt her. Was still hurting her.

Deciding to give him a taste of his own medicine and hoping that he'd choke on it, Wilhemina raised her hands to lift the heavy mound of hair off her neck, securing it into a knot. She watched his eyes darken as they followed her movement, and she smiled seductively.

"I'm sure I won't have any trouble at all meeting eligible men in Denver as well, Ethan. It looks like Denver is going to be very good for both of us." Turning on her heel, she walked toward the riverbank to gather up her clothes, unaware of the outrage and murderous look Ethan cast her way.

Chapter Eleven

Denver, Late Autumn 1879

DENVER WAS A FAR CRY FROM GOOD FOR EITHER OF
them, despite Wilhemina's words. The city was frightfully expensive, and her meager funds had depleted to the point where she would need to find employment soon. She didn't know how long they would remain in the city, only that she needed to work while they searched for leads to Rafe's whereabouts.

Upon leaving home, she had brought with her the last of her savings, but that was nearly gone. The trip to find Rafe Bodine was proving more costly than she'd originally planned. Her intent to sleep under the stars and live off the land had been impractical at best. And there was still the matter of that lavender gingham dress.

The boardinghouse where they had secured lodgings last night charged two dollars each a day. Highway robbery, in Wilhemina's opinion, if the meal they'd been served last evening was an indication of Mabel Turner's culinary expertise.

The chicken had been stringy, the biscuits hard, and the company dour. Mrs. Turner was short on hospitality but long on wind. She had a penchant for complaining, and Wilhemina's ears had tired after listening to the woman's two-hour diatribe on the drawbacks of widowhood and supporting oneself.

But at least she and Ethan had a roof over their heads. And separate rooms. Wilhemina had been insistent on that point, even though her decision had not set well at all with the testy Texas Ranger, who'd shouted, cursed his fate and women in general, and finally given in.

Now, staring out the grimy front window of Mrs. Turner's sparsely decorated parlor, she wondered when Ethan would return. *If* Ethan would return.

They'd been at each other's throats for days since the near drowning episode, and the confrontation over the sleeping arrangements last evening had only worsened matters. This morning at breakfast Ethan's mood had been downright surly, if not rude, for not only was he frustrated by her unwillingness to bed him, he was still faced with the daunting task of finding his brother.

To that end, or maybe both, he'd announced with a confident smirk that he intended to pay a visit to an acquaintance this morning. Loretta Goodman ran a boarding establishment at the other end of town and was a good friend of Rafe's. And it was likely, Ethan had said, that the woman knew something about his brother's whereabouts.

Ethan hadn't bothered to hide the fact—rather, he'd embellished it—that Loretta Goodman used to practice the world's oldest profession and was his close, very personal friend as well.

Though Wilhemina had feigned indifference at the time he'd regaled her with these impertinent facts, she was now frothing with fury at the idea that he would bed a prostitute, or even a former prostitute. The man had absolutely no—

"Miss Granville?"

Mabel barreled into the room—all two hundred fifty pounds of her—and waited impatiently, tapping her foot against the oval braided rug, to gain Wilhemina's attention.

"You mentioned during breakfast that you was looking for work. I heard they was looking for someone to serve the meals over at the Busy Bee." She wiped wet hands on her apron as she talked. "You might want to check it out."

The prospect of employment snapped Wilhemina out of her pique over Ethan, and she gave the woman her full attention. "Really? Well, how kind of you to mention it to me, Mrs. Turner."

"Kindness ain't got nothin' to do with it, young woman. If you can't pay your board, I lose money. And if I don't got money, I can't eat."

Mrs. Turner's triple chins wagged as she turned on her heel and quit the room, and Wilhemina thought the obese woman could stand to miss more than a few meals, but she refrained from stating her opinion.

The benefit of working at the restaurant would be twofold, Wilhemina realized. Not only could she earn some much needed money, she might be able to glean information about the whereabouts of Rafe. While Ethan occupied his time with that prostitute, she intended to question the patrons of the Busy Bee Cafe.

Ethan was in a mood as sour as a dill pickle when he approached the Goodman boardinghouse. The garishness of the yellow, two-story structure with the red shutters did little to improve it. And nothing was likely to until he bedded Wilhemina again.

It seemed at present his hands were full of difficult women.

Despite what he had led Willy to believe, he and Loretta Goodman were far from fast friends. They'd had a caustic, somewhat antagonistic, relationship from their very first meeting, and nothing had changed much over the years. He thought her tongue sharp and her opinions just as pointed, and he'd never understood Rafe's reasons for helping the annoying woman escape a life she had chosen for herself.

Ethan believed that folks should pay for their own foolish decisions and mistakes, instead of asking others for charity or help.

He knew damn well that Loretta would be reluctant to give him any information regarding his brother's whereabouts. She and Rafe were as thick as fleas on a hound dog. And if nothing else, Loretta was loyal to her friends. But even knowing all that, he had to try, so he knocked on the door.

"Well, well, Ethan Bodine! As I live and breathe, I never expected to see you standing on my doorstep."

Loretta's too bright smile was strained, and Ethan grew immediately suspicious. "You're looking good, Loretta." The short, curvaceous blonde wasn't his type at all. He preferred dark-haired women with brown eyes and—

"Why, thank you, Ranger Bodine. I believe that's the first time you've ever paid me a compliment. You must be softening in your old age."

Doing his best to ignore the gibe, though the words pricked his skin as they were meant to, he said, "Do you mind if I come in? I need to ask you a few questions."

She hesitated. "Actually, I do. I'm . . ." A soft blush covered her face, and her right brow arched. "I'm entertaining a friend at the moment."

Ethan didn't bother to hide his disgust. So much for Loretta starting a new life. It appeared the former prostitute was up to her old tricks—and turning a few of them as well.

"I'm looking for Rafe. Have you seen him? I heard he might be traveling with a woman and five children."

Fear entered her blue eyes and she nodded slowly, her words measured when she spoke. "He was here a while back."

"He's wanted by the law, Loretta, and if you're harboring a fugitive, then you're breaking the law as well."

Her posture grew defensive immediately, and Ethan cursed his lack of restraint. Tact had never been his strong suit, as Travis was so fond of pointing out.

"I told you Rafe was here, but he ain't any longer. He took off weeks ago. Said he might be going to Oregon—Portland, maybe. I can't rightly recall."

Frowning, Ethan puffed his cigar, and the smoke rings rose up, curling over his head like a halo. "If you're trying to protect Rafe, then think again. He's after the Slaughter gang, and they're likely to shoot him down on sight if they get the chance. And if he finds them first and kills one of them, there'll be nothing I can do to save his hide. He'll hang for sure."

The woman wrung her hands nervously, wiping them on the skirt of her dress; she appeared genuinely distressed. "Rafe told me he was in some trouble, Ethan, but I had no idea it was this serious. You can be sure I'd tell you if I knew where he was. I wouldn't want any harm to come to him. After all, he's my friend."

Though Ethan suspected she wasn't telling the truth, he had no way to prove it, so he thanked Loretta and walked away. The sound of the door slamming shut had him looking back over his shoulder; the hairs on his neck prickled, making him wonder if he shouldn't have insisted on searching the house.

But Rafe was too clever to stay in one place too long and had likely left weeks ago, just as Loretta claimed. No doubt after he'd deposited Miss St. Joseph and her brood at the train station, he'd replenished his supplies and been on his way to find the Slaughters.

At least Ethan now knew for sure that Rafe had been in Denver. If only he'd been able to get here sooner, he might have caught up with him.

But he wouldn't have given up the opportunity of meeting Willy and taking her to bed. As exasperating and troublesome as the woman was, making love to her had been the highlight of this whole miserable trip.

Determined that he would experience that pleasure yet again—for one taste of Willy wasn't enough, and he aimed to satisfy his appetite—Ethan headed back to the Turner boardinghouse.

It had taken Wilhemina over twenty-five minutes to locate the Busy Bee Cafe. Now that she'd found it, she was sorry she'd ever set foot in the place.

The proprietor, a tiny, gnomelike man named Tyrell Botts who reached only to her waist, had hired her on the spot, not seeming to care if she had any waitressing experience. After handing her an apron, he had pushed her out the kitchen door and into the dining room with an admonition not to break anything. That had been nearly two hours ago. But to Wilhemina it seemed like a lifetime.

Propping the heavy tray of dishes on her hip, she made her way gingerly across the dining room to the waiting customer near the window.

"Hurry up with my food, miss. I told you when I came in that I had no time to waste," grumbled a dust-laden cowboy.

"Yes, sir," she replied, breathing a sigh of relief that she hadn't dropped any of the dishes or broken any glassware. "I'm sorry it took so long." After setting the bowl of thick beef stew and basket of sourdough bread on the table, she turned to leave—and felt a hand caressing her buttocks.

"Hey, honey," said the man at the next table, "what are you doing after work? If you need some money . . ."

The lecherous oaf reminded her of Rufus Bowers. Fighting to keep her temper in check, Wilhemina forced a thin smile, "I'm not interested in what you're offering, sir, but if you'd care to answer a few questions, I'd be most appreciative."

"Questions? I ain't interested in your questions." He rubbed his chin. "But maybe we could work something—"

Moving quickly before he had a chance to grope her again, Wilhemina wondered if she'd made the right decision in her selection of employment or if she'd been too confident in her abilities to play detective. Obviously investigating took a bit more finesse than she possessed.

A few minutes later Ethan slid into the corner table at the rear of the restaurant and watched in amusement and admiration as Wilhemina struggled to balance her tray. Mabel Turner had informed him of her whereabouts. Since he had thought it highly unlikely that a career-minded woman like Willy would accept a job waiting tables, he decided he had to see for himself.

The woman had grit, he'd give her that. She was totally inept at what she was doing, but he gave her credit for trying. She had told him of her financial difficulties and desire to find employment. And though he had enough money to support both of them, he hadn't said as much, thinking that Willy would never accept his support under the present circumstances.

He'd never really thought that she would go out and find a job. But she had proven him wrong once again. It seemed she'd been doing that a lot lately.

Wilhemina spotted Ethan and was making her way over to his table when a customer reached out to grasp her wrist and forced her to a halt.

"Bring me some coffee. And be quick about it. Can't you see I'm out?"

Ethan almost rose out of his chair to teach the burly, redheaded oaf some manners, but he sat back down when she nodded and smiled at the man, telling him she'd be right back. She returned a moment later and began pouring hot coffee into his cup.

"It's about time. I ain't got all day."

"Hey, hurry up with my food," yelled someone across the dining room.

"Miss, oh, miss!" An elderly lady waved her napkin in the air like a flag, trying to gain Wilhemina's attention. "Where's the tea I ordered? And may I have a piece of apple pie to go with it?"

Soon half a dozen people were shouting orders at her, and Wilhemina's head began to spin like a top as she tried to keep track of them all. All of a sudden the rude redheaded man tugged on her skirt, causing her hand to jerk and the coffeepot to dip, spilling the hot liquid contents over his lap.

Willy looked horrified. "Oh, dear! I'm so sorry, sir!"

"Eeeoww!" He jumped up, pulling his wet pants away from his legs. "You stupid bitch!"

Ethan lurched from his chair just as Wilhemina brought the coffeepot down hard on the man's head. Ethan rushed toward her, as did the café's owner.

"Here now, young woman! What do you think you're doing?"

"This horrible man called me names, Mr. Botts."

The man rubbed the large lump forming on his head and stared daggers at Wilhemina. "This stupid bitch spilled coffee all over my lap."

Wilhemina brought the pot up again, intending to strike the man a second time, but Ethan grabbed it out of her hand. In the next instant he tossed her over his shoulder and carried her out of the restaurant, smiling apologetically at the patrons who stared wide-eyed at the commotion.

"Put me down, Ethan!" she screeched, pummeling his back. "I'm going to bash that man's brains out. How dare he call me vile names! I was only trying to help."

When they got a respectable distance from the café, Ethan lowered Wilhemina to the ground. She was red-faced and mad enough to spit nails, and even the chilly air couldn't cool her temper. "Try to get hold of yourself, woman."

She looked up at him with big, mournful eyes, then burst into tears. Ethan stared back, totally at a loss as to what he should do. He'd never been much good with crying women. They made him feel powerless and inept.

"I was doing my best." She sniffed several times, then hiccuped. "And those pe . . . people were so rude. I . . . I couldn't move fast enough to suit them, though I tried."

She covered her face, hiccuped two more times, and resumed crying.

"Willy darlin'." He drew her into his arms and patted her back and head as if she were a child, ignoring the curious stares of the passersby. "Don't be fretting over things that aren't important."

"But I needed that job. I'm almost out of money. And I was hoping to find out something useful about Rafe's whereabouts. I failed miserably at both."

"I've got plenty of money. There's no need for you to work. And I told you that I don't want you sticking that pretty nose of yours into things that don't concern you and asking a lot of questions. One of these days you're going to ask the wrong person, then . . ." He couldn't bring himself to think about what the Slaughters would do if they got their hands on her.

"I'm supposed to be your partner, Ethan, not your kept woman. I can't take your money. I'm supposed to be earning the reward money for Rafe's capture. That was the whole idea of becoming a bounty hunter in the first place."

As upset as she was, he didn't think it prudent to point out that kept women usually warmed their keepers' beds. Or that becoming a bounty hunter was the dumbest plan ever concocted by a woman. "You can keep track of what you owe me and pay me back after you collect the reward money for Rafe. How's that?"

She wiped her eyes with the back of her hand, seemingly appeased by his suggestion. "Are you sure? Because I don't want to be beholden to you for anything."

He took her elbow and began walking toward the boardinghouse. "There'll be no strings attached to the loan. And as for your working at the café, we're not going to be in Denver long enough for you to draw your first paycheck."

She ground to a halt, ignoring the whistles and catcalls she received from a group of cowboys riding by on horseback. Ethan didn't and reached for his gun.

"Stop that!" she chided, slapping his hand. "They're just feeling their oats after being out on the trail for months on end."

Jealousy was an alien emotion to Ethan, but he felt it now as keenly as his need for this woman. "After observing your behavior in the café, I was led to believe you weren't partial to rude behavior."

Blushing, she replied with a smile, "I tolerate yours, don't I? Now tell me about your visit with Loretta Goodman. And don't leave anything out."

His grin was naughty. "You want *all* the details? I'm not sure that's such a good idea, Willy. I wouldn't want to shock you." Her eyes filled with hurt, and he cursed himself for teasing her. "Nothing happened between me and Loretta, if that's what you're getting at. She despises me. Always has."

Relief flooded Wilhemina. "Really? I find that so hard to believe, you being so agreeable and all."

Ethan leveled a look of annoyance at her. "You want to hear about Rafe or not?"

Grinning, and feeling one hundred percent better, she nodded.

"Loretta claims he went to Oregon, but I don't believe her. I think she's hiding something, but I've got no way of knowing what it is. And I can't very well accuse her of it." Though he'd done his best to try, in a roundabout sort of way.

"Why would your brother go to Oregon? Do you have family there, someone who might take him in?"

"Nope. That's why I don't believe her."

She considered the possibility, then said, "On the other hand, Oregon's not that far from California, and if Rafe decided to go to California with the St. Joseph woman, as Frau Muehler suggested, then maybe Oregon wouldn't be so farfetched after all."

When they reached the walk in front of Mrs. Turner's boardinghouse, they paused. "I'm going over to Holladay Street to see what else I can find out about Rafe. I want you to stay put until I get back."

"But why can't I go with you? I may be able to help gather information."

"Holladay Street is full of brothels and gambling houses. I don't want you near that part of town. Women have been known to disappear there."

Wilhemina gasped, her eyes widening in fright. "Murdered?"

He nodded gravely. "Some. But most are drugged and sold into prostitution. I don't want that happening to you, Willy. Do you understand? From here on out, no one but me is going to know that sweet little body of yours."

Willy's pleasure at the compliment was mixed with annoyance. But the pleasure of Ethan's proprietary manner far outweighed the annoyance of his arrogance. "Your conceit and self-confidence continue to astound me, Ranger Bodine." And they also continued to fill her with hope that maybe, just maybe, things would work out between them. After all, a man as determined as Ethan might feel something other than lust and not even realize it. As obtuse as Ethan was, that was a likely possibility.

Patting his cheek, she mimicked. "Don't hold your breath, *darlin'*."

He grabbed her then and kissed her right on the sidewalk in front of God and everybody, including Mrs. Turner, who was standing at the front door, staring aghast, and who'd already declared emphatically that she wouldn't tolerate any hanky-panky going on in her house.

The intensity of Ethan's kiss was so great, it put all of Mrs. Turner's dire warnings right out of Willy's head. Instead Wilhemina thought she might faint.

When the kiss finally ended, Ethan smiled at her dazed expression and chucked her playfully under the chin. "You can breathe now, Willy." Then he marched off down the street, whistling a cheerful ditty.

Wilhemina stared after him with tingling lips and the uneasy prospect of facing Mabel Turner.

As soon as Ethan entered the brothel and gambling hall known as La Petite Chatte, an uneasy feeling came over him. Maybe it was intuition, or maybe it was the fact he'd been on his guard too long, but there was something about the place that set him on edge.

Strolling up to the long mahogany bar, he decided to have a drink and see what information he could ferret out of the barkeep. "Howdy," he said. "How's business?"

The bartender took one look at the tin star on Ethan's chest and his eyes filled with panic. "We don't want trouble here, Ranger. This is a respectable place."

Ethan's laugh was mocking. "If this place is respectable, then I'm Billy the Kid. But I didn't come here to cause you any trouble, I came for information. Give it to me and I'll be on my way."

"I'm only the bartender, and I mind my own business."

"Then perhaps I should speak to the owner of the place. Most of the other saloon owners I've spoken to have been cooperative, but if you're not inclined . . ." Ethan shrugged and left the threat hanging.

"Mr. DuMonde is the owner. He's in his office this time of day, working on the books. What is it you need to speak to him about?"

"I'm looking for a man by the name of Rafe Bodine. Or he may be using another name—St. Joseph, or even his first name, Rafferty."

At the mention of Rafferty, the man's eyes widened in recognition, then darkened. "I'll let Mr. DuMonde know you're here and that you wish to speak to him."

A few minutes later Ethan was being escorted into Simon DuMonde's private office at the back of the gambling parlor. The man seated in the oak swivel chair behind the desk could have been drawn from any dime novel. His dark hair was slicked down, and he had a long handlebar mustache groomed with wax. His eyes were rimmed red, and Ethan suspected the man was fond of either drink or opium or both.

"Monsieur, my bartender, Maurice, informs me that you are looking for the man named Rafferty. May I ask why?"

"The name's Bodine—Ethan Bodine, up from Misery, Texas. I'm on the trail of my brother Rafe, or as you may know him—Rafferty Bodine."

Simon DuMonde's eyes narrowed into thin slits, his hands balling into fists. "A man by that name worked for me some weeks ago, but he's gone. I'm not surprised to hear that he's in trouble with the law. He seemed the type. Very disagreeable, if I recall correctly."

Ethan was darn tempted to gouge out the man's bloodshot eyes with his thumbs, but he held his temper. "Your opinions don't interest me, DuMonde, just your information."

"You look alike, you and your brother. But the eyes are different shades of blue."

"Look, mister, I ain't lookin' for a date; I'm looking for information. Now if I was to sniff around long enough, I'm sure I could find something illegal to pin on you. But since I'm not the law in these parts, and I need to be moving on, I'll get out of your face if you cooperate."

Simon DuMonde smiled coldly and said, "Your brother and I had an argument over a whore named Loretta Goodman. We came to an understanding and he left. I hope never to set eyes on him again. He caused me a great deal of trouble."

Ethan's eyes widened imperceptibly at the mention of Loretta. Just as he suspected, the woman knew more than she'd let on and had been up to her skinny neck in dealings with Rafe. "Do you know where Rafe was headed?"

DuMonde lit a cigarette and puffed agitatedly on it. "There's been talk that he left town with a woman and five children. Rumor has it that he's gone to Utah and is now passing himself off as a Mormon to hide among the saints. He has a beard and mustache, and with the woman and children in tow, it's possible that he could be living in Provo and getting away with the deception."

Utah made a lot more sense than Oregon, Ethan decided. And DuMonde, who had reason for gaining revenge on Rafe, was likely telling the truth as he knew it.

"I hope your brother lands in hell, Monsieur Bodine. It is where he belongs."

Ethan leaned down on the desk, his face inches from the Frenchman, and grasped the man by the shirtfront, nearly strangling him. "You'll be there a lot sooner, DuMonde, if you keep talking. My brother may be wanted by the law, and I may have to bring him back to stand trial, but I don't have to listen to you or any other piece of shit malign him. Do I make myself clear? Because if I don't, I sure as hell can."

DuMonde nodded and the sweat dripping off his brow landed on his inkpad. "Yes, Monsieur Bodine," he choked out. "I understand."

Ethan released him. "Good. Because if Rafe's not in Utah, I'll likely come back here. And if I do, I might just pay you another visit."

The man paled and Ethan stalked out, trying to figure out how he and Wilhemina could pass themselves off as Mormons and how he was going to convince her to pose as his wife.

Chapter Twelve

"**Y**OU WANT ME TO BE YOUR WIFE!**"

An unexpected surge of pleasure spread through Wilhemina. She nearly dropped the vial of perfume she held, until she noticed Ethan's horrified expression reflecting back at her in the dresser mirror.

"Not for real, Willy. I need you to pretend to be my wife when we get to Utah." He shut the bedroom door behind him, wondering when she would notice that they were sequestered in the same room and kick him out.

Her excitement, which she silently chided herself for, deflated as quickly as a punctured hot-air balloon, and she wondered why the prospect of marrying Ethan Bodine had been so damned appealing.

Sucking in her breath, she turned from the mirror to face him. "Let me get this straight: you want us to go to Utah and pretend to be married? Why?"

"Because one of the saloon owners I spoke with today heard that Rafe may be hiding in Provo. The place is full of Mormons, and we'll fit in better if we pretend to be one of them. From what I hear, the community is pretty much closed to outsiders."

Crossing her arms over her chest, she pursed her lips in disgust. "Considering that those Mormon men have more than one wife, I'm not at all surprised." The place was a man's fantasy, that's what it was. Imagine anyone believing that crock of horse manure that some angel or whatever came down from heaven and spoke to Joseph Smith, gave him a few golden tablets, and told him to start a religion whereby he could have more than one wife.

She snorted at that, and at Ethan's ridiculous idea of going there. "This is the craziest idea you've had yet, Ethan. First of all, you're not at all sure that your brother is in Utah, despite what some saloon owner claims, and Provo must be at least four hundred miles from here."

"Closer to five, actually."

"And even if he were there, what makes you think you can find him? Provo is a fairly large city. And Rafe's not going to make himself accessible to you."

"If he's there, I'll find him. I just need to get there first."

"I don't think Rafe is hiding among the Mormons. The woman he's traveling with, Miss St. Joseph, would never subject children in her care to such . . . such depravity and un-Christian thinking as the Mormon lifestyle permits. Polygamy is against everything we Christians believe in."

"For chrissake, Willy! You don't even know the St. Joseph woman. For all you know she's been raised among heathens and practices voodoo.

"And I know a little bit more about desperate men than you do. My brother is running from the law, and he's going to look for the safest place to hide. What better place than among religious fanatics?"

"But why do we have to pretend to be married? We could say we're brother and sister. Or friends. I don't—"

"Now, Willy," he said, his voice as smooth as a bottle of twenty-year-old Scotch. Stepping closer, he clasped her hand. "A husband and wife traveling together will draw far less speculation. Besides, we've been traveling together for weeks, living as close as any man and wife. What harm could it do?"

She swallowed as heat traveled up her arm to spear her heart. *What harm indeed?*

"As long as you agree that this ruse will be in name only, and that we won't be sharing a bed, I might consider it."

He pulled her into his arms, and she fought against the memory of what being with him could be like. "You wound me, Willy darlin'."

"Don't tempt me, Bodine," she said, twisting out of his hold. "I'll go to Utah with you, because I'm your partner and you have money and I have none. And I'll pretend to be your Mormon wife in name only. But that's as far as it goes. Once we find your brother we'll be parting ways. I don't think either one of us wants anything to start between us."

She stared meaningfully at him, but he didn't grasp what she was hinting at, so she added. "Like Lorna Mae Murray."

When her insinuation became clear, Ethan's eyes darkened to midnight, his face reddening at her belief that he'd gotten Lorna Mae pregnant. "There are ways to prevent that sort of thing from happening."

"Too bad you didn't inform Lorna Mae of them." She knew she was purposely goading him, but she needed to put distance between them. And making him mad seemed as good a way as any.

"I told you, Lorna Mae's not carrying my child."

"And if she were?"

He took a moment to ponder the question. "I'm not the kind of man who's interested in settling down with a wife and family, but I'd see that the child was cared for, given my name. I'm not in the business of making bastards. Bodines take care of their own. Despite what you choose to think."

Though his self-serving speech merely confirmed her previous belief that Ethan wasn't a man capable of commitment, it still incited anger and resentment within her. "How magnanimous of you, Ranger Bodine."

"There you go with those ten-dollar words again."

"I think it's time for you to leave. I'll pack and be ready to get started for Utah in the morning."

"But—" He noted her resolve and cursed, "Oh, hell!" before stomping out of her room and moving down the hall to his. She heard him reel off several more descriptive epithets before slamming the door behind him.

Wilhemina stared at the wall separating their rooms and knew that more than wood and plaster were keeping them apart. And it would take more than Ethan's sweet kisses and smooth words to bring them together.

It would take commitment.

And that was something she'd never get from the footloose Texas Ranger.

The train trip to Utah Territory was tiring. They had not been able to secure sleeping cars on such short notice and had been forced to remain sitting upright for the two-day journey.

Wilhemina had always despised traveling by train. She considered them smelly, uncomfortable, and dusty contraptions, though she knew it was a necessary evil when time was of the essence.

Having convinced himself that his brother would be found hiding there, Ethan had been chomping at the bit to get to Provo. But Wilhemina held on to her conviction—silently, since Ethan sneered whenever she offered an opposing opinion—that Miss St. Joseph would never run to such a heathenish place. Even for a man she might be in love with. That thought had entered Wilhemina's mind more and more of late. For she couldn't fathom any other reason that a sane woman would go on the run with an outlaw. Unless, of course, she didn't know Rafe was an outlaw.

Treachery and men seemed to go hand in hand.

Clutching a leather-bound book in her lap, Wilhemina frowned at that reality, and at the Mormon's belief in polygamous marriages. Ann Eliza Young, the nineteenth and last wife of Brigham Young—though there were some who believed he'd had as many as twenty-seven—had divorced the now deceased ruler of the church in a scandalous public denunciation of the religion and had written a book: *Wife No. 19, or The Story of a Life in Bondage.*

Having already read a good portion of the narrative, Wilhemina was not looking forward to her arrival into the Mormon stronghold of Provo. The woman's life had sounded like a living hell, and she couldn't countenance any religion that held women in bondage. Slavery had long since ended, but apparently not in Utah.

"Will you put that book down!" Ethan, seated across from her, ordered in a low voice. "We've been getting a lot of strange looks, and if we're to pull off this ruse, we can't have these folks questioning our beliefs. I doubt that a true Mormon wife would read such drivel."

She looked up, unfazed by his objection. "I'll have you know that this is not drivel, but a full and accurate report of life within the Mormon religion. If I'm to pretend to be something I'm not, at least I should learn something about it, don't you think? And I doubt that anyone will question our beliefs since you insisted on dressing us up like crows. I feel like an elderly widow in these weeds you've forced me to don. Or at the very least like Sister Theresa. And that preacher's garb you're wearing hardly suits you at all."

He tugged at the stiff collar encircling his neck and wished he had on his comfortable clothes, knowing that if Rafe or Travis could see him dressed like this, they'd laugh their heads off. "I thought we needed to look conservative. Trust me, I didn't relish spending my hard-earned money on such ugly duds. I feel naked as hell without my gun. But it can't be helped. We don't want to stick out like sore thumbs."

Wilhemina was to remember Ethan's words when they stepped onto the railway platform in Provo to discover that most of the women were dressed in gaily decorated fabrics and didn't look at all as though they'd spent most of their life in a monastery.

"I am so embarrassed," Wilhemina ground out between clenched teeth, clasping Ethan's arm as she smiled at a young couple they'd recently met on the train. "We do stand out like sore thumbs, but not for any of the reasons you've cited."

"*Sssh!* Someone might hear you." He turned and waved at Orrin Falkish and his new bride, who had just returned from visiting her gentile parents in Colorado City and had ridden the train west with them.

The bearded young man greeted them. "Welcome to our city, Brother and Sister Bodine. We are happy you will be joining us."

"That's neighborly of you, Brother Falkish," Ethan parroted. "We're eager to meet as many of the town's inhabitants as we can and settle in." And he was anxious to begin the search for his brother.

"Of course you'll want to attend temple as soon as possible to offer thanks to God for bringing you here. And perhaps you will want to preach to the brethren."

Ethan ignored the soft choking sounds his "wife" made and swallowed with some difficulty. "Preach?"

"As you know, since we have no professional clergy, we are always open to new members bearing witness."

"You must come visit us, Mrs. Bodine," Sarah Falkish said to Wilhemina, who was having a difficult time not laughing aloud at the horrified expression on Ethan's face. "I will introduce you to the ladies in the congregation."

"I'd like that. Thank you." Wilhemina smiled back at the lovely young woman, wondering how this new bride would feel when her husband decided to take another wife. She would hate to think that Sarah's illusions would be shattered by having to share her husband with other women.

Though the church preached that plural marriage was essential to an individual obtaining eternal happiness, not all men subscribed to the belief. She hoped for Sarah's sake that Orrin was one of them.

After bidding the Falkishes good-bye and promising to come to tea the following day, Wilhemina tugged Ethan's coat sleeve, staring at her surroundings with a great deal of uncertainty.

The town was lovely, with its uniform streets and attractively landscaped one-acre building lots. Manicured yards and thriving vegetable gardens seemed to be the norm, and Wilhemina couldn't fault the Mormons for their knowledge of horticulture. There were fruit trees in abundance, and she'd read that they'd managed to devise an irrigation system that would make an engineer proud.

But though Provo had all the outward trappings of normalcy, she knew that beneath the neat rows of radishes and well-tended rosebushes lay cultural and religious beliefs that would never meld with her own. She might as well have traveled to a foreign country—another planet—as strange as all this seemed.

"What now?" she asked Ethan. "I feel like a fish out of water here."

"We observe and mimic. That shouldn't be too hard."

"Well, I guess you'd better get your hands on the Book of Mormon, then, if you're going to be preaching in the temple."

Ignoring the gibe, he reached for a cigar, but she stayed his hand and shook her head in warning. "It said in the book I read that tobacco, alcohol, tea, and coffee are frowned upon. They'll spot you as an impostor if you even think about lighting up a cheroot."

He groaned. "Jesus! I might be able to give up smoking for the time being, but I'm not giving up coffee. Who'd make such a ridiculous rule?"

"It's their belief that it stimulates unnecessarily. In your case, it might be a good idea to quit."

"The only thing that stimulates me, Willy darlin', is you. So if you don't want a demonstration, I suggest you keep quiet."

"Does this mean you won't be taking another wife into our home, *husband* dear?" she asked, her eyes twinkling.

"You're already one wife more than I want or need, so you needn't worry about that."

The statement stung, but she recovered quickly, eager to have the last word with the lawman, whose convictions seemed to be as hard as his head. "Oh, I'm not worried,

Ethan. The man I marry will have little need for more than one wife to keep him happy. Especially in the bedroom." She patted his cheek and felt his jaw tense.

"For a woman who insists on a platonic relationship, you're treading on thin ice, Willy."

She noted the definite bulge in his pants and smiled inwardly. "Oh, dear! It must be this dress. It makes me feel so utterly wicked and depraved." At his look of outrage, she burst out laughing and marched off ahead of him, determined to make the best of their present situation.

Seated in Sarah Falkish's front parlor, holding a cup of tea while balancing a plate of shortbread cookies on her lap, Wilhemina was doing her best to fit in among the ladies of Provo, whom she'd been invited to meet, and found herself constantly biting her tongue at the outrageous comments being put forth.

Many of the women present were sealed in polygamous marriages and talked of their husbands as if it were the most normal thing in the world to share them with other women.

"Herbert visited this morning," stated a straitlaced, fashionably dressed, thin-as-a-rail woman named Mona Lucas. "He cut two cord of firewood before leaving, and promised to return next week for his regular visit."

"Don't you miss your husband when he's gone, Sister Lucas?" Wilhemina couldn't help asking. "I would think having your husband gone so much of the time would be lonely for you."

Many of the women stared at her strangely, but Mona only smirked at the foolish assumption. "It is not my place to ask or yearn for more of my husband's time than is proportionately due me. The true Principle teaches that we must conquer feelings of possessiveness and any desire for romantic love or feelings of an earthly nature.

"I am content to raise my children and do my duty, as a good wife should. Obedience is a woman's highest duty. I am well taken care of and content to remain such."

Murmurs of approval sounded from several of the ladies. Then an older, gray-haired matron asked, "Were things so different in Denver, Sister Bodine? Or do you feel superior because your husband has not yet taken another wife?"

A warm blush covered Wilhemina's cheeks, and she fought to cover her mistake. The last thing she wanted to do was insult these women and make them suspicious of her. "I feel no superiority over any of you. Please forgive me if it sounded that way."

"I'm sure Sister Bodine meant no disrespect," Sarah pointed out quickly, smiling kindly at Wilhemina. "Sister Bodine is new here and is no doubt just trying to make polite and interesting conversation. We had several lively conversations on the train ride here. Isn't that right, Sister?"

Wilhemina started to agree when a buxom blonde, who'd been introduced as Eliza Adamson, stood and came forward. She was lovely, even dressed in her widow's weeds, but there was something in the depths of her green eyes that made Wilhemina uncomfortable.

"A man has a spiritual duty to marry as many wives as he can support. You should be magnanimous and allow your husband to submit to the true teachings of the church. I, for one, would not object to being sealed in marriage to your husband, if only you would consent. My economic status since my husband died is poor, and it would be advantageous to join your household."

At the woman's audacious suggestion, Wilhemina's mouth nearly dropped to her chest, and she had to shut it forcibly. She took a moment to regain her composure. "My husband does not desire another wife, Mrs. Adamson. Ethan and I have discussed it many times, and he assures me that is the case."

Eliza's smile was as sure as a siren's, the look in her eyes predatory, and Wilhemina sensed that this woman was going to be trouble. "That is because he knows you would object, and a man cannot take another wife if his first wife objects."

"I'm very sorry for your present circumstances, Sister, but I do not wish to share my husband with you or anyone else." Actually, the mere thought of it brought forth all kinds of turbulent feelings in Wilhemina, murder being at the top of the list.

Later that afternoon, at the small house on Winthorp Street that Ethan had rented for them, Wilhemina recounted her meeting.

"You cannot imagine how shocked and totally disgusted I was by the women's assertions that I should willingly share my husband with them. I was made to feel like

an insensitive witch when I refused to do any such thing."
She paused, pulling off her gloves.

"I'd read that Brigham Young used to put a chalk
mark on the door of the wife he'd chosen to bestow his fa-
vors upon for the evening, but I had assumed that the author was given to gross exaggeration. I guess she wasn't.

"Imagine those women being willing to share their
husbands! Well, if I were really married, I certainly would
not share my husband with anyone." She crossed her arms
over her chest, as if the matter were settled.

Ethan looked up from the newspaper he was reading
and grinned. "I didn't know you cared, Willy darlin'."

"It's not the least bit funny, Ethan. And if you possessed as much sense as a mule, you'd know that." Tossing
her bonnet on the side table, she flopped into the wing
chair, looking terribly put out by the whole situation.

Leaning forward, Ethan clasped her hand in his. "No
one said this would be easy, Willy. We're bound to find
these folks' beliefs different from our own, but we have to
pretend to understand. It won't take us long to look around
and ask questions about Rafe."

"We've only been here two days, and it already seems
like a lifetime, Ethan. I know the women think I'm odd—
Sarah's the only one who's really taken to me—and I'm
not sure how many more times I can bite my tongue before
it falls off."

"I told you from the beginning that being a bounty
hunter wasn't going to be easy." He cocked an eyebrow.
"Are you willing to admit that I was right and give up your
search for Rafe?"

Sighing, she shook her head. "No. I would never admit that you're right about anything, Ethan. You know that," she said, finally smiling. "But I'd like to conclude our investigation into your brother's whereabouts as quickly as possible, so we can leave this place. It feels ungodly to me."

"You know," he began, "there's something to be said for the practice of polygamy."

Her eyes widened. "You can't be serious?"

"Many believe it eliminates the need for prostitution. In fact, I read that very thing in *Harper's* magazine."

"Only you would consider that a benefit. I don't believe there's a need for prostitution any more than I believe that there's a need for plural marriages. Man is by nature monogamous, and he can damn well learn to curb—"

"Man isn't monogamous by nature, Willy. Look around you. There are very few animals who mate for life. Most have more than one partner."

"Well, if you're so convinced of that, perhaps you'd like to take Eliza Adamson for your wife. She's definitely interested in the position." And Wilhemina doubted the other woman had only monetary reasons for her suggestions. Once a woman laid eyes on Ethan Bodine's rugged, handsome countenance, even briefly, she wasn't likely to forget him.

"Do I detect a hint of jealousy?"

"It's hard to be jealous of something you don't really have, Ethan," she said, rising to her feet. She turned away from him so he couldn't see how utterly miserable she felt, but he followed, grasping her shoulders.

"Let's not fight, Willy darlin'. After all, this is the first night in our new home."

"This is not *our* new home. We're merely living here until the Morgans return from Salt Lake City, thanks to the Falkishes' intervention." Though it was certainly an adorable house, with its red and green chintz-covered sofa and chairs and highly polished pine floors. It even had indoor plumbing, a rarity for houses in the West.

He nuzzled her neck, and gooseflesh erupted everywhere. "I've got a powerful hunger, woman."

"I told you, Ethan, you'll be sleeping on that lovely chintz sofa tonight."

He grinned and turned her to face him, kissing the tip of his nose. "I was speaking of my stomach. Though the other certainly applies as well." He pulled her into him to demonstrate just how much, and she could feel the hard swell of his manhood against her thigh.

"You did say that you were capable of satisfying your husband, Willy. Then I would need no other woman in my bed."

She pushed against his chest to put distance between them. "I did. But you're not my husband, Ethan. Not really. And you're not ever likely to be." She marched off to the kitchen, and Ethan wondered why all of a sudden the truth of her words had the power to sting.

Marriage was a deathtrap for a man. He'd always thought so anyway. But damn if making love to Willy wasn't pure heaven.

And having her so close and not being able to do a damn thing about it was pure hell!

Chapter Thirteen

ETHAN RUBBED THE SMALL OF HIS BACK AND CURSED both the damned uncomfortable sofa he'd been forced to sleep on and Willy's unrelenting stubbornness about keeping him at arm's length.

Having spent a sleepless night, and feeling as if he'd been pistol-whipped soundly, he rubbed his burning eyes and yawned widely before stepping into the mercantile. The sign above the door read "Jacob Stein and Sons".

Much to his surprise, he'd found that there were many gentiles living in Utah among the Mormons, and he thought it ironic that a Jew would now have to consider himself a gentile among the saints—a chosen one among the chosen ones.

"Good day, Brother." The bearded man behind the counter greeted him and introduced himself as Jacob Stein. "Can I interest you in a new shovel or rake? They're made of the finest tempered steel, and we have a special on them this week."

Ethan glanced at the gardening implements and shook his head. "They look like fine tools, but I'm actually looking for information. I was hoping you might be able to help me."

He stared quizzically at Ethan. "I'll do my best."

"I'm looking for my brother and his family. The last letter I received said they were living in Provo." Ethan gave the man a brief description of Rafe and went on to explain that his brother's family consisted of a wife and five children.

Of course in Utah bearded men with large families weren't likely to attract much notice.

"St. Joseph, you say?" The proprietor pulled his wiry chin whiskers and considered the matter. "The name sounds familiar, but . . ." Finally he shook his head. "I'm sorry, but I just can't seem to place it."

Disheartened but not discouraged, he thanked the proprietor and moved away from the counter to the rear of the store to inspect the women's ready-made dresses hanging on the rack, thinking that perhaps he should rectify his earlier error in judgment by buying Willy a new gown.

Women put a great deal of store in frills and furbelows, and she had been a good sport about accompanying him to Utah.

The bell over the door tinkled and a trio of ladies entered. They were dressed fashionably in colorful silk gowns, and Ethan felt another tinge of regret that he had made Wilhemina don such unflattering attire.

Deciding that Willy definitely needed a new gown, he considered the selection carefully, finally choosing a rust-colored taffeta that was sure to bring out the highlights in her glorious sable hair. He started to turn when the sound of his name caught his attention. Stepping back, he peeked around the dress rack to see who was speaking.

"Imagine Sister Bodine's unreasonable views on the subject of marriage," an attractive blonde said to her two companions. "The way she spoke of her husband made one think she thought herself better and luckier than everyone else."

"Perhaps she's truly in love with him, Eliza. Not all Mormon women aspire to polygamous unions. And we should be gracious enough to accept her ways as we expect her to accept ours."

Ethan sucked in his breath at the possibility of Willy loving him, then chided himself, realizing the notion was ridiculous. He and Willy mixed together as well as oil and water—not at all. Except, he reconsidered, in bed.

The blonde sniffed disdainfully at the older woman. "There's something strange about Sister Bodine, if you ask me. She doesn't seem at all convinced of the doctrines of our faith."

Their suspicions made Ethan uneasy; he couldn't afford to have their deception discovered before his search for Rafe concluded. He waited to hear what else they would say on the matter.

"Perhaps she's a new convert," counseled the short, dark-haired friend. "Or a new bride. It takes time to accept the inevitable. I never thought Mr. Butler would take another wife after being married to him for eleven years and bearing six children, but now he has four wives, and I have reconciled myself to it."

The woman's unhappiness showed on her face, indicating to Ethan that she may have reconciled herself to the arrangement but she didn't like it one bit.

"Be that as it may, Bethany, I intend to call upon the Bodines and present my case to Mr. Bodine myself. Once he hears of my financial situation I'm sure he'll be convinced to take me as wife. After all, I have much to recommend me. And Wilhemina Bodine is far from a great beauty."

Ethan's eyes narrowed at the woman's catty remark.

"The husband might be toothless, hunched over, and nearing one hundred," the woman named Bethany pointed out.

Running his tongue over his teeth, Ethan did a quick inventory.

"The way Sister Bodine's eyes softened when she spoke of her husband, I daresay he's an attractive man. Sarah said that he's far from ancient and has the widest pair of shoulders she's ever seen. I doubt he's hunched at all, but rather as erect as a sturdy tree trunk."

She flashed a smile that was far from innocent, and Bethany gasped, then the two women started giggling and whispering to each other. Ethan felt suddenly as if his manhood had been violated.

"Stop that kind of talk, you two," the older woman chided, shaking her head and *tsk*ing loudly several times, before purchasing the two spools of thread they had come for. "I'm going to pretend that I didn't hear you say such a scandalous thing, Sister Adamson."

The younger women exchanged amused glances, then the three ladies linked arms and strolled out the door.

Ethan swallowed, stared at the dress he held, and wondered if the gift was going to be enough to assuage Willy's temper when she found out Eliza Adamson, the husband hunter, was coming to call.

Convinced that his brother was hiding somewhere in Provo and determined to find him, Ethan set out later that day for another tour of the town. Willy, unwilling to allow Ethan to search for Rafe a second time without her, rushed to keep up with him.

"Don't walk so fast. I can hardly keep up."

Ethan smiled spitefully, not slowing his stride. "That's too bad. You should have stayed home like a good wife and let your husband do the investigating, Mrs. Bodine," he said through gritted teeth, smiling in greeting at an elderly couple passing by. "I told you that I would find Rafe on my own."

"We're in this together, if you care to remember. And two heads are always better than one."

He was about to dispute her words when the sight of a bearded man herding a group of children into the back of a hay wagon caught his eye. "Let's go."

"Stop yanking my arm, Ethan! You're pulling it out of its—" She gasped, finally noting the reason for Ethan's impatience. "It's hard to tell, but that woman looks like she might have red hair beneath her bonnet."

Ethan's voice filled with excitement. "It's them. I'm sure of it."

They hurried their pace, their walk turning into a run as they hurried after the family. "Excuse me," Ethan called out, waving, and the man in question stopped what he was doing and turned.

"Yes? Was there something you needed, Brother?"

The man's beard was graying, his eyes a deep brown, and Ethan knew immediately that the stranger was not Rafe. Bitter disappointment lodged in his throat. After a moment he said, "I thought you were someone else."

The man smiled kindly, as did his wife. "It happens all too frequently. The beard and the clothing are similar to many others, are they not?"

Ethan nodded and, after making his apologies, bade the couple good day and escorted Wilhemina across the street. The frustration masking his face made Wilhemina's heart ache.

"I'm so sorry, Ethan. If it's any consolation, I thought it might be them, too."

He shrugged. "No matter. We'll find them yet. It's only a minor setback."

But how many more could they take, she wondered, before admitting defeat and giving up?

"I still can't believe the audacity of the woman!" Wilhemina had received Eliza Adamson's neatly scrawled note this morning, informing her that she intended to call upon her and Ethan at precisely one o'clock that afternoon to discuss, as she put it, "matters of grave importance to both of us."

Seething with indignation that the woman would dare go around her to get her needy hands on Ethan, Willy added, "Well, it doesn't take a genius to figure out why she's coming here, does it? Not after what she said to me the other day at Sarah's and what you overheard at the mercantile."

Ethan had given Willy a brief synopsis of the conversation he'd heard, omitting the most inflammatory of the comments—the ones that were likely to cause another coffeepot incident. He thought it best to change the subject.

"You look mighty pretty in that dress. It fits you like a glove."

Noting how intently he stared at her breasts, she pursed her lips, which puckered up like a tart lemon. "Are you sure you didn't buy this gown a size too small on purpose, Ethan? I wouldn't put such a thing past you." At his crestfallen expression, she grew immediately contrite and clutched his arm. "I'm sorry. I love the dress, you know that. And it was very kind of you to buy it. But that woman has put me in a foul mood. I feel as if we're trapped in a nightmare of our own making."

He patted her hand. "Let's just wait and see what she's up to. Perhaps you're frettin' for nothing."

"*Hmph!* The woman is a piranha. As soon as she sets eyes on you, she's likely to eat you alive."

His eyebrow arched. "Now, Willy, calm down. She might be a little desperate, but I'm sure if she were some femme fatale, as you claim, she'd have been banished from the community long ago. Mormon women are respectable for the most part." Though he knew that some folks characterized the women of polygamous marriages as no better than prostitutes, the ones he'd met seemed wholesome, charitable, and downright pious.

"Ha! Eliza Adamson is a wolf in sheep's clothing. She's exactly like a Venus flytrap. *Dionaea muscipula* entraps its prey and swallows it whole." She demonstrated by cupping her hands and slapping them closed, and he started at the noise. "They never know what hit 'em."

A knock sounded at the door, and Ethan leveled a warning look at her. "Be on your best behavior, Willy. Don't forget—we can't afford to raise suspicion."

"I'll remember that, as long as you remember to behave like a married man." He winked before crossing to the door to answer it, and Wilhemina steeled herself for the husband-stealing woman.

The visit proved every bit as awful as Willy had predicted.

"As I explained to your wife the other day, Brother Bodine"—Eliza sipped her tea, smiling in what Wilhemina could only call a gloating fashion—"I am a widow. My husband's death left me in dire financial straits, and I am in need of a protector."

She leaned forward to pick up a sugar cookie from the china plate, displaying an indecent amount of bosom for a Mormon woman, or any woman, Wilhemina decided. She wished she'd added a bit of hemlock to the dough, especially after noting that Ethan, who was seated across from

Eliza, could hardly keep his eyes off the woman's voluptuous white breasts.

Wilhemina kicked him swiftly but discreetly in his shins to let him know she had noticed.

"Owww!" he cried. Then, recovering: "Oh, well . . . ," he said, and smiled benignly at the woman in case Wilhemina decided to aim her foot a bit higher. "That is tragic, Mrs. Adamson, but as I'm sure my wife has already explained, I do not believe in the practice of polygamy."

Wilhemina's "I told you so" smile did not last long.

"Mrs. Bodine, would you mind fetching me a headache powder?" Eliza rubbed her temples. "I have a terrible pounding in my head."

Probably because her brains were so much smaller than her bosom, Willy decided ungraciously. Loath to leave Ethan alone with the piranha for even a few minutes, but knowing that to do otherwise would have been considered rude, she nodded. "Of course. I won't be a minute."

Swallowing with some difficulty, Ethan wished he could have a smoke, a whiskey, or both. The woman was looking at him in a very seductive manner, as if she intended to devour him whole, just as Willy had predicted. Under other circumstances, in another time, he might have been willing to take her up on what she was offering, but now he was married. Or pretending to be. And much to his surprise, a sense of duty and respect for Willy squelched all temptation.

Eliza Adamson, for all her beauty and allure, just wasn't Willy.

"Mr. Bodine," she said, taking the recently vacated seat next to Ethan and leaning into him, "although you don't believe in polygamous marriages, let me assure you that you won't be disappointed if you decide to take me for wife. I am very good-natured, an excellent cook"—she stared disdainfully at the cookies—"and my appetite is considerable, if you understand my meaning."

She reached for his hand, but Ethan managed to avoid contact by reaching for his teacup. He'd known many women like Eliza Adamson, who used their looks and body to get what they wanted. One, in particular, came to mind, and he frowned. Lorna Mae may have fooled him for a time, but this Mormon hussy wasn't going to.

"I'd better see what's detaining my wife," he said. "She's probably having some difficulty finding the powders."

When he stood, she reached up to touch his thigh. "Don't be too long, Ethan. We have much to discuss."

"Do we?" he responded with a smile that failed to reached his eyes. He left for the kitchen.

"Looks like you were right, Willy. Eliza Adamson is doing her best to seduce me."

Wilhemina turned from the cupboard, saw the gloating, self-satisfied smile on his face, and her brown eyes darkened to black. Unwilling to give him the satisfaction of knowing just how angry she felt, she said, "Well, Ethan, if we were really husband and wife, I guess I'd have reason to care, but we're not, so . . ." She shrugged.

"Don't pretend you don't care, Willy. I know you better than that. And I've had just about all the teasing I can take for one day, woman," he said, pulling her hard against him before grinding his lips down upon hers.

Absorbed in their mutual pleasure, neither saw the swinging door open or the vengeful, determined look on Eliza Adamson's face.

The gunmetal sky was awash with color as the sun dipped slowly beneath the horizon. Ethan stepped onto the porch to smoke a cheroot and to think about the kiss he and Willy had shared not long ago and the fact that Eliza Adamson had been nowhere to be found when they'd finally ended it and come back into the parlor.

"Ah, Willy," he muttered, feeling a longing so strong, so intense, it frightened the hell out of him.

She was cleaning up the dinner dishes, probably trying, as he himself tried, to put their attraction for each other into proper perspective. "Lust" was the word that came to mind when he thought of his feelings for Willy. But somehow the word just wasn't strong enough, meaningful enough.

Ethan threw his cigar to the porch and ground it out beneath his boot heel before someone saw him smoking. It was a damn waste of a good cigar, considering it wasn't half-smoked, but he'd found out in the two days they'd lived on Winthorp Street that his neighbors made it their business to know everything about his.

Angry voices caught his attention, and he looked down the road to see a mob of men approaching. They were carrying torches, looking not the least bit friendly or pious. A blond woman, who looked very much like Eliza Adamson, headed up the processional.

Ethan cursed and rushed into the house, bolting the door behind him; he shouted for Willy. "Grab your things, and let's get the hell outta here. I think the piranha has given us away."

Willy emerged from the kitchen, wiping her hands on her apron. She'd been so totally absorbed in her thoughts over Ethan's kiss that she hadn't heard anything out of the ordinary. "What is it? What's wrong?" The look on Ethan's face filled her with dread.

"Eliza must have overheard our conversation about not being married. There's an angry mob heading our way, and unless you want to be the target of their wrath, I suggest you get a move on."

She thought of the new dress hanging in the wardrobe and winced. "But my clothes . . . I have to pack my things. I can't just rush off and leave them behind." Granted, her wardrobe wasn't much to brag about, but it was all she had.

He shook his head, unable to believe the irrational way a woman's mind worked during a crisis, and grasped her hand. "There's no time for that. We'll buy new clothes if we escape from these outraged Mormons. And that's a big *if.*"

"But where will we go? Where will we hide?"

Not taking the time to answer, Ethan yanked her toward the back door and into the evening's dusk.

"This hay smells."

"*Sssh!* Keep quiet, and keep your head down. We don't want anyone to know we're up here."

The hayloft was moldy and stank of things Willy would rather not think about. She made a face, though Ethan couldn't see it since her head was buried under a mound of the smelly stuff. "But it's sticking to my skin."

"Dammit, Willy! Will you shut up? Maybe you've got a hankerin' to be made an example of, but I don't. And if they discover we're hiding in this poor excuse for a barn, we're done for." He was lucky to have spotted it not a mile from where they'd been living.

"It's been nearly an hour and no one has found us. Besides, it's dark out now. No doubt they've called off their search."

"Maybe. But I'm not taking any chances." He doubted the Mormon hierarchy would be amused by their deception and feared that they might even think he and Willy were government spies. The government in Washington had resisted Utah's pleas for statehood because of the polygamy issue, and feelings were tense between the Mormons and Congress.

"How long do we have to stay buried under here? I'm starting to feel like I'm suffocating. And it's cold."

"Willy!" The exasperation in his voice was evident when he reached out and pulled her to him. "For a bounty hunter you sure do complain a lot."

She nestled against him, seeking warmth and whatever else he might be willing to give. "I always complain when I'm scared, Ethan. It takes my mind off things and gives me something to do."

He frowned into the darkness. "Don't be scared. I'll protect you. I'd never let anything happen to you, Willy." And he knew it was true.

Maybe it was the imminent danger, or maybe the excitement of discovery, but Wilhemina was starting to feel awfully amorous as she snuggled closer to Ethan's hard body and nestled her face in his neck. "I know," she whispered against his hot flesh.

Ethan's heart started pounding like an untried youth's. His member was so hard, he could drill holes clean through the pine planks of the hayloft, and his hands were actually sweating.

Wilhemina reached out to touch his face, caressing the sharp angles, smoothing his soft mustache. "I'm glad you didn't want to take Eliza Adamson for your wife, Ethan. I don't think you would have suited at all."

He turned his head to reply to her amusing comment and found her lips waiting for his kiss. There wasn't a darn thing funny about the desire in her eyes—desire that matched his own.

"If I kiss you again, Willy, I won't be able to stop. You know that, don't you?"

Her decision amazed even as it frightened her, and she swallowed before answering. "I'm not going to ask you to stop this time."

Throwing off the hay covering her, Ethan replaced it with his own body and took her face between his hands. "I've been waiting a long time for this, Willy. Longer than I've ever waited for any woman. And I want you more than I've ever wanted any woman." Then he kissed her slowly, languorously, thoroughly, until Wilhemina grew weak with passion.

He undressed her quickly, then shed his own clothes, not caring or thinking about being discovered, wanting only to be inside Willy, to feel her incredible warmth, to take her to places she'd never gone before.

He feathered kisses down her neck, her chest, then trailed his tongue down and over her breasts, he kissed their soft underside, and drew the taut nipples into his mouth.

"*Hmmm...*" She purred like a contented cat. "You make me feel so womanly, Ethan." She arched her back, and the invitation was too hard to resist.

"You're every bit of that, Willy darlin'," he said, his eyes riveted on the vee of her womanhood. He lowered his head to lap at the tiny bud of her femininity, separating the folds to gain greater access.

Blood pounded hard and hot through Wilhemina's veins, centering between her legs, and she felt as though she might explode at any moment. "Ethan! Please!"

Just then the barn door banged open below and voices could be heard, but Wilhemina's brain was too fogged by passion to hear anything but the sound of her own heartbeat.

"Ethan, hurry!" she urged.

Quickly he smothered her urgent cries with his mouth, praying that the men would make short work of their search.

"I don't see anyone," a deep voice bellowed. "This barn's empty."

"What about the loft? Someone could be up there."

Ethan tensed and felt Willy stiffen beneath him.

The first man laughed. "Not likely. That hayloft is old and rotted. I doubt those boards could support any weight. And there's creatures up there. Rats."

Willy's eyes widened in fear.

A moment later the men departed; Ethan lifted his head, giving Willy the chance to speak.

"Rats, Ethan! Creatures!"

He smiled reassuringly. "The only creature you're going to come in contact with this evening, darlin', is the one between your legs." He covered her mouth once again, and soon all thoughts of rodents and Mormons disappeared from Willy's mind.

After easing his hardened shaft into her, Ethan replicated the motion of his tongue with his pelvis, and she could taste her musky scent upon his lips.

For such a strong, stern man, Ethan's touch was surprisingly gentle in its urgency, and she matched him stroke for stroke. Caressing the tendons of his back, the furred muscles of his chest, she rose up to meet him as waves of passion began to wash over her, lifting her up and over the edge.

They climaxed quickly, unable to sustain the intensity of their passionate union, though they wanted it to go on forever. Breathing hard, hearts pounding in staccato rhythm, their bodies still moist with sweat from their lovemaking, they lay wrapped in each other's arms, waiting to regain control of their senses and emotions.

There was no doubt in either of their minds that they had just shared something special, experienced what few couples could ever lay claim to. And it was humbling.

When she was finally able to speak, Willy's voice was filled with emotion. "You promised to protect me, Ethan. But who's going to protect me from you?"

He had no answer and so remained silent. But the question she posed was to haunt Ethan in the day to come.

Chapter Fourteen

B ACK IN DENVER, THEY STOOD IN FRONT OF THE PO-
lice department, huddling in their winter coats. Ethan's
scowl was menacing and Wilhemina's expression was
worried as she tried her best to comfort him.

It had been a crushing blow to the Texas Ranger's
self-confidence that Rafe hadn't been in Provo and that
they had been run out of town. Now, to make matters
worse, it looked as if they were going to be sent on yet another wild goose chase.

"Maybe the police officer was wrong, Ethan. After all,
it took them an awfully long time to come up with the fact
that your brother and Miss St. Joseph were seen boarding
a train for California. Who knows what else they'll come
up with if we wait around long enough."

He palmed the frustration from his face, wishing like
hell she was right but knowing she wasn't. It was obvious
that Loretta Goodman had purposely steered him in the
wrong direction, and Simon DuMonde had formed hasty, un-
informed opinions in his need to revenge himself on Rafe.

The trip to Utah had been a total waste of time and money. The only saving grace had been making love to Willy. That made up for all of the disappointment he'd encountered of late. But even their lovemaking, as wonderful as it had been, had its drawbacks, for it made him think about things he had no desire to question: like what his life would be like when the search for Rafe was over and Willy was no longer a part of it.

He sighed at the futility of the whole situation and shook his head. "The police aren't wrong, Willy. They've got an eyewitness. Some old lady who happened to be at the railway station the day they departed. I spoke to her myself. The description she gave of Rafe was deadly accurate."

"But why didn't she come forward sooner?"

"She's been out of town visiting relatives and just returned last week."

His frustration evident, he finally spoke aloud what had been on his mind since he'd heard the woman's account. "If Rafe's gone to California, then perhaps he's no longer in danger. Maybe I should just give up on finding him. I can't go gallivanting all over this damn country looking for my brother." And the longer he spent in Willy's company, the harder it would be for him to leave her.

Willy crossed her arms over her chest, and her chin jutted out mutinously. "What kind of a way is that to talk? Have you forgotten why I got involved with this search to begin with? Let me assure you, Ethan, that I am not that fond of bounty hunting. I've had my fill of sleeping on the

cold ground, eating beans and weevily biscuits, and sharing my bedroll with itchy, crawly insects.

"But my aunts need the money I'll get for finding
Rafe. The last letter I received from Aunt Birdy said that
Rufus Bowers had called three times, threatening to evict
them. The only thing preventing him from doing so has
been the intervention of Reverend Green, who pleaded on
my aunts' behalf for more time.

"So you see, I can't afford to give up. And neither can
you."

Knowing the truth of her words, but not liking them,
Ethan clasped her arm and dragged her along the sidewalk
to the hotel. "I haven't forgotten any of that. I'm just sick
and tired of beating my head against the wall, that's all. I
told you when we started that finding Rafe wouldn't be
easy. He's just as experienced as I am in hiding his tracks,
and he's done a damn good job of it so far."

She hurried her pace to keep up with his longer stride.
"Your family is counting on you every bit as much as mine
is counting on me, Bodine, and *I* don't intend to let mine
down."

He smiled inwardly at the way she always called him
"Bodine" when she was angry. The cuddly kitten had
turned into a spitting she-cat.

"You want to go to California, even if it means taking
a train all the way there? You know how much you hate the
damn things. All you did the entire way back from Provo
was complain. 'It's too cold, Ethan. . . . It smells bad,
Ethan. . . . When are we getting there, Ethan?'"

His falsetto impersonation brought a smile, and Wilhemina caressed his cheek. "As I recall, you didn't seem to mind most of the time. And we could get a sleeping compartment in the drawing room sleeper car this time."

He didn't look at all impressed. "Great. We can listen to consumptives coughing all night, babies crying, and old men snoring. It sounds just peachy."

"I doubt we'll be doing much sleeping anyway," she added.

A low growl emanating from his chest, Ethan turned on his heel and began to walk in the opposite direction.

"Ethan, where on earth are you going? I thought we were going back to the hotel to get something to eat."

"We are," he said, shouting over his shoulder. "But first we're going to buy us two train tickets to California."

Brown. That was Wilhemina's first impression of California as she gazed out the window of the luxurious Pullman car, which Ethan had insisted paying extra for.

Due to a recent drought, the Golden State was brown, dreary, and desolate. As desolate as she felt at the moment.

Though she and Ethan had made love countless times since boarding the Pacific Railroad's westbound train in Denver, there had been no avowals of love from the taciturn Texas Ranger. He hadn't uttered even the slightest endearment, other than "darlin'," which she suspected he called any woman under the age of one hundred.

His silence had kept her own lips sealed equally tight, for she had her own fears to conquer. She loved Ethan with all her heart and soul, with an intensity that frightened her, but she was afraid to admit it. Afraid that by telling him her true feelings, he would abandon her, just as Thomas had abandoned her.

She had often wondered if it hadn't been Thomas's fear of commitment and not just her work that had caused him to flee. And she didn't want to scare Ethan off in a similar fashion.

He had been wounded by Lorna Mae Murray's betrayal and was leery of anything smacking of commitment. Though he hadn't come right out and said so, he'd talked around the subject often enough. And she knew that the Murray woman had taken Ethan's fragile heart and stomped all over it, making him bitter and resentful.

Wilhemina had told him only last night about her affair with Thomas and their subsequent breakup. He had offered the appropriate words of condolence, expressed his outrage at the man's stupidity in leaving her, but had made no further declaration, given no assurance that a similar thing wouldn't happen with them.

And he wasn't likely to.

She looked back over her shoulder at the way he slept so peacefully, the blanket tugged up to his chin, a small smile lighting his face, like a child having the most delicious of dreams, and she sighed.

Wilhemina had always been a practical woman. Falling in love with Ethan had been the most impractical thing she had ever done. One of these days he would leave her. She knew that with a certainty and tried to prepare herself for that eventuality.

He was a man who loved his work, his freedom, his horse—which even now rode in one of the baggage cars.

A man who found it difficult to trust. And he was a man who had no place for a woman in his life.

But knowing all these things didn't make it any easier to accept. If only she could put aside her emotions and think about their relationship in purely scientific terms and form an intelligent hypothesis of how best to approach her subject.

If Ethan had been a plant, she would have pulled him apart, layer by layer, dissected him into tiny pieces, and studied him under a powerful microscope, until she learned every nuance of what made him what he was.

But Ethan was a man—and, as such, totally out of her realm of expertise. So she would muddle through somehow, make the best of what time they had left, and learn to accept what she could not change.

Her life would be better for having known and loved him. But once he was gone from it, she would never be happy again.

Through slitted eyes, Ethan stared at the pain etched on Willy's face, and his gut wrenched at the thought that he might be the cause of it.

Though he wasn't privy to the depth of her feelings, he knew that she wasn't the kind of woman to go easily to a man's bed, as she had gone many times to his, and he feared that her attachment to him was growing far deeper than he was ready to accept.

Willy wore her heart on her sleeve. He had only to look into her soft brown eyes to know that she was falling in love with him. Though she hadn't said the words, she'd communicated her feelings through her kiss, her touch, the urgent way she drew him into her body when they made love.

Their need for each other was mutual. Ethan had never experienced such complete satisfaction as he did when making love with Willy. But he had vowed never to love another woman, never to give his heart again. Never to feel the pain of betrayal deep in his soul.

He didn't know exactly what he felt for Willy. He cared about her, felt protective toward her, wanted to be with her constantly. But he didn't love her.

He couldn't love her. Or any woman.

He had his career, his family, his freedom. They had served him well over the years and would again when his time with Willy was through.

So when the conductor called out, "Sacramento City, California," it was with a great deal of relief and a measure of sadness that Ethan accepted that his time with Willy would soon be at an end. If Rafe was found residing here, his search, as well as his conflicted feelings for Willy, would be over.

His heart gave a funny, painful lurch, but he didn't pause to question why.

The Lucas St. Joseph Home for Foundlings and Orphans was an impressive structure. Made out of brick, which was as uncommon in California as green grass, the three-story multiwinged building was an architectural marvel.

Even Ethan, who knew little of such things, was quite impressed and let loose with a shrill whistle. "That St. Joseph woman has money. And lots of it. This place must have cost a fortune to build."

Wilhemina was tired and dusty, and her back ached. The trip by buckboard had been uncomfortably long, and she wasn't as appreciative of her surroundings as Ethan. Unlike the died-in-the-wool Texan, she'd had many opportunities to view large buildings while living in Boston.

"If you recall, Ethan, the station manager said it was actually her brother who had the orphanage built. Miss St. Joseph merely took over in his stead after Lucas St. Joseph's untimely death."

"Well, at least now we know why Rafe hooked up with the woman in the first place." Ethan drew the buckboard to a halt, placing his foot on the break. "Her being stranded out in the wilderness with five little ones explains why he couldn't just abandon them."

"Your brother sounds like a decent man despite everything that's happened." The more details she learned about Rafe's character, the more difficult it became to justify her search. But her aunts were counting on her, and she knew she couldn't abandon her quest.

"Rafe's never been one to take his duties lightly," Ethan said. "And he's never killed a man without good cause. I just hope to hell he's here so we can take him back to Misery and let Travis prove his innocence."

She clutched his arm, her heart heavy with concern, her need to protect strong. "Ethan, you must brace yourself for the possibility that if Rafe does return to Misery, he may hang for Bobby Slaughter's murder. After all, the outlaw is dead, and your brother's been on the run. It may not look good to a jury of his peers that Rafe took matters into his own hands. You yourself said something similar once."

Ethan's blue eyes hardened with fierce determination. "There's no way in hell that I'd ever let my brother hang, Willy. Not even if I have to break the law myself to save him."

His words shot fear through her heart. "You don't know what you're saying, Ethan. You've been sworn to uphold the law. Think of your career as a Ranger, all you believe in. It would destroy you as a person to go against your code of justice and honor."

"I hope to God it never comes to that, for the oath I've taken to uphold the law I do not take lightly. But if it does, my brother's life comes first. And the hell with everything else. For once in his life, my father was right: family comes first." Ethan's duty to the law, and the love he felt for Rafe, were creating great conflicts inside him, ones he had to resolve before they tore him and his family apart.

He jumped down from the buckboard and came around the wagon to help her alight.

"Trust me when I say that I'm not looking forward to arresting my own brother. Now let's get inside and get this over with."

Upon entering, they were met by an elderly woman who guided them into the handsomely decorated office of the orphanage's director, Mr. Luckaday, and asked them to wait.

Ethan paced nervously across the green-and-gold Oriental carpet, walking from one side of the large walnut-paneled room to the other. Wilhemina chose to remain seated in the green leather wing chair in front of the desk and fidget with the folds of her skirt.

"It shouldn't be much longer," she tried to reassure him. As she spoke, the door opened and a short, thin, white-haired man entered. He wore wire-rimmed spectacles and a somber black suit, and he reminded Wilhemina of an undertaker.

"Sorry to keep you waiting." Harlan Luckaday moved to take a seat behind his desk, motioning for Ethan to take the vacant chair next to Willy. "My secretary said you were looking for Miss St. Joseph. May I ask why?"

Ethan explained the reason for his visit, leaving out several significant details. "I have reason to believe that my brother may be traveling with Miss St. Joseph. We've recently had a death in the family, and it's urgent that I find him and bring him back home. Ma's been grievin' and said that the only thing that would make things better was if Rafe would come home."

Surprised at the blatant lie Ethan reeled off with such unexpected ease, Wilhemina shot him a stunned look.

The director merely shook his head at the alleged tragedy. "I'm terribly sorry for your family's loss, Mr. Bodine. Of course you would want to find your brother as soon as possible. But I'm afraid the news isn't good. You see, although Miss St. Joseph . . . I mean, Mrs. Bodine, was here—"

Wilhemina couldn't contain her gasp, even as Ethan jumped to his feet. "Mrs. Bodine? You mean they're married?"

Mr. Luckaday smiled quite happily. "Why, yes. They were married in Denver. And Miss St. Joseph . . . I mean, Mrs. Bodine, seemed as happy as a lark when they arrived here. Of course, the children were quite beside themselves with joy."

Ethan swallowed. "The children?"

"The Bodines have adopted the children as their own. Isn't that just the most wonderful thing you've ever heard?"

"All five?" Wilhemina couldn't keep from asking.

"Mr. Bodine insisted upon it. Said he wouldn't have it any other way. He's quite a man, your brother is, Mr. Bodine. Why, we would never have gotten the orphanage opened in time if he hadn't pitched in to help."

Ethan dropped down in his chair and nodded absently. "I'm glad Rafe could help."

"I wish I could be of more help to you and your dear mother, but I'm afraid your search is not over yet. The entire family left weeks ago for Boston. Mrs. Bodine is executor of her family's vast estate and holdings there, and she had to return to take care of some personal matters."

Wilhemina's face brightened. "Boston! They've gone to Boston? Why, how extraordinary!" She could see by Ethan's dark visage that he wasn't at all pleased by the news. She, on the other hand, was ecstatic, having thought that she'd never again step foot in the exciting cosmopolitan city.

Ethan thanked Mr. Luckaday and propelled Willy out the door. "This news is hardly cause for celebration," he said after the door shut behind them. "I don't have unlimited funds, and a trip to Boston would be very expensive. Not to mention long. And we can't afford another Pullman car." The last impulsive extravagance had about depleted the money he'd brought along.

"You should telegraph your family right away. I'm sure once your father hears the news of Rafe's whereabouts, he'll send you the required funds. And we'll need a little bit extra to buy suitable clothes. We can't possibly go to Boston dressed like this."

Though she hated becoming more indebted to Ethan, her pride would not allow her to return to Boston looking any less grand than when she'd departed. Foolish, yes. But her pride was the only thing intact when she'd left the city, the one thing she still had despite all the hurt and bitter disappointments she'd endured.

"And why not?" His look was indignant as he gave their appearance a quick once-over and found nothing amiss. "What's wrong with the way we're dressed?"

"It's just different in the East, that's all. They tend to be more formal—conservative, really. The men all wear suits, and the women are usually outfitted in elegant, fashionable dresses."

"I can tell already that I'm going to hate it there."

"Does that mean you'll go?"

"Don't see that I have much choice. You'd just go off half-cocked if I don't and get yourself into all kinds of trouble."

She grinned, barely able to contain her excitement. "That's true."

"You're not thinking about seeing that old boyfriend of yours while we're there, are you?" His face darkened at the prospect, and unfamiliar surges of jealousy shot through him. "Because I might have to kill him if you do."

"Why would you do that? You don't even know Thomas."

But Thomas knew Wilhemina, in the biblical sense, and Ethan wasn't about to forget that any time soon.

"You must be so excited, miss, traveling all the way to Boston. Oh, I hear it's a lovely city," the shopkeeper said, handing Wilhemina a selection of dresses in various colors and styles to try on. "I've picked out the nicest ones in your size."

"Yes, I'm very excited," Wilhemina admitted, even knowing that Ethan did not share her enthusiasm one bit. She had urged him to purchase a suit and some shirts, but he'd refused, saying that his arrival in Boston would be soon enough to turn him into a dandified sissy.

She pulled the lovely red-and-green taffeta dress over her head, then smoothed it over her hips, but she couldn't seem to get the front of it fastened over her bosom. Frowning, she called out through the curtained partition. "I'm afraid you've given me the wrong size, Mrs. Daily. This one doesn't seem to fit. I'll try on another." But after trying on all five dresses the dressmaker had brought her, Wilhemina was dismayed to discover that all of them were too small in the bust.

She stared at her reflection and sighed, pulling open the curtain to find Mrs. Daily waiting patiently. "Apparently I've gained weight. I guess I'd better try on a larger size." Suddenly she grew dizzy and reached for the small stool located in the corner of the dressing room.

"Miss, are you all right?" the shopkeeper asked, instructing Wilhemina to bend over at the waist and place her head between her knees. "Take some deep breaths. That's a good girl."

A few moments later the color returned to Willy's cheeks, and the woman said, "I was the same way when I got with child, miss. I didn't want anyone to know, especially Mr. Dailey, and I just kept buying larger sizes until eventually I got up enough courage to tell my husband. We had just opened this shop, had little money, and I—"

Mrs. Daily continued on, but Wilhemina had stopped listening as the realization that she might be pregnant reverberated through her brain, sending a chill into her soul and butterflies into her stomach. Even though she had known the possibility of conceiving a child existed, like most foolish women, she'd never really thought it would happen to her. And there was a whole lot more going on in her mind and body during her lovemaking episodes with Ethan than thoughts of contraceptive devices, not that she had any to use anyway.

Despite great strides for women's equality, and despite her own college education and scientific training, sexual practices and contraception were not matters bandied about in polite society. Women were taught to abstain. Too bad they weren't also taught how it felt to be overwhelmed by their bodies' natural urges.

She sighed, gazed down at her abdomen, and saw that it was still relatively flat. Her breasts were a bit fuller, though. She hadn't been sick at all or felt the least bit uncomfortable. Except during that horrible buckboard ride to the orphanage when her lower back had ached so terribly.

I am pregnant!

The reality that she would bear a child out of wedlock hit her like a ton of bricks, and her excitement about traveling to Boston fizzled faster than champagne gone flat.

She, who had been so determined to avoid falling into the pregnancy trap, now found herself in the same situation as Lorna Mae Murray: unmarried and with child. Only Wilhemina knew with a certainty who the father of her child was. She swallowed.

When the kind woman returned, handing her another batch of dresses, Wilhemina donned them one by one, going through the motions but not really paying much attention to what they looked like, noting only that they seemed to fit better.

"Will those do, Mrs. . . . I'm sorry. You didn't tell me your name."

Wilhemina felt her face flame. "It's Mrs. Bodine," she said, biting her lip, grateful that the woman couldn't see her face to tell she was lying. "I'd appreciate it if you didn't mention any of this to my husband when he arrives to pay for the clothes, Mrs. Daily. He doesn't know about the baby, and I'd like to surprise him myself with the news."

"Of course, dear. I understand perfectly. Just hand me the gowns and I'll wrap them up, so you can be on your way."

A few minutes later the bell over the front door tinkled. Wilhemina suspected that Ethan had finally concluded his business at the barbershop and arrived as previously scheduled to escort her back to the hotel.

She dressed hurriedly, trying to decide how best to handle this awkward and difficult situation. There was no way she was going to tell Ethan of her dilemma. He wasn't the kind of man who'd appreciate being trapped into marriage. Hadn't she already learned that lesson after his dealings with Lorna Mae?

"Good grief," she muttered, buttoning her gown, her fingers shaking so badly that she could barely fit the bone buttons through the holes. She and Ethan had been sharing a hotel room, not to mention intimacies, and that was going to have to stop. She couldn't take the risk of his finding out about her condition. Apparently he hadn't noticed her recent weight gain or the increased size of her breasts. Or, if he had, he had merely chalked it up to her fondness for desserts. She'd been ravenously hungry of late, eating everything in sight. Now she knew why.

But if they continued sleeping together, he was sure to find out she was pregnant.

Entering the front of the store a few moments later, she breathed deeply, pasted on a serene smile, and went forward to greet the unsuspecting father-to-be, though she was trembling within. Ethan chatted with Mrs. Dailey, seemingly just as at ease in a ladies' dress shop as in a saloon. However, his manly presence seemed incongruous amid the delicate laces and fancy ribbons.

"Hello, Ethan. I hope I haven't kept you waiting long."

He smiled in greeting, even as the woman said, "Oh, there you are, Mrs.—"

"I don't know how I can ever thank you for all your help, Mrs. Dailey," she interrupted, hoping Ethan hadn't noticed the way she'd been addressed. "I just love the gowns you picked out for me." Her ploy to distract the woman worked, and Mrs. Daily beamed with pleasure at the compliment.

"Why, thank you. I hope you and Mr. Bodine will have a lovely time in Boston. Though I'm sure the weather will be dreadful this time of year. Not like our mild California winters at all, I'm afraid."

Ethan considered the comment a moment, then said, "You're quite right, ma'am. You'd better find us a warm coat for Willy. I don't want her catching her death while we're traveling."

"But, Ethan—" Wilhemina felt guilty enough about all the money he'd spent. Despite her suggestion to have his father wire money, Ethan had decided to withdraw the last of his savings from his bank in Texas and fund the trip himself. Old habits were hard to break, he had told her. And he didn't intend to be indebted to his father for any reason.

"You can hardly wear that jacket you arrived in, Willy. If you recall, you said we needed new duds for the trip."

"He's right, dear. And I have just the thing." The proprietress returned a few minutes later carrying a large brown box. "I ordered this for someone else, but she died before she could claim it. It was a terribly tragic accident. But it's a perfectly lovely coat and will look stunning on you."

She unwrapped it to reveal an ankle-length red wool coat lined with rabbit fur, and Wilhemina gasped at the sheer beauty of it. But then she shook her head. "I'm afraid it's much too expensive. Do you have anything else?"

"Wrap it up. We'll take it."

Wilhemina stared at Ethan as if he'd lost his mind, then excused herself to Mrs. Dailey and pulled him out of earshot. "Have you forgotten that our funds are limited? We can't afford such an extravagance. And I would never be able to repay you."

"You already have. So let's just leave it at that."

She thought about his words, his kindness, later that day when they arrived back at the hotel. Knowing that necessity now dictated what she must do, she entered their room with a heavy heart. Ethan would despise her for what she was about to say, and that hurt most of all.

"I'm grateful for the lovely wardrobe, Ethan. I know you can ill afford it."

"I'll never understand the way a woman's mind works. First you complain that our clothes aren't good enough to travel to Boston, then when we buy new clothes you complain that I'm spending too much money. You can't have it both ways, Willy darlin'." He reached for her, but she pulled back and tried not to think about the confused look on his face.

"I've been doing a lot of thinking, Ethan, and I've come to a rather difficult decision."

He flopped down on the bed and leaned back against the headboard, his hands resting behind his head, his feet crossed comfortably at the ankles. "What's that? Have you changed your mind about going to Boston?"

She shook her head. "No. Just about the way we should travel there."

His forehead wrinkled. "You don't want to travel by train? Well, it's a hell of a long ride on horseback, and I don't think you're up to it."

She wrung her hands nervously and began pacing back and forth in an agitated manner. "I don't think we should continue sleeping together, Ethan. I think it might be better to resume our former platonic relationship."

His eyes widened at first, then narrowed dangerously as he rose to his feet and stepped toward her. "And when did you come to this conclusion? After you discovered that Rafe was in Boston and we'd be traveling to the city where your former lover resides?"

She gasped, rocking back on her heels as if slapped, never thinking in a million years that he would form such an outrageous conclusion. "No! That's not true. It's just—"

Just what?

That I'm pregnant.

She could hardly confess to that.

That I don't love him?

She would never lie to him.

What choice do I have but to let him think the worst?

She remained silent, and he took that silence for confirmation.

"Far be it from me to come between you and the dashing Thomas Fullerton, Willy. Even if the man did dump you on your pretty behind."

His words immediately angered her. "Isn't that what you plan to do, Ethan? Dump me when you've had your fill? Isn't that what all men do when they tire of a woman? When they don't want the responsibility of a relationship?"

"I've been up front with you from the beginning. I've never made you any promises."

"Nor I you," she reminded him. "So don't go acting the outraged suitor. We've both enjoyed our relationship. But now it's time to end it. You have your brother's arrest to contend with and—"

"You have Thomas Fullerton to take to your bed," he finished.

"I'm sorry you think me so shallow, Ethan. But you told me once that we all have to do what we have to do."

He grabbed his hat and walked to the door. "You're far more calculating than I'd originally given you credit for. I thought you were different from most women, but I can see you're not."

His words cut to her heart like a blade, and she blinked back the tears in her eyes. "Believe what you will, Ethan. But know that what I'm doing is for the good of both of us."

"Why do I find that hard to believe?" He slammed the door behind him, exiting on a curse.

Wilhemina collapsed on the bed, giving in to her tears of despair and feeling as if her life had just ended. But she knew that a far more precious life now grew deep inside her. One she would have to protect at all costs.

Chapter Fifteen

Boston, Massachusetts, Late February 1880

THE CITY OF BOSTON WAS HIT BY ONE OF THE WORST snowstorms in decades just after Wilhemina and Ethan arrived. A nor'easter had blown in, dumping several feet of snow on the roadways and bringing the bustling seaport city to a halt.

The frigidity of the temperature seemed to replicate Ethan's mood toward Wilhemina. His animosity hadn't lessened; if anything, it had grown worse.

Frustrated that the weather was causing yet another delay in locating his brother, and doubly frustrated that he couldn't make love to the woman who occupied his every waking moment, Ethan was running on a short fuse, with a temper that threatened to explode at any moment.

Trapped inside his hotel room, which adjoined the contrary, fickle horticulturist's and fronted the picturesque Boston Common area, Ethan paced the confines like a caged animal. Puffing agitatedly on his cigar, he tried to work out why his life was in such an uproar and what the hell he was going to do about it.

To make matters worse, Wilhemina continued on as if nothing were wrong. She still smiled frequently, told an occasional joke, related stories from her childhood, and looked more beautiful than ever. And she behaved as if they'd been nothing more than good friends from the beginning. That they had ever shared a bed and the intimacy of a sexual affair was never addressed. They had reverted back to a relationship that was platonic, friendly—at least on her part—and businesslike.

And Ethan hated it.

He hated not being able to hold Willy in his arms, not being able to kiss her and make love to her into the wee hours of the morning. He hated waking up at dawn and finding her side of the bed cold. He hated hearing her bustling about in the next room, drawing her bath, picturing her naked glistening body and not being able to touch it.

Though he was loath to admit it, and doubted he ever would, Ethan Bodine had finally met the woman of his dreams. The woman he wanted to spend the rest of his life with. The woman he loved.

And there wasn't a damn thing he could do about it.

For the woman he loved was still in love with another man.

To think he had actually thought—no, feared—that Wilhemina had fallen in love with him when all the time her thoughts had been centered on Thomas Fullerton.

Her passionate, ardent response during their love-making had fooled him into thinking that their joining had been special—magical. But he guessed that Willy was just an affectionate and responsive woman.

Damn her for loving another man! And an Easterner to boot!

Ethan had spent a great deal of time wondering about Thomas Fullerton, the esteemed Boston horticulturist and Willy's ex-fiancé. He wondered what he looked like, what kind of man he must be to lose interest in a vibrant, beautiful, intelligent woman like Wilhemina. And he wondered what special quality Fullerton had that would draw Wilhemina back to him.

Ethan had no answers to any of these questions. But he knew one thing for certain: he hated Thomas Fullerton with a passion. And if he ever met the man, he intended to tear him apart limb from limb. Fitting, he thought, considering the man was a horticulturist.

Ethan had never been a gracious loser. He especially didn't like losing Willy to some dandified eastern dude.

A soft knock sounded on the adjoining door, interrupting his murderous thoughts, and he shouted for Willy to enter.

"Jesus!" he said, noting her chalky complexion when she stepped through the doorway, clearly alarmed. "You look whiter than the snow falling outside the window."

Not about to reveal that she'd just had another bout of nausea and had thrown up her entire breakfast, she smiled wanly. "I'm a bit under the weather. I think I may have eaten something that didn't agree with me."

Worry knitted his brows. "You want me to call a doctor?"

She shook her head vehemently. If there was one thing she didn't want, it was a doctor confirming her pregnancy. A doctor who would no doubt relate her condition to a persistent Ethan. "No! I'll be fine in a few days. We won't be doing anything strenuous anyway, so I'll just stay indoors and rest."

Her comment brought a frown, and he turned toward the window. "You've got that right. This weather has made searching for Rafe impossible. Roads are buried under several feet of snow, and most of the businesses are closed. We'll just have to cool our heels for a few more days and hope it lets up." And hope Rafe didn't get wind of their arrival and flee.

Wilhemina could see the strain on his face and wanted to move forward and comfort him, but she knew that her efforts would only be rebuffed or misconstrued as something other than worry and friendship.

"How shall we occupy our time while we wait?"

It was an innocent enough question, but the look Ethan conveyed sent tingles up her spine and down to her toes. "I brought a few books with me," she said when she could breathe again.

"I'm not much for reading. It reminds me of being in school. I wasn't partial to school."

"How about cards? We could play poker or rummy."

His right brow arched. "You're not planning to cheat again, are you?"

She smiled. "Just because I won the last time we played is no reason to accuse me of cheating. I beat you fair and square. And I'll be happy to do so again." She sat at the small mahogany table in front of the fireplace and pulled a deck of cards from her pocket, holding them out to him. "Would you care to assure yourself that the deck's not marked?" He grumbled something, taking the seat across from her.

The fire crackled and hissed, the snow fell silently outside the window, and Willy and Ethan settled in for an afternoon's amusement.

Wilhemina shuffled the cards and dealt, feeling mildly encouraged by Ethan's somewhat friendlier attitude. At least he was talking in complete sentences, something he hadn't done on the trip here.

The two weeks spent on the train had been the longest of her life. Not only because of the irksome delays they'd experienced from the weather, cows on the track, collapsed bridges, and the like, but because Ethan's manner had been mean and moody.

She guessed she couldn't blame him. He was a prideful man. And she had wounded that pride. But there had been times when she'd wanted to take the Colt .45 out of his holster and shoot him with it. Like when he'd struck up a conversation with a bleached blonde from Albuquerque and had spent the entire day with her. Or when he had gotten drunk and had urinated from the back of the train, nearly falling onto the track in the process.

Smiling inwardly at the memory, she studied him beneath lowered lashes and knew that she missed Ethan in more ways than she would have ever imagined. Their lack of lovemaking was a great loss, but it was their friendship, their easy banter, even their squabbling, that she missed most of all.

After drawing a card from the deck, she rearranged her hand and laid down her cards. "Gin."

He looked at them in disbelief, then at her. "I know you're cheating. I just haven't figured out how." He made to light his cigar, but she held up her hand.

"Please don't. The smell of the smoke doesn't sit well with my stomach." Not much did these days. Even the scent of Ethan's aftershave had the power to send her stomach rolling.

A measured look followed, then Ethan admitted, "I've been meaning to quit anyway," and laid aside his cigar. Wilhemina wanted to kiss him for the grand gesture. She knew how much he loved his smokes.

As she settled back in her chair, the warmth of the fire soon filled her with lethargy, and she felt her eyelids grow heavy. Vowing to rest for only a moment, she was soon fast asleep.

Ethan started to speak when he noted Willy had dozed off. She looked frail and wan sitting in the great wing chair, and a surge of protectiveness washed over him. He grabbed the quilt off the bed and covered her with it, then bent down to graze her lips with a soft kiss.

She smiled in response but didn't awaken, and Ethan knew in that moment that he intended to fight for the love of this woman.

*   *   *

On the third day after their arrival in Boston, as they sat in the hotel dining room having breakfast, Wilhemina suggested an outing. She was feeling much improved, but claustrophobic, and thought that some fresh air would do much to improve her health and Ethan's tension. She knew the time they'd lost because of her illness and the weather had made Ethan even more eager to resume their search for Rafe, but she needed this time to sort out a few things of her own.

"The Horticultural Society is not far from the hotel, Ethan. Let's walk down and spend some time there. It'll be much better than playing cards or pacing the hotel room, which is all we've done since our arrival."

Setting down his fork, he leveled her with a disbelieving look across the table. "In case it's escaped your notice, it's snowing meaner than a naggin' woman's disposition." He nodded toward the window at the heavy precipitation, which hadn't seen fit to abate. "And you haven't been well. I don't want you going out in this weather." He shook his head. "No. We'll stay put."

Eyes flashing, she threw down her napkin, clearly ready to do battle. "Well, I'm going to the Horticultural Society. I'm sick and tired of staying indoors just because it's snowing. I happen to like the snow. And I may have a chance to meet up with some of my former colleagues."

Like Thomas Fullerton? Ethan wanted to ask, wondering at her motive for risking the elements.

At the next table, a young couple purportedly on their honeymoon, if the "Do Not Disturb" sign on their door could be believed, had finally emerged from their hotel suite. They were now staring aghast at Wilhemina, who had dared to defy her male companion with such vehemence and insolence.

Ethan wished Willy were half as compliant as the new bride, for he was not at all pleased by her stubbornness in this matter or by his sudden decision to accommodate the headstrong woman.

"All right," he heard himself saying. "But if you have a relapse, you only have yourself to blame."

"Don't worry. The Murrays didn't do me in. And neither did near drowning or the Mormons. I sincerely doubt that a little snow is going to, either. You won't get rid of me that easily, Ethan. We're in this together to the very end."

But how long would that be?

The Massachusetts Horticultural Society was located on Tremont Street, not far from the Boston Common area. The spacious granite building had been constructed on its present site in 1865 in the French Renaissance manner, and the sight of it never failed to thrill Wilhemina.

"Look, Ethan! Isn't it wonderful?" She'd always taken such pride in the impressive structure, marveling that she'd actually been a part of the important work conducted within its walls.

Ethan, whose feet had numbed many minutes ago and who thought that his blood must surely have coagulated in his veins like ice water by now, didn't share her sentiments. "Is it heated? That's all I care about. I'm freezing my butt off out here."

Sucking in the brisk morning air, she brushed the snow from her new coat. "For a hardy Texan you surprise me, Ranger. I wouldn't think a little snowstorm would get to you. Not after all we've endured these past months.

"And look at all of this history surrounding you." She motioned at the structures with a wave of her hand. "Our country was formed amid these very buildings.

"Benjamin Franklin served his printing apprenticeship in this city, Paul Revere fashioned elegant silver pieces not far from where we're standing, and the Boston Common, which we just crossed, is one of the most historic places in the United States."

Clearly unimpressed, he snorted disdainfully, saying, "It'll never hold a candle to the Alamo, Willy darlin'," and Wilhemina knew that the history lesson was over for the time being.

Officious-looking men in white laboratory coats and tailored suits buzzed about the building like worker bees in pursuit of the queen bee's business. Ethan had never given much thought to flowers, trees, and grasses, but judging by the serious looks on these men's faces, that was all they thought about, talked about, cared about.

Wilhemina dragged him from hall to hall, room to room, showing him the various experiments being conducted, explaining the importance of each procedure, and taking great care to explain things to him in terms even he would understand.

He supposed she was trying to be nice, but she was succeeding only in making him feel like a dunce and a fool. He'd never professed to being a learned man, and he felt totally out of his element here.

She smiled, waving in greeting at folks she obviously knew, stopping to chat briefly with a former co-worker, a cleaning lady, then said, "Upstairs is where I used to work. Would you like to see my former office?"

It was clear by the animation on her face that she was dying to show it to him—or dying to run into her former colleague Thomas Fullerton, he wasn't sure which—so he nodded, pretending an interest he didn't feel.

"Sure. Why not? It's not as exciting as a trip to a bordello. But hey . . . I've got the time."

She flashed him an annoyed look. "I doubt you learned anything in a bordello."

He grinned. "You'd be surprised, Willy darlin', what I learned in my youth. How do you think I got to be such a good lover?"

Wondering how the innocent conversation had gotten so totally out of hand, how mere words could conjure up images best forgotten, she smiled spitefully. "What makes you think you are?" Not waiting for his reply, she opened the door to her former office to find Thomas Fullerton seated behind her desk, looking not a day older than when she'd last seen him over a year ago.

Ethan was still recovering from her comment when he heard Wilhemina's sharp intake of breath and saw the welcoming smile of the stranger seated behind the oak desk. A feeling of unease swept over him.

"Wilhemina!" The man jumped up and rushed forward, the joy on his face evident as he pulled Wilhemina into his arms and kissed her soundly on the lips. "My God! I never thought to see you again." He stared as if he couldn't believe his eyes, and joy clearly suffused his features.

Ethan definitely couldn't believe his and took two menacing steps forward, but Wilhemina, anticipating his reaction, stepped quickly in front of him.

"Hello, Thomas. It's nice to see you again," she said, confused by the enthusiastic reception. Thomas had been anything but enthused, more like relieved, the last time she'd seen him, but he was acting as though he'd actually missed her.

"Wilhemina, we have so much to talk about, so much—"

She held up her hand to halt whatever it was he was about to say, wanting no remorseful declarations in front of Ethan. "Thomas, this is my friend, Ethan Bodine. Ethan's with the Texas Rangers."

At the sight of the menacing-looking gun strapped to the man's hip, the snow-covered cowboy boots, the battered felt hat, and the totally inappropriate casual attire, Thomas's eyes widened. "How do you do?" He held out his hand, but it was obvious there was no warmth in the greeting, only disdain—the same disdain Ethan felt.

The closest thing to a cow this pilgrim had ever seen was a T-bone steak, Ethan decided, sizing up the short man in a heartbeat: sissy, pretty boy, breaker of women's hearts. He decided in that instant he would have to keep his original vow to tear Thomas Fullerton limb from limb.

And he immediately did just that, letting loose with a punch to the man's jaw and knocking him back onto his desk.

Wilhemina screamed in outrage, unable to believe her eyes at what had just transpired. "Ethan! Are you crazy? What are you doing?" Before she could stop him, Ethan picked up Thomas by his shirtfront and hit him again, this time smashing his nose. She heard the crunch of breaking bone even before she saw the blood squirting out of his nostrils.

Yanking on the crazed Ranger's arm, she pulled him back. "Stop this madness! Stop this at once!" Her voice was shrill, nearly hysterical.

"Isn't this the man you told me about, Willy? The one who broke your heart?" Ethan reminded her, believing that a broken nose wasn't nearly enough compensation for Wilhemina's heartache.

She didn't answer. Instead she rushed forward to attend to the sniveling whelp's injuries. "Thomas, are you all right?" She pulled the handkerchief from his pocket and held it to his nose, trying to stanch the flow of blood. "You've broken his nose!" she shouted at Ethan. "How could you?" There was a wealth of reproach in those words.

"I did it for you, Willy. I'd think you'd be thanking me instead of condemning me for it."

Her mouth dropped open, then her eyes narrowed into slits. "For *me?* You know damn well that you did it for yourself, Ethan Bodine, and don't try to tell me any differently."

He had the grace to blush. She knew him too well. "Okay. So I did it for both of us. And it felt damn good."

"Wilhemina . . ." The feeble voice drew her immediate attention.

"Yes, Thomas. I'm here. Are you all right?" She patted his cheek, and Ethan cursed under his breath.

"Who *ith* that barbaric man? And why *ith* he hitting me? I don't recall ether meeting him before!" His broken nose had swollen, making speech difficult.

She remembered the first time she'd ever laid eyes on Ethan and said by way of explanation, "He's from Texas. That's how men greet each other in Texas."

The handkerchief she held over his nose saturated quickly with blood. "I think he broke my *nothe.*"

"I'd like to break every damn bone in your body, you bastard!"

"Ethan!" She flashed him a condemning look. "Please help me get Thomas into the chair."

Thomas took one look at the Texan's menacing visage and shook his head. "No! I can manage."

"Are you sure?" she asked.

"*Yeth, yeth,*" he replied, and Ethan wanted to smile. The only thing that kept him from it was the angry look on Willy's face. It was a look that promised retribution.

Watching her fawn over her former lover made Ethan physically sick to the point where he couldn't stomach it any longer. "I'll wait for you downstairs, Willy. Don't be long."

Relieved, she nodded. "Yes. I think that would be best."

When the door closed she filled a glass with water and handed it to Thomas. "Here, drink this. It might make you feel better." It wasn't going to make him look better, that was for certain. Already his right eye was turning a sickly bluish purplish color.

"I'm not thure I approve of the company you keep, Wilhemina," Thomas said, setting down the now empty glass. "He'th a bit rough around the edgeth."

"Ethan's a good man. He's just been a bit touchy of late due to some family problems." She thought it best not to elaborate. They couldn't afford for Rafe or Emmaline St. Joseph to discover their presence in Boston, and Thomas was well acquainted with a great many people. And not above a little gossip if it suited his purposes.

"How did you come to be with him? And what are you doing back in Bothton? Dare I hope you came becoth of me? I've mithed you."

She perched herself on the edge of the desk, trying frantically to think up a plausible excuse for returning. "Ethan is a friend of my aunts'. I'm helping him with some personal business. Since I knew my way around Boston, they suggested that I help him."

"Oh."

He seemed crestfallen by her explanation, but she chose to ignore his reaction. "How is your work going? Judging by the piles of papers strewn all over the floor, you seem to be keeping busy as ever."

"Yeth. Dr. Merriam and I are working on a project together. And I'm preparing to addreth the Horticultural Thothiety at the end of the month. I've been invited to give the keynote addreth thith year."

She smiled, genuinely happy for him despite everything that had happened between them. Thomas was very dedicated to his work, and he loved the recognition of his peers. He enjoyed the spotlight and didn't like sharing center stage with anyone.

"Congratulations! That's wonderful, Thomas."

"It could be, if only thingth had turned out differently between us, Wilhemina. You can't imagine how much I regret what happened."

Uncomfortable with where the conversation was headed, and unwilling to dredge up old wounds, Wilhemina stood. "I'd best go before Ethan takes it in his head to come back."

That prospect alarmed Thomas, and his eyes widened. "Yeth, perhapth you thould. But would it be all right if I called upon you at your hotel tomorrow evening? I'd love to hath dinner, catch up on all you'th been doing."

"That would be lovely," she said, and told him where she was staying, then added, "You might want to consult a physician about your nose. And you should put some ice on it to reduce the swelling."

"I hope it won't affect my ability to thmell the thpethimenth. You know how important that ith."

It was really a shame, she thought, that Thomas didn't know what "stopping to smell the roses" was truly all about. He was a man who would benefit greatly from tearing his injured nose away from the grindstone and enjoying the simpler pleasures life had to offer.

She had discovered, much to her surprise, that she had taken much for granted over the years. Her brush with death, her time spent with Ethan, had taught her that life was too short to waste, too precious to be ignored.

She had lived more in the past few months than she'd lived her entire life before meeting Ethan Bodine.

And she had loved more in that short time than she would ever love again.

In her hotel room, Wilhemina sat at the dressing table and pondered the offer she had received tonight. The offer that would solve all of her problems, save one.

Thomas had proposed marriage. Again. He had declared over two glasses of port and a large piece of sponge cake his undying love and unconscionable stupidity in letting her go in the first place.

Due to her present circumstances, it was a tempting proposition, and she had thought as much at the time he'd made it.

"Wilhemina, you must forgive my lapse in judgment that allowed us to part. I realized after seeing you again yesterday that I'm still very much in love with you. I want to marry you and put things right between us."

Totally taken aback by his heartfelt pledge, she froze, and her fork clattered noisily to her plate, drawing the attention of the elderly couple at the next table. "I don't know what to say, Thomas. This is so terribly sudden, especially after all that has happened between us. We've been apart a long time; we're very different people now."

He reached for her hand and patted it reassuringly in a gesture that was familiar and comfortable, but not the least bit arousing. "But we still have so much in common—our work, our past together. Surely we could begin again. I know I was selfish in wanting you to give up your work. I realized afterward how much it meant to you, and that I should never have asked it of you."

She sat stunned and even now, hours later, was still confused by his seemingly total reversal in character and opinion. A year ago she would have been ecstatic to have had him admit his mistakes and declare his undying love and devotion. A year ago she would have been starry-eyed and grateful to be singled out by such an esteemed colleague.

But now . . .

Now there was Ethan to consider. The one problem that Thomas's declaration could not solve.

Ethan, who'd shown definite signs of jealousy and possessiveness yesterday during his barbaric attack on Thomas, but who had still made no declarations of his own.

Ethan, who was the father of the child she carried within her.

Ethan, who would never marry her and give their child his name.

But Thomas would. He would marry her, and her child would not be branded a bastard. She could fall back into her old life in Boston, pick up the threads of a shattered relationship, and begin anew.

She would be living a lie, for she didn't love Thomas and knew now that she never would. But she had a child to consider and would do what she must, make any sacrifice, to protect and insure that child's future.

And therein lay the problem.

* * *

Next door Ethan was having problems of his own. The half bottle of whiskey he'd drunk hadn't made him feel any better. In fact, his head was pounding like a kettledrum and his mouth felt like somebody had stuffed it with a wad of cotton.

Wilhemina had told him this morning of her planned dinner engagement with Fullerton and had asked him to act civilly toward the man she now called friend, if he should happen upon him.

He hadn't, choosing instead to spy from a discreet distance. Through the adjoining door, Ethan had watched the two together, had seen the smitten look on the dandy's face as he devoured Wilhemina's beauty, had observed the smiles exchanged, and knew Fullerton intended to make an all-out effort to win back Wilhemina's love.

"Damn the man!" he cursed, throwing his naked body into the wing chair and staring into the flickering flames of the dying fire. It was nearing midnight and the mantel clock ticked off the minutes with sickening regularity.

There had to be something he could do. He'd made a mess of it yesterday. Beating Fullerton to a pulp had been a mistake. He could see that now. His actions had only made Wilhemina feel sympathetic toward the spineless dandy, instead of making her see how weak and useless he was. And though she hadn't dragged him over the coals for it, Ethan knew she was disappointed and shocked by his behavior.

He could see her disappointment every time he closed his eyes, hear it in her voice every time she spoke in that controlled, precise manner, and it hurt. It hurt so damn bad that he knew he'd have to apologize or go crazy thinking about it. About her.

He yanked on his pants and approached the adjoining door; knocking softly, he opened it, not waiting for an answer.

"Willy . . ."

Wilhemina spun at the sound of her name, and her eyes widened at Ethan's disheveled appearance. He was barefoot and bare chested, and hadn't bothered to button the fly of his pants. She could see the dark line of hair curling there, soft and tempting. She swallowed.

"Ethan, is something the matter? It's rather late." She pulled the edges of her robe together, as if it could protect her from the ardent look on his face and the hot flashes of wanting running through and over her.

"Willy, I—"

They stared at one another, the tension between them palpable, their need and desire so thick, Willy felt it like a fog in the air.

Ethan stepped toward her, his hand outstretched. "You look very pretty tonight." Dressed in the white virginal nightgown and robe, she looked tempting as hell. Realizing that he was about to touch her, he lowered his arm. "I waited up for you."

"You shouldn't have."

"There's something I need to tell you."

Her heart went into double time, and she held her breath, praying that Ethan would finally declare himself and say the words she longed to hear. Her voice was barely a whisper when she spoke. "What is it?"

He guided her to the bed and pulled her down next to him on the edge of the mattress. Her nervousness mirrored his own. "I—" He swallowed, wondering why an apology should be so difficult, wondering why he just didn't kiss her senseless and communicate his feelings in that elemental way. But he knew that demands and brute force wouldn't work this time. Wilhemina would have to be wooed, gently and considerately.

"Yes?" she prompted in a voice as soft as velvet.

"I'm sorry."

She appeared startled by the declaration. "Sorry?"

"For the way I behaved yesterday with your friend Fullerton. I shouldn't have lost my temper. I wanted to say I'm sorry."

An apology. He had come to offer an apology. And though she knew she should be grateful, for Ethan was not the kind of man to offer one easily, she was crushed. The words of love she hoped to hear remained only that—a hope, and a false one at that.

She knew now that Ethan would never say the words she desired. For the truth of the matter was he just didn't love her.

Knowing that made her decision that much easier.

Chapter Sixteen

"*I* THINK I'VE FOUND RAFE!"

Ethan burst into Wilhemina's room the following day, holding a slip of paper and waving it at her, his voice boiling with excitement. "I've been making the rounds of the local businesses, and they are all quite familiar with the St. Joseph name.

"Apparently Emmaline St. Joseph . . . Bodine"—he paused, obviously still ill at ease with the idea of a woman he'd never met being married to his brother—"is quite generous with her money, doing all sorts of charity work and that sort of thing. The St. Joseph name is very well respected in the community. At any rate, I've got the address."

Not feeling a smidgen of the enthusiasm Ethan did, Wilhemina smiled nevertheless. She was still smarting over her disappointment from last evening and didn't feel in a victorious mood. But she knew how important finding Rafe was to Ethan, and she didn't want to dampen his pleasure in finally locating his brother. And she was still hoping to claim that reward money and bring Rafe back home.

Besides, she had already resigned herself to the inevitable where Ethan was concerned.

"What can't be cured must be endured," her aunts had always counseled.

Outside, the sun shone brightly, so she guessed it was a good omen of sorts. At least it would help melt some of the snow that had accumulated waist high over the past few days.

Realizing that Ethan was waiting for her to comment, she said, "That's wonderful! Is it far?"

He shook his head at the irony of what he'd discovered. "We've practically been living right on top of them. They're in a section of the city known as Beacon Hill, which isn't far from here. From what I understand, it's quite *the* place to live if you've got the wherewithal. And they do."

She laughed at his speech affectation and squeezed his arm. "I'm happy for you, even though I know this is going to be hard once you meet Rafe. What will you say to your brother when you finally meet him face-to-face?"

Ethan had thought long and hard about that eventuality. Rafe would not be at all happy to see him. And Ethan didn't relish busting up a family that contained five small children, especially his own brother's. And though he'd thought about just walking away and leaving Rafe be, he knew he couldn't do that. Justice had to be served. Rafe had to be arrested, and Ethan would be the one to do it.

"There's really only one thing I can say, Willy, when the time comes."

She cringed inwardly at the sorrow reflected in his eyes, hating to ask the question. "What's that?"

He heaved a sigh. "You're under arrest."

The affluent area known as Beacon Hill was bounded by Statehouse and Charles, Beacon, and Pickney Streets. Many of the Federal–Greek Revival houses had been designed by the golden-dome Statehouse architect, Charles Bullfinch, and were a sight to behold.

As the carriage lumbered down the historic cobbled streets still mired in snow, Ethan couldn't help but be impressed as he viewed the collection of attractive, substantial homes.

The entire area bespoke money and refinement, and the St. Joseph wealth was reconfirmed when the carriage halted in front of a three-story brick mansion, which could only be described as opulent.

It didn't take a great deal of imagination to picture the tall maple trees now devoid of foliage in full bloom. Around the entire residence stood a black wrought-iron fence, which could adequately keep in five rambunctious children or keep out unwanted visitors, such as themselves.

"It looks like little brother has married quite well," Ethan commented, pleased for Rafe despite the circumstances. His brother deserved some happiness after all he had gone through with Ellie and the baby. Unfortunately his happiness was about to be interrupted.

Sensing Ethan's discomfort and conflicted feelings, Wilhemina clutched his arm. "Try to remember that you're only doing your job, Ethan. I know it's tearing you up inside having to bring Rafe in, but it'll be easier for Rafe having you as the arresting officer. Someone else might shoot first and ask questions later."

He chucked her under the chin, grateful for her support and understanding. "Like a bounty hunter?"

"I admit that I've got no stomach for this, either. Chasing your brother around the country was one thing, but having to arrest him in front of his wife and children is something else entirely." The more she thought about it, the more she just wanted to give up on the idea of arresting Rafe and bringing him back to stand trial. She wished now she had listened to Ethan and had returned to Texas.

"Speaking of stomachs . . ." He cast her a measured look. "Have you gained weight? I noticed that despite your bout of illness you're a bit more well-rounded in places." Though Ethan hadn't slept with her in a while, he had noticed that her breasts were much fuller than they used to be.

At Ethan's words, Wilhemina crimsoned and decided to brazen it out, her voice filling with indignation. "What an ungentlemanly thing to say, Ethan Bodine! But coming from you that's no surprise. Maybe I have gained a few pounds. What's wrong with that?"

"Nothing. I was merely making an observation. No need to get your corset all tied up in knots." He had touched on a sensitive subject. He sure as hell wouldn't make that mistake again. Women! he thought with a sigh.

After lighting from the conveyance, Ethan paid the driver and helped Wilhemina down, then returned the topic to their earlier conversation. "I'll try to be as circumspect as possible when I arrest Rafe so the kids won't get alarmed."

"But you're wearing a gun! How circumspect can you be with a firearm strapped to your hip?"

"For chrissake, Willy! I'm here to arrest a man for murder. What'd you expect me to do? Bring him flowers?"

"But you might scare the little ones."

"If I know Rafe, he's got those kids trained in the use of firearms by now. Probably Emmaline St. Joseph, too. Just because he's living in the lap of luxury don't mean he's forgotten where he came from."

Reluctantly Wilhemina followed Ethan down the path to the gate, praying that the difficult ordeal would be painless and over with soon for everyone's sake.

They were greeted at the door by a black-suited butler, who stared down his long, aquiline nose at Ethan's western attire, not bothering to hide his distaste at the gun he sighted at the Ranger's hip. Before the man could speak, a soft, cultured voice called out.

"Who is it, Jefferson? Who's calling at such an early hour?"

The female speaking sounded tired and a little annoyed, and both Willy and Ethan figured correctly that Emmaline St. Joseph was at home and not at all pleased to be receiving visitors this early in the day. Willy could hardly fault her for that.

"Don't bother announcing us," Ethan told the startled man as he pushed past him through the doorway. "We can find our own way."

"But, but—" the servant sputtered, righting his wire-rimmed glasses and looking very put out.

Smiling apologetically at the gasping man, Wilhemina hurried after Ethan.

The dining room stood to the left of the wide black-and-white marble-tiled entry hall, and its double, intricately carved walnut doors were open. Inside, children's voices could be heard babbling, and a man's gruff orders for them to keep quiet and eat their breakfast reverberated loudly off the floral-papered walls.

But all sounds of normalcy stopped when Ethan strolled into the room and cleared his throat.

The handsome man at the head of the long table looked up, his blue eyes widening in shock as recognition hit him squarely. His resemblance to Ethan was startling.

"Howdy, little brother," Ethan said in greeting, his hat held behind his back in an uncharacteristically self-conscious gesture.

As soon as she spotted Wilhemina and Ethan, the lovely redheaded woman burst into tears.

All five children started shouting at once, and the youngest child, a girl, began crying loudly as well.

Wilhemina, observing all of it, and the wretched look on Ethan's face, felt like sobbing herself.

Rafe Bodine, a resigned look on his face, pushed his chair back and came forward to greet them. "I was expecting you a whole lot sooner, Ethan." He clasped his brother's hand. "I've been worried about you. Heard those Murray boys had finally caught up with you."

"They did," the Ranger admitted. "But you haven't been all that easy to find."

Smiling ruefully, Rafe turned his attention to Willy. "Is this your . . . wife?"

Ethan's face crimsoned to nearly the same shade as Willy's. "No. This is Wilhemina Granville, a bounty hunter. She's been traveling with me to find you."

Rafe's brow arched ever so slightly, and the gesture reminded Willy so much of Ethan. She held out her hand. "I'm actually a horticulturist by profession, Mr. Bodine, but circumstances have forced me into this rather unsavory profession. It's nothing personal."

He nodded in understanding, and there was not a trace of condemnation in his eyes. "Come and meet my family. As you've probably heard, I'm married now, Ethan."

Rafe put his arm around his brother's shoulder and guided him toward the table. His wife, Emmaline, was still weeping softly into her napkin. The children, all silent and wide-eyed, stared at the intruders with fear and uncertainty.

"Emma, we're all going to drown if you keep up that caterwauling. And you know I can't stand it when you cry. Now come and meet my brother, the Texas Ranger."

At the mention of his brother, the woman's demeanor changed drastically. Throwing down her napkin, she stood, and it was clear when she did that she was as pregnant as the silence that resulted.

Ethan and Willy exchanged meaningful looks.

There was anger in her eyes, as well as defiance, as she faced her nemesis. "I won't say 'Welcome' because you're not, Ethan Bodine. I've heard about you and your woman-hating ways, and I'll not allow you to take Rafe back to Texas. Not after all we've been through to make a home for these children. What kind of man would hunt down his own brother like an animal?"

Wilhemina's heart went out to the woman, and to Ethan, who stood silent and stone-faced.

"Papa! Papa!" The small child, who couldn't have been more than two, toddled forward on chubby legs, holding out her hands to Rafe. He obliged her instantly by picking her up and hugging her to his broad chest.

"Don't cry, little flowerpot," he said, nudging her soft cheek and giving her a kiss. "This is Theodora," he explained. "But we call her Pansy. She's the youngest of the five."

"She's adorable," Willy said, smiling widely at the child and receiving a grin in return.

Ethan felt a lump rising in his throat at the sight of Rafe with the child, and he did his best to ignore the red-headed woman's hateful glare, though it wasn't easy, as guilty as he felt. "I'm sorry to bust in on you like this, Rafe, but I think we need to talk."

Emmaline moved nearer to her husband and twined her arm through his. "There's nothing to talk about, Mr. Bodine. You have no jurisdiction in this state, and you are trespassing on my property. Please leave, or I will have you thrown out."

"Emma!" Rafe's voice filled with censure as he patted his wife's hand reassuringly. "Take the kids upstairs while I talk to Ethan. I know you're upset, but we've discussed this possibility a thousand times, and now it's time we face it. Perhaps Miss Granville will help you get the kids settled down." He looked at Willy beseechingly.

"Of course." Willy held out her hands for the baby. "I just adore children, Mrs. Bodine. And I'd love to see your house. It's very beautiful."

At Rafe's intractable expression, Emmaline relented, bestowing a small smile on the unwelcome bounty hunter. "Come with me, Miss Granville. I'm anxious to hear all about how you've turned from a life of respectability into a bounty hunter."

"Yeah! Can you tell us all about the men you've hunted and killed?" asked a small blond boy with an engaging grin. Wilhemina got the distinct impression that the boy often asked a lot of frank questions.

"That will be quite enough, David!" Emmaline warned with a shake of her head. "Daniel," she told the oldest boy, who appeared to be about thirteen, "quit staring in awe at that Texas Ranger and get upstairs with your brother. Miriam and Miranda," she told the two sisters, "that goes for you, too."

"Yes, Mama," they replied in unison.

"Shall we tell Aunt Loretta it's time for our lessons?" Daniel asked.

Emmaline looked quickly at Rafe, then at Ethan, whose face reddened in anger.

"Loretta Goodman is here from Denver? What about her boardinghouse and her new life of respectability?"

Rafe shrugged. "Actually she was, but she's not at the moment. She left early this morning to attend a sick friend."

"A male friend, no doubt," Ethan said with no small amount of derision, still angry about how the woman had tried to mislead him concerning Rafe's whereabouts. Emmaline nearly bared her teeth at the lawman.

"Loretta's with a lady friend. An elderly woman who's too ill to care for herself. Loretta has taken it upon herself to nurse the woman back to health."

Ethan's disbelieving look made her voice chill to arctic proportions. "Some people do change, Mr. Bodine. Except, perhaps, for you." With that, she swept regally out of the room, dragging the two girls with her.

"Mama sure is mad at you, Ranger," David said before his older brother grabbed his arm and hauled him out of the room.

Wilhemina shook her head at Ethan and heaved a sigh. "So much for circumspection," she said, then quit the room as well.

"Guess I didn't handle things too well," Ethan admitted once he and Rafe were alone and sequestered in the library. The room smelled of leather and the old books that lined the oak shelves in great profusion.

"There wasn't a good way to handle it, Ethan, so don't go blaming yourself. Emmaline's been high-strung and nervous lately because of the pregnancy. She's usually not so rude."

"I'm sorry about all this, Rafe. I—"

Rafe held up his hand. "I knew all along that you'd be coming for me. I told Emma as much. But she thought we'd be safe back here in Boston, far removed from the grisly happenings out west."

"Truth be told, the thought had crossed my mind a time or two about giving up on finding you, but Willy is stubborn as a mule." He explained about her circumstances and the events that led her to becoming a bounty hunter. "So you see, she didn't really have much choice. It was either find you or see her aunts thrown out in the street. If I ever get my hands on that damn banker . . ."

"You're in love with the woman." Rafe's disbelief soon turned to laughter at the sheer irony of his woman-hating brother finally meeting his match in a small slip of a woman, knowing what that was like all too well.

"I never thought I'd live to see the day, Ethan. Not after all the lectures you gave me. And certainly not after your experience with Lorna Mae Murray."

Ethan wore a mask of despondency. "Willy doesn't know I love her, and I want to keep it that way for now. She thinks she's in love with someone else—a man she was once engaged to—but when the time's right I'm going to show her that it's me she loves."

"Is this lovesick fool standing before me the same Ethan Bodine who swore it wasn't normal for a man to marry and go against his natural inclination? Who used to say that women couldn't provide the same feeling of camaraderie as a camp full of men? Who did his damnedest to convince me never to marry?"

Ethan tugged self-consciously on his mustache. "That was before I met Willy. She's different."

"How long you gonna wait before you tell her you love her? Your success rate with women isn't that good. And she may up and decide to marry this other fella."

Over my dead body, Ethan vowed silently. "I'm not much good at this man-woman stuff. I've already botched it with Willy by beating up her former fiancé."

Rafe grinned. "You never were known for your tact, Ethan."

"And you never were known for your brains, little brother. Why in hell didn't you wait for me? I told you I'd help you track down the Slaughters. Instead you go off half-cocked and shoot the son of a bitch."

"I didn't shoot Bobby in cold blood like that whore claimed. He drew first. I merely put him out of his misery."

"So why run? If you were innocent, you should have come back and faced the music. You would have gotten a fair trial in Misery. Even now Travis is fixing to prepare your defense."

Rafe, who didn't seem at all surprised by the revelation—Bodines always took care of their own—stood and began to pace the room. "First off, I couldn't let the Slaughters get away with what they'd done to Ellie and the baby. You know you'd have done the same if it were you.

"Revenge might not be the smartest course, but it felt damn good."

"I take it you found the bastards."

A pained look washed Rafe's face as memories of his encounter with the Slaughters came flooding back. "More like they found me. They took me and Emma hostage and were fixing to rape her, or worse, to get back at me. I did what I had to do."

"Are they all dead?"

"All but Roy Lee. He passed out drunk, and Emma convinced me to spare his life. He's currently residing in the territorial prison in Wyoming. Luther and Hank are dead."

"You got any whiskey?"

"It's a mite early for whiskey, big brother. Or is Miss Granville driving you to drink already?" He grinned.

"It's you who's driving me to drink. After what you just told me I need a little fortification."

Rafe obliged, and Ethan swallowed whole the contents of the glass Rafe handed him. His voice was hoarse when he finally spoke. "You're in a shitload of trouble, little brother. Not only do you have to answer for the murder of Bobby, but now there's Luther's and Hank's deaths to consider. Keeping you from hanging's going to be nigh on to impossible."

Rafe took the seat next to Ethan. "Nevertheless, I've decided to go back to Texas. I can't stand always looking over my shoulder, wondering when or if I'll be found. It's no way to live. And it's no way to raise a family.

"Emma's my life. We're expecting a child of our own. And those kids are depending on me to give them some sort of decent upbringing. Lord knows they haven't had a fair shake up till now. I can't let any of them down. If I'm ever going to have a normal life, I've got to go back and stand trial."

"Goddamn it, Rafe! I should be happy as hell to hear you say such a thing, but going back means facing the hangman. I'm not sure now that push has come to shove that I can allow you to take that chance. Not with your wife and children to consider. And a baby on the way."

"You don't have a hell of a lot of choice, Captain Bodine. You swore an oath to bring me in, and you wouldn't be the man I know you to be if you did any less. Besides, I'm ready to go back. There's a lot I left unsettled—Ellie, the baby, her parents, my own. I let a lot of folks down, including you, and now I have to make it right."

There were times when Ethan hated being a lawman, and he realized now was one of them. But he also knew that Rafe was right: no matter how painful, no matter how difficult, his brother needed to go back to Misery to stand trial and clear his name.

Willy and Emmaline were having a similar conversation. The children were occupied in the schoolroom, Pansy had been put down for a nap, and now the two women were sharing a pot of tea in the upstairs parlor.

"I'm sorry if I acted rude earlier, Miss Granville. I just haven't been myself lately. And now this horrible turn of events has me worried to death. If you knew what Rafe and I have gone through just to be together . . ." Her dispirited sigh spoke volumes.

Wilhemina studied the woman before her while she sipped chamomile tea from a Wedgwood cup. Emmaline Bodine was lovely. Curly red hair framed a piquant face, and a splattering of freckles danced across the bridge of her nose, giving her a youthful appearance. She was spare of frame but looked sturdy enough to spit nails if the situation warranted, which Willy was sure it had.

"I understand perfectly the strain you've been under, Mrs. Bodine. Please don't apologize. I feel terribly awkward coming into your home under such dreadful circumstances."

"Are you the same Wilhemina Granville I've read about? The one who did such interesting work with tulips?"

Wilhemina's face flushed with pleasure. "Why, yes! I wasn't sure anyone had read my paper on fire-blight, which is among the most serious of diseases to attack the genus *Tulipa.*"

"We have some lovely gardens here, and I try to keep up on disease prevention and that sort of thing. Or I used to, before traveling west with my brother and subsequently with Rafe."

"Ethan and I visited the Lucas St. Joseph Home for Foundlings and Orphans. I'm sure your brother would be proud that the institution he founded bears his name."

"It was the least I could do. Lucas gave his life for a very noble cause."

"It was indeed noble of you and Mr. Bodine to adopt those five orphans."

"Please call me Emma, and I'm sure Rafe wouldn't want you to stand on formality, either." Wilhemina insisted that they do the same, and the woman continued.

"By the time Rafe and I returned from our search for the Slaughters, we realized that we didn't want to live without the children, so we adopted them as soon as we reached California."

"They're delightful. I envy you such a fine family."

Emmaline cast Wilhemina a searching look. "Unless I miss my guess, Willy, you'll be having a family of your own soon."

Wilhemina's face paled at the woman's unerring accuracy. "I—"

Smiling knowingly, Emma said, "I was pregnant before I married Rafe, so I'm quite familiar with all the symptoms. And the healthy glow you wear is impossible to hide. Does the Ranger know?"

Noting that Emma couldn't quite bring herself to mention Ethan's name, she shook her head. "No. I don't think so. I've convinced him that my weight gain is caused from overeating. I'd appreciate it if you didn't mention my pregnancy to anyone. Ethan and I are not going to get married. In fact, I may be marrying someone else entirely."

"Really? Well, I can't say I blame you. Ethan Bodine is a hateful man."

"He's really not. Ethan loves his brother a great deal, and hunting Rafe down has been very difficult for him. I think he would have given up long ago, but I prodded him to continue for purely selfish reasons. I needed the reward money to save my aunts' home." She explained further her current predicament.

"You love him very much, don't you?"

"Yes. But he doesn't feel the same way about me. I've resigned myself to that, and I've decided that I must go on with my life for the sake of the child."

"If Ethan's like Rafe, and I'm sure he is after seeing them together, then he's not a very communicative sort. Perhaps he does love you, but just hasn't found the right way to tell you. I despaired of ever hearing those words from Rafe, and it wasn't until it was almost too late that he admitted his feelings." Her face filled with painful memories.

"Perhaps you're right. I'd like to think so, anyway. But with the baby I can't afford to wait. I've received a proposal of marriage from my former fiancé, Thomas Fullerton. I'm considering accepting it. It would solve a lot of problems."

"This sounds all too familiar to me. It's a good thing Loretta's not here or she'd be lecturing you on the thickheadedness of Texans and about fighting for the man you love."

The corners of Willy's mouth tipped up. "I take it you received such a lecture."

"Several times. She even loaned me a dress so I could seduce Rafe."

"Well, by the looks of your stomach it worked."

Emmaline laughed, reached for a cookie, and nibbled. "I like you, Wilhemina Granville. I think we're going to be good friends."

"Even though I came with the intention of bringing your husband back to Misery to stand trial for murder?"

"The shock of seeing Ethan Bodine in the flesh rendered me senseless for a while, but I know deep in my heart that the only way Rafe and I can ever live a normal life is for him to go back and stand trial. He's innocent and will be found as such."

"Rafe's lucky to have you."

"Yes, I know. I tell him that every single day."

The longer Wilhemina spent in Emmaline's company, the fonder she grew of the woman. "I doubt we'll be traveling back to Texas any time soon. The weather is still unsettled and the snow has made travel impossible for the time being."

"Then you and Ethan must move in here and stay with us. It's foolish for you to be living at a hotel, spending money unnecessarily, when you could be living here. We have plenty of room, and it would be such fun to have another woman around. Especially one who is also expecting a baby."

"That's very kind of you, Emma. And I'm sure Ethan would love to spend more time with his brother and nieces and nephews. But as I told you, I'm considering a marriage proposal, and it might be necessary to entertain my gentleman friend, which, under the circumstances, might be very awkward."

A calculating look entered Emma Bodine's soft brown eyes. "And what better place to entertain him than right under Ethan's nose? The possibilities are endless, and I welcome a chance to give the arrogant Texas Ranger a little of his own medicine. From what Rafe's told me, his brother's attitude toward women is a bit cavalier, if not downright archaic."

Wilhemina's mouth dropped open, then she snapped it shut. "I don't think that's a very good idea, Emma. Ethan has already given poor Thomas a severe beating, and—"

"Excellent! Then he's not as indifferent to you as he might let on. Leave everything to me."

"But—"

Emma patted Willy's hand. "Trust me, Wilhemina. Ethan Bodine will never know what hit him."

Chapter Seventeen

ETHAN WELCOMED THE OPPORTUNITY TO MOVE INTO the St. Joseph–Bodine mansion for several reasons. It enabled him to keep a closer eye on his brother and to get to know his nieces, nephews, and sister-in-law better, and it afforded him the opportunity of living under the same roof with Wilhemina.

Once Willy had a chance to observe how happy Rafe and Emma were in their marital bliss, how the joys of motherhood were so fulfilling to a woman, perhaps she would look upon his suit with interest. Once he decided to press it.

Ethan figured it wouldn't take much to make Wilhemina see the error of her ways where Thomas Fullerton was concerned. After all, Ethan was the better man of the two, had never broken her heart the way Fullerton had, and they had shared a number of passionate moments. And he doubted that Fullerton had an ounce of passion in his sissified body.

"Hello, Ethan. Are you finding your accommodations satisfactory?"

Ethan turned from the library window to find his new sister-in-law entering. She'd become a tad more civil since their first encounter yesterday, but he still felt as if he were walking on eggshells around her.

Rafe had mentioned that his wife was in the habit of performing daily calisthenics, and Ethan wasn't taking any chances that she was going to use her muscles on him. He'd already had a taste of her acerbic tongue.

"Yeah. Thanks. It's much nicer than the room at the hotel. Is Willy settled in? Has she eaten?"

An eyebrow arched. "My my, but you're certainly solicitous of Miss Granville's welfare." His face colored, and she smiled inwardly. "Willy's just fine. She was tired this morning, so I encouraged her to sleep in. I know what it's like to be on the trail with a Bodine brother."

The censure in her voice was unmistakable, making those eggshells under his feet start to crack. "Is Rafe around? I haven't seen him yet this morning." At least with a man like his brother he knew where he stood. To Ethan's surprise, Rafe hadn't shown any bitterness over his brother's coming to arrest him. Ethan guessed he was still more Texas Ranger than anyone'd given him credit for.

"Rafe always arises with the dawn. It's a habit of his I haven't been able to break."

"I'd think having a beautiful woman in his bed would make my brother reluctant to leave it."

The compliment was unexpected and warmed Emma's heart just a little. Men of her acquaintance had always found her money far more attractive than her person. Except Rafe. And now his brother.

"Rafe had some errands to run for me. Being with child has slowed me down a bit, so he offered to deliver the invitations for me."

"Invitations?"

"Why, yes. Didn't I tell you? We had already planned a fund raiser before you arrived to solicit additional funds for the new orphanage we're intending to build here in Boston. I'm planning to hold a masquerade ball to kick off the event."

"A ball? Are you outta your mind? We've got no time for such frivolous things. I've got to bring Rafe back to Misery to stand trial, and we need to leave soon." He'd be damned if he was going to any fancy ball with a bunch of stiff-shirts. Just the thought gave him hives.

She waved off the objection as if it were of no importance. "The weather is still dreadful, Ethan, and I'm sure you wouldn't want to deprive innocent children of an adequate place to live.

"Children like Pansy, whose mother was an alcoholic, find themselves on the street with no one to care for them. They need help from people like us who can afford it."

What she said made sense, but he still couldn't help feeling that he was being manipulated in some way. And he had no intention of going to any ball.

"Rafe tells me you do quite a bit of charity work."

"Privilege has a price. My father drilled those words into my head since I was a child Pansy's age. It's my duty to help those less fortunate than myself. And I'm happy to do it. I couldn't possibly spend all the money I have on myself or my own family in several lifetimes, so I believe in spending on those who need it."

He took measure of her words, thought of Willy's predicament, and asked, "Is your generosity limited to orphans, or do you give to anyone who's in need?"

"Are you asking for yourself, Ranger Bodine? You don't look terribly deprived to me."

Heat rose up his neck to land squarely on his cheeks. "Willy's in some financial difficulty. She needed the reward money on Rafe to help out her aunts, and now she's decided she couldn't possibly take it. I can tell she's worrying herself over it. And I don't have the money to give her. I spent the last of it traveling here to find Rafe."

Emma toyed with the Waterford paperweight on the desk, weighing his words and the paperweight in the palm of her hand. "You care for her a great deal, don't you?" she asked, delighting in the possibilities.

He shrugged, unwilling to admit a thing to this woman he barely knew; he hoped to hell Rafe had kept his counsel. "We're friends. Good friends." There was a wealth left unsaid in those words.

"It's such a pity, then."

"A pity?" His forehead wrinkled in confusion. "I'm afraid I don't follow your drift, ma'am. Is there a problem about Willy?"

"What I mean is, you two are such good friends, and you do seem genuinely concerned for Wilhemina's welfare, but she told me just yesterday that she is considering a proposal of marriage from a former fiancé of hers."

Ethan rocked back on his heels, and his face blanched whiter than the ivory lace curtains hanging at the windows. Emma almost felt sorry for him. Almost. But not quite. She wasn't ready to forgive the Texas Ranger just yet.

"You speaking about Fullerton? That panty-waist horticulturist she was once engaged to?"

Emma bit the inside of her cheek. "Why, yes. I do believe that was the name she mentioned. She said he was quite handsome and very urbane. I take it they have a great deal in common, what with their work and all."

While he and Willy had nothing in common but a mutual passion and friendship. Would that be enough? he wondered.

"And Willy said he proposed?"

"Not an indecent proposal, I assure you. From what I understand, he's madly in love with her and wants to make an honest woman out of her."

"I'll see him in hell first."

"Oh, dear! Well, I'm afraid that you're going to see him a whole lot sooner than that, Ethan. Mr. Fullerton is coming to dinner this evening."

"What!" A killing rage turned Ethan's face bright red, and Emma took a step back, thinking that perhaps she had pushed him a bit too far as she watched him stalk to the door.

"I trust that you'll be on your best behavior tonight, Ethan. Willy told me what happened the last time you encountered Mr. Fullerton. Your behavior was really quite barbaric, if you ask me."

He glared at her. "Well, nobody did. And I don't need no woman telling me to mind my *p*'s and *q*'s." He disappeared out the door, not bothering to acknowledge Loretta Goodman, who had just entered.

"Merciful heavens! Who on earth put a burr under that man's saddle? Ethan Bodine looks mad enough to kill. Though he sure as heck is a handsome devil. In my day a man like that wouldn't have had to pay the usual fare, if you get my meaning."

Emmaline smiled indulgently at the former prostitute, now her dearest friend, and instructed her to close the door behind her. "But does he look mad enough to propose, Loretta? That's what I'm wondering."

"Something tells me you're up to no good, Emma." Loretta moved farther into the room, and a huge grin split her face. "You have always been a woman after my own heart. I knew that from the first moment I laid eyes on you."

Rafe had brought Emmaline and the children to Denver, and to Loretta at the boardinghouse she owned, intending to go after the Slaughter gang once they were safe and secure. But Emma, who had a mind of her own, and was madly in love with Rafe, followed him to join in his search to find the men who had murdered his first wife.

"Playing matchmaker is a role I was born to."

"You are as devious as you are lovely, honey."

Emma grinned and wrapped her arm about the petite blonde. "Why, thank you, Loretta. Coming from a canny woman such as yourself, that's quite a compliment."

"I taught you well, did I?"

"Very well. Very well indeed."

* * *

Brooding over his third cup of coffee while he waited for Willy to put in an appearance, Ethan was beginning to wonder if this miserable day could possibly get any worse. Four of the five Bodine children entered the dining room, and he soon discovered that it could.

The children had locked hands, as if presenting a united front, and approached the table cautiously. Ethan had never before seen such serious faces on a group of youngsters.

"You come in here to eat?" he asked, feeling ill at ease. "The ham, biscuits, and eggs are pretty good. And there's plenty left."

Daniel stepped forward. "We've already eaten, Uncle Ethan, but thanks anyway."

The crisp bacon Ethan had just wrapped his teeth around lodged in his throat. *Uncle Ethan.* For some reason, he liked the sound of that, and thought that "Pa" might not be half bad, either, *if* he and Willy were to marry.

She'd want children, and though he'd never given them much thought up until now, it wasn't an altogether displeasing idea, though a bit unsettling. His father would surely be pleased, for Ben Bodine thought of little else besides marrying off his sons and having grandsons to carry on his name.

The loss of Rafe and Ellie's child had been a severe blow to the old man, but when he discovered that Rafe now had five children and another on the way, he'd be beside himself with joy.

Ethan turned his attention back to the children. "So, if you haven't come to eat, why are you here? Were you thinking that we should get better acquainted?"

"We want you to leave our papa alone," the child called Miranda stated, brown eyes flashing fire. "You shouldn't take Papa away from us. He's the only one we got."

Miriam stepped forward. "Papa says prayers with us at night and tucks us in bed. And sometimes he reads us stories from the big storybook. We'd miss him if he had to go away. Our real parents had to go away, and we never got to see them again." She started to cry.

Touched by the young girl's tears, Ethan held out his arms for the weeping child to come to him. "Don't cry, little darlin'. I'm going to do everything in my power to see that your pa comes back to you safe and sound. He's my brother and I love him, just like you love your sister."

The child sniffed and crawled up on his lap. "Will you read us a story tonight before bed, Uncle Ethan? Papa says you used to tell him stories every night when he was a small boy."

Choking at the memory, and the fact that Rafe had thought enough to mention him to his children, Ethan nodded, remembering how he used to tell Rafe tales of Indian attacks and the calvary coming to the rescue and how his little brother used to hang on to his every word. "I'd like that."

David stepped closer to the table. "Can I see your badge? Is that the badge all Texas Rangers wear?"

Ethan removed the distinctive tin badge from his shirtfront and pinned it on the excited youngster. "Now take care of it, Davey. It's the only one I've got with me."

His blue eyes wide with wonder, David brushed at the star with his shirtsleeve, polishing it to a high sheen. "Look, Danny! I'm a Texas Ranger."

"I'm going to be a Texas Ranger when I grow up," Daniel stated, staring enviously at the star and wishing his uncle had two of the precious objects. "I want to be just like Pa when I'm old enough."

"Your pa was a damn . . . darn good Ranger, son. You'd be smart to follow in his footsteps, But you're forgetting something."

His forehead wrinkled in confusion. "What's that, Uncle Ethan?"

"A Texas Ranger's got to live in Texas."

The boy thought for a moment, then said, "And Texas is where you'll be taking our pa?"

"Danny! You traitor!" Miranda stared daggers at her brother, stamping her foot in anger.

Pressing the advantage he'd just been given, Ethan replied, "Yep. Maybe you'll all be able to come with us when we travel back to Texas. My pa, your grandfather, would love to meet all of you. He lives on a ranch."

"With cows and horses?" Miranda asked, weakening a tad.

"Yep. And my stepmother, who just loves little kids, makes wonderful pies and cookies. My other brother, Travis, your uncle, is a lawyer who is going to help me clear Rafe's name."

"But what if he can't, Uncle Ethan? What if Papa goes to jail?"

He brushed Miriam's soft face with a kiss, his face turned solemn. "Your pa will have to go to jail for a while when we get there. He's going to have to stand trial."

"Because he shot Bobby Slaughter?" Daniel asked, and Ethan's brows lifted in surprise. "We know all about what happened. Mama and Papa told us, so we wouldn't hear it from strangers."

Rafe and Emmaline had been wise to confide in them. Gossip could be cruel and devastating to a child. "That's right. Travis is a lawyer, and he'll be defending your pa in court. We'll find witnesses who'll testify on his behalf, and gather evidence to declare his innocence." Ethan sounded far more confident than he felt at the moment, especially knowing that Luther's and Hank's murders would also have to be faced.

Miranda stepped forward and clasped his large hand trustingly in her small one, squeezing it tightly. "We know you'll help our pa, Uncle Ethan. He said you were a good man, and that if anything ever happened to him, we could always come to you for help."

He drew her up on his other knee. "Your pa's right, darlin'. I'm going to do everything I can to help all of you. We're family now. And Bodines stick together."

In the hallway, Emma and Loretta listened, and the older woman wiped teary eyes on the edge of her apron. "That man's got a good heart, Emma. I never thought so until this moment, but I do now."

Emma nodded in agreement. "Willy said as much, but I had a hard time believing her. I guess there's more to these Bodine men than meets the eye. Guess I should have learned that lesson with Rafe, and not have judged Ethan quite so harshly."

"Don't go blaming yourself, honey. After everything that's happened, you had a right to be upset. And you can always make it up to him."

She sighed, feeling guilty that she'd spoken to Ethan so bitterly yesterday. "I hope so. He must think me an awful shrew."

"You just fix it so he and Miss Granville get together, and I'm sure he'll forgive you anything."

Chewing her lower lip thoughtfully, Emma said, "But what about the hell I'm going to have to put him through first? Maybe this idea isn't such a good one after all."

" 'All's well that ends well,' my Cal used to say, and I have a feeling that my dearly departed husband was right. This is going to turn out just fine and dandy. See if it don't."

"Well, it's too late now, anyway. Rafe was to deliver the dinner invitation to Mr. Fullerton this morning and not come back unless he had an affirmative answer." She smiled impishly. "And you know how persuasive he can be when he puts his mind to something."

Loretta patted her friend's swollen tummy. "I'll say. That man has you on your back more than most of the working girls I know."

Emma's face reddened, then she gasped. "Loretta Goodman! For shame!" The two women broke into a fit of giggles as they ascended the wide staircase to find Wilhemina.

Wilhemina wasn't asleep as everyone thought, but pacing her room, indecision weighing heavily on her shoulders. Emma's plan to bring Ethan to his knees and eventually to the altar had been tempting, and she'd finally agreed to allow the insistent woman to try her hand at matchmaking.

But now that the dinner invitation to Thomas had been issued, and she knew Ethan waited downstairs and would demand an explanation, Wilhemina wasn't so sure she had made the right judgment.

In fact, she was pretty darn positive that she hadn't.

She tensed at the knock on her door, believing it was Ethan, and was relieved to hear the sound of Emma's voice.

"Willy, are you awake? It's Emma and Loretta."

Tightening the sash on her robe, she called for them to enter, knowing that her wisest course would be to call a halt to the subterfuge before it got out of hand.

Before Ethan permanently disabled Thomas.

Wilhemina had met Loretta the previous night over a strained dinner of duck à l'orange punctuated with grunts, growls, and disapproving looks from Ethan. She had liked the feisty little woman instantly. Her good nature and ribald jokes had brought levity to what could have been a dreadfully awkward situation. Even Ethan had lightened his mood after a while, unable to resist Loretta's humor.

"Good morning." She pasted on a lighthearted smile she didn't feel.

"Oh, posh!" Loretta said, taking one look at the distraught woman. "You look as nervous as a virgin her first time out." She came forward to clasp Willy's hand, which was cold and clammy. "You ain't having second thoughts about this plan of Emma's, are you?"

"You mustn't worry, Willy dear," Emmaline said. "I have everything under control. Rafe will be back shortly, and Mr. Fullerton will be here for dinner this evening."

"But Ethan is likely to kill him. And then what'll I do for a husband?"

Ignoring the protestation, Emmaline crossed to the tall mahogany wardrobe. "Let me see what you've chosen to wear for this evening. It has to be something special and captivating."

"Wish I still had the 'Salivating Cal' dress," Loretta stated, mostly to herself, but Emma smiled, recalling her one occasion to wear the risqué gown: the night she lost her virginity.

"I'm afraid my wardrobe is lacking. Ethan purchased a few gowns for me before we left Denver, but there's nothing fancy or suitable enough for a dinner party."

The pretty socialite tapped her chin, sized up Wilhemina from head to toe, then nodded. "I think I've got several gowns that will fit you. We can try them on and see. You're bigger than me in the bust, so they'll probably have the same effect as Loretta's famous dress of seduction."

Wilhemina's eyes widened in disbelief and horror. "You want me to seduce Thomas tonight?" She shook her head. "That is quite impossible." Ethan would, no doubt, disembowel the man. "Besides, Thomas isn't the type of man who's interested in things of a . . . a sexual nature."

Loretta's mouth unhinged. "And you was planning to marry this fella? Girl, if a man can't cut it between the sheets, then he's just no good to a woman. There ain't all that much fun in life for us gals. If we don't have our pleasure in bed, where the heck else are we gonna get it?"

"I take it you didn't have the same problem with Ethan?" Emmaline asked, her eyebrow arching in question. Her relationship with Rafe was wonderfully romantic and fulfilling, and she couldn't imagine that every woman wasn't as fortunate as she.

Flushing to the tips of her bare toes, Wilhemina shook her head. "No. Ethan is quite an accomplished lover. I have no complaints on that score."

"I should say not," Loretta declared. "The Bodine brothers are known far and wide for their ability to pleasure their women. Why, their prowess, not to mention the size of their—"

Wilhemina gasped, making Emmaline say in a censure-filled voice, "You forget yourself once again, Loretta! Willy is not used to your salty tongue."

The short woman looked genuinely offended. *"Hmph!* Never had many complaints about my tongue in the old days."

Wilhemina and Emmaline exchanged amused glances, then Emma said, "Ethan is waiting for you downstairs, Willy, but I suggest that you avoid him until dinner. We want you to make an entrance that he isn't likely to forget."

"He sure as heck was put out when he found out you was thinking of hitching yourself to that horticulturist fella. Ain't that right, Emma honey?"

"That's correct. I don't think it's going to take much persuasion at all to bring Ethan around to our way of thinking."

Plopping down on the large tester bed, Wilhemina wasn't nearly as convinced as her two friends. "You don't know Ethan very well. The man is as stubborn as a mule sometimes. This plan might just backfire and start him running in the opposite direction." Then she'd have no choice but to marry Thomas.

"Would you care to place a wager on that, Wilhemina?"

"A wager? But I have no money."

"But I do. And I'm willing to wager, say, five hundred dollars, that you and Ethan Bodine will be married before summer."

"You'd better be," Loretta said, "or you'll be sticking out like a ripe watermelon."

Her hands resting on the soft swell of her abdomen, Wilhemina observed raw determination on both women's faces and it strengthened her own resolve.

"I'll agree to the wager, but only if you'll agree to play poker with me should I lose. That's the only way I'll be able to make restitution. I'm much better at poker than I am at matters of the heart."

"They're both games of chance, but I intend to stack the deck in my favor."

The proper Bostonian woman had spunk and continued to astound Willy with her boldness. "You intend to cheat?"

Emma smiled. "I certainly do."

Chapter Eighteen

"I FEEL LIKE A DAMN FOOL IN THIS GETUP," ETHAN complained, tugging at the stiff shirt collar that strangled his neck like a hangman's noose. "Pour me another whiskey, will you?"

"Quit your bellyachin'," Rafe scolded. "You told me to help you get ready for tonight, so I did. The suit looks just fine on you. We're about the same size. I don't see what the problem is."

"The problem is that you can't turn a sow's ear into a silk purse, which is what I'm trying to do. I can't be something I'm not, Rafe. Maybe you have no trouble fitting into Emma's society life, but I feel like a duck out of water. And a damn fool to boot."

"You are a damn fool if you let that lovely woman get away from you. Rest assured that Thomas Fullerton is going to be rigged out in his finery. The pompous ass practically drooled over me when I handed him the dinner invitation."

The elegant parlor was softly lit by the crystal chandelier overhead, but it was bright enough to illuminate the anger and disgust on Ethan's face. "You should have shot the bastard. As my brother it was your duty."

"Ha! You're a fine one to be talking about familial duty and sibling love after hunting me down the way you did."

"Point taken," Ethan said, chugging down his whiskey and looking chagrined.

"Fullerton's going to be here at any moment, so I hope you've got enough sense in that thick skull of yours to behave. Emma won't like it if you bust up any of the furniture, and Willy's going to think you're an animal, if she doesn't already, and run headlong into Fullerton's arms."

"And what makes you such an expert on romance, I'd like to know?"

"I'm a married man with a family. That puts me way ahead of you in the romance department, Ethan. And you'd be wise to listen to me. I won my woman; you've still got a ways to go."

The grandmother clock in the corner struck seven, and both men stared at it, listening to the gongs and then to the loud banging of the front door knocker.

"Just keep telling yourself that you love Willy, no matter what happens, no matter what she might say or do." Emma had confided to him about the dress Willy was going to wear tonight, and Rafe was pretty certain that Ethan was going to go off like a stick of dynamite when he saw his lady love in it. Rafe had taken one look at the indecently low-cut red velvet gown when Emmaline purchased it and had refused to let his wife wear it.

"Only hookers wear red," he had told her. And Loretta had howled until her sides ached.

"What do you mean anything she might—"

"Mr. Thomas Fullerton has arrived, sir," Jefferson announced in an imperious voice, leading Ethan's rival into the parlor, the man's coat draped over his arm, sparing Rafe from answering his brother's question.

"Will there be anything else, sir?" the butler asked.

Rafe shook his head, figuring that Jefferson was about to make a beeline for the kitchen to see if Loretta was within. He'd seen the old man's eyes follow her whenever he thought no one was looking, and he suspected that love had smitten Milton Jefferson.

Clasping Fullerton's hand, Rafe noted how limp the man's handshake was, like a fish floundering on dry land. He also noted how his brother's hands were clenched into fists—a good indication that Ethan had no intention of shaking the man's hand and burying the hatchet. Unless, of course, he buried it in the middle of Fullerton's back.

"Thank you for inviting me to your lovely home, Mr. Bodine. I'm so very pleased to be here."

Noting that Fullerton's eye was still an ugly, unattractive shade of purple, Ethan felt a large measure of satisfaction. His broken nose had been bandaged, and he wasn't talking like he had cotton stuffed up his nose anymore. "Fullerton," he said grudgingly, nodding at the man, who responded in kind.

"Would you care for a drink?" Rafe offered. "My wife and Willy should be down to join us at any moment."

The horticulturist cringed at the abbreviated version of Wilhemina's name and indicated with a nod of his head that he would. "Thank you. A small amount of sherry would be most welcome. It's quite cold outside."

"Sherry! What kind of pissant drink is that?" Ethan muttered, removing himself to the sofa, much to Rafe's relief.

Rafe fetched the man his cordial, then said, "I understand you and Willy are well acquainted."

The man glimpsed Ethan's darkening visage, the way his lips thinned into a nonexistent line, and apparently decided that some discretion was in order. "Wilhemina and I were co-workers some time back. She's a delightful young woman. So full of passion f—"

"Now hold on, pilgrim!" Ethan jumped to his feet.

"For her work," he added quickly, mopping a perspiring brow with a pristine linen handkerchief. "She's very dedicated to her work. It's a shame she left Boston to return home to Texas. She had such a promising career with the Horticultural Society."

"Maybe she wouldn't have, if she'd been treated with some respect."

Rafe's eyebrows lifted at his brother's remark. Ethan was the last man, he thought, who would ever have given thought to respecting a woman's career, let alone declaring such a thing aloud. It was obvious big brother had changed.

"Your collection of Dresden porcelain is exquisite, Mr. Bodine. Have you been a collector long?"

"Not really," Rafe said, following the man's gaze to the brass etagere in the corner and the lovely figurines placed there lovingly by his wife. "I used to collect scalps, but I gave up the hobby when I married Emma."

At the bald-faced lie his brother told with such facility, Ethan choked on his whiskey, hiding his chuckle behind a discreet cough.

The man paled considerably. "Scalps?" he asked, clearly shocked. "But that's positively—"

"It's a living, Fullerton. Why, you can't imagine how much these city folks pay for human hair. Where do you think those fancy wigs the ladies all wear come from?"

"Scalps?" Horror shone within the depths of his eyes.

"Exactly."

Thomas was saved from more of Rafe's teasing by the arrival of the ladies. If Ethan thought his brother's ribbing of the dandified horticulturist was amusing, his mood turned sour quickly at the sight of Willy decked out in a red velvet gown, displaying her assets for all to see.

"Jesus!" he said, his eyes rounding as he stared at the daring amount of cleavage she displayed, unwilling to believe that this brazen woman before him was his little horticulturist.

Fighting to hold on to his fragile self-control, he poured himself another whiskey and downed it, then crossed the room to greet her.

Wilhemina felt like a lamb entering a den of lions. She knew she was indecently dressed. One had only to look in the mirror to see that too much bosom flowed over the low-cut bodice of the gown. One had only to look at

Ethan's glowering face to know the same thing. He was furious.

On the other hand, Thomas was looking at her breasts with unconcealed admiration, as if he'd never before seen them. As if they were the most thrilling and important work he'd ever had occasion to feast his eyes upon.

She found it flattering compared to the terse welcome Ethan had muttered through gritted teeth when she entered.

Emma clasped Wilhemina's hand, dragging her forward. "Here we are. And doesn't Wilhemina look just captivating this evening? This dress looks far lovelier on her than it ever did on me. Don't you agree, Rafe?" she asked, pinning her husband with a look that said he'd better not disagree.

Rafe said a quick prayer of thanks that he'd had the good sense to refuse to allow his wife to wear the scandalous garment. And the fact that Ethan hadn't yet exploded in anger all over the room. "You look lovely, Willy," he finally choked out, hoping his brother wasn't going to shoot him in the back.

Fortunately for everyone, the Ranger had left his sidearm upstairs in his room, though his hand had sought the weapon several times already this evening.

Ethan lit a cigar and was blowing enough smoke rings into the room to warrant a visit from the fire department. Willy was nauseated by the odor.

"You look rather wan, Wilhemina," Thomas noted, ever solicitous of her welfare. "Shall I fetch you a sherry? Perhaps it will restore some color to your cheeks?"

Deciphering the problem correctly, Emma said to her brother-in-law, "Would you mind putting out your cigar, Ethan? I'm afraid the smoke bothers me in my present condition."

He looked at the cigar and at Emma, then his eyes drifted to Wilhemina, who was doing her best to avoid his gaze. Without saying a word, he crushed out the smoke and wondered if Willy's recent bouts of nausea and noticeable weight gain hadn't been caused by something entirely different from bad food or overeating—something like pregnancy.

Fool! he told himself. He'd been a goddamn fool letting Wilhemina pull the wool over his eyes when the truth had been before him all along. It should have been a joyous moment to discover he was going to be a father, but Willy's deception had ruined that for him.

A simmering rage started to boil within him.

The rest of the evening passed by in agonizing slowness. Though Rafe and Emma had done their best to be gracious hosts, none of their guests, with the exception of Thomas Fullerton, was the least bit talkative.

Ethan had barely spoken a word since the cigar smoke incident, preferring instead to drink whiskey.

Willy had spent a great deal of her time tugging up her bodice, avoiding Thomas's leering gaze, and staring discreetly at Ethan, who looked quite handsome in the dark navy suit he had borrowed from his brother.

Thomas, oblivious of anything beyond Wilhemina's breasts, regaled everyone with incessant chatter on every topic known to man. And some that weren't.

"Did you know that flies mate in midair? I was completely taken aback by the discovery myself, and if—"

"Will you look at the time?" Emma said, purposefully interrupting the pompous man as she gazed meaningfully, hopefully, at the clock. "Guess I'm a great deal more tired than I thought. I can hardly keep my eyes open." She yawned several times for effect.

It was barely ten o'clock, so Willy surmised that Emma was as tired of listening to Thomas's dissertations as everyone else.

Did I really think his conversation interesting at one time? Did I really think his lovemaking adequate? His fawning ways endearing? His arrogance and supercilious comments acceptable?

Because she didn't think so now.

"Why don't I walk Thomas to the door?" she offered, accepting a grateful smile from Emma and Rafe. "I'm sure he wouldn't want to tire out a lady in your delicate condition."

After a few moments of steady stares from the four other inhabitants of the room, Thomas closed his mouth and stood, making a great pretense of checking his watch. "It is late, isn't it? Well, I guess I'll be on my way. I have to be at work early tomorrow. Another presentation, you know." He conveyed his appreciation in his usual fawning fashion and allowed Wilhemina to escort him to the door.

Ethan remained behind, conspicuously silent.

"I've been anxious to talk to you privately all evening, Wilhemina," Thomas said when they were finally alone. "Have you given any more thought to my proposal of marriage?"

Chewing her lower lip thoughtfully, she contemplated the best way to relate the decision she had made this evening: she couldn't and wouldn't marry Thomas Fullerton. No matter what happened. Even if she had to raise her child alone and be branded a woman of ill repute, she could not marry Thomas.

But she didn't want to hurt him, for she knew how fragile his ego was, and he had been kind to her in his own fashion. She said softly, hoping it would cushion the blow somewhat, "I've given your generous offer a great deal of thought, Thomas, and—"

His face lit. "Splendid!"

"And I've decided that I cannot marry you."

"What?" He tapped his ear, unsure he had heard her correctly. "Surely I've misunderstood you, Wilhemina. I thought you just said that you couldn't marry me."

"I can't marry you, Thomas. I'm sorry. I wish you only the best, but I am no longer in love with you. And I realize that it would be unfair to both of us if I married you under those circumstances."

"But . . . but surely you know what a wonderful catch I—"

She pressed his hat and coat into his hands, not allowing him to finish what was sure to be a lengthy discussion of his greatest attributes. "Good-bye, dear friend. I wish you well and hope you find the happiness you seek."

He stiffened his spine. "Very well. I can take no for an answer. But I'm sure after you reconsider things, Wilhemina, you'll come crawling back. Your friend Rafe Bodine is a scalp collector, and I don't understand why you would associate with someone . . ."

Thomas continued babbling about scalps all the way down the slippery steps, and Willy, who had no earthly idea what he was talking about, watched in alarm as he nearly fell on his face before righting himself. Finally she closed the door behind him. And on the relationship they had once shared.

The confrontation had exhausted her, and she wanted nothing more than to go to her room and to bed. Lately she couldn't seem to get enough rest. Emma had explained it was because the baby sapped so much of her strength. But she knew it would be rude not to thank Emma and Rafe for their kindness in inviting Thomas to dinner this evening. After all, they thought they were doing her a favor. Most likely they didn't think so now, after spending an entire evening with the man.

Returning to the parlor, Willy noted that Emma and Rafe were gone, and a sick feeling of dread formed quickly in the pit of her stomach. Ethan waited, pacing the room like a predator on the prowl.

She supposed she was his prey.

Ethan's look was feral when he spoke. "You thought to keep it from me, didn't you, Willy? Thought I'd be too stupid to guess."

She blanched, reaching for the arm of the sofa.

He knew.

Ethan knew about the baby. But she opted to brazen it out just in case she was wrong.

"If you're speaking about Thomas, Ethan, then I've got nothing to say. My association with him is none of your business. I am an unmarried woman, and whom I associate with is nobody's business but mine and the gentleman's in question."

The mention of Thomas had the power to distract Ethan momentarily, and his face reddened in anger. "What you see in that lily-livered bastard is beyond me."

"The genus *Lilium* does not have a liver, and you are the only bastard that I know, Ethan Bodine. Now, if you will excuse me, it's late and I'm going to bed." She turned to leave, had taken three steps and nearly made it through the wide double doors, when Ethan's next words halted her in midstride, chilling her to the bone.

"You're pregnant, aren't you, Willy? You're pregnant and you're carrying my child?" The questions came out as ringing accusations, reverberating like clanging cymbals as they banged against the walls of her mind and heart.

Taught by her aunts and father to always own up to the truth, even if it was painful, she stiffened her spine and turned back to face him. "And what if I am? This has nothing to do with you."

His mouth dropped open in disbelief. "You saying this ain't my kid?"

"No. It's definitely your child." She chose to ignore the brief flash of pleasure covering his face. He didn't love her. They had no future because of that. And she could find no solace in his joy, only bitter sadness. "What I'm saying, Ethan, is that although you may have planted the seed for this child, I will be the one to nurture it, feel it grow, bring it to life, and watch it blossom.

"This is my child, and has nothing to do with you beyond an accident of nature during a very passionate moment between us."

Rage replaced pleasure. "Goddamn it, Willy! Don't you be spouting off all that horticultural crap about seeds and blossoming. This is my baby we're talking about. Not some damn plant."

"No, Ethan! That's where you're wrong. This is my baby. We're not married, and as such the child belongs to me."

"Then by God we'll get hitched and pronto."

Her heart soared, but only briefly, for she knew it was the child he wanted and not her. She wondered at the irony of receiving two marriage proposals in one day and not being able to accept either one of them. Fate was indeed cruel.

"I'm afraid that's not possible. I won't marry just for the sake of the child. I thought I could, but—"

"You were going to marry Fullerton and allow that pissant bastard to raise my son? A Bodine raised by a horticulturist!" He shook his head, anger and hurt making his words bitter.

"Jesus! You're just like all the rest of the women I've known. Liars. Conniving, self-serving . . . Why, you're no better than Lorna Mae Murray."

His words pricked her heart like a thousand sharp needles. "Think what you like. You have in the past, as I recall." The barb made him whiten. "I'll do whatever is best for my child . . . my *daughter,*" she added to annoy him, and she succeeded. His mustache was twitching.

"Now good night, Ethan. I have nothing further to say on the subject." Running from the room before his senses had a chance to return and he could chase after her, she hurried upstairs to her room.

Tomorrow would be soon enough to face another verbal battle with Ethan. Tonight she would sleep. If she could.

Ethan wasn't the least bit tired. What he was was foxed. Inebriated. Falling-down-on-his-ass drunk.

And he intended to get a whole lot more intoxicated before this night was through.

Willy was pregnant! Had planned to marry Fullerton and raise his child as a plant. A pissant plant just like Fullerton. Goddamn, but it was too much to bear!

He stared at the near empty bottle of whiskey, at the glass in his hand, and threw the expensive crystal goblet angrily at the fireplace, not caring if Rafe or his wife got upset. Upending the bottle, he finished it off in one swallow, then wiped his mouth with the sleeve of Rafe's expensive suit jacket. He didn't care about that, either.

Ethan decided he'd be damned if he'd allow some conniving, sweet-talking woman to get the best of him again. Willy thought she was done with him, with discussing their child and their marriage, but he wasn't. Not by a long shot.

He intended to have it out with her, once and for all. He intended to convince the stubborn, mule-headed woman that the only reasonable, the only sensible, thing she could do was to marry him and give the baby his name.

After all, it was his baby. She'd admitted as much. And it was obvious that she wasn't going to marry the pissant now, so she might as well marry him and be done with it.

He loved her, goddamn it! Didn't the foolish woman know? Just because he didn't make flowery speeches like the pissant, she obviously thought he didn't care about her. Just because he didn't call her "my dear" and fawn over her hand like she had chocolate dripping all over it. Just because he didn't simper and smile like some lovesick dandified fool, she thought he didn't care.

But he did care. He cared a great deal. And he was going to convince her of that, or there'd be hell to pay for the both of them.

Chapter Nineteen

"WILLY! WILLY, COME BACK HERE! WE'RE NOT done hashing this mess out yet."

Ethan's shouts as he staggered drunkenly up the stairs boomed off the walls like cannon fire, bringing a sleeping Wilhemina awake, along with everyone else in the household.

He pounded on the bedroom door with his fist. "Open up this door or I'm going to kick it in. You hear me, Willy? I said open the damn door!"

"Go away," came the sleepy response. "Go to bed and sober up. You're drunk."

"I'm not drunk. And even if I am, who are you to tell me what to do? I'm a goddamn Texas Ranger. I can drink any man, woman, or child under the table any damn time I feel like it. Now open up this door. We ain't done discussing things yet."

"You're going to wake up everyone, Ethan. Keep your voice down."

Ethan nearly fell on his face when the door suddenly

opened and Willy stood there, looking madder than a wet hen. "It's about time you came to your senses, woman. Now move aside and let me in."

"Go away. You're drunk, and I'll not discuss things with you in your present intoxicated condition."

"Get out of my way, woman. I'm warning you."

She folded her arms across her chest and shook her head defiantly. "No! I will not. Now go to bed."

"I intend to do just that." With one fell swoop, he scooped her into his arms and began to carry her toward the bed. "It's time we got a few things straight about who's going to wear the pants in this family once we're married."

"I'm never going to marry you, Ethan Bodine!" Willy screamed at the top of her lungs. "Put me down! Put me down at once!"

Hearing the loud commotion, Rafe ran into the room to find Willy slung over his brother's shoulder, Ethan's hand resting on her backside, as he staggered toward the large tester bed. "Ethan! Put that woman down. What the hell do you think you're doing? Are you crazy, you dumb son of a bitch?"

Emma, following close on Rafe's heels, gasped at the sight before her. "Put Willy down at once, you stupid cowboy, before you injure her. Rafe, make him stop."

"How come Uncle Ethan's holding Miss Wilhemina over his shoulder, Mama?"

All heads turned to find David standing in the hallway, the other children stacked at his back, trying to peer over his shoulder at the happenings in the guest bedroom.

"You children get back to bed!" Rafe shouted, his voice brooking no refusal. "I mean now. Get moving."

Knowing the wisdom of retreat, Daniel yanked his younger brother by the pajama top and pulled him back and out the door; Miriam and Miranda, wide-eyed at the goings-on, followed suit, shutting the door behind them.

"There's no need to take out your anger on the children, Rafe. It's your brother who's causing all of the trouble here." Emma stared daggers at her brother-in-law, who still had Willy hoisted over his shoulder and who didn't look the least bit inclined to comply with everyone's wishes that he put her down.

Annoyed that he was now the target of his wife's wrath, Rafe took a menacing step toward his brother. "Unhand the woman, Ethan, or I'm going to beat the living crap outta you. You hear me?"

Ethan swayed on unsteady feet, and Willy screamed, looking pleadingly at Rafe for help.

"You can try, little brother, but I wouldn't advise it. You know you can't beat me. Remember when we were kids and I forced you to eat that stick of poison oak? Ha! You had sores all over your mouth for a month."

Apparently Rafe remembered quite well, because his fists were balled and ready for action.

Emma noted her husband's state and said, "Stop this! Stop this at once! I'll have no fighting within my house. Now put Willy down this instant, Ethan Bodine, or I'll crack you over the head with that fireplace poker and put you out of your misery once and for all."

Ethan stared at his sister-in-law's furious expression, then at the poker propped near the marble hearth, and decided through his alcohol-induced haze that she meant business. He moved back to the bed and gently lowered Wilhemina onto the mattress.

"Damn you for a fool, Ethan!" Wilhemina shouted, and immediately jumped up and began pummeling his back with her fists.

"Now, Willy darlin'," he cajoled in a drunken slur, trying to grab hold of her wrists and falling onto the bed in the process.

"What the hell is all this about, anyway?" Rafe asked. "Will somebody please tell me what's going on? And why we're all shouting at one another in the middle of the night?"

Emmaline looked for confirmation at Wilhemina, who nodded. "Willy's with child, Rafe. She's going to have your brother's baby, and I suspect that he's just put two and two together. Is that correct, Wilhemina?" The embarrassed woman nodded, then covered her face with her hands and began to sob. Emma stepped forward to comfort her, casting her brother-in-law a dangerous look.

"She won't marry me, Rafe. I asked her to marry me and she won't. She was going to marry that pissant Fullerton, and pass my kid off as his. Imagine—a Bodine being raised by a horticulturist. What would Pa say?" Ethan held his head between his hands, as if the possibility were just too awful to contemplate.

"He'd say you're a goddamn stupid fool, Ethan! That's what he'd say."

"I know it." There was a wealth of regret in those words.

Rafe's voice gentled as he addressed the distraught woman. "Willy, is it true? Are you going to have Ethan's child?"

She sniffed a few times and nodded. "Yes. But it's . . . it's my child, not . . . not his. He was only the instrument of its conception."

Ethan stiffened in outrage. "Well, you sure as hell didn't mind that instrument when it was—"

"Hold on, Ethan! I think we get the point," Rafe ordered, and his brother quieted.

"I'll not marry a man who doesn't love me. It's as simple as that."

Ethan's head snapped up. "But I do love you, Willy darlin'. Truly I do."

Wilhemina listened to Ethan's drunken avowal, and her eyes flashed fire. "You most certainly do not! You're only saying you do because of the child. I'm not a total idiot, Ethan. You've never so much as even hinted that you cared about me. And now that I've confessed to being pregnant, you're suddenly madly in love with me. Well, I'm not buying such drivel."

"But it's true, Willy. I swear it's true." He lunged for her, but Emma held out her arm and forced her hand into Ethan's chest, halting his advance.

"Stop right there, Bodine!" Her look was as feral as a mother hen protecting her chicks. "I won't have you accosting this woman under my roof. Now get out of here. You've done enough damage for one evening. Go to bed."

"But—" He held out his hands beseechingly. "She wants to raise my son as a plant. You don't understand, Emma. Willy wants to raise my boy as a pissant plant."

Rafe gazed at Willy and could see she was just as confused as he by the statement. "Come on, big brother. Let's go down to the kitchen and get some coffee. We can work all this out after you've sobered up some."

Ethan allowed Rafe to haul him to his feet, then said, "I ain't drunk, Rafe. You've seen me when I'm drunk and you know I'm as sober as you. Christ. We hunted Indians drunker'n this. We cleaned out swarms of Mexican bandits on a few bottles of mescal."

Rafe made the appropriate responses as he guided and cajoled his brother out the door. Once they were gone, Emma drew Willy into her arms. "I know you're upset right now, Willy. You've had a rough evening. But trust me when I say that things will look much better in the morning."

Blowing her nose on her handkerchief, Willy said, "Everything's such a mess, Emma. I thought I could marry Thomas and give my child a name, but I realized tonight that I could never do that. I don't love Thomas Fullerton; I love Ethan. And I can't marry him because he doesn't love me back."

"He says he does, Willy. And I'm inclined to believe him, despite his drunkenness and general stupidity in dealing with women."

"It's because of the baby that he says he does. Don't you see—it's the child he wants, not me. Oh sure, he'll take me to get to the child. But it's a son that he covets. Sons are very big in the Bodine family."

"I know your fears, Willy. I had similar ones myself when I discovered I was pregnant with Rafe's child. I didn't tell him about the baby until after we were married, though I'm sure he suspected.

"Women want assurances, need to feel that they're loved for themselves, and your concerns are natural and just. But I think you need to give Ethan a chance."

"But if I marry him, how will I ever know if he truly loves me?"

Emmaline suspected—in fact, she was pretty darn certain—that Ethan was very much in love with Wilhemina. She felt it in her gut, and Rafe always said you should go with your gut instincts when you think you're right. And women's intuition wasn't half bad, either.

"How do any of us really know if we're loved, Willy? Saying the words doesn't make it so. It's the way a person acts toward you, treats you, respects you. The way his eyes follow you when he doesn't think you're looking. The way he gets all miserable when you aren't around. The feeling of joy your heart gets when you've been apart and you see each other again."

"I'm so confused."

"You don't have to make any decisions right now. Go back to sleep and think on things for a while. Your heart will tell you the right thing to do. And it may take time to do it."

Wilhemina squeezed her friend's hand. "Thank you for caring, Emma. You've been a wonderful friend. I've felt so alone without my aunts."

At the mention of the aunts, Emma's cheeks filled with color. "That reminds me—a telegram came for you just before dinner. I believe it's from your aunts. It completely slipped my mind. Wait one second and I'll fetch it." She disappeared and was back a moment later, holding an envelope and looking very contrite. "Please forgive me."

"Don't be silly. I just hope nothing's wrong. I feel so guilty about leaving those two dear souls all alone for so long." Willy ripped open the missive and read it, and her face paled.

"What is it? What's wrong?"

"I must leave at once. Rufus Bowers has begun foreclosure proceedings on my aunts' home. They must be in a terrible state." She handed Emma the missive.

"I'll not allow you to travel across country by yourself, Willy, especially in your condition. Leave Rufus Bowers to me. I'll contact my lawyer in the morning and have him take care of everything. You're not to worry."

"But I can't allow you to do that. I appreciate your kindness, but—"

"It's only money, Willy, and I've got plenty to spare. Now hush. As soon as I can find someone to take over the charity ball for the orphanage, and make the arrangements for the children to travel, we'll leave for Texas."

"You're coming, too? You're bringing the children and traveling to Texas when Ethan brings Rafe back to stand trial?"

"Of course. You didn't think I'd allow my husband to face such an ordeal by himself. He'll need his family by his side at such a difficult time. And I couldn't bear to be apart from him for any length of time."

"Rafe's lucky to have you."

"We're lucky to have each other, as you and Ethan will soon discover."

Wilhemina prayed with all her might that the optimistic woman was right.

The following afternoon, Ethan paused in the doorway of the library to find Wilhemina reading quietly by the crackling fire. She was curled up with a book, totally absorbed in the story.

The firelight played across her face and hair, her cheeks were flushed pink from the heat, and Ethan's gut knotted at the thought of how much he loved her, wanted to be with her.

He'd really made a mess of things last night, but now he aimed to rectify that, no matter how low he had to crawl to do it. And from what Rafe had said about his behavior—most of which he didn't remember too clearly—that was going to be pretty low.

The flowers he held behind his back jiggled nervously as he cleared his throat and entered the room.

Wilhemina looked up and a knot of apprehension formed in her stomach. She didn't feel like sparring with the obstinate man this early in the day. Determined to appear indifferent—though she felt anything but—she ignored him and went back to reading her book, hoping he would just go away and leave her alone.

"Good afternoon, Willy. Hope I'm not disturbing you."

She didn't meet his gaze, and her voice was as cold as the weather. "Actually, you are. I'm quite busy at the moment, as you can see."

He moved forward to where she was seated and squatted beside her. "I came to apologize for my rude behavior last night, Willy darlin'. I hope you'll forgive me."

Astonished by the apology and contriteness in his voice, she turned to find a lovely bouquet of pink roses being thrust in her direction. "These are for you. To say how sorry I am about what happened."

Touched by the gesture, she accepted them, inhaling deeply of their sweet fragrance. No man, including Thomas, who would never have spent a dime on such a frivolous gesture, had ever gifted her with flowers. "Thank you. They're exquisite. But you shouldn't have spent your money so extravagantly. I know how dear hothouse roses are this time of year."

"I tried to buy a bouquet of morning glories, but they didn't have any."

Swallowing the lump in her throat, she willed her heart to stop beating so quickly. Morning glories meant hearth, home, and roots to a footloose man like Ethan, and Willy didn't dare let herself believe that he truly wanted to settle down and make a home with her.

If only he loved me for myself, and not just the child.

"I know I acted like a damn fool last night. I don't re-member everything, but my brother was only too happy to relate most of it." He grinned sheepishly. "Rafe always did like getting one up on me.

"Anyway, I guess I was just upset about the baby and all and drank too much. And then there was the matter of that damn Fullerton—"

She grasped his arm before he could go off on that tangent again. "Why don't we just forget it ever happened? We both said things we didn't mean, and I want us to re-main friends."

He took the roses from her hand, laid them aside, and drew her into his embrace. "I want to be more than your friend, Willy. I want us to be married. And I want to be a proper husband to you and a father to the baby."

Patting his cheek, she brushed her thumb across his soft mustache, wishing with all her heart that she could be-lieve him. "I'm afraid that I'm not ready to make such an important decision just yet, Ethan. I feel very confused right now about a great many things. I have this baby to consider—"

"*Our* baby," he interrupted, and she smiled softly.

"Our baby to consider. And I want to make the right decision. I can't afford to make any mistakes."

"Marrying me won't be a mistake, Willy. I promise you that."

"But you've always led me to believe that marriage wasn't right for you, Ethan. I know how much you distrust women, and—"

"But that doesn't mean I don't love you, Willy."

"Love and trust go hand in hand. I can't marry a man who says he loves me, then turns around and accuses me of deceiving him at the drop of a hat."

He cringed at the reminder of what he'd said last night in a moment of anger and wished he could take it all back. Willy was nothing like Lorna Mae. Nothing at all.

"Just because you've been hurt in the past, Ethan, doesn't mean that you should mistrust every woman you come in contact with."

"A man can't be perfect."

"No, he can't. And neither can a woman. But a woman can love a man who has flaws, and vice versa, if there's trust between them. Without trust, they have nothing to build a relationship on."

"You love me, Willy. I know you do. I can see it in your eyes every time you look at me."

"Yes, I do. I love you very much. But I'm still not going to accept your offer of marriage."

"I knew you did." His euphoric state lasted but a moment, his grin melting quickly into a frown. "But if that's so, then why won't you marry me?"

"Because I'm not convinced of your feelings for me, and until I am, I won't."

"But I told you I loved you, Willy. Let's go upstairs to bed and I'll show you how much."

"As tempting as that sounds, Ethan"—and it did sound tempting, because her body missed Ethan as much as her heart—"I don't think making love is going to prove anything. You wanted to make love to me when you hardly knew me. And I confess to feeling the same way about you."

He brushed her hair with his lips. "I think of little else except burying myself deep inside you, darlin'. Hearing you make those kittenish little mewling sounds when you're about to reach your climax. Jesus! I'm getting hard just thinking about it."

Heat that had absolutely nothing to do with the fire in the hearth infused every pore of Wilhemina's body. She bit the inside of her cheek to retain her equilibrium. "I need more than just the commitment of your body, Ethan. I need to know that I have your heart as well."

Frustration filled his voice. "Goddamn it, Willy! How the hell am I supposed to show you that? You want me to cut it out and give it to you on a silver platter?"

She kissed him softly on the lips, then stood. "That'll be a start, *darlin'*," she mimicked, her eyes twinkling. "Now, I've promised the children a story. I must go upstairs to the nursery."

"But . . . but what about us? What about us getting married and all that?"

She paused at the door and looked back. "It's a long way to Texas, Ethan. You'll have plenty of time to convince me of your sincerity." She blew him a kiss and was gone.

Ethan stared into the fire and felt totally out of his element for the first time in his life. For all his reputation as a ladies' man, he'd been a dismal failure with the opposite sex as far as lasting relationships went.

He knew far more than the average man about tracking and shooting, drinking and whoring. He'd excelled in every one of those things. He could shoot the eye out of a buffalo at two hundred yards, could catch a fish from a running stream with his bare hands, could wrestle a mountain lion to the ground the same way.

But wooing a woman, making her feel loved and wanted . . . That was another thing entirely, and something he was totally inadequate at.

How the hell am I going to convince a smart woman like Willy that I'm in love with her?

He needed help. And from the opposite sex. But Emma had already made it clear that she wanted nothing more to do with him. Rafe had warned him to stay out of her way. And that sounded like sound advice to Ethan. Emma Bodine was a firecracker beneath that prim and proper facade. Redheaded women were known to have a temper, and she was no exception.

Miriam and Miranda were females, but they were too little to know about such matters. That left only one woman he could think of who might be willing to help him. And though it galled him no end to ask her for help, Loretta Goodman was his only option.

Like Willy said: it was a long way to Texas. And during the time it took to reach Misery, he intended to woo him a wife and gain him a son to boot.

Chapter Twenty

Misery, Texas, March 1880

Tempers and nerves were stretched parchment thin by the time the Bodines and Wilhemina reached the town of Misery a few weeks later.

Rafe was understandably nervous about the prospect of going to trial and facing the murder charges against him. There was a good possibility he would hang.

In addition to her fear for her husband, Emmaline's pregnancy had already shortened her temper and heightened her emotions to the boiling point, and she was frequently bursting into tears at the drop of a hat. The ordeal of being cooped up on the train with five young children had frazzled what was left of her nerves, and everyone had given her a wide berth.

Ethan had made little progress convincing Willy to marry him. He'd said and done everything Loretta had advised, even resorting to begging on occasion, and still she refused to accept his proposal. This standoff had put the

Ranger in a foul mood, but he was determined to have his way come hell or high water and had no intention of giving up.

Wilhemina had been the picture of serenity on the train ride to Texas, helping Emma with the children, trying to lift Rafe's spirits about the upcoming trial, avoiding Ethan's advances as best she could—though the man had attempted every type of seduction known, and a few he'd invented himself.

Three nights ago he had attempted to get her rip-roaring drunk by plying her with champagne and chocolates and luring her into his sleeping compartment. This had resulted in her vomiting all over his bed, then passing out cold.

But rather than be put off by her behavior, Ethan had only become more solicitous of her. His fawning behavior had come straight from the Thomas Fullerton Instructional Guide, and it was driving Wilhemina quite insane. If Ethan asked her one more time how she was feeling, if she needed anything, she thought she'd have to haul off and smack him alongside the head.

Ben Bodine had sent his ranch foreman, Woody Hamlin, with a buckboard to fetch them from the train station. He was a rangy cowboy with a salt-and-pepper beard and a face mapped with age lines that looked tough and tanned as shoe leather. Wilhemina suspected from the way he limped that he had earned his nickname the hard way.

It was a bright, sunny day, but the air still held the nip of winter, as spring had not quite made an appearance as yet. The ground, muddy from a previous rain, made the going slow in the old buckboard, despite Woody's sure handling of it.

"Mr. Bodine and the missus sure are excited about seeing you boys again," the foreman informed Rafe and Ethan. "Mr. B. said it was going to be good having his boys home again."

"Yeah. Too bad it won't be permanent," Rafe said dispiritedly, then wrapped his arm about his wife's shoulder when he saw she'd begun to cry again. "Hush, darlin'. I'm sorry I made such a stupid remark."

"It's just like you to speak without thinking, little brother. I'm learning how to treat my woman right. Ain't that so, Willy darlin'?" Ethan hugged Wilhemina, seated next to him in the wagon. "Can I get you anything? Are you warm enough? Do you need a blanket?"

The annoyed woman gritted her teeth. "I'm fine. Just enjoying the ride and the fresh air. And the quiet."

Emmaline had let it slip that Loretta was to blame for Ethan's drastic change of behavior, and Wilhemina was relieved that the well-meaning woman had decided to stay behind in Boston, because Willy would have been sorely tempted to strangle her for interfering.

Maybe Loretta found Milton Jefferson's solicitous behavior endearing, but Wilhemina definitely did not think the same of Ethan's. She wanted the surly Ranger back the way he was: rude, fun loving, and insensitive. This new and improved version was killing her with kindness.

Be careful what you wish for, Wilhemina; you might get it. . . .

Wasn't that the awful truth? she thought, wishing she had heeded her aunts' sound advice long ago.

"Miss Wilhemina?" Miranda tugged impatiently on her coat sleeve, and Willy gazed fondly at the lovely child.

"Yes, honey?"

"Is it true you're gonna have a baby?"

"Miranda!" Emma chastised, offering an apologetic smile to the distraught woman. "Mind your manners and say you're sorry."

The child did neither. Instead she folded her arms across her chest and sank down in her seat, trying to avoid her parent's stern glare.

Willy's cheeks glowed bright red, and she didn't know quite how to answer the girl. Ethan was pinning her with a look that said "I told you to marry me," and the other children had turned to stare, waiting for her reply.

"Yes. I'm going to have a baby," she finally answered. "It's not necessary for a woman to be married to have a baby, but it's preferred."

"How come you don't marry Uncle Ethan?" David wanted to know. "I heard him ask you a thousand times."

Ethan leaned toward her. "Yes, Willy, how come?"

Willy's eyes narrowed, for she wouldn't put it past Ethan to have coerced the children into coming to his aid, and she had no intention of giving in, no matter how embarrassing the situation became.

And she suspected that when she reached the ranch, and had to face Ethan's family, the situation was going to be very embarrassing indeed.

* * *

Wilhemina wasn't wrong. As soon as she stepped through the front door and into the rustic but attractively furnished Bodine home, the patriarch, Ethan's father, descended on her.

Ben Bodine was a handsome man, with white hair and the same startling blue eyes as his sons, and it was easy to see where the boys got their rugged good looks. Unfortunately he was wearing the same look of determination that she'd seen on Ethan's face countless times, and she hid her groan behind a smile.

"My boy tells me you're pregnant. If that's so, then I guess Lavinia will be planning a wedding soon. Can't have my grandchild being born without a proper name. And Bodine is a name any child would be proud to have. Any woman, too, for that matter."

Willy unbuttoned her red wool coat and draped it on the brass coatrack by the door. "Are you always this direct, Mr. Bodine? I haven't even had a chance to say how nice it is to finally meet all of you."

Lavinia Bodine came forward, casting her husband a censorious look; he took the hint and departed, but without an apology.

"He's as blunt as a dull knife blade most of the time, dear. But pay him no mind. You'll get used to his blustering ways soon enough. Now come in and sit down. I've made hot tea and oatmeal cakes." She ushered Willy into the parlor, complete with comfortable leather chairs and a cowhide hanging over the fireplace.

"Thank you, Mrs. Bodine." Willy found herself alone with the woman. "Where has everyone gone?"

"It's Lavinia, dear. And most everyone's gone upstairs to rest. The children were dead tired, as was sweet Emmaline. Rafe and Ethan have gone off to talk things out with their father. He'll give them a proper grilling before he sets his teeth into you again."

Willy warmed to the kind woman instantly and returned her smile. "I can see where Ethan gets his bossy manner."

"It's the truth. Those boys are just like their father. Ethan especially, though he'd never admit to such a thing. He and Ben have butted heads for years over just about everything imaginable."

"So Ethan said."

"Ben's been worried to death about Rafe. I can't tell you how relieved we all were when we received Ethan's telegram from Boston, informing us of Rafe's whereabouts and marriage.

"I thought Ben would burst at the seams when he learned about the five children, and another on the way. And now we find out that you're with child, too." She squeezed Wilhemina's hand affectionately. "We've been dying for grandchildren, so you must forgive our enthusiasm."

"I haven't decided to marry Ethan yet, Lavinia."

Lavinia's knowing smile lit up her face. "Oh, I think you have, dear. You're just going to make him sweat a bit before you accept. I think that's a perfectly logical thing to do. Ethan has never been known for his tact when it comes to women, and I'm sure he's led you a merry chase since you've met."

"The man is utterly impossible. One minute accusing me of all kinds of vile things, the next fawning over me until I can't stand it." Her expression turned mutinous. "I may decide not to marry him just to escape his confounded solicitous manner."

Lavinia chuckled, refilling their teacups. "I never thought I'd live to see the day Ethan would woo a woman so . . ."

"Annoyingly?"

"Completely. Though I'm sure he's overdone it. That man doesn't know how to do anything halfway once he sets his mind to it. His brother Travis is of a similar nature."

"Will Travis be here soon? I've heard so much about him. I can't wait to meet the other 'little brother' that Ethan speaks so fondly of."

"Travis is taking care of some paperwork having to do with Rafe's trial. He's hoping to post bail, so Rafe won't have to spend time in jail. He'll be here in time for supper."

The young woman's dark eyes clouded with concern. "Emma will be devastated if Rafe goes to jail."

Lavinia nodded. "But she's strong. I could sense that right off. Any woman who'd do what she did to help her man is made of strong stuff. She'll be all right. And she'll have us to help her with the children."

"I'm afraid I can't stay long, Lavinia. I must return to Justiceburg. My aunts are expecting me, and I've been gone an awfully long time." The last letter she'd received from them just before leaving Boston had been downright maudlin, if not frantic. Birdy had expressed fears of impending death, while Eunice had complained unendingly of her rheumatism. Willy suspected that their hints were a direct message for her to come home.

"Well, we'll cherish the time we have with you, dear, and hope you'll come back and visit whenever you can." She patted her hand. "Justiceburg's not all that far from here."

"I suspect it's much closer than the distance separating me and Ethan."

"Honey, Bodine men are a loud, insensitive bunch of braggarts, and it's a miracle that any of us women fell in love with them to begin with. But they're loyal and loving, and I don't know what I'd have done if my Ben hadn't come along when he did. The man's impossible, but I can't live without him, and I suspect you'll find the same's true of Ethan.

"Once they burrow their way into your heart, there's just no getting rid of them."

"Kind of like tics?" Wilhemina grinned, and Lavinia started to laugh, then the two women settled in to spend another hour getting acquainted.

Outside, the Bodine men gathered on the wide front porch. The tip of Ben's cigarette glowed in the approaching darkness, while Rafe paced the boards nervously and listened to his father vent his frustration over recent events.

"You boys have really messed things up this time," Ben told his two eldest sons, shaking his head in disgust. "Rafe's wanted for murder, and you've gone and gotten some young woman pregnant, Ethan—a woman who obviously wants nothing to do with marrying you."

Ethan's eyes narrowed. "Don't you discuss my future wife in that tone, Pa. Willy will marry me. It's just going to take a little more time to convince her, that's all."

"Ha! The child will be in grade school before that happens. You finally get around to giving me a grandchild, and you ain't even married to the child's mother."

Sensing his brother was about to explode, Rafe stepped between the two men. Refereeing arguments between his father and brother had become second nature to Rafe over the years. "I hate butting in on your stupid argument, but I think there're more important things to discuss right now. Like how I'm gonna save my neck from being stretched by the hangman's rope."

Ben turned on his middle son. "It's a fine thing to be worrying about it now, boy. You shoulda thought about that before riding off half-cocked to murder that scum Bobby Slaughter. I thought I taught you better than that."

"It wasn't your wife, Pa, who was butchered and left to die a cruel, senseless death. Think if it had been Ma."

Noting Rafe's anguish, Ben encircled his son's shoulder in a comforting gesture. "I'm sorry, boy. I never told you how sorry I was about little Ellie. She was a sweet girl, and I know you only did what you thought best. But damn it, Rafe! You've got yourself into quite a mess. I ain't so sure Travis is going to be able to help you."

"He'll do his best. Travis is smart." Ethan glared at the old man, daring him to deny it.

"True. But the boy's not had a lot of experience with murder trials and such. Then again, I wouldn't trust no fancy eastern lawyer to defend Rafe."

"Just don't let on to Emma that you're worried. She's got enough on her mind, what with the kids and the new baby coming. I don't want her making herself ill worrying over me."

"And don't be grilling Willy about her marrying me, either, Pa. She don't need that kind of pressure. I'm giving her enough of it already."

Ben ignored his sons' advice, asking Ethan, "How come you ain't smoking, boy? You always had a real fondness for cigars."

Embarrassed to reveal the reason he'd given them up, because he knew damn well what his father's reaction would be, Ethan hemmed and hawed, finally replying, "I quit smoking them. They made Willy sick to her stomach."

The response was predictable: Ben howled with laughter and slapped his knee. "Damn, but that woman's turned you into a soft son of a bitch."

Rafe stepped in front of his brother again and sighed at the old man's lack of tact and ability to rile Ethan. "You know damn well, Pa, that Lavinia don't allow you to smoke in the house, which is why you're out here doing it now. So don't be taking Ethan to task for the same thing."

His father had the grace to blush. "How long you known about that?"

Ethan and Rafe exchanged grins, then said in unison, "About five years."

Ben smiled sheepishly, then said to Ethan, "Well, at least your brother and me had the good sense to marry our women. We didn't let them lead us around by our tails."

Rafe rolled his eyes at that, grateful his father didn't know the whole of his relationship with Emma.

"Willy thinks I only want to marry her because of the baby. And it's just not true."

"You've never made no secret about hating being tied down. Guess it's coming back to haunt you now, son."

"Well, if you want another grandchild, Pa, then I guess you'd better start singing my praises instead of belittling me in front of Willy. No doubt you've already scared her off by your domineering, opinionated questions."

Ben threw back his head and howled, and even Rafe joined in the laughter, causing Ethan to stiffen in anger.

"What the hell's so damn funny? Why are you two baying like a couple of wolves?"

"Because, son, no woman who joins up with a Texas Ranger pretending to be a damn bounty hunter when she's really a . . . a horticulturist"—he started laughing again until his eyes watered—"is going to be scared of an old man like me."

"Tell 'im, Rafe."

"Pa's right. That's woman's got more sand in her veins than the whole Mojave Desert. I think she's leading you on, and you don't even realize it."

"What?" Ethan's face paled slightly at the possibility.

"I bet she's in there now telling Vin all about how much she loves you and can't wait to hitch up with you.

She's just going to make your life miserable until she decides to give in. Don't you know nothing about women, boy?"

Rafe and his father continued to laugh at Ethan's expense, but Ethan wasn't finding this latest revelation the least bit funny. And he aimed to do something about it.

Dinner that evening was a lively affair. Travis arrived shortly after sundown, and the reunion of the three brothers was heartwarming and wonderful. And, of course, full of the usual teasing that was known to go on between siblings.

"So, Travis," Ethan said around a bite of crispy fried chicken, "did you ever lose your virginity? I can't seem to recall. . . ."

Rafe chuckled. "You should recall, Ethan. After you got Travis liquored up, he puked all over that whore you paid to teach him how to do the deed right. If I remember correctly, it ended up costing you double."

Emmaline and Wilhemina exchanged indulgent looks, then Emma cleared her throat and said, "I don't think this is a proper discussion for the dinner table, do you, Rafe?" She cast Lavinia an embarrassed smile.

"The kids are in bed, Emma, so what's the harm?"

Wilhemina clasped her friend's arm before she could respond and whispered, "Let them have their fun, Emma. It may be a while before they get to again."

Emmaline's eyes clouded in pain, but she saw the wisdom in her friend's words and tried to join in the lighthearted banter, though her heart was anything but light.

"Rafe, you'll have to tell your brothers about the incident at the whorehouse, when I told those whores you were riddled with disease and your privates were about to fall off."

Rafe's face reddened, and Ben let loose with a loud guffaw. "I knew I liked you, little gal, from the moment I laid eyes on you. Any woman who can best my son is all right with me." Though he was speaking to Emma, he winked at Wilhemina, who blushed in response.

"So, Ethan, what kind of stories do you and your lovely lady have to share?" Travis prodded, sipping his wine, his blue eyes twinkling. "I'd like to hear the one about how Willy saved you from a vicious beating at the hands of the Murray brothers while using her umbrella as a weapon." He grinned as Ethan's eyes widened in surprise, then shifted to Willy.

"I see you've been telling tales again, woman. You should know better than to tell my brothers anything. They always use it against me."

"Travis and I were merely getting acquainted. And I only told the absolute truth, didn't I, Travis?"

Wilhemina turned to her hostess, who was smiling happily at the warm affection being bandied about. "This fried chicken is absolutely heavenly, Lavinia. Travis tells me that you won a blue ribbon for it at the fair last summer. I'd love to have the recipe. I'm not all that fond of cooking, but if I could cook as good as you, then maybe I'd like doing it much better."

"You do some things real well, Willy," Ethan said suggestively, and the color rose to her cheeks once again.

"Of course, dear," Lavinia said, directing a disapproving look at her stepson. "I'll teach both you and Emma how to make this dish."

This produced a loud guffaw from Rafe. "Don't bother showing Emma, Lavinia. She can't cook worth a damn. Why, if it wasn't for me fixing meals on the trail, those kids would have starved to death. Ain't that right, darlin'?"

"Hmph!" Emma stiffened in her seat. "I've never professed to be domestic. But I did hire a wonderful French chef who handles the cooking chores quite adequately. You've got no cause to complain . . . Rafferty." She watched her husband's eyes narrow at the use of the hated name—a name only his deceased mother had dared use.

"How's that lawyering been going, Travis?" Ethan asked, leaning back in his chair, feeling replete in all areas save one. "Guess you must keep pretty busy."

"I handle mostly civil complaints and such. Rafe's criminal defense . . ." At Emma's gasp, he stopped, patting her hand apologetically. "I'm sorry, Emma. I didn't mean to bring up unpleasantness during dinner."

She waved off the apology. "It's all right. I need to get used to the fact that Rafe will be standing trial soon."

"I'm afraid you'll need to get used to a bit more than that."

"Travis," Rafe said with a note of warning.

"What is it? What are you keeping from me?"

"Rafe's bail has been denied, Emma. I'm afraid Ethan's going to have to take him into custody tomorrow. He'll have to remain in jail until the trial."

"Oh, dear Lord!" Lavinia said, her hand flying to her throat. "But we were so sure . . ."

The young lawyer banged on the table, nearly upsetting his wineglass. "I told that fool Barkley that Rafe wasn't going to run, that he was a married man now and had responsibilities. But I had a hell of a time convincing him of that because of Rafe's previous flight. I'm afraid Judge Barkley has denied bail."

"I thought Barkley was retiring," Ethan said. "Why the hell is that old codger still sitting on the bench? He should be looking after that sour-pussed daughter of his instead of—" He stopped at the deadly look Travis shot him at the mention of Hannah Barkley, the woman he was once engaged to.

"The judge is retiring. But his replacement hasn't arrived yet, and he's filling in until he does. You know how slow the justice system works out here, Ethan. There was nothing I could do." He turned to Emma and Rafe. "I'm sorry. I did my best."

"We know you did, Travis. Rafe tells me you're a fine lawyer with a good head on your shoulders. I know my husband is in good hands with you handling his defense."

"Who's prosecuting the case?" Ben asked. "Anyone we know?"

Travis nodded. "Most likely Will McGrath."

Ethan snickered in contempt. "You'll be able to outwit him, Travis. See if you don't."

Rafe pushed back his chair. "Well, seeing as how this is my last night as a free man, I'd like to spend it with my wife. So, if you'll excuse us, we'll be turning in now.

"Emma?" He held out his hand, which she gladly took.

No one made any ribald comments because the couple was retiring so early. The situation for Rafe, his wife, and his family was too depressing to mock. Soon a pall settled over the room, and Travis made his excuses to leave as well.

"I've got an early day tomorrow. I need to get back to town."

"We'll walk you out, son," Ben said, his chair scraping against the floor as he stood. "I'm sure Lavinia will want to give you a big good-night kiss." He winked at his wife. "Ain't that right, Lavinia darlin'?"

The older woman smiled. "I never turn down a chance to kiss a handsome man." Bending down, she bussed Ethan's cheek, then allowed her husband to escort her out the door.

Ethan and Wilhemina were left alone at the big table. "We need to talk, Willy. I'd like to come to your room for a few minutes if that's all right."

At the determined look flashing in his eyes, she swallowed the lump in her throat. "I'm rather tired. . . ."

"I'm not taking no for an answer tonight, Willy, so you might as well agree. I'd hate to make a scene in my parents' home, but I will."

She sighed and rose to her feet. "Very well. But you can only stay for a moment. After all, it's hardly proper for me to entertain a man in my room."

He rolled his eyes. "Woman, we've spent many nights together in each other's company, so I don't think propriety means a rat's ass 'long about now."

Something was different about Ethan. His fawning politeness and forced gentlemanly behavior had apparently come to an end.

It was what I wanted, wasn't it?

But now that she was faced with the Ethan of old— arrogant, stubborn, determined to get his way at any cost— she found that she was terrified.

Chapter Twenty-one

WILHEMINA WAS DETERMINED NOT TO LET HER ANX-
iety show as she led Ethan into the bedroom she'd been as-
signed—his bedroom.

The room reeked of his manly scent, and on the walls
hung mementos and treasures from his childhood—a small
set of elegantly tooled silver spurs, a well-worn pair of
leather chaps, a rifle whose stock held the imprint of a
child's hand.

A photograph of Ethan's mother sat on the maple
nightstand right next to the kerosene lantern, which flick-
ered softly. Patsy Bodine was a pretty woman, though the
years and the harshness of the land hadn't been as kind to
her as her smile had been to others.

She avoided the brass bedstead and took a seat in the
rocker by the hearth, fighting to keep the nervousness she
felt out of her voice. "What is it you wish to speak to me
about, Ethan? I thought we had already discussed things
pretty thoroughly."

He kicked the door closed behind him, and the sound was ominous, final and alarming. His massive presence filled the small room, making the space between them seem nonexistent.

"It seems every member of my family knows you've been playing me for a fool, Willy, except me."

Color filled her cheeks, and she shook her head in denial. "No. I—"

He didn't allow her to continue. "Everyone knows that you love me, Willy, and that you've already made up your mind to marry me. So why have you been playing these games? I've never been a man who liked playing games. I thought you knew that." Resting his hands on the arms of the rocker, he tilted it back until Willy's feet hung suspended in midair and she was forced to look into his passion-filled eyes.

"If you want to play games, darlin', I've thought of one we can play right now."

A familiar yearning filled her, and she could hardly catch her breath at the ardent desire reflected in his eyes. She was trapped. Not only by the position of the rocker, but by her own undeniable feelings of love, her sexual attraction and hunger for this man. "I . . . I haven't been toying with you, Ethan. I've made no secret of my feelings for you."

"No?" There was disbelief in that one word, and he leaned closer until their lips almost touched. "But you've made no secret of your determination not to marry me, either. You wanted me to convince you of my love, Willy, and I've tried. I acted the fool for you. I fawned and scraped and played the gentleman because I thought that was what you wanted. But I think I know now what you really want." His tongue came out to flick over her lips and taste her, and Willy's heart slammed into the back of her chest.

"You want the same thing I do. I can see it in your eyes when you look at me. I can smell the scent of your need when we're in the same room together. I can feel the pull of your desire when we're miles apart.

"Unbutton your dress, Willy. Do it now, and do it fast." His words were like silken steel, soft yet strong and unyielding.

"Ethan . . ." Her heart was hammering so rapidly, she couldn't catch her breath, let alone make her fingers work. "I don't think we should. This isn't going to solve anything." Though she wanted to make love with him. God, how she wanted to!

He took her hand and placed it on the hard length of him, while keeping the rocker tilted back with the other. "Making love is going to solve a great many things, darlin'. One of them is sitting in the palm of your hand." Suddenly the chair rocked forward, and she tumbled headlong into his arms.

He lifted her gently and carried her to bed, covering her mouth with his hungrily before she could utter a protest. "I've never wanted a woman the way I want you, Willy. I love you more than life itself, and if you don't believe me, then you're just plum crazy."

His words filled her heart with joy, but there was still a niggling doubt in the back of her mind—a doubt that wouldn't go away, no matter how much she willed it to. The baby stood between them, and she would never know for sure if it was her or the child that he truly wanted.

"I love you, Ethan. I think I always have."

He stripped off her garments, then quickly shed his own. Worshiping her body with his eyes and lips, he said in an awe-filled voice, "This is my child, Willy. The proof of my love for you." Placing the palms of his hands gently on the swelling mound of her abdomen, he reverently examined every inch of the growing life within her, then trailed lingering kisses over her soft flesh with his lips.

"Ethan . . ." Warm wanting flooded Wilhemina's womanhood, and her breasts grew heavy with need—the same need and desire that punctuated her every rational thought. She drew his mouth to her turgid nipples, urging him to suckle.

Ethan's tongue swirled around and around the dark areolae of her sensitive breasts, then he flicked the ends of both nipples until Wilhemina was forced to grasp the coverlet to keep from flying to the ceiling.

"Oh, God!" Her head lolled back and forth at the glorious sensations he created with his clever mouth and inquisitive fingers.

"It's been too long, darlin'," he said huskily. "A woman's got needs the same as a man, and yours have been denied too long." His palms moved up and down her legs, over the soft flesh of her buttocks, glancing over the damp curls of her femininity, until Wilhemina bucked against them.

"Please, Ethan! You're torturing me." Every inch of her skin was on fire.

He flicked the pulsing bud with his thumb, over and over, sensing her need as acutely as he felt his own. "Tell me what you want, Willy. Tell me now."

She swallowed, and the fever within her raged. "I want you. Only you."

"And do you want to marry me, darlin'? Do you want to spend the rest of your life making love with me?"

"Yes, yes. I do. Now please, please give me release. I need you so badly."

Her admission filled him with relief and satisfaction. He spread her legs wide, inserted his finger deep inside her to make sure she was ready, and felt the glistening proof of her need. Covering her body with his, he plunged his tongue into her mouth as his long shaft slid into her, filling her completely.

With strong, sure strokes he rode her, pumping hard and fast, gentle and slow; over and over he replicated the motion, until she was a writhing mass beneath him.

"Oh! Oh!" came Willy's sharp gasps of anticipation as the tension mounted and her whole body tightened like the taut strings of a finely tuned instrument.

Ethan played her well, lifting her buttocks off the mattress, then plunging himself to the hilt, taking her over the top and into nirvana.

Wilhemina screamed out her climax, and Ethan swallowed her cries with his mouth as he filled her again with his seed.

"You're mine, Willy," he said when he could breathe normally again; droplets of sweat glistened off his forehead and mustache. "Never forget that. Mine, tonight and for always."

She basked in the glow of his lovemaking, felt the warmth of his words, and prayed with all her heart and soul that he was telling her the truth.

A shaft of sunlight shone through the bedroom window, landing on Ethan's face and forcing him into wakefulness. Reaching out to the woman who lay beside him, he encountered only empty space and grew suddenly wide awake.

"Willy?" He glanced around the room but could find no sign of her, no sign that she'd ever been there. The valise she had carted around the countryside was no longer sitting on the chair by the door where she had placed it the night before. The closet door stood ajar, and he could see that none of her garments resided within.

A sick feeling of dread replaced his euphoria of moments before, then anger obliterated that. "Willy, damn you!" He threw back the covers and jumped out of bed, still able to smell the scent of her on the sheets. It was then he noticed the note that had fallen off the dresser and onto the floor.

With nervous fingers, he opened it and read Wilhemina's good-bye:

Ethan, last night was wonderful. A woman only dreams of having a lover as skilled and considerate as you.

"A lover! Is that what you think of me, Willy?" His lips thinned and he read on.

Though you say you love me, and have shown me in countless ways, my foolish heart will not allow me to believe the words just yet. Please forgive me, but I must return home to see to my aunts' welfare and sort out this situation between us.

I love you deeply, but I cannot marry you.

Liar! he thought. Only last night she had promised she would when he asked her if she wanted to marry him and spend the rest of their lives making love. *"Yes, yes. I do,"* she had said.

I can't help but think that you loved once before and became totally disenchanted with your intended bride. I do not wish for that to happen to us. And I have been hurt deeply in the past, and those doubts and fears still haunt me.

"Fullerton!" The name came out as a curse.

So I've decided that if absence truly does make the heart grow fonder, our love for each other will only flourish and blossom by our separation, as does the child growing inside me.

Please forgive my hasty departure, but I thought it would be for the best. Love, Willy.

Ethan reread the note just to make sure he was reading her words correctly, then crumpled it in the palm of his hand, shaking his fist in midair. After everything he'd said and done, after their tender lovemaking of the night before and his earnest avowals of love, Wilhemina still did not believe him.

The pain in his heart became tangible, and he rubbed at his chest with the palm of his hand. "Go on, Willy, and run away. I'm through making a fool of myself for you. Go home and take care of those two crazy aunts of yours. If it hadn't been for them, I'd have never met you, and my life would have remained simple and sane."

A pounding on the door interrupted his bitter diatribe. "Ethan? Ethan, are you in there? It's Lavinia. May I come in?"

Still naked, he scooted under the covers so he wouldn't shock his stepmother and called for her to enter. "Sure. Why not? I'm alone." And he intended to remain as such for the remainder of his days.

Lavinia floated through the doorway, holding a note and looking very concerned. Her usually flawless complexion was lined with worry. "Do you know what could have prompted Willy's sudden departure, Ethan? She asked Paco to drive her to town this morning. Did you two have a quarrel?"

Wilhemina had left a note for Lavinia as well. How considerate, he thought, smiling ruefully at his stepmother's question. "Quite the opposite, in fact. I guess my lovemaking scares women off these days."

Her cheeks filled with color, and she stepped closer to the bed, clearly distressed by the implication of his words. "I'm so sorry, dear. I had no idea."

"Willy's gone. She didn't believe me when I told her that I loved her."

"She's confused. Pregnant women get like that, full of insecurities about their appearance, about who loves them. You must get dressed and go after her, Ethan. You must bring her back."

He shook his head. "Hell, no! I'm through with the woman. I've done everything in my power to convince Willy of how I feel about her, and none of it's done a damn bit of good. That one woman's more mule-headed than a whole herd of jackasses put together!"

"But you love her, Ethan. And she loves you."

He sneered. "I'll get over it."

Lavinia sat on the edge of the bed, holding his hand as if he were a small child and she was explaining the facts of life to him. "Son, you're in love, and the feelings you have aren't going to go away. This is not like sweating off the remnants of a fifth of whiskey after a good drunk. That woman is in your blood, and she's in there to stay."

To display the deep affection he felt for his step-mother, he kissed her hand and squeezed it gently. "Lavinia, you're a good woman. I only wish I had met someone with half your common sense, instead of some flighty, headstrong woman who fancied herself a damn bounty hunter.

"Wilhemina Granville's been nothing but a pain in the butt since the moment I laid eyes on her. I'm better off without her. We're better off without each other."

"It's because of the way Willy is that you love her."

He thought of how she'd run headlong into the fracas with the Murrays, how she'd nearly drowned in the rushing river, the way she'd looked last night when she'd experienced her woman's pleasure. He thought of a great many things, and his mouth went dry. "Maybe so. But I'm through with her. I won't beg Willy to marry me. She's made up her mind, and there's nothing I can do to convince her otherwise."

"But the child, Ethan? What of the child? It's your flesh and blood. Are you sure you can just walk away from it?"

His face filled with pain, his heart with longing. "I'll send money for his upbringing. And I'll visit him as often as she'll let me. Maybe in time I can convince her to let him come live with me part of the year, or permanently, if she decides to go back to Boston."

Lavinia stood, and there was great sadness in her voice when she spoke. "And that's it? That's what you've decided about your future and your child? Your son?" She hadn't missed the way he kept referring to the child as *him*. This child had already become quite real for Ethan. As real as his love for Wilhemina.

"Yep. That about sums it up."

"I've never known you to be a foolish man, Ethan. And God knows you've got more courage than most. But what you've decided is not only stupid, it's downright cowardly." Ethan flinched at her words but remained silent. "I know I don't have enough words to convince you of that right now; only time will be able to do that. I just pray to the good Lord that yours doesn't run out before you can come to your senses.

"The heart is a funny thing. Once it's broken it takes a lifetime to heal."

Chapter Twenty-two

THREE WEEKS LATER WILHEMINA WAS SEATED IN THE small parlor of her aunts' Justiceburg home, staring into the dying flames of the fire and thinking about the disquieting conclusions she'd formed since leaving Misery: absence did not make the heart grow fonder, and she'd been a fool to run away from Ethan the way she had.

Only the heartwarming and enthusiastic reception she'd received from her aunts upon her return had made her homecoming worthwhile. And the absence of worry on their faces, knowing that Rufus Bowers could never bother any of them again, was indeed gratifying.

"I understand Mr. Bowers has left town entirely," Birdie announced, unable to keep the glee from her voice, blowing on her tea and then sipping it gently. "I heard he got fired from his job at the savings and loan and was forced to leave town in disgrace."

"Well, good riddance, I say!" Eunice added. "The man was a nefarious lecher, and this town is much better off without him."

Wilhemina didn't know what miracle Emmaline had wrought to rid the town of Rufus Bowers, but she would remember to thank the kind woman the next time she saw her. Not only had she paid the overdue amount owed on the loan, she had paid off the mortgage entirely.

Emmaline had Willy's undying gratitude, love, and friendship. And she'd tell her so, if she ever saw her again. But that was a big "if," considering the way things stood between her and Ethan at the moment.

Wilhemina had been so sure Ethan would come after her, believing that if he truly loved her, he would let nothing, not even pride, stand in his way.

But she had been wrong. He hadn't come. He hadn't even written. And she could only conclude, though it tore her heart in two, that he hadn't really loved her.

"My dear, you've worn the longest face since you've been home. It breaks our hearts to see you this way. Won't you tell us what's troubling you? Maybe we can help."

She had told her aunts about the baby upon her return, unwilling to lie about something so important that would impact on their lives so dramatically.

She'd been uncertain of their reaction. Though they had always supported her in the past, had always loved her unconditionally, the prospect of having an unwed mother in the house was sure to raise eyebrows. Bernadette and Eunice were quite proud of their standing in the community, and Wilhemina knew she would likely be the topic of discussion at everyone's dinner table. And the last thing she wanted to do was bring shame upon her aunts.

But she needn't have worried. As they had with everything else she'd ever done, her aunts met her condition with calm acceptance and joy. Eunice had taken a few gulps of the medicinal peach-flavored brandy that she was so fond of, but other than that both her aunts seemed quite accepting of the news.

Forcing a small smile, she said, "I'm fine. Truly I am. I'm just tired from the trip and . . . and the baby." She still had difficulty talking about the child with them.

"Birdy and I don't understand why that nice Texas Ranger hasn't come around. After all the time you two spent together on the trail, and after his getting you with child, we thought surely he would have done the right thing and married you by now." Eunice exchanged a knowing look with her sister, then asked, "Did you two have a falling-out, dear? Is that why you're not getting married?"

Pain stabbed her breast, and she pinched her lips together. "I really don't want to discuss it right now, Aunt. Perhaps another time."

"You've been as quiet as a church mouse since you've come home, Willy." Birdy's arms fluttered about nervously as she gestured. "So wan and listless. You used to chirp like a virtual magpie, and now we can hardly get a word out of you. I know the baby is sapping your strength, but I sense it's more than that. Won't you take us into your confidence?"

"I . . . I . . ." Suddenly the floodgates opened and Wilhemina burst into tears. "I'm . . . I'm just so dreadfully unhappy. I thought Ethan would come after me, but he hasn't. He doesn't love me, and . . ."

Their faces filled with alarm, the two elderly ladies
rose from their seats and surrounded their niece. Birdy patted her hand. "Willy, dear, things always seem much worse
than they really are. I'm sure the Ranger will come to his
senses eventually. You must remember that Mr. Bodine is
a man and as such is just horribly obstinate and obtuse."

Willy sniffed several times. "He doesn't want me.
I've ruined everything by my stupidity."

The women exchanged puzzled looks, then Birdy
said, "What do you mean, you've ruined everything, dear?
Surely not. Why, any man would welcome a lovely woman
like you for a wife."

Eunice pinched her niece's cheek affectionately.
"Have faith, Wilhemina. You have much to offer a man.
And I don't believe you are giving Mr. Bodine enough
credit. It's true men aren't as wise as we about matters of
the heart, but I'm sure in time your Ranger will see the
error of his ways and propose marriage. Mark my words."

"Ethan would have married me, but I refused because
he only wanted me for the child and not myself."

"What poppycock!" Eunice said, shaking her head.
"That is utterly ridiculous."

"I told you I was stupid."

"Stupidity doesn't have a thing to do with it, Willy.
You're in love, that's all. Your heart has clouded up your
mind with all kinds of nonsense."

Bernadette's face broke into a smile. "You're going to
have a baby, Willy! Think of it. And that's far more wonderful than anything I could ever have imagined. We're

going to be great-aunts. Oh, how much fun it will be to have a baby in the house again."

"Birdy, have you lost your mind?" Eunice said with a shake of her double chins. "Wilhemina's not married. And though I intend to support her in any way I can, I don't think being pregnant and unmarried is cause for celebration. As much as I hate to say it, she's going to be branded a loose woman."

Wilhemina rose to her feet, her face set with determination. "I will not let my condition lower your standing in the community. I will leave here and find somewhere else to stay. I have no intention of bringing shame upon either of you. I love you too much to risk that.

"I can travel farther west and pass myself off as a widow, or I can stay with the Sisters of the Sacred Heart until after the baby is born. I know they'll take me in." She began to pace, the ideas she'd been contemplating taking shape.

Eunice gasped, looking clearly distressed. "What nonsense are you speaking, Wilhemina? I won't hear another word of your leaving. You are not going anywhere."

Birdy cast her sister an annoyed look. "See what you've done by your thoughtless remark, Eunice." She turned to Willy. "Is there no hope for you and Mr. Bodine, dear?"

"None at all, I'm afraid. I've made a mess of things with him. And even if Ethan were to propose again, I could not accept him."

Both women looked at her as if she had lost whatever sense she'd been born with.

"I'm sorry to lay this trouble on your doorstep, Aunts, but I thought I was doing the right thing. I don't want to marry a man who doesn't love me."

"But he says he loves you!" Birdy thought to point out, wondering what other kind of clarification the stubborn girl needed.

"I'm grateful your father didn't live to see the day that his only daughter turned into a foolish young woman with not a shred of common sense.

"Of course you are going to marry Mr. Bodine," Eunice stated. "It's the only sensible thing to do."

Willy blanched at her aunt's harsh tone. Eunice had never been one to mince words, but she'd never been as direct as this, either. Her manner bore a striking resemblance to that of Ben Bodine.

"I'm afraid Ethan no longer wants me."

Birdy wasn't buying that excuse for a moment. "What nonsense! Of course he still wants you. You've wounded his pride, that's all."

That's all, Willy thought. To a man like Ethan, pride was everything—the only thing. "I'm going outside to work in the garden. It's a lovely spring day, perhaps the exercise will do me good."

"Flowers again?" Eunice shook her head. "Young woman, you'd better hope sniffing those tulips and daffodils you've got planted out back helps to clear your mind of cobwebs. I've a good mind to take you over my knee and spank some sense into you."

Willy smiled and kissed both her aunts on the cheek. For some reason, baring her soul had made her feel so much better. "I love you both. And this will all work out, you'll see. So don't worry. I'll handle everything." She left, leaving Eunice and Birdy not the least bit confident in her prediction, their heads bowed in prayer.

It wasn't fifteen minutes later that a knock sounded on the front door. Birdy rose to peek out the window, screeching in delight for her sister to come see who their caller was.

"I'm not in the mood for your shenanigans right now, Birdy. I'm still annoyed with you. Imagine—" She gasped at the sight before her. "Good heavenly Father! Our prayers have been answered."

They rushed to the door and threw it open, and their beaming smiles could have lighted a city the size of San Francisco.

"Why, Ranger Bodine! We've been expecting you," Eunice said, escorting him into the house. "What's taken you so long to come to your senses?"

"Eunice, must you be so blunt?" Birdy smiled apologetically. "Please forgive my sister, Ranger Bodine. We're delighted to see you again." She jabbed Eunice gently in the ribs.

After riding as if the devil were on his heels to get to Willy, Ethan was in no mood for the elderly sisters' silly banter. In his opinion, they were fruitier than Lavinia's peach cobbler.

"Is your niece here, by any chance?" he asked, holding back his shortened temper.

They nodded in unison. "She's out back. Tending to her garden," Eunice explained. "Would you care to join her?"

"I would. And I don't want to be announced, or interrupted." He spoke with the authority of a man used to being obeyed.

The two women looked at each other, then began giggling like schoolgirls behind their hands. "Of course. We wouldn't dream of it," Birdy finally assured him.

Trying hard to convince himself that Willy was actually related to these two scatterbrains, Ethan made his way to the rear of the house, glanced out the door, and spotted her instantly. She was dressed in a faded blue gingham dress, squatting on her knees beside her flower garden. Before her, rows of yellow daffodils bloomed, and tulips in every color of the rainbow danced in the sunlight. And he remembered that she was something of an expert when it came to tulips.

Nervously he approached; when he was only a few feet away he cleared his throat.

Wilhemina didn't look up, just kept on working. "I told you, Aunt Birdy, that I'm not ready for lunch right now. I've got weeds choking the life out of my flowers, and—"

"Your aunts are still in the house, Willy."

The breath caught in her throat, and she turned to find a pair of black boots rooted beside her. Her eyes drifted up long muscular legs housed in dark pants to the familiar sheepskin jacket that smelled of cigars and brandy.

"Ethan!" She began to rise, but he motioned her back down, squatting beside her.

"I've missed you, Willy. I thought I could forget all about you. But my stepmother was right: I couldn't get you out of my mind. You were all I could think about from morning till night. Travis has practically disowned me for not being more help with Rafe's case."

She looked crestfallen. "You wanted to forget about me?"

He clasped her hand in his and chose his words carefully. "You hurt me, Willy. Hurt me like no woman has ever done before. I guess it threw me for a loop that my heart was such a fragile thing. Me bein' a grown man and all." He swallowed the lump in his throat. "I love you, Willy."

Tears filled her eyes. "Oh, Ethan! I love you, too."

From beneath his coat, he withdrew a small container and handed it to her. "Just in case you weren't inclined to believe me this time, I had Lavinia make me a cutting. I thought it would look nice crawling up the side of our new house."

The pink morning glory vine had a single blossom on it, and what it symbolized made Willy's heart leap to her throat: Ethan loved her. He truly loved her. He wanted to make a home for her and the baby. He wanted her.

"It's beautiful," she said, clutching it to her heart. "Can you ever forgive me for leaving the way I did? For doubting your love for me?"

He drew her into his arms and felt he had come home. "I might. If you'll finally agree to marry me, and let me make an honest woman out of you."

She sniffed, wiping her nose on her dress sleeve. "I will. I promise."

"In that case . . ." He reached into his vest pocket and brought forth a small box. Opening it, he got down on one knee and presented her with a gold wedding band. "Will you do me the honor of becoming my wife, Wilhemina Granville? I promise to love and cherish you from this day forward until death do us part. Which I hope won't be any-time soon." He grinned.

"Oh, Ethan! Yes! Yes, I will." She took the ring and placed it on her finger, then threw herself at him, knocking him backward in her exuberance to hug him and falling on top of him.

"Oh, dear!" Eunice said, glancing out the window. "I do hope the neighbors aren't watching."

Birdy pushed her sister aside and drew back the curtain, then she grinned. "Wo cares what the neighbors think, Eunice? We're going to have us a new baby to love. And Wilhemina's found the man of her dreams. I'm so happy I could cry."

"Well, go ahead. I already have."

The two women hugged each other, then bawled tears of happiness.

Some second sense told Wilhemina to glance at the house, and she spotted her aunts at the window. "I fear we have company, Ethan."

He frowned. "Those two old ladies have been a thorn in my backside since the day I first met them. I hope they're not an indication of how dotty you're going to be in your old age."

"Well, your father is hardly a sterling example of civility and decorum. You're already too much like him, if you ask me."

"Speaking of Pa, he told me to tell you to get on back to the ranch and help him with his pasture grasses. He said you should be putting that horticultural expertise of yours to work instead of resting on your laurels."

She laughed. "Ben Bodine needing my help? Will wonders never cease. And here I thought he'd be treating me like a hothouse flower because of my delicate condition."

"Not Pa. He'd have you out herding cattle if he thought I'd let him get away with it. Which I won't."

She caressed his cheek. "But you have something else in mind for me to do besides tending cattle and learning to cook Lavinia's fried chicken, don't you?"

"You're damn right I do, woman!" He kissed her then, hungrily and thoroughly, and Wilhemina might have fainted if she hadn't already been in a reclining position.

"Goodness!" she exclaimed. "You really did miss me."

He placed her hand on his crotch, which was hard and pulsing. "Darlin', is there any doubt how much?"

"Ethan! Shame on you. Aunt Eunice and Aunt Birdy will be—"

"Jealous?" His grin was wildly erotic. "Well, hell, woman, there's plenty to go—"

She gasped, covering his mouth with her fingertips. "Shocked. I was going to say shocked. What on earth has gotten into you?" She darted a quick glance at the window, relieved to find they no longer had an audience.

He flipped her onto her back, then blanketed her body with his. "The same thing that's going to get into you in just about half a minute, Willy darlin'." He reached under her skirts, and she felt his hot hand on her thigh.

She swallowed. "But, Ethan! The neighbors . . . my aunts . . ."

He tensed at the reminder and rolled off reluctantly. "Does this house of yours have a bedroom? Because if it doesn't, those old ladies are in for the shock of their lives."

Shyly she nodded, and in one fell swoop he bounded to his feet, lifted her in his arms, and tossed her over his shoulder. "Lead the way, darlin'. I'm ready to commence our wedding night."

"But, Ethan!" she protested. "We aren't married yet."

He chuckled. "The preacher should be here at any moment to marry us, Willy darlin'. I wasn't taking any chances about you changing your mind this time."

"But my hair is a mess. And I'm filthy. My dress is covered with dirt, and my hands—"

When they reached the house, he lowered her to the ground and clasped her face in his hands. "Willy darlin', you're lovelier than any of those flowers you're always fussing over. You mean more to me than anything in this world, and I intend to spend the rest of my life proving that to you."

Her eyes filled with tears. "Oh, Ethan."

"You do love me, Willy? You do want to marry me, don't you?"

He looked so serious, so vulnerable, it melted her heart. Wrapping herself about him like the morning glory vine that symbolized their love, she confessed, "I do."

Please read on for
a special bonus excerpt from

DEFIANT
BOOK III: THE LAWMEN TRILOGY
by Millie Criswell

Coming August 1998 from
WARNER BOOKS

Chapter One

Misery, Texas, Spring 1880

"Your brother's going to hang. You've got my word on that, Bodine."

Travis stared at the cocky smirk on the prosecutor's face and his lips flattened into a thin line. He and Will McGrath had developed a hostile, competitive relationship in grade school and nothing much had changed since then. His brother's murder trial would likely stretch their tenuous truce to the limit. Travis intended to get Rafe acquitted. No matter what he had to do.

"Don't count on it, McGrath. Your conviction rate here in Taylor County stinks. It's likely you won't even be re-elected the next time."

The prosecutor's face crimsoned, nearly matching the color of his russet hair. He turned on his heel and stomped out, slamming the door behind him. Releasing the breath he'd been holding, Travis seated himself behind the battered oak desk and reached for the bag of gumdrops he always kept close by, popping a sugar-coated candy into his mouth.

If bluster and arrogance could win this case, then he hadn't a care in the world. Unfortunately it was going to take a lot more than gall to get his brother Rafe acquitted of the murder of Bobby Slaughter. Slaughter had been one of the men his brother held responsible for the brutal murder of his first wife after Rafe had quit the Texas Rangers. But Bobby Slaughter was a man Rafe claimed he had shot in self-defense.

Travis knew his limitations in a court of law. He was a damn good civil attorney, but criminal law wasn't his area of expertise. With evidence and witnesses piling up against Rafe, his brother was going to need excellent representation. No mistakes, no errors in judgment could be made.

Though he'd done his best to convince his family, especially his bull-headed father, that Rafe would be better off with an experienced eastern lawyer, Ben Bodine would hear none of it, insisting in his blustering manner that "Bodines took care of their own." Even his eldest brother Ethan, the Texas Ranger who'd brought Rafe back to Misery to stand trial, had chosen to take their father's side. Considering Ben and Ethan's long-standing antagonistic relationship, that was nothing short of miraculous.

Three short raps on the door interrupted Travis's disquieting thoughts, and he looked up to find Enos Richards poking his head through the doorway.

"Got an empty chair downstairs, if you're still looking to get your hair cut today, Travis. Looks like you could stand to lose an inch or so. I reckon your family's going to expect you to attend church service come Easter Sunday."

Travis tugged absently at the dark hair brushing the collar of his shirt and wondered if there was anything that went on in town that the affable barber wasn't privy to. "I'll be down directly, Enos. Thanks." The barber disappeared, and Travis heard heavy footfalls on the stairway leading to the barbershop directly below his law office.

Misery wasn't so different from many other towns of its size. Everyone knew everyone else's business. As irritating as that could be on occasion, it was also an endearing quality for a town to have. Folks cared about each other, helped each other out in times of trouble, and Travis found he liked the feeling of being part of one big extended family.

He had attended law school in Boston and found it to be a cold, unfriendly city. Maybe that's because his thick Texas drawl had proclaimed him a stranger from the beginning, and he'd never warmed up to those clipped-speaking New Englanders. The exception to that was his brother Rafe's wife, Emmaline. She was a woman with a warm heart, a hot temper, and a quick smile, despite her New England heritage.

Thinking of Emma brought Rafe to mind. Who would have thought all those years ago when he was trailing after Rafe and Ethan, worshipping the ground they walked on, as only a younger brother can do, that Rafe would one day be in jail and on trial for murder? And that Travis would bear the responsibility for getting the former Texas Ranger freed?

He hadn't done a good job so far of reaching that goal. Judge Barkley, now retired but still presiding until the new judge arrived, had denied Rafe bail, and his brother was presently biding his time in the Misery jail.

Though Travis had pleaded Rafe's case as eloquently as he could in an attempt to reassure the judge that a married man with five adopted children and another on the way wasn't likely to run, the judge had denied the request based on Rafe's past history of having been a fugitive from the law.

Travis admired Judge Barkley despite their difference of opinion in the matter, and despite everything that had gone on in the past regarding Travis's failed relationship with his daughter, Hannah Louise, but he also knew the old man could be stubborn, opinionated, and a pompous pain in the butt at times.

At the moment, the pompous pain in the butt was allowing his housekeeper to fuss over him. Thaddeus Barkley had been feeling poorly of late, though Doc Leahy couldn't find any medical reason why that was so, and had told the judge in no uncertain terms that his malady was all in his head.

"Imagine Doc telling you that you was making things up, like you was one of them hypochondriacs or something," Maude Fogarty stated, clearly annoyed and snorting her disdain as she fluffed down bed pillows and covered the judge's shoulders with a crocheted shawl. "I think you should see someone more knowledgeable than that quack Doc Leahy. In my opinion, he's no better than a snake oil salesman."

"Be that as it may, Mrs. Fogarty, he's the only doctor we have at the moment, and I don't intend to go traipsing off to Denver or San Francisco to consult a specialist. I'm pretty much stuck here in Misery until the new judge arrives." And that wouldn't be any time soon, according to what he'd heard. Maude gave his shoulder a comforting pat, and his lips pinched into a frown. He may very well be sick, but Thaddeus James Barkley wouldn't tolerate being treated like a child.

"You'll be feeling like your old self again when Hannah Louise arrives, Judge," the housekeeper assured him. "The sight of that gal's face is sure to put a smile on yours and perk your spirits right up."

"When did the letter say she'd be arriving?"

Retrieving the missive from her apron pocket, she smoothed it out, as she had the ten previous times she'd read it. Maude Fogarty's baby girl was coming home, and no one was more pleased about that fact than Maude.

"Says here she'll be arriving this coming Saturday. I can hardly believe we'll be setting eyes on our Hannah

Louise again after five long years. I sure have missed my darling girl." The older woman's eyes misted, and anyone who knew Maude well knew that her tears were a rare occurrence. The woman had a hide as tough as bark on a cottonwood, a spine as stiff as the steely color of her hair, and a heart as tender as young asparagus.

"It'll be good to see her again," Thaddeus concurred, tugging the shawl more securely around him. He'd written to Hannah of his extreme tiredness, the twinges in his chest, but never dreamed that she'd drop everything and come running home to care for him. But he was pleased that she had, nonetheless.

It wasn't fair that her mother'd had the privilege of being with Hannah Louise all these years, while he and Maude had been deprived of her company. But then, Fiona Barkley wasn't what he considered a fair woman. Far from it, in fact. He and Fiona had been separated for nearly ten years for what she insisted were irreconcilable differences.

His wife was a woman who never gave an inch without taking a yard in return, who was never satisfied unless she had the last word in any conversation. Marriage to Fiona had been a mixture of heaven and hell, love and hate. But never boring.

Maude's lips puckered in distaste. "That gal would never have left for New York City if it hadn't been for that Bodine boy." She shook her head, and the graying knot at the nape of her neck threatened to spring loose. "Imagine him breaking our gal's heart like he did? I'll never forgive Travis Bodine for that."

The judge heaved a sigh at the painful memory, and the stubbornness of women in general. Hannah Louise was too much like her mother for her own good—stubborn, opinionated, and put on this earth to make a man suffer.

"Now, Maude, you know I chose not to take sides in the matter. What's done is done. I'm just happy our girl is coming home where she belongs." For how long, no one knew.

"Travis has a tough road ahead of him with the upcoming trial and all. I bear the boy no ill will for what's happened, and neither should you. Let bygones be bygones, I say."

Maude crossed her arms over her ample chest, not the least bit swayed by her employer's generosity of spirit. "*Hmph!* I ain't as forgiving as you seem to be, Judge, and I doubt very much that Hannah Louise will be either."

"Tell me again, Rafe, the circumstances surrounding the shooting of Bobby Slaughter. And don't leave anything out. Even the smallest detail may be important."

"For chrissake, Travis! You've asked Rafe to tell that story ten times over. How many more times are you gonna need to hear it? I can practically recite it by rote."

Travis's blue eyes narrowed, and he shot his eldest brother an annoyed look. "You might be a damn good Texas Ranger, Ethan, but you know nothing about preparing a defense case, so I suggest you keep your big mouth shut, your opinions to yourself, and let me interrogate Rafe as I see fit."

"Travis is right," Rafe said, leaning back against the cold wall of his jail cell, the narrow bunk he'd been forced to sit and sleep on a painful reminder of how quickly his circumstances had changed for the worse. "Let Travis do his job."

Ethan hated losing an argument to anyone, especially his brothers, but by the stubborn set of both men's jaws it was plain that this was one he wasn't likely to win. "Oh, all right! But it seems to me we should be doing something a lot more useful than asking a bunch of questions we already know the answers to." Removing a cigar from his vest pocket, he lit it, prompting Rafe to raise an eyebrow in question.

"I thought you'd quit smoking because of Willy's pregnancy." If anyone had told Rafe eight months ago that his confirmed-bachelor, woman-hating brother Ethan would be married and expecting a first child, Rafe would have told them they were nuts. But newly married Ethan was head-over-heels in love with his bride, horticulturist turned bounty hunter Wilhemina Granville, a spirited woman he'd met while looking for Rafe after the murder of Bobby Slaughter.

"I did. But Willy's not here and I feel the need for a smoke. Unless you and Travis want to object to that, too."

Used to Ethan's irascible ways, Travis let the comment pass. Leaning forward in his chair, he directed his next words to Rafe. "Tell me again what happened."

"I returned to the ranch house to find Ellie gone. I discovered her body in the barn. She was dead, as was our unborn child. I knew in my gut that it was Hank Slaughter's gang that had done the murders. The bastard had threatened to get even with me after I'd put him in prison."

"It was you and Ethan who had arrested him, right?" Travis asked and Rafe nodded.

"I took out after them. It wasn't hard to pick up their tracks, and I soon discovered that they had split up. I followed a set of the horse tracks to Justiceburg, and that's where I found Bobby Slaughter, Hank's younger brother."

"At Madam DeBerry's bordello, correct?"

"That's right. Bobby was screwing his brains out with Judy when I walked in on them. Bobby was terrified when he saw me. I never saw a guiltier looking son of a bitch. And even though I went there with the intention of killing him, I didn't shoot him in cold blood."

"Judy DeBerry claims you did."

"That's right," Ethan concurred. "When I interviewed her she said you pulled your gun and shot Bobby down in cold blood. Of course, I knew she was lying straight off, but there was no way I could get her to change her story."

"She was in love with the bastard. What did you expect her to say? But it didn't happen the way she claims. Bobby's gun was beneath his pillow. He reached for it, aimed it at me, and fired. He had every intention of killing me, but my draw was quicker, truer, and I shot him dead."

"The whore claims you threatened her life."

As he gazed at his younger brother, who was writing fast and furiously, and taking notes of everything he said, Rafe's expression filled with regret. "I won't deny that I tried to intimidate her in an attempt to get her to talk. I needed to know where the Slaughters were headed, and she was the only one who could help me find them."

"So you might have threatened her with bodily harm?"

"I think I told her that if she didn't stop screaming she was going to get some of what Bobby got."

"Shit, Rafe! You told her that?" Ethan paced back and forth across the narrow jail cell and puffed his cigar agitatedly, creating a smoky haze about him.

"She was screaming at the top of her lungs that I'd killed Bobby. What the hell else was I supposed to do?"

"Is there anything else you can remember?" Travis's voice remained much calmer than his brother's. "Anything at all?"

"I remember thinking that I had to get out of there before the sheriff showed up. And that I had to find the Slaughters."

"You sure as hell are in a shit-load of trouble, little brother. But I guess you already know that."

"Yeah. But thanks for telling me anyway, Ethan. It was something I was just dying to hear."

Ethan winced at the disheartenment in Rafe's voice. "Jesus! I'm sorry. I—"

"Forget it. Just find some evidence that's going to get me out of this place. I want to go home to my wife and kids. With Emma expecting our first child, I'm worried that this is all going to be too much for her, that something's going to happen, and that I'm going to lose her, too, just like I lost Ellie."

"That's not going to happen, Rafe. Travis here is going to get you off. You and me didn't spend all that money on that fancy eastern law school for nothing. Ain't that right, Travis?" Ethan prodded.

Wanting to give Rafe the reassurance he needed, Travis smiled confidently and nodded in agreement, but he wished now that he'd never thought of becoming a lawyer, never allowed Rafe and Ethan to pay for his expenses to Harvard.

A formal legal education was a rarity out West. Many lawyers were self-taught and apprenticed themselves to experienced practicing attorneys to learn the ropes. For Travis to have been given the opportunity to study law at one of the most prestigious law schools in the East had been nothing short of a miracle. And a dream come true. A dream paid for by Rafe and Ethan.

Travis knew early on that he wanted to do something with his life besides ranching. Unlike his brothers, Travis had always preferred reading to roping and using his wits not his brawn to defeat an opponent.

Despite his father's strenuous insistence that he stay on the ranch and follow in his footsteps, Travis was determined to succeed in his goal to study law and live life as he saw fit.

Rafe and Ethan had taken his side in the matter, and his father had finally come to terms with Travis's decision, grudgingly accepting it. He owed them for that, and for so much more, and he couldn't let them down now that they needed his help.

But as much as he wanted to believe that he'd be able to get Rafe acquitted, he just wasn't sure. The prosecutor was out for blood, the DeBerry woman, too, and Travis was facing the biggest battle of his life with very little ammunition.

In the front room of the ranch house, the women of the Bodine family pondered Rafe's upcoming trial. The boys' stepmother, Lavinia, had just set a steaming pot of tea and plate of oatmeal cakes on the table before her two daughters-in-law, filling the air with the enticing aroma of cinnamon and nutmeg.

"It's not good for you girls to fret so, especially in your condition. There's not much we can do at this point, except pray that Travis and Ethan will be able to find evidence to help Rafe's case. Worrying never did a body any good. And it's definitely not helping those babes of yours."

Emmaline nibbled the chewy cookie halfheartedly, grateful her five adopted children were presently occupied with her father-in-law and his foreman. The two men had taken the children out to the barn to see the new piglets. As depressed as she was about Rafe's situation, Emma didn't think she could keep up much longer the happy face she'd put on for their benefit. "I know you're right, Lavinia, but I can't help worrying over Rafe. He's my husband, the father of my unborn child and those five adorable children we adopted. I don't know what I'll do if the worst happens."

Fear clouded Willy's eyes, for she worried that if Rafe were convicted, Ethan was likely to do something rash. Despite his being a Texas Ranger, and despite his proclivity to carry out his duties to the letter of the law, she distinctly remembered him telling her once that he'd never let Rafe hang, no matter what he had to do to prevent it.

Knowing that he was a man of his word, that gave her great cause for concern.

"We've just got to have faith in Travis's abilities," she told her new sister-in-law, hoping to reassure Emmaline, as well as herself. "He's a fine lawyer. And Ethan's going to do everything he can to find evidence that will help secure Rafe's release."

"Willy's right. You must have faith in Travis, and in the Lord. At times like this, faith is all we women have."

Lavinia's face was drawn, dark circles smudged her eyes, and Emmaline felt guilty that she'd put her burdens onto the older woman's shoulders. Her mother-in-law seemed awfully tired of late. "I'm sorry to be so gloomy. I know you're both right. I've told myself the same thing a hundred times over. But still, it's difficult not to worry."

"Why don't we talk about something else?" Lavinia suggested. "We've been too preoccupied with this subject as it is, and it's not doing us any good."

Willy's face lit with a mischievous smile. "I understand that a woman by the name of Olive Fasbinder has set her cap for Travis. According to Myra Semple at the post office, all the eligible women in town are talking about the fact that he's building himself a house."

"I heard the same thing when I went to town to visit Rafe. The clerk at Robinson's General Store was only too happy to give me all the details, only he mentioned a woman by the name of Margaret Willoughby."

Lavinia nodded. "Margaret's mother would love nothing better than to see her eldest daughter hitched to Travis. Olive Fasbinder's, too. Every mama with an eligible daughter's been after that boy. But I doubt they'll have much luck. Travis is dead set against matrimony."

"I seem to recall Ethan saying the very same thing once," Wilhemina reminded her mother-in-law with a wink.

"True. Ethan was hurt by that hussy from Nogales."

Willy smiled triumphantly, pleased that she'd managed to bring the woman-hating Ranger to his knees. It hadn't been easy, but then, nothing worth having ever was.

"You're a much different type of woman than either Olive or Margaret, Willy. You've got spunk, spine, and spirit, all the things Ethan admires in a woman. I'm afraid Olive and Margaret are sadly lacking in those areas and aren't a suitable match for Travis, either emotionally or intellectually."

"But I was led to believe that he was engaged to a woman who was perfectly suited for him and that he broke off their engagement for some mysterious reason." Emmaline sipped her tea, enjoying the gossip, and the opportunity to take her mind off Rafe's upcoming trial, if only for a little while.

"I guess Travis thought he was justified in what he did, though none of us really understood his reasons at the time. I'm still not sure I do." An apologetic look crossed Lavinia's face. "But Travis's personal business is not something I'm comfortable talking about. If you want to know more about what happened between him and Hannah Louise, then I'm afraid you'll have to ask Travis."

"From what Ethan tells me, Travis is unusually close-mouthed for a lawyer," Willy remarked. "We'd probably have better luck asking him about that new home he's constructing rather than his ex-fiancee."

Laughing, Lavinia's eyes twinkled. "You won't have any trouble getting Travis to talk about that new house of his. He's proud as a peacock of it. And I doubt that he's given a moment's notice to the fact that his new home is drawing Misery's spinsters to him like bees to a hive.

"I declare, Travis Bodine! We had no idea you were so talented with your hands. Did we, Margaret?"

The faint buzzing of women's voices had Travis glancing up from the nail he was pounding in place as he secured the floor joists to the porch frame. He groaned inwardly at the sight of Olive and Margaret standing on the street in front of his half-finished house. With everything he had to contend with at the moment, he sure as heck didn't need two husband-hunting spinsters breathing down his neck.

Setting the hammer aside, he pasted on an affable smile, wishing he could turn himself into smoke and disappear into thin air. "Good afternoon, ladies. What brings you to this end of town today?"

A soft blush crossed Margaret's freckled cheeks, and her voice trembled slightly when she spoke. "Olive and I are here to invite you to sit with us at church Easter Sunday, Travis. That is, if you don't already have other plans."

He opened his mouth to refuse the invitation, but Olive was quicker, adding, "We checked with your brother and Ethan assured us that you didn't."

Gritting his teeth, he replied, "Really?", thinking that the only recourse he had left was to kill that damn interfering brother of his when he got the chance. Rafe wouldn't be the only Bodine standing trial for murder. "That's very kind of you, ladies. But I hadn't really—"

"We won't take no for an answer," Olive said, devouring him with her eyes, until Travis felt the need to fasten the two top buttons on his shirt and roll down his sleeves in self-protection. He was starting to feel downright naked in front of the two spinsters from hell, as he and Ethan had always referred to the women.

"We understand your stepmother is holding her annual Easter celebration after church service Sunday, Travis. Olive and I have already received invitations to attend. We're really looking forward to it."

"Well, isn't that just . . ." *the worst possible news I've ever received.* ". . . terribly kind of Lavinia. She's so thoughtful."

"How come you're not at your office working on your brother's case? Margaret and I were surprised when Mr. Richards told us you were here at the new house." She stared wistfully at the structure.

The house was two storied with a wide wrap-around porch. The kind of porch where a handsome young attorney and his wife could sit of an evening and enjoy the cool night air. There would be many windows when it was completed to allow in lots of sunlight, and two fireplaces to snuggle before on a brisk winter's evening.

Olive released a sigh. "It's certainly going to be splendid when it's finished. Isn't it, Margaret?"

Margaret's faint blush turned into a full-fledged crimson hue. "Oh yes! Why, any woman would be proud to live in such a fine house. Are you building it for any special reason?"

Retrieving his coat from the nail where he'd left it hanging, he shrugged it on, realizing that he had no more stomach for construction today. The pleasure and solace he normally found while working on the new house had disappeared the moment Olive and Margaret made their presence known.

"I'm building it to live in. That's all. Nothing more. I want to be closer to my office, and I'm tired of living at the boarding house." And he wanted something of his own, something permanent. Something that would last.

"Mama always says that a man should have a proper roof over his head and a proper wife to go under it," Olive stated, obviously applying for the position.

"I'm content to live under my roof . . . *alone* as a bachelor." He had made his feelings on the subject clear, but could see by Margaret's determined expression that she wasn't buying his explanation for a second.

"That's because you haven't met the right woman yet," the carrot-topped spinster insisted. "When you do, you'll jump at the chance to enjoy matrimonial bliss. Why look at your brothers. They're both married now and happy as larks, from what I hear."

It was true: Rafe and Ethan were content with their new brides and impending fatherhood, but that didn't mean for an instant that Travis had any intention of joining them in their matrimonial bliss. He'd nearly gone down that road once before with disastrous results, and he had no intention of traveling it again.

Hannah Louise Barkley had made the journey far more aggravating than he'd ever thought possible. He'd learned his lesson the hard way about the contrariness of women, about headstrong females who relished a career over home and family life, about promises made but never kept.

He was well rid of Hannah Louise, who'd gone off to New York City to live, and he wasn't in the market for another fiancee, or another round of heartache.